A PAPER STATUE

*To my good friend Don Bates
with best wishes,
Roger Naylor*

BOOKS BY ROGER NAYLOR

A PAPER STATUE – **WW II Fiction** – Fighter pilot Lee Marks finds himself face-to-face with Japanese fighters, abominable weather, and a manipulative CO who defines the war on his own terms.

ARK II – **A Thriller** – Buck Barnum serves as point-man to lead a high-tech project for environmental protection against an unlikely coalition of NIMBYs and crime syndicate.

BLACK ROCK BAY – **A Thriller** – Hud Bryant offers to help an old friend and his neighbors on a beautiful Northern Minnesota lake and finds himself caught up in a showdown with home-grown terrorists to whom murder is only a means to an end.

CALIFORNIA TRIVIA – A collection of trivia, often humorous and always fascinating, about the Golden State

A PAPER STATUE

A Novel

Roger Naylor
Author of Black Rock Bay

iUniverse, Inc.
New York Lincoln Shanghai

A PAPER STATUE

Copyright © 2006 by Roger A. Naylor

All rights reserved. No part of this book may be used or reproduced by any means, graphic, electronic, or mechanical, including photocopying, recording, taping or by any information storage retrieval system without the written permission of the publisher except in the case of brief quotations embodied in critical articles and reviews.

iUniverse books may be ordered through booksellers or by contacting:

iUniverse
2021 Pine Lake Road, Suite 100
Lincoln, NE 68512
www.iuniverse.com
1-800-Authors (1-800-288-4677)

This is a work of fiction. All of the characters, names, incidents, organizations and dialogue in this novel are either the products of the author's imagination or are used fictitiously.

ISBN-13: 978-0-595-40768-2 (pbk)
ISBN-13: 978-0-595-85132-4 (ebk)
ISBN-10: 0-595-40768-4 (pbk)
ISBN-10: 0-595-85132-0 (ebk)

Printed in the United States of America

A Paper Statue is dedicated to all those men and women who had roles in designing, building, flying, servicing, or restoring the incredible Lockheed P-38 Lightning. Their efforts have made the world a better place.

Acknowledgments

It is always my goal to tell a compelling story set in realism. To this end, I am deeply indebted to fellow members of the P-38 National Association for their encouragement and assistance with my research. President Stan Jones contributed pieces of his fine art work and Lee Northrop granted access to the 475th Fighter Group Museum archives. Others of the association who offered their expertise on the P-38, war-time life on southwest Pacific islands, or both included: Pat Connolly, Dick Willsie, Jack Mullan, Ed Baquet, Seymour Prell, Phil Wiltsie, and Robert Maxwell. Col. J.A. Saavedra (Ret) of the Air Force History Support Office at Bolling AFB provided some precious links when I had hit a wall on a couple of points. If I have missed on something, it's my error, not theirs. For their encouragement I thank Kelly Kalcheim and Sharon Greene, strong Association members. But without question, the project could not have been completed without the ongoing support, tolerance, and scrutiny of my dear wife, Jeanne.

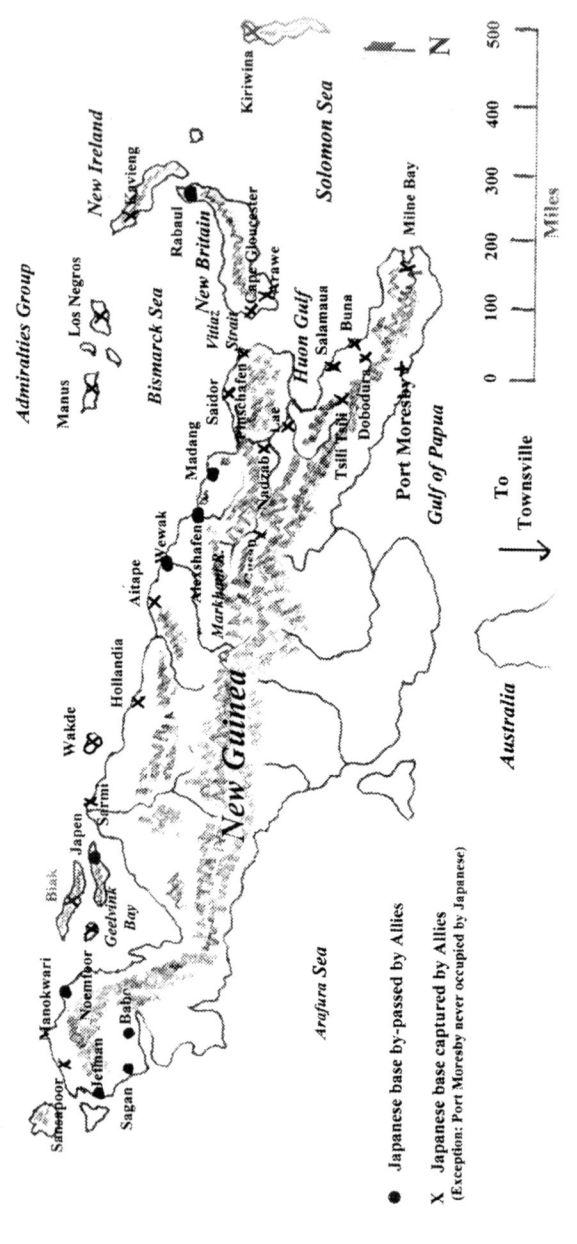

Chapter 1

▼

January 27, 1944—Somewhere over the Coral Sea

"Perhaps the longest journey a man can take is that of half-circling the globe to an unfamiliar land with the ordained task of entering ill-prepared into battle against an enemy he has never seen, an enemy he can never understand, an enemy who will inevitably choose death over defeat."

Second Lieutenant Lee Marks recalled the words of his CO at advanced fighter training. Lee still knew little about the enemy, but he knew it had been a long, tedious trip. Oh, man, my butt hurts, he thought, and this is the *good* part.

The C-47, the olive drab aluminum whale in which he rode, suddenly lurched and Lee Marks found himself tipped on his back into a trough formed by the bench seat and the curved side of the fuselage. Twisting his neck he looked straight downward through the porthole of the old Gooneybird to the blue sea 10,000 feet below. A chorus of yelps and profanity overrode the metallic din of the airplane as it continued its sharp bank, climbed slightly, and slipped ghostlike into a neighboring cloud.

"What was *that* all about?" asked Bubba Nash, the skinny young pilot next to Marks.

Lee Marks looked to the captain who sat across the aisle for an explanation. The senior officer calmly surveyed the fledgling fighter pilots as they struggled to regain lost composure and hide their fear.

"Probably saw some Japs," the captain finally shouted. "One of their small carrier groups was messing around northwest of here yesterday. He patted the metal bench seat with the shallow indentations to accommodate the human anatomy and added, "Good old ship, but she'll never beat a Zeke."

Lee settled in again as the aircraft righted itself. The pain in his hips and tailbone told him the respite at Townsville, Australia, had been too short. He took a deep breath and tried to relax, but the pungent mix of dust, aluminum, mildew, and body odor that he had come to think of as Army Air Force reminded him all too clearly of where he was, and more important, why he was there.

A recently commissioned fighter pilot, Lee Marks had just turned twenty-one. His black, wavy hair was combed back, and his deep-set, brown eyes probed intensely from behind a slender, almost hawkish face to give him a somewhat forbidding countenance. Lee Marks was handsome when he smiled, but in recent weeks his smile had seldom been seen by strangers.

Last leg to New Guinea, thought Lee as he mopped the sweat from his forehead with a shirtsleeve. By tomorrow, I'll be in the damned war—if we don't get shot down today. He tensed at the thought. He'd try to deal with the fear as he always had, like facing a dive into a cold, dark swimming hole—deny his dread, hold his breath, and dive right in. The captain across the aisle seemed to be watching him. Lee reacted by looking down the line at the others, where a glib line had just drawn a burst of laughter. He smiled inwardly at himself. He hadn't even heard the joke. Would he ever break that self-conscious habit of looking away from strangers? He forced his attention back to the captain.

The lines in the captain's Atabrine-yellow-tan, weather-beaten face suggested he was old, perhaps even twenty-five. His shapeless visored officer hat was tipped at a jaunty angle. Brown eyes peered through slits formed by puffed eyelids. Except for the age, he fit Lee's image of a veteran combat pilot. Huh, Lee thought, he's probably a desk jockey from Port Moresby.

Smiling, the captain leaned across the aisle. He said, "I'm Captain Dick Robesky. My friends call me Roby."

"Second Lieutenant Marks, Sir, Lee Marks," he replied, wondering if he was now a friend or still only a lieutenant.

"You assigned to the new Fighter Group?" Robesky asked.

"Yes, sir, the 483rd Fighter Group, 125th Squadron, I guess."

"Ohhh, so you're one of Mo Brennan's new birds," the captain said. "You want to learn your way around? You listen up and learn. Nobody in the Air Force gets things done like Major Brennan."

"Thank you, sir," Lee said. "I'll listen."

He glanced back down the line at the other passengers. Several older-looking strangers with lines of experience lacing their yellowish-tan faces sat among the sixteen fresh, young, khaki-clad officers who had made the trip from the States together. The new officers were being attached to the recently formed 483rd Fighter Group, Fifth Air Force, at Dobodura, New Guinea.

Six of them would join the 127th Fighter Squadron, while Lee and eight others were to merge with three veterans to form the 125th Fighter Squadron.

Lee had known two of the pilots since primary flight training and had become acquainted with others during advanced training and the subsequent long trip. He had watched the behavior of the young eagles as they flew closer and closer to the combat zone. One small cluster talked endlessly about their athletic prowess during high school and college years. Another group had spent over ten thousand miles boasting about and probably embellishing their sexual conquests. Still others had matched up in pairs and were quietly discussing their families, the war, flying, or the uncertain future. Lee had spent much of his time alone, thinking. Nerves, he mused, all of us coping with nerves. How differently we do it.

He glanced at his watch. They should be over half way in their seven-hundred mile flight from Townsville, Australia, to Port Moresby on the south coast of New Guinea. Only half-way? Lee slid down in the uncomfortable seat, tipped his hat over his face, and begged for sleep. The sweaty smell of the cap stung his nostrils, so he moved it higher on his forehead. But the high-pitched voices, staccato sounds, and boisterous laughter pronged his consciousness, reminding him of the countless excursions on buses, trains, and ships over the last year.

The vibrations of the two radial engines produced a monotonous backdrop to the voices and teased Lee with their hypnotic effect. While their rhythm induced drowsiness, their heavy drone reminded him that they were over water far from the nearest land. He found himself listening for the slightest miss or sign of engine trouble. He had searched and searched for that small chunk of pleasant relief called sleep, but he had seldom found it.

Lee began to retrace his long journey back across the wide Pacific, back along the railroad tracks to South Chicago and home. Ever since his leave prior to shipping out, thoughts of home meant thoughts of his sister Marie—thoughts of trouble. At a time when his military mates found sanctity in memories of home, Lee tried desperately to avoid such reminiscence, for it brought only pain and confusion, frustration and anger.

Home had always been the center of Lee's world, that place where his victories were lauded and his defeats quickly laid to rest. He had received frequent encouragement from his mother, though in his youth he had often felt her disciplining hand.

"You study hard—you work hard, Lee Marklevitz," she had said when he was very young, "and someday you be president. Someday you make up for that no good, foolish father of yours."

Lee had always felt the shivers when his mother berated his father like that. He knew she had the right. His father had left them soon after the birth of Lee's younger sister, Marie. No warning—he just left. And the remaining trio of Marklevitzes had never found their way out of that cold, dark hole. His mother eventually shortened the name, moved them to a small, rented house in a lesser neighborhood, and set about raising a "good American family." Still, whenever she began to malign his father, Lee had felt threatened, for perhaps someday she would turn on him. Ultimately, as it turned out, she did.

It came when he got into trouble over Marie, who was now sixteen. Despite his warnings, Marie had been sneaking out with a spoiled, rich punk who was three years older than she. Having made love to more than one girl during his high school and college years, Lee was alert to the signs. He had only seen Pete Loren with his sister once, but he knew what Loren was after. It would only be a matter of time until the smug Casanova had her in the back seat of his new convertible.

The trouble erupted one night when Lee was hanging around the local pool hall while home on leave. An acquaintance cornered Lee and told him that Pete Loren had boasted openly that he had been screwing Marie Marks and that she was "a real hot fuck." Lee remembered the fight in the alley—every blow. He had methodically chopped Loren down to a bleeding mass in a fetal position on the alley bricks. He could still remember the strange feelings he'd had during the fight. His initial anger had somehow become an overwhelming compulsion to punish, hurt, destroy the other man. And he *had* hurt Loren, though he never really knew how badly.

Two policemen had hauled Lee off to the station, where he was told there was a good chance that Loren's father would file charges. Officer Crowder advised Lee not to leave town, then winked. Lee would never forget his mother's angry tears as she assailed his bad judgment and compared him to his father. And now, barely two weeks later, he found himself on the opposite side of the world. Aware of his quickening pulse, Lee knew he could work himself into a useless frenzy, so he sat up and looked around.

"Feel like talking now?" Captain Robesky asked.

"Well, yes, sir. I guess I do."

"Come on over," the captain said, motioning to the vacant seat beside him. As Lee settled in, Robesky asked, "You like the P-38, Lieutenant?"

"Sure do, sir. Any idea which model we'll get?" Lee noted that he was still a lieutenant, not a friend.

"Hard to say, maybe Model Js, probably not the new Model L," the captain answered. "Where you from?"

"Chicago."

"How old are you, Marks?" Robesky asked, looking directly at Lee.

"Twenty-one, sir."

"Is that all? You seem a lot older than the rest of these kids."

"It's just—I'm a little different, I guess, sir. I don't seem to need crowds," Lee said. An uncomfortable silence set in, finally broken by Captain Robesky.

"You know, Marks, when I first broke in over here, flying P-40's out of Darwin, I had an older flight leader who had been with Chennault's AVG's in China. He used to say, 'If you want the toughest fighter pilot around, choose a scrappy loner.'" The captain looked seriously at Lee. "But, if I've got a Zero on *my* tail, I think I want a *friend* for a wingman. What do *you* think?"

"Guess I really shouldn't have an opinion, sir," Lee replied, "being just a rookie."

"Oh, come on, Lieutenant," pressed the captain. "You *must* have an opinion."

Lee studied the senior officer. Was this a sincere conversation, or was the captain baiting him? The twinkle in Robesky's eyes suggested the latter. Lee felt annoyed. He resented being manipulated. He wanted to move back to his original seat, but he found himself responding instead.

"If I had that Zero on *my* tail," he began, "I think I'd prefer a scrappy loner who can *shoot* to a wonderful friend who can't find his ass with both hands."

Robesky laughed. "Can you shoot?"

"Yes, sir," Lee responded, still bristling.

"I like that—confident, too."

Lee backed off. "Sir, I didn't mean to sound cocky. What I meant was, even as a kid with my slingshot, I never hit anything I thought I was going to miss."

"No, Marks, I'm sure you didn't." Robesky laughed again.

A natural silence blanketed the conversation. Lee glanced at his watch. About two more hours and they should be landing at Seven-mile Drome, the large marshalling base near Port Moresby. He almost asked the captain about the name Seven-mile Drome, but he decided not to renew the conversation. He leaned back, willed the pain from his body, and dozed off again.

He awakened an hour later to violent bumping and tossing by the Gooneybird. The cabin grew dark, and the loud splatter of rain against the craft's thin aluminum skin silenced its passengers.

Captain Robesky shouted down the line, "Seatbelts on! It's probably just a squall, but it could get rough."

"Sir," Lee began, forgetting his vow in the face of the new element, "how do you tell the difference between a squall and something worse out here?"

"If you survive it, it was a squall," Robesky said with a smile. "Over the water you can see a storm from many miles away. You can gauge its height, width, and movement. Out here, you'll spend a lot of time over water, and you'll see storms almost every day, but they're *all* taken seriously. You can't show a tropical storm too much respect. Once you're in it, you're blind as a bat and you've probably lost your radio."

By 1630 hours, they had found clear skies and begun letting down. At 1745, the tires of the Gooneybird screeched against one of three parallel strips seven miles east of Port Moresby. The airmen disembarked, standing in a huddle and gawking as they awaited the canvas-covered truck that rolled across the tarmac to meet them.

"Je-sus! Look at all the B-25's," a young voice exclaimed.

"Yeah, and over there—B-24's."

"Where are the fighters?" someone asked.

"Ohh, no! Look over there—P-39's! You don't think they'd put us in *those* relics, do you?" a disheartened second lieutenant groaned.

"Nah," a voice answered. "I heard they're pawning those off on the Aussies."

"God, I hope you're right."

"Hey, here's the truck."

They tossed their bags up, climbed aboard, and plopped onto the wooden bench seats.

"Damn, I think we're in another squall!" Sandy Sadler shouted, standing and bending to exhibit his wet butt. The truck lurched forward, sending the jokester tumbling onto his mates. In minutes, the vehicle ground to a squeaky stop, and the men piled out. Two enlisted men, obviously familiar with the base, hoisted up their duffels and took off on their own. The newcomers gawked in all directions, trying to assimilate everything at once.

"Grab your gear and meet over there," Captain Robesky directed, "next to the mess hall."

As the group neared the mess hall, a jeep rounded the corner and jerked to a stop before them. Captain Robesky walked to the jeep and engaged the driver, a major, in serious discussion. Lee edged a little closer to the conversation.

"Hell no, I won't trade you, Roby," the major was saying, the fixed grin on his face contradicting an emphatic voice. "*You* rolled the damned dice yourself—got first pick. Now, get these yardbirds fed and settled in for the night. Big day tomorrow." He jammed the gearshift into low and the jeep scooted around a corner and out of sight.

Captain Robesky rolled his eyes, turned, and introduced himself to the group. "I'll be commanding the 127th Squadron. That was Major Brennan, CO of the 125th." He went on to outline bunking assignments and procedures for the evening mess. "We'll see you right here in the morning, ready for work at 0630 hours. Any questions?"

"Place is sure big," said one of the newcomers. "Not exactly posh, is it?"

"Enjoy it, Lieutenant," Captain Robesky countered. "If you *ever* see anything this nice again, it won't be for at least six months."

Chapter 2

The prong of petulance jabbed Lee the next morning when he saw the line at the mess hall. How he hated lines. He had *always* hated lines, even those at games, movies, dances, and especially at college registration. Then came the Army. He must have spent half of his Army Air Force time waiting in lines. Each time he had found himself locked into a line he swore it would be the last time. If there was anything in this world worth waiting in line for, he'd not yet found it. Once again, peaceful images of the laid-back Swiss Family Robinson flitted through his mind. When he reached the serving counter, his conviction that nothing was worth a wait was even further reinforced as the servers spooned a wad of greenish, half-cooked powdered eggs and some black strips that might once have been bacon onto his tray. When he got to the toast and coffee, he felt better. What could they do to toast and coffee?

He scanned the mess hall, spotted Bubba Nash, the tall, gangly young man who had been with Lee since basic training, and headed his way. Bubba's white hair stood out in the crowd like a beacon, and despite constant exposure to the sun, the complexion of his baby face progressed only from baby pink to dark baby pink. As Lee took his seat, he noticed the steamy, pout on the face of his cohort and wondered how Bubba would deal with the food this time. While the glob of eggs still lay there, Bubba had at least eaten his bacon and toast.

"Good morning, Bubba," Lee said.

"Morning."

Lee abandoned the social endeavor and prepared to confront the abominable breakfast in his customary manner. He simply bolted it down, the faster the better. He had but a half-cup of the bitter, black coffee left when he noticed the man across from Bubba.

At first, the stranger seemed to be performing some ritual. As Lee watched, however, he realized the man was holding the slices of toast up to the light and then picking small objects from the toast. Methodically, he placed the pickings to one side of his tray. Seeming to sense his audience, the man looked at Bubba.

"Weevils," he commented dryly. As Bubba lurched to his feet and bolted for the door, baby pink was rolling to green.

Poor Bubba, thought Lee, he's still coping with that problem. Too bad they wouldn't let his mother come along as his special cook. I'll bet these guys are wondering how he got this far. Lee smiled to himself. Gifted, simply gifted, Bubba had mastered every aircraft, from the Ryan PT-22 primary trainer to the P-38 Lightning, in half the prescribed time. I'm pretty good, Lee thought, better than most. But that skinny guy who looks and acts like a sixteen-year-old kid can make a plane do things nobody ever thought of. He'll be an ace, if he can shoot, and if he can somehow keep his food down. The latter might be the bigger challenge for Bubba.

By 0630 hours, the new pilots of the 125th Fighter Squadron had gathered outside the mess hall. Bubba Nash stood sheepishly off to one side. Major Brennan casually strolled back and forth before the group, puffing on a cigarette and casting an occasional glance at the blue-gray sky. Lee studied the major. Slightly shorter than Lee's six-foot height, he had the broad shoulders and full chest of an athlete. He had blue eyes, sandy-colored hair, a deep, yellowish tan, sparkling teeth, and dimples that made him strikingly handsome when he smiled. But Lee sensed something else there, a commanding presence that compelled one to listen, even when the major was not speaking, and suggested that he was not as casual and relaxed as he appeared.

Major Brennan glanced at his watch, then said, "Okay, fall in, alphabetically from your right." The first command struck Lee as less than military. Referring to a clipboard, the major moved down the line, attaching names to faces and adding an occasional word to one of his new charges. "Lieutenant Marks?" he asked, staring into Lee's eyes with a steely penetration that belied the gentle smile on his face.

"Sir," Lee replied.

Major Brennan paused silently for a moment, his eyes fixed on Lee's. Lee studied the major as he moved on down the line. He wanted to learn everything there was to know about this unusual man. When the major smiled his weathered skin showed lines on his forehead and around his bright blue eyes. Yeah, Lee thought, the smile. He's almost always smiling—even makes me want to smile.

When the CO had accounted for the nine newcomers, he led the group single-file to a grassy area near the jungle's edge. Lee noted that the major did not march them over. In fact, he'd not yet called them to attention.

"Flop here in a semi-circle facing me," he said, squatting before them. For a full minute of nervous silence, the major studied his group. His expression became cold.

"I've spoken to many groups of pilots," Major Brennan said. "I've never faced a group that was not intelligent, bright, intuitive, and highly motivated—until now."

Lee felt his body twang with tension. The men seemed to be holding their breath collectively as one. Lee knew he would be very careful in dealing with this officer.

Then, the major casually reached into his shirt pocket, came out with a cigarette, lit it, took a long slow drag, and smoothly exhaled. And as he did, his smile returned. The ominous, black cloud of moments before had mysteriously transformed into bright sunshine.

"Observations so far?" he asked, scanning the group.

"Yes, sir," said Sandy Sadler with devilish eyes glinting from his freckled face. "Bubba blew his breakfast again." After a moment of electric silence, Brennan smiled and the group broke into laughter. Lee glanced over at Bubba. The face had reached a crimson that glowed in the morning sun, but not without an embarrassed, boyish grin.

"Lieutenant Nash will, I repeat, *will* get over that very soon," he said, looking sternly at Bubba. "You can't *fly* and you certainly can't *fight* on an empty stomach. Anything else?"

So much for the smile, Lee thought. The silence told him that, despite the seemingly relaxed atmosphere, no one but Sandy would test the waters.

With a serious, almost menacing countenance, the major continued, "On the ground in my outfit, we're somewhat loose on military protocol. But make no mistake. We haven't thrown the book away. And in the air, we are not only military—we are a *military machine*. I expect you to learn my methods so well that you can execute correctly at just the click of my mike."

Lee saw no warmth in the smile that accompanied the pronouncement. Not a sound came from the men.

"Now, I've been given one of the shitty jobs our Air Force has to offer—organizing, training, and leading a new, rookie squadron. As your CO I'm expected to keep you healthy," he said with a burning glance at Bubba, "and I'm expected to teach you, see that you have the best equipment, lead you in combat—and write letters to the families of those who fuck up."

Lee felt a shiver run up his spine. Major Brennan now spoke in ominous GI dialect, and he certainly had their attention. With a minimum of words, he had said a lot. Lee began to think he might like their commander's approach.

"Now, I'll do *my* job," Brennan continued, "and I'll do it very well," he took another drag in his cigarette, "except that I don't want to write those damned letters."

Lee heard a few subdued chuckles. "You will listen, learn, and work, so I don't have to sharpen my pencil too often. For the next three days, you go to school. You'll learn more than you have in the last three months. If you don't, you won't be around three months from now."

The major paused, glared menacingly, and scanned his audience. The glare changed suddenly into a slight grin.

"I've brought two experienced pilots with me who were transferred over from the 49th Fighter Group. Each of the three flights, which we'll make up later, will have one of us experienced pilots to head things up. Any questions?" Without waiting for a response, he said, "Good. Let's go to work. Lieutenant Green will take you on that truck over there to pick up your gear and side arms. From there, you'll go to Geography and Current Affairs Class. Lieutenant Gustafson will teach you all about New Guinea and the area. Pay attention to what he has to say. Dismissed."

Lee caught up with Bubba Nash as the enthusiastic, young flyers walked toward the truck. Bubba's color had returned to normal. The gaunt rookie stalked along beside Lee like a stoop-shouldered country boy walking barefoot through a thistle patch.

Within the hour they had been issued their flight gear and weapons and transported to still another tin hut for the class. Lieutenant Gustafson, a short, stocky man with large, brown eyes, a mechanical smile, and a prematurely balding head launched into his presentation. Despite the lieutenant's robot-like manner, Lee found the lecture interesting. The lieutenant's vocabulary and phrasing seemed to supply the enthusiasm that his droning monotone lacked. Working from a large map of New Guinea and the surrounding island groups, Lieutenant Gustafson traced events from the point early in the war when the Japanese troops had come south over the Owen Stanley Mountains to a point within thirty-two miles of taking Port Moresby. They were finally stopped and pushed back by a small contingent of fierce, determined Australians.

Since that time, General MacArthur's American and Australian troops had collaborated with General Kenney's Fifth Air Force to seize several bases along the northern New Guinea coast. The Allied strategy had changed for the New Guinea effort. Previously, the American invaders had captured and occupied whole island groups in a broad, sweeping movement toward the west. But MacArthur had changed to what Lieutenant Gustafson called a "the biggest game of hopscotch in history."

Developing a protective barrier for Australia and moving swiftly toward the liberation of the Philippines were the primary goals. In the process, the Allies hoped to destroy the Japanese air capabilities in the area, seize Japanese air bases for Allied use, and engage enemy ground forces only when they guarded Allied objectives or were simply too large to be ignored.

The American and Australian forces had hopped and skipped from east to west along the northern coast, from Milne Bay at the southeastern tip of New Guinea to Finschafen and Saidor farther west on the Huon Peninsula. The plan was to pick off strategic Japanese bases and bypass the others which, because of U.S. air and sea blockades, would simply "die on the vine." And since most of the coastal jungles were impassable to vehicles and barely passable to foot soldiers, the Allied assaults were usually amphibious. One exception had been the Jap base at Nadzab, an airbase that lay in the Markham River Valley forty miles inland from Lae. The first major airborne assault in the Pacific War had caught the Japanese defenders completely by surprise.

"Up to now," Lieutenant Gustafson said, "we control a heavy concentration of air bases from Milne to Lae. but that's only about one-fifth of the northern coast. From Lae on to the west, the enemy bases are fewer and farther between, but they are much larger and tougher. Jap bases like Wewak and Hollandia, for example, each control several airfields."

Apparently neither side was interested in the interior of the island. Because of the huge ranges of high mountains and the untenable jungles, the land was of little strategic value, and much of it would remain unexplored by civilized man.

"General MacArthur has drawn some flak over his hopscotch plan. Some say he's obsessed with freeing the Phillipines. You know, his famous, 'I shall return,' line. But so far, it seems to be working—with one exception. He skipped over New Britain, this island group only a hundred miles northeast of New Guinea." The lieutenant pointed to the northern tip of New Britain. "Right here is Rabaul—probably the most powerful Jap base in the Pacific. Six large airdromes. The Fourth Japanese Air Army at Rabaul includes some of their best pilots in this theater. But we can tell they're absorbing large numbers of new and very inexperienced pilots—a reason our kill ratio is going up. But n*ever*, I repeat, *never* assume the ones you face are beginners. The rest of them are *very* good. Any time you're working the coast, you want to keep an eye to the east. They like to hit us from high in the morning sun. Remember, as long as they're *there* they're apt to be *here.*"

After a brief question period, the lieutenant gave each man a map of the area to be thoroughly memorized. "Know where you are at all times. If you take some hits and get separated, there's no time to drag out your road map. Oh, if you're bleeding, *don't* go down in the water if you can avoid it. The area is lousy with sharks. But if you ditch over the jungle, try to stay close to the coast or at least a river, so you have a chance to find your way out."

Lee wasn't sure if the shudder that ran through him was provoked by the mention of the Rabaul pilots, the bleeding, or the sharks, but he now knew the real meaning of the title, "Geography and Current Affairs."

The men talked quietly as they walked to the mess hall. Lee purposely sat next to Bubba. Though he had to be hungry, Bubba simply sat over his tray and stared at the ceiling. His thin, wispy, white hair lay plastered to his forehead by sweat.

"I can't do it, Lee. I just can't," Bubba moaned softly, "specially the breakfasts. I keep trying, but every time we move to another base, the food gets worse. And *this* stuff—"

"Bubba," Lee cut in, "do you remember that horse's butt we had for a sergeant in boot?"

"Jeez, who could forget old Volcano Mouth?"

"Well, Bubba, he told me when we finished basic that you'd never cut it," said Lee.

"He told you *that?*"

"Sure did. He said you weren't man enough to even eat Army chow, let alone fight Japs," Lee said. "Was he right? Don't you think it's about time you get over this nonsen—"

"Okay—okay, Lee, I get the point," Bubba replied, "but *how?*"

"Simple, Bubba. Keep your mind on something else—off the food. Each time you take a bite, think of old Volcano Mouth, chew faster than hell, and swallow. In no time, you'll be done. And after you've won the battle a few times you'll get used to this garbage."

"That what *you* do?" asked Bubba. "That why you eat so fast?"

Lee nodded.

Bubba hesitated a moment, then attacked the food ferociously with Lee reciting anecdotes about the sergeant to keep him going. In minutes, Bubba had cleared the tray.

"You know? I think it worked. I did it!"

"Sure it did. Now let's get out of here and get our minds on something else."

As they picked up their trays and turned to leave the table, a Seven-mile pilot who had been observing the lesson said loudly, "Well, fer Jesus Christ! Look at the size of this goddamned worm in my gravy!"

Bubba stiffened, tossed his tray onto Lee's, and charged outside. As the rangy pilot, much younger than his years, raced from the mess hall, he reminded Lee of Ichabod Crane. Despite some guilt, Lee couldn't resist joining the raucous laughter.

That afternoon, with Colt .45s, machetes, and jungle kits strapped on, the trainees were led on a long hike, "survival refresher" it was called, into the jungle. Lieutenant Green, who had once been shot down and forced to spend a week hacking his way back to the nearest base, served as their guide. He showed them edible fruits that were plentiful, how to crack coconuts, locate water, improvise shelters, and use machetes against the thick undergrowth. As the troop staggered out of the dense jungle hours later, Lee concluded the session may have been "survival," but there was nothing "refreshing" about it, except perhaps for Bubba. He had filled up on fruits and coconut milk.

By the time they had trudged the last mile to their hut, the men were tired, sweaty, scratched, and covered with insect bites. Lee doubted that a man in the jungle for any length of time could actually survive the mosquitoes and other parasites. He dreaded the prospect. One might be wiser to choose the sharks.

Rather than release the pilots after the ordeal, Lieutenant Green took them directly to Major Brennan, who gave them a short break, then herded them back onto the truck.

"This guy is turning more GI by the minute," groaned Sandy Sadler.

"Christ, it's 1730 now. Couldn't he let us off after all that?" groused Callahan.

Shortly, the truck squeaked to a stop and the men reluctantly jumped down. Spirits soared quickly, however, for they found themselves standing on the flight line before a long row of beautiful Lockheed P-38 Lightnings. The huge fighters stood proudly in their olive drab skins, their four 50-caliber machine guns and 20-millimeter cannons bristling from their noses.

Whistles, sighs, and other expressions abounded, and Lee found himself caught up in the spirit with the rest of the men. Gorgeous, he thought, gorgeous!

"Men," announced a smiling Major Brennan, "here are your new toys. In case you're wondering, no, they aren't the latest, the Model Ls. But they *are* brand new Model Js. Most new pilots don't rate new aircraft. They get the left over crap." He punctuated the statement with a slight grin. "We've had the squadron markings, ID numbers, and your names painted on them. Now, go find your birds!"

Lee quickly found his, the one with the large numerals 161 painted on the outboard side of each engine. He circled it slowly, taking in every detail. While the original XP-38 was an older design than the Bell P-39 and the Curtiss P-40, both of which were being phased into obsolescence, the Lightning had proven to be an extremely effective all-purpose fighter plane, and improved models were being shipped to both theaters of the war in large numbers.

The conventional fighters of the war were single-fuselage, low-wing monoplanes in which the pilot's cockpit was placed midway between the engine and the tail. In contrast, the P-38 was what Lee's advanced instructor back in the States had called "a three-piecer." Two long, slender booms containing Allison in-line engines extended back to a horizontal stabilizer that joined them at the rear. A streamlined cockpit pod was mounted on the center of the wing between the twin engine booms with their huge three-bladed propellers. German pilots had labeled the aircraft "Der Gabelschwantz Teufel," the Fork-tailed Devil.

The lettering, LT. LEE MARKS, beneath the side cockpit window swelled Lee's pride. He climbed up onto the wing, opened the canopy, and gazed at the fresh, unmarred interior. He had never seen a brand new ship before, let alone one with his own name painted on the side. The exterior details and the instrument panel and controls looked similar to those of the older Model F on which he had trained back in the States. But there had to be differences. He was anxious to learn about them.

"Okay, button them up!" called Major Brennan. "Just time to get back for chow. Tomorrow, we fly. Oh, and don't look a gift horse in the mouth…I bite."

Early in the evening, the pilots of the 125th Squadron gathered to watch a variety of warbirds landing on the three parallel runways of Seven-mile Drome. The fledglings' excitement ran high, and it merged with anxiety to prompt a steady flow of questions and debates.

"Still can't figure it," Bubba said, "How did *we* end up with new aircraft?"

"Can't tell you *how* the major did it," Lieutenant Green answered. "He has ways of getting what he wants." He paused, then added, "But then you'll find that out."

Chapter 3

Lee awoke with a start and turned his head to scan the Quonset hut. He had known darkness that merely restricted vision. He had known darkness that nearly subdued all light. But the darkness that greeted him had obliterated all light forever. He raised a sweaty hand and slowly drew the back of it close to his face. He smelled it, but he never saw it.

He might have been drifting through a black hole in space but for two things, the pain caused by the unyielding GI cot and the dissonance of the invisible menagerie of jungle birds outside the hut. It was the shrieker that had wakened him. Some of the birds sang sweet, lyrical melodies, not unlike those he had heard in the States. Others produced no melody but rather a shrill, high-pitched trilling sound. Then there were those who shrieked their primitive jungle dialogue. They were the loudest, and Lee vowed that, should he ever get the chance, he would reduce their population.

His thoughts returned to the evening in the mess hall with Major Brennan. The major had outlined many specific characteristics of their new aircraft and compared their strengths and weaknesses with those of the principal Japanese craft they would be meeting in combat. One rule he had stressed over and over was, "Never try to turn with a Zero, or for that matter any of the smaller Japanese planes." The propeller torque of the enemy's single engines gave them a particular advantage in short left turns. The heavy Lightning weighed nearly eight tons, and its two counter-rotating Allison engines neutralized torque, thus favoring neither direction. While it moved well for a craft its size, agile it was not.

But those Allisons did offer enormous power. The new Model J could outrun the Zero in straight-and-level flight, a dive, and a long, shallow climb. "But in climbing," Major Brennan had added, "never climb so steep you give away your speed. And if you get caught in a stall or even close to one, you're dead. Altitude, speed, power, weapons, and a ship that can take hits and still bring you home are your advantages. Use 'em or lose 'em. But *don't* count on taking hits. Your job is to *give* them, not *take* them."

Then their new CO presented to his new charges the highlight of the meeting. Throughout its history, dating back to the late-thirties, the P-38 had been plagued by a ghostlike problem in power dives, an aerodynamic design phenomenon called compressibility. It had brought down many planes and killed many pilots. When the airspeed in a power dive was allowed to increase much beyond 450 mph the P-38 would develop a nose heavy attitude and begin to shudder. Unless the pilot reacted immediately by reducing speed he could be caught in a dive from which there was no recovery.

"Now they've finally given us the solution on these late Model Js," Brennan had said. He went on to explain the new dive brakes, flaps built into the undersides of the outer wing sections. The four-inch by four-foot flaps could be lowered at any speed. In addition to quickly slowing the craft, the new flaps would pull the nose up, even without assistance from the pilot. "We hope," he had added, "that they might also help shorten our turn radius. But don't think for a minute that you'll be able to turn with a Zero." Lee's pulse quickened with the thoughts of flying the new ship and of combat.

That night, the twisting and turning that Lee heard coming from the other bunks told him he wasn't the only one too charged to sleep. It seemed he had hardly drifted off when he came awake again.

There would be no more sleep. He somehow got dressed and headed for the mess hall. At least he'd beat the lines. Rain had begun to fall, a lazy, light rain, that glittered slightly against the lonely, distant yard light. He popped into the mess hall, closed the screen door behind him, and quickly surveyed the long, wood-floored room. Serving had not yet begun, but small clusters of men sat drinking coffee and quietly talking. He drew a cup and added some milk mix to it. He looked at it, blinked, looked away, then looked again. The brew had turned gray! Lee glanced around. Apparently nobody had noticed his reaction. Unsure he should drink the concoction, he decided he'd watch and follow the lead of the others. He turned to choose a seat.

"Hey, Marks!" a voice called. "Over here." It was Major Brennan, sitting with Captain Robesky. He moved to join them, spilling some hot coffee or whatever it was on one leg as he walked.

"Damn it," he said softly, plunking the hot mug on the table. "Good way to start the day."

"Trouble sleeping?" quizzed Brennan, a revealing twinkle in his eyes. "I figured you'd be one of the first ones over. I'll bet the others won't be too far behind you."

"You'll bet?" Captain Robesky shot at the major. "You *did* bet, remember, Mo? I bet you two-bits that Marks *would* be the first one over. Now, pay up!" They laughed together and Major Brennan dug for the quarter, came up empty, and flipped a buck on the table. The major's natural, robust belly-laugh and the infectious impact it had on those around him fascinated Lee. It compelled him to laugh right along, even when he felt outside the humor.

Then Brennan suddenly became serious. "I'm glad you *are* here, Lieutenant. We were just talking about your friend, Lieutenant Nash, and his problem. Maybe you can be of some help. Is it really as serious as it's beginning to look?"

"Well, yes—and no." Lee caught their perplexed reactions. "Bubba has had this problem off and on a few times during training, but then he got over it. It's just a weak stomach, I guess."

"Weak stomach or weak head?" the captain asked.

"Well, okay, I guess it's in his head, but he'll get over it." Lee hesitated. "I don't have to tell *you* about the adjustment to Army food. But the food here yesterday was by far the worst we've had." Lee sipped his coffee, surprised that the taste did, in fact, resemble coffee. Then he added, "I didn't know Bubba then, but I imagine his momma spoiled him, at least on the food thing."

"Lots of spoiled kids here," Brennan acknowledged. "I don't particularly want the job of unspoiling them. Can Nash fly? Is he any good *off* the ground?"

"Right up with the best in our Advanced Class."

"Well, Marks, is there any helping the kid? Anything we can do?"

Lee stalled momentarily, fearful that he might betray his friend, but the officers seemed sincere. He told them of his nearly successful attempt of the previous evening. Then he added the business of the bananas and coconut milk.

"Is there any chance of getting some special consideration from *them?*" Lee asked, nodding toward the kitchen.

"Hell, that's an idea," Major Brennan replied. "I don't know *these* guys. Back at Dobo I'm sure we can work it. Anyway, it's worth a try," he added as he jumped up and struck out for the kitchen. A few minutes later he returned, a broad smile on his face.

"I guess I don't need to ask," said Captain Robesky.

"In the bag, Marks. You catch Nash before he gets here and send him to the back door of the kitchen. They'll fix him up with something to calm his gut down. Then maybe he'll learn to eat the garbage they give us out here."

"How'd you do it, Mo?" asked the captain.

"Simple. I told them the kid is a really hot pilot and we need him. They laughed. Then I told them Nash has a really bad ulcer and it's got to be controlled right away, or he'll be grounded." He paused to light a cigarette. "Cost me a jug of Scotch, Marks. He'd better be worth it." Captain Robesky rolled his eyes and laughed. Lee grinned nervously, gulped his remaining coffee, and headed out to find Bubba Nash.

When Lee returned for his breakfast and was asked by others about Bubba's absence, he simply muttered something about "probably out looking for bananas and coconuts." The subject was dropped.

As the cadre of newcomers stepped out of the mess hall into a soft but steady rain, they were met by Major Brennan. One glance told Lee the upcoming announcement would be more serious than anything they'd previously heard from their CO. A second glance suggested the major was more than serious; he was angry. And getting completely soaked through would probably not ease his disposition.

"All right, you yardbirds," Brennan said. "Listen up. It wasn't supposed to go this way, but once in a while things happen that I can't control. On this one—" He paused to run a sweeping glare over the group, "I'm thoroughly pissed off, so don't do anything to make it worse. We were scheduled for a couple of days of orientation and flying with our new birds before heading to our base at Dobodura. Unfortunately, someone fucked up. Now we're told we have to clear out this morning to make room for more pilots and planes coming in from Australia. You've got ten minutes to pack up and catch the truck to the flight line." With that, Major Brennan wheeled, climbed into his jeep, and spattered mud as he jerked the clutch out and sped off.

"Wow," said Bubba, "he doesn't leave much doubt about what he wants, does he?"

By the time the rookie pilots had gathered their gear and trucked to the flight line, the rain had stopped, and the sky to the northeast was clearing. While the morning sun would take another two hours to clear the Owen Stanley Mountains, the sky had lightened enough for an appraisal of conditions. The scattered cirrus clouds that remained seemed to be chasing the rolling, gray rain clouds away.

"Gather 'round, men," Major Brennan instructed.

First, he introduced Sergeant Worley, the squadron line chief, a wiry, little man, unlike the burly mechanic stereotype Lee had come to expect.

"Sergeant Worley is the best damned line chief in the Pacific, so when he tells you something about your aircraft, you'd be wise to listen. The maintenance problem he doesn't know about hasn't been invented yet."

The impish line chief smiled proudly and then introduced the two crew chiefs and two mechanics who had accompanied him from their base at Dobodura.

"They're all ready, sir," Sergeant Worley informed the major, "except that the oil pressure on the port engine of Number 164 is showing a tad low. She sounds fine. I think it's just the gauge." Then he turned to the pilots. "We only have five of us to tuck all of you in for this take-off, so you'll have to be a little patient." He motioned back to Major Brennan.

"Your flight leaders will give you final instructions, and from this minute on, you do exactly as they say." The major paused long enough to send a menacing glare to each man. "And the guy who breaks his airplane," he continued, "had better hope the Japs will adopt him. Now let's get ready and head for home." Lieutenants Gustafson and Green each gathered three of the new pilots and led them down the flight line.

"Nash," Major Brennan said, "you'll fly Number Two slot on my wing. Barton, you're Number Three, and Marks, you're Tail End Charlie. You know what that means?"

"Yes, sir," Lee replied. "Watch our backsides."

"Let's hope you don't see anything behind us but eight of our birds, but once we cross over the mountains, anyone might show up. All of you, check that sun every few seconds. This is Nippy's favorite time of day."

Lee's excitement raced within him as he pulled the tiny retractable ladder out and down from the rear of the cockpit pod. After a brief hesitation, he stepped up in the prescribed routine. He remembered the time at advanced training when he carelessly rushed the routine, slipped off the first rung and skinned his shin.

His heart pounded as he climbed down into the cockpit and settled into the bucket seat. Sergeant Worley climbed up and helped Lee secure his parachute and harness straps. The kindly little man tapped Lee on the shoulder, flipped a quick, careless salute, and disappeared. Lee heard the retractable ladder thunk into place, and soon he saw the sergeant off to his left giving the start-up signal.

Lee adjusted his throttle and mixture controls on the left and then reached awkwardly around the control column to the ignition and starter switches with his right hand. The powerful V-12 Allison coughed and shook for a few seconds before settling into the smooth, lusty roar that brought to mind a powerful stallion lurching forward, anxious to run faster and farther than the others. He repeated the process with the starboard engine. The five ground crewmen hustled from one ship to the next, pulling the wheel chocks and signaling the "all clear" to each pilot.

"Red Flight, taxi in order of position," came Major Brennan's voice through the headphones.

Lee kept his toes on the right and left brake pedals, jockeying the red knobs of the twin throttles gently with his left hand, as he watched the first three planes in his flight pull out of the line and head south on the hard surface taxiway. He followed cautiously, getting the feel of the brakes as he rolled along. They turned into position for their final run-up of the engines and the last check of the instruments before commencing their take-off roll. One by one, Major Brennan called them for a final "ready" signal.

"Red Flight rolling," came the major's voice.

The pounding of Lee's heart surprised him. Calm down, he thought. You've done this lots of times. When the Number Three plane piloted by Lieutenant Barton cleared the runway, Lee pushed the throttles forward enough to start the sleek machine moving once more. He turned his head one last time to check for incoming traffic and then rolled onto the runway. He stopped the ship briefly, checked his propeller setting, and shoved the two throttles forward to the war emergency stops. Reaching maximum power, he released the brakes. The acceleration pressed him back into the seat. At 50 mph he felt a slight crosswind from the left and compensated.

Lee held the big ship down until well past flying speed. Then he eased back on the yoke and rotated the Lightning upward. This was the moment that pilots loved most dearly, that moment that made men sacrifice to be pilots, that moment when the clumsy, gravity-stricken Homo sapien defies nature and becomes a bird. If he lived to fly a thousand years, Lee Marks would never tire of it, would never experience a take-off as purely a physical phenomenon. It was a spiritual rite, a transcendent denial of the laws.

Lee jolted himself back to reality, retracted his landing gear, checked his instruments, and followed the other ships in a gentle climbing turn to the right.

"Red One," came Major Brennan's voice. "Come on up, boys. Close it up on me. Tend to business."

He knew, Lee thought, he knew what we were experiencing, what we were thinking. As fast as Lee was climbing, he could barely close the gap. About a mile ahead he saw his leader begin another slight turn to the right, the turn that would set their compass heading at zero-five-zero to the northeast and over the Owen

Stanley Mountains. Lee seized the opportunity to cut the corner, a move that almost took him past the Number Three man, Barton.

Gradually, the Red Flight closed up into the finger-four formation designed to hold the four-plane group close together while at the same time providing the visibility required for protection from attack by other planes. Theoretically, what one pilot couldn't see from the formation, another could. Their dangerous blind spot lay in that area below and behind the formation. Lee knew that area was his responsibility and would lead to a stiff neck. He quickly developed a focus routine that ran clockwise 360 degrees, beginning with the overhead rearview mirror attached to the windshield on the outside of the cockpit. From there, he rotated to check to the right side, right rear upper, then right rear lower, back to the mirror, then to the left side, left rear upper, then left rear lower, and finally around to straight ahead, instrument panel, check his formation position off Barton's right wing, and begin the routine all over again.

The dark gray, shadowy side of the Owen Stanleys rose before them, demanding a steep climb for sufficient altitude. At 10,000 feet Lee had just secured his oxygen mask when he felt the automatic unit kick in. The sky had cleared and their altitude had finally put them in a visual line with the rising morning sun. It seemed to smile in at Lee over his starboard engine. He looked down with fascination as they reached 16,000 feet and cleared the rugged summit of the mountains. The glorious moment blended a swell of pride and appreciation within him. Then he reminded himself to check for enemy planes so that the experience didn't come to an abrupt ending.

Once across, Major Brennan led them in a shallow descent following the terrain downward on the north side of the mountains. Lee throttled back accordingly to hold his position and checked his instruments, then the sun, once more. He had just completed his cycle when the full impact of what lay before them struck.

Beneath them at approximately 10,000 feet stood an ugly mass of storms, each made up of clusters of clouds that seem to be competing with one another for dominance. Lee felt himself tighten. Training flights had taken them into, over, and around storms, but he had never seen weather like this. The silver-white tops of the cumulonimbus monsters darkened to threatening gray near their bottoms.

"Red One," crackled Lee's headset. "Now we'll see how good you are," came the major's voice. "Tighten it up, follow your flight leader, trust your wingman, and everything will be fine. Down we go."

Lee snuggled up as closely as he dared to Lieutenant Barton's aircraft. He had known that sooner or later things would come to this. Aloysius "Black Bart" Barton was not Lee's favorite squadron member. He was a selfish, aggressive loud-mouth who seemed to get his kicks by stirring up trouble. But worse, he flew with a similar style, brash, careless, and unpredictable. And now Lee found his very survival dependent upon Black Bart's ability to stay on Major Brennan's wing, no matter how bad the visibility became. What if Bart panicked and suddenly veered off, right into Lee's flight path? Lee heard his mind say, "It'll be over quickly."

As they descended through the upper layer, their leader eased smoothly to the right, then left, picking his way from one opening to another as though the whole threatening mass was mapped out before him. By the time they had changed course a half-dozen times, Lee began to feel a resurging confidence, especially when he caught a glimpse of jungle terrain some 7,000 feet below. When they broke clear of the clouds and into steady rain at 3,000 feet, Lee became aware that he was already soaking wet from perspiration.

On the major's command they broke into single file string formation and reduced their airspeed to allow large gaps between planes. Lee could barely make out three, perhaps four landing strips passing to his left as they flew their downwind leg. He recalled that Major Brennan had told them they'd be landing on Strip 4-Y, a 4,000-foot strip surfaced with steel Marston matting. He reduced his airspeed to 130 mph to widen the gap before him. When he saw Black Bart's landing gear and flaps go down, he followed suit.

Almost before he knew it, Lee had made his two left turns and found himself flaring out and settling in. The rain increased, blurring his view of the steel matting. When his main gear touched down, the vibrations and whirring noise were unlike anything he had heard or felt. Gently, he eased his nose down. He applied his brakes, gradually increasing the pressure as he gained a feel for the Lightning's traction on the slippery matting, much of which was obscured by slimy mud. At one point, his brakes locked and he began a skid. Quickly, he eased off, then reapplied the pressure. Up ahead, he saw Bart turn left off the runway. As Lee slowed and gained control of his ship, the end of the runway came up quickly, only to be lost again in a blinding burst of rain.

He made an impulsive guess and turned left at the spot where he thought Bart had turned. Suddenly, his Lightning shuddered, slowed, and sank into mud that dragged the big craft to a stop. Lee felt like he'd been struck by a muddy thunderbolt when he realized he had turned a few feet short of the taxiway and slipped off the steel matting. He tried revving up the engines and rocking the Lightning's nose slightly with up and down elevator movements, but the nose wheel was buried in the mud. Better his own nose was buried in the mud, he thought.

As his frustration became panic, Lee looked out to see a ground crewman waving for him to cut his engines. He responded, and within a minute a truck had backed up toward him, hooked a cable to his nose gear, and began to ease him out of the muck. He sat there helplessly as a tractor tug took over and dragged him around the corner and down a series of curved taxiways to a spot where he deftly maneuvered Lee's ship backwards into its assigned spot.

As he extricated himself from the cockpit and closed it up, Lee turned to find Major Brennan standing in the rain, waiting. Lee struggled down the slippery ladder and made for his commanding officer. Brennan stood there, rain dripping off his visor, coldly surveying Lee as he approached.

"You got bad eyes?" Brennan bellowed over the roar of engines and the slapping of huge three-bladed propellers against the rain. Before Lee could think or respond, his superior continued, "Doesn't matter how goddamned good you can fly if you smash the son of a bitch up on the ground!"

"Yes, sir!" he responded snappily, adding a nervous, involuntary salute. "That thick rain suddenly blinded me and—"

"Cut the happy horseshit!" Brennan roared. "We don't salute in battle zones. You'd better hope all those birds up there who had to wait for you to make your mud pies get down all right."

Lee felt the major's eyes burning holes right through him.

"And remember this, yardbird," Major Brennan continued. "You've just had *your* snafu. Used it up—no more coming!"

Chapter 4

▼

Second Lieutenant Lee Marks stood there slouching in the rain as his CO stomped off. He had prided himself on being exempt from such verbal abuse since early in basic training. But the self-designed banner of success had been jerked from his grip by a muddy mistake.

"Hey, stupid!" A shoulder bumped him hard from behind. Lee spun around, his fists clenched, but Black Bart was already a couple of steps away and swaggering down the flight line. He shouted back over his shoulder, "Next time, follow me like you were told to!"

Lee started after Bart, but before he could close the gap, the familiar voice of his mother, that life-time force he called his "regulator" spoke from within. He could see her stern face and the familiar index finger that jabbed at him as she talked.

"If you're really sure you're right, you fight like an angry tiger and you win! But if there's any doubt, any doubt at all, you take your lumps and walk away." Then came the words he always tried not to hear, "Your good-for-nothing father never learned that."

Struggling to file away his anger and reassemble his shattered pride, Lee joined the group of saturated khaki-clad pilots as they gathered around Major Brennan. Their leader was pointing out the B-24s, B-25s, and P-40s that belonged to other detachments of the Fifth Air Force. He explained that there were many more aircraft than they could see from their vantage point. The base had grown from a single strip to four, and staff projections called for as many as eleven.

The major smiled then extended his hands palms up and glanced upward to a silvery spot in the clouds where the sun threatened to break through. As though commanded by his gesture, the rain abruptly stopped.

"That, men, is New Guinea weather. It rains every day for nine months. Then comes the monsoon season—which we are into right now. Take a good look," he went on. "That weather up there takes as many of us out as the Japs do. Come on." He turned and led them up a pathway that had been blessed with a topping of heavy gravel. Its crunch beneath their boots was tempered by a squishy sound, but it did not quite yield mud.

"This is Operations, Briefing, and Intel," said the major, waving to an open-sided structure, little more than a corrugated roof supported by long, crooked poles. "Wait here while I report in."

He returned shortly, and as they resumed their trek he pointed out the mess hall and the hospital tents. He led them back toward the edge of the jungle to an area that brought home to Lee who they were and where they were. Ahead of them, to the west, on an upward slope stood a vast city of four-sided tents with peaked, pyramid-shaped tops. A groan went up among the men.

"Sorry—really sorry," Major Brennan said with a smirk. "I tried to get you reservations at the Waldorf, but they gave us the Ritz instead. Your gear will be in on The Golden Goose about noon. Head for that tent with the little rag flag above it." He gestured up the hill. "You should find a Sergeant Rommel there. He can tell you which tents to choose from. If you need me, I live here," he concluded, turning to enter a nearby tent.

The nine newcomers followed their two experienced mates into the maze of wet, musty smelling canvas.

"God damn it," sputtered Black Bart. "This is worse than fuckin' basic."

"Oh, it's not so bad," countered Bubba, "and you heard what he said. It's only temporary."

"Bubba," scoffed Sandy Sadler, "everything in this war is temporary—including us."

"And you think it's going to get better where we're going, Bubba?" fired Barton. "Shit, we won't even get tents up there!"

Lee felt his anger bubbling once more. It was more than Black Bart's recent jab at him. It was an accumulation of ongoing bitching that had begun in basic, continued through flight training to advanced training, and all the way across the Pacific. The husky lieutenant had little going for him, and his inappropriate comments did nothing to lend him charm. He was a product of crooked genes. An immense, hooked nose centered his angry face with its dark eyes and pronounced cheekbones, and unruly black hair stuck out rakishly, no matter how often the bullish agitator combed it or slicked it down with ointments. He reminded Lee of an angry porcupine. Someone in basic had suggested a crewcut and received a bloody lip for an answer.

"Hey! Look at this!" a voice from up front called. Lee moved up to see. There was a large sign with amateurish lettering that read: FUNGUS FIELD, POPULATION 305. The five had been crossed out and a four substituted beneath it.

Soon they came to another sign, a directional one with two large arrows. Someone had crossed out the large letters that spelled LATRINE. Below, they had printed in crooked letters, DYSENTARY DROPPINGS. One arrow pointed toward the latrine area with the added words, IF YOU CAN MAKE IT! The other arrow pointed to the nearby jungle and said, IF YOU CAN'T!

Lieutenants Green and Gustafson went on ahead, stopped briefly to talk with another man, then disappeared among the tents. The man, dressed in fatigue trousers and G.I. undershirt soaked with perspiration approached the group. He had a large, angular head with thinning wisps of red hair that had long before failed to cover the top. Beads of sweat hung on his forehead defying gravity. His cold, angry eyes were separated by a large, rumpled nose that attested to more than one bar brawl. His mouth, clamped on an old cigar stub, seemed to be fixed in a perpetual scowl. His enormous arms and shoulders were covered with tattoos.

"This way," the man grunted, leading them back among the tents. He stopped, held up four fingers, and motioned toward a tent. Lee stepped out, but four others from the back of the line had the jump on him, and he was destined once more to endure the plague of Black Bart. He scanned the remaining faces. His misery would be shared by Bubba Nash, a nice but ever serious guy named Robert Logan, and Sandy Sadler, the bright squadron clown. It could be worse.

"Is your name really Sergeant Rommel?" Bubba asked.

The man said nothing, but Lee saw his eyes narrow, the scowl deepen, the cigar twitch, and the awesome fists clench momentarily.

"I suppose then they call you the Jungle Fox," said Bubba triumphantly.

The gargantuan sergeant turned on Bubba and glared down at him. He said nothing, but his face twisted into a mask of contempt that threatened to melt the skinny second lieutenant on the spot.

Bubba finally got the message.

"Well, ahhh, you know, ahhh, most of us have nicknames. You know, like my name's Bubba." He turned timidly to Lee for support. Lee hadn't seen Bubba turn quite that pale since the time back in primary when he threw up all over Sandy Sadler in the mess hall.

Sergeant Rommel turned and led them far back into the city of tents, stopping at one that was perched right at the jungle's edge. He motioned with his bird finger at the tent.

"Get your blankets and shit down at the supply tent," he said. He turned and disappeared among the peaked tents.

The five pilots looked over their new abode. The open sides were screened with mosquito netting. The floor was raised about a foot above ground level and was planked with rough-sawn mahogany. Lee considered the tent a lucky draw, since most of the other tent floors were elevated three feet or more above ground level. He and his mates would have it much easier than those other guys who had to scramble up and down rickety stairs. But the cracks he saw in the wooden floor were an obvious invitation to the creepy crawlies of the jungle.

The tent could accommodate six men; the numbers had worked out in the group's favor. There were four portable canvas cots matched to the four open sides of the tent and two more lined up parallel to each other, sandwiching the tall, center pole that held the tent roof up. Apparently newcomers didn't even rate sturdy cots with springs and mattresses.

The five men all but filled the aisle between the center island of tents and the perimeter. Yet, when each had chosen a cot and stretched out, the tent seemed adequate in size. Lee broke the silence.

"Bubba, have you ever been pounded, pounded really good?"

"Well, ahhh—"

"He couldn't do that," interrupted Bart. "Bubba's an officer!"

"Yeah," said Bubba. "I'm an officer."

"Ohhh, Bubba," groaned Robert Logan, usually the quietest man in their group. "That Rommel probably eats second lieutenants for lunch."

"He doesn't even spit their bars out," added Sandy Sadler. "He just grinds them up and squeezes them into his cavities with his tongue."

"Anyway, Bubba," Lee advised, "I'd stay away from him. He's awfully mad at somebody for something."

"Ah, he's all bluff," said Black Bart. "I could take him."

"Yeah, yeah, yeah," answered Sandy. "We know, Bart. We know."

Their conversation drifted to a review of the flight from Port Moresby. As Lee might have predicted, Bubba and Bart both seemed to have missed the beauty of the scene just prior to their mountain crossing as well as any feelings they might have had when they cleared the range and started down into the weather. Bubba's mind had been on his flying, and Black Bart's mind? No one would ever know. Lee retired from the discussion when it became a speculative debate on the future of their squadron.

"I'll bet they send us up to that new strip at Gusap," said Bubba. "Jeez, that's less than a hundred miles from the big Jap base at Madang!"

Lee looked over to see Sandy Sadler sit up and swing his legs over the side of his canvas cot. He pulled a large, hunting knife from a leg holster and began whittling on a piece of wood.

"Shit, Bubba, use your head," said Bart. "They can use the old equipment, the P-40s, for that short range. They won't take us that far west. They'll put us at Nadzab where we can fly east, north, or west. That way they can use us against the Jap airbases at Hollandia, Kavieng, and Rabaul and still have us in good position to hit the Jap shipping all over the place."

For once Lee agreed with Bart. He pulled the mosquito netting down around his bunk, rolled over, and tried to sleep.

"I hope not," Bubba went on. "I don't want to go around shooting at ships, and besides I don't like flying over all that water—and those sharks."

Whack!

Startled, Lee turned. Sandy's knife stood upright, its large, sturdy blade stuck in the rough wooden floor, its handle still quivering. Separate halves of a nine-inch centipede scampered off in opposite directions.

"Ooooh, yuck!" exclaimed Bubba.

"Kind of reminds me of my two-faced sister-in-law," drawled Robert Logan. The handsome blond with a crewcut seldom contributed more than one line. Lee regarded the Georgia Tech graduate as intelligent, a capable and reliable pilot, and an honest and dependable friend. He had the characteristics essential for leadership, except for one thing. Robert was a follower.

"Nash in there?" came a voice from outside. "Lieutenant Nash in there?" It was Major Brennan.

Bubba catapulted from his bunk right into an entanglement with his mosquito netting.

"Be right there!" he called as he tipped the cot over in his effort to escape. Then to save face, he hopped lithely off the step just outside the tent. But on landing his feet found slippery ground and he gyrated like a khaki-clad spider before landing on his butt in the mud.

"Bubba, you're clumsier than a three-legged horse on a diving board," hooted Sandy Sadler.

Lee couldn't hear the major's words, but he concluded that the major was once again outlining a special chow program for the gangly, young tent-mate. Lee thought about Bubba. He knew that the twenty-year-old was the only child of a St. Louis druggist and his wife. Bubba had a good head, one year of junior college, and a sincere, childlike devotion to his role in the war. But Bubba was indeed a spoiled child, and he was a paradox. On the ground he appeared to be a simple, uncoordinated boob, but at the controls of a P-38 Lightning he had the natural sense of flight and the quick reactions that come from within, the talents that belong to a select few.

Lee considered himself to be among the few. His own aptitude and love for flying had been discovered during the summer after high school. A neighbor in their Polish district worked as an aircraft mechanic at a small field west of Chicago. The kind man had invited the fatherless Lee Marklevitz to go up for a ride. One ride had led to another. Soon, Lee's mentor had begun a series of informal flying lessons in his yellow J-3 Piper Cub. Lee saved his part-time job money so that he could at least help pay for the gas.

The fever had immediately infected Lee. While he couldn't afford to go for his private license, he began to lay plans—plans for Uncle Sam to pay the bill. He knew in that summer of 1940 that his mother had been scrimping to add to the college fund that he had been building. He also knew that the Army Air Corps preferred some college experience as a prerequisite to flight training. He could not know that by the time he had finished two years of college the United States would be embroiled in World War II. But, he reasoned, he had gotten what he wanted. Now it was payback time. If he survived to return home again, he would have done everything right. If not, none of it would really matter.

"Come on, Guys! Let's go!" someone shouted from outside the tent.

First Lieutenants Gustafson and Green had stopped by to guide the nine newcomers through the day. They made two long treks down the hill and back. First they went through processing at the supply tent and returned with their atabrine and salt tablets, mess kits, and woolen blankets. Then their guides led them all the way down to the aircraft flight line where they were introduced to, as Lieutenant Green put it, "one of the best friends you could have over here—the Golden Goose."

The Goose, the product of a midnight requisition credited to Major Brennan, was an older glass-nosed B-25 medium bomber with surprisingly low flight time on it. It had been stripped of all weapons but the .50-calibers in the top turret and tail. Its bomb bay doors had been sealed and a sturdy floor had been added above them. A door had been cut into the left side of the fuselage just aft of the wing to convert the ship to a personnel and supply transport plane for the 483rd Fighter Group. On each side of its nose was painted a large, smiling golden goose wearing long, blond hair, panties and a bra. The B-25 served primarily to haul needed parts and supplies from Townsville, Australia, but it often carried members of the fighter group to Australia for staff meetings, medical treatment, or R and R.

A sweaty corporal tossed their duffels down to them, then scrambled down and plopped in the Goose's shadow for a snort from a newly acquired bottle of gin.

By the time they reached their tents the second time, some grumbling about the half-mile, uphill trek had begun. The hot sun bore down on the saturated landscape, and Lee felt like he was inhaling steam.

"It's so hot the chili peppers will be screaming for mercy!" offered Sandy.

"You'll get used to it," Lieutenant Gustafson said with an encouraging smile. "Now that you have all your gear together, we'll turn around and hike back down to the mess hall. Then at 1300 hours, Mo wants you to have an orientation session. From 1400 hours on, we work on our aircraft, mostly painting, stuff like that. Grab your mess kits."

Lee spent no effort in analyzing the lunch; he forked it down, washed his kit, and headed for the Ops Shack and their orientation meeting. Bubba was already there when Lee arrived. He greeted Lee with a grin and a thumbs-up sign.

"It's great, Lee. I don't know where they found food like that—I'm not allowed to tell you—but it's only for a week. The major says by then I have to eat the regular stuff or starve to death."

"I'm betting you won't starve, Bubba."

Within minutes, the rest of the squadron members had settled in. Major Brennan strode to the front and then paused for a moment to look over his new charges. His khakis showed surprisingly few wrinkles. His cap sat as usual at a jaunty angle. His sleeves were rolled up above the elbows. He lit a cigarette, then sat on the edge of a table.

"The meek shall inherit the earth," the major said, gesturing through the open side of the shack to the muddy road outside. "Look at that mud. Anybody want it?" He paused. "I've got just a few things to say. Then I'll turn it over to Greenie and Gus." He paused once again and scanned the group with his sharp, blue eyes. "You have the best aircraft available. You have the best Air Force in the world backing you. On those days when you have doubts, just take a look at the Aussies. For equipment, they have Commonwealth Boomerangs and Wirraways, Lockheed Hudsons, Vultee Vengeances—*we* call them Vultee Vibrators; *they* call them dive bombers—Bristol Beauforts, Bristol Beaufighters, and a few Douglas Boston A-20s.

The only planes they have that we'd even consider flying might be the A-20s and the Bristol Beaufighters. But they're getting the job done. Compared to them, we're spoiled, spoiled rotten. Can you believe? Their Commonwealth Wirraway is nothing but the old AT-6 that you used in training with a few miserable guns added. You'd like to take that against a Zero?" He stood and eased to one side. "Now, Greenie and Gus are going to give you a head start on dealing with your situation here. Listen up and learn so you don't have to learn too many things the hard way." He flicked the ash from his cigarette and strode from the tent.

Lieutenants Green and Gustafson split the lead role for what they called the "greet 'em and beat 'em" session in which they outlined the problems, the "greet 'em" portion that came with jungle life in New Guinea, and the "beat 'em" suggestions for overcoming the hardships.

"First, let's deal with the larger picture," began Lieutenant Gustafson. "There are three kinds of guys out here: one, those who recognize the problems and solve them; two, those who sit around and bitch full-time; and three, those who do neither—nothing. Mo won't carry any squadron members who fit into the two or three slot. He says, 'We are *going* to be—I didn't say *hope to be*. I said *going* to be the leadership squadron in the Fifth Fighter Command.' Now, there are three excellent squadrons over in the 475th Fighter Group who have a big head start on us, and I'm sure they won't agree with that prediction. But the major's mind is made up—period."

The short, heavyset lieutenant paused to light a cigarette. Lee had watched Gus closely and he had watched the others react to the first lieutenant. Despite his robot-like presentations, Lee knew that he was already building a following. The men liked Gus and his pleasant smile, his warmth, and his apparent respect for each of them.

"Okay," he said, "here we go. Take notes," he added, pointing to his head. "We Gophers usually use first names or nicknames for call signs, both on the ground and in the air, so you decide who you are and that's the way it'll be. The major likes this in the air. It's simple and clean for us, yet it tells the Japs, if they are monitoring our frequencies, very little. If, for example, he calls for Red Flight to do something, that tells the Japs that four planes are about to do that. But if he calls for the flight leader by name to stay up or come down, or whatever. Well, you get the picture. Now, some situations, we still have to use the colors. By the way, the Major goes by Mo, Lieutenant Green is Greenie, and I'm Gus. In case you're wondering, Mo has eleven kills, I have nine, and Greenie has six, so all three of us have made 'ace.'

"The squadron will be named the Golden Gophers after the University of Minnesota football team where Mo played his college ball. We already have our ID numbers and names painted on our ships. This afternoon, we'll finish trimming them out with gold spinners and Jap flags for the three of us. Before you do any nose art on your ships, hold off until we can take a look at Mo's Golden Gopher, that is, when it's done. We've talked about maybe painting the same mean, old gopher on each of our ships, sort of an intimidating thing like the Flying Tigers. He said he'd leave that up to us.

"Always be alert around camp for Japs. Some of them didn't know what to do or had no place to go when we moved in, so they took off into the jungle. We've caught a few of the sneaky little devils coming into camp at night. Some say they came in to slit our throats; some say they were starving, just looking for food."

Gus," asked Robert Logan, "what did the Japs say they were after?"

"You turnee over. I needee placee to sleepee," injected Sandy.

"So far," said Gus, "I don't think any of them have had a chance to explain." He gestured with his hands, as though to say, "What are you going to do?" Following a stony silence, Gus moved on. "You'll meet your ground crews today and tomorrow, three per aircraft. Treat these guys right. Your lives depend on the quality of their work and their loyalty to you."

Gus paused to light another cigarette.

"I'm about done for now. Just a couple more things. The terrain. You've got low flat lands and some swamp between here and the coast. And obviously, big, big mountains right behind us. Have respect for the mountains. Don't hedge hop in there. Some of the down drafts can even toss a Lightning ass over teakettle. Here," he said, reaching into a bag and tossing small packets, one by one, to each pilot.

He waited quietly as his fledglings unwrapped and opened up colorful silk scarves. "These will fit in your pockets. Or, you can wear them around your necks like they do in the movies. Whatever. But if you'll take a closer look, you'll find a pretty good map of northeastern New Guinea there, including many bases, rivers, mountains, and even some native villages. If you go down, that little piece of silk will become very important. It can really help in communicating with the natives, trying to show them where you are and where you need to go. Just one thing, don't mark anything additional on the map, not your home base, nothing. I think you can see why. Greenie?"

Lieutenant Green stepped in. He was a tall, slender man with curly light brown hair, hazel eyes, and two sets of sharp dimple-ridges down his cheeks to his jaw. He moved about in a bent posture with a sliding step that could be called slinky.

"He looks like a spook to me," Sandy Sadler had said after their first meeting in Port Moresby. Later, Sandy had conceded that Greenie was a regular, everyday guy who might, in fact, be the ultimate authority on survival in New Guinea.

"I don't have any long paragraphs to recite to you, just a lot of short one-liners that *could* save you a lot of grief. Ready?"

"Ready," several voices responded.

"Okay. First, the climate. Accept it, deal with it," he said seriously, "because you'll never change it. The real rains begin in September and last until April, although the monsoon season is usually considered to be December through March. Okay, a bunch of things that relate to weather. Keep your feet as dry as you can. Once your boots get wet you'll play hell getting them dry again. Any chance you get, grab onto an extra pair or two. Many of us like the slip-on engineer boots. They're higher, easy to slip in and out of, easier to dry out, and they protect your legs from the little biters. Some guys prefer to cut the tops down some. But one warning, they'll pop right off when your parachute opens. Because of that, a lot of the guys have opted for paratrooper boots that are tied and buckled on.

"You're living and working in the biggest disease factory known to man. Admittedly our facilities don't encourage personal hygiene, but the better you do at it, the better you'll feel. The two biggest threats have been malaria and dysentery. We're learning to control the dysentery, mainly with treated water and lots of canned cheese. Don't even *think* of skipping your daily Atabrine tablets. They can't totally prevent malaria, but they sure as hell increase your chances. Here's a survival summary that's easy to remember: Atabrine and salt tabs, eat right, don't drink untreated water, use mosquito netting at night, keep boots, socks, and feet as dry as possible.

"Okay, let's go on." He paused and scratched his crotch. "Stay dry there, too," he advised. "We do have some pests that can make life miserable if you let them, like foot-long rats, plus leeches, flies, bugs, worms, and mosquitoes. The chiggers will get onto your legs and burrow into your skin to lay their eggs whenever you move through the grass or brush. Best to tuck your pants into your socks if you're out there. Helps to boil your socks when you get back. There are a few poisonous snakes in the area, and they *don't* rattle. Occasionally a good-sized constrictor is seen, probably not big enough to squeeze you to death. They're not poisonous, but they do bite when they're pissed off—nasty guys. Just watch where you walk, especially at night.

"What about Cement Mixer Charlie, or whatever he's called?" someone asked.

"Some call him Bedcheck Charlie or Washing Machine Charlie. I call him Piss Call Paul. That's the Jap bomber harassment, usually a single Betty, during the night. You can hear him coming because his engines are purposely out of sync. One plane can't do too much damage.

His main objective is to keep us awake. Our AA gives three warning shots for air raids. And they're supposed to limit their range of fire to reduce falling shrapnel, but don't count on it. And keep in mind, Paul's not dropping chocolate chips. Dig your foxholes near your tent so you're ready. Oh, and try to dig your hole more like a trench with slots so it can drain.

"Okay," Greenie said as he checked his watch. "Let's finish this up. Keep your weapons cleaned and oiled. They'll rust in a few days out here. Be careful about buying into rumors or scuttlebutt. Leaves to the mainland generally come only after six months, but there's no guarantee. The mail takes at least a month, packages up to six months. For recreation, we have pick-up baseball and volleyball games, cards, inventing things to deal with the bad elements, some fishing in the rivers or lagoons, a few gardens, Tokyo Rose, and an occasional party where you can even dance—if you like dancing with men. If your tent is wired at all, you're allowed one forty-watt light bulb. The generators can't handle more than that. Watch out for jungle juice. These brews are made from every conceivable source, from dehydrated potatoes, bananas, to dirty socks, and they can kick like a mule. They can also make you very, very sick. I'll tell you right now, you get into juice trouble and Mo'll be all over you! Last thing, no uniform code. Some of the guys go almost naked. But remember, it's not ninety-five degrees with ninety-five percent humidity at 20,000 feet. Your mission may last for hours, and you can't run back to the base for your sweater."

"Ah, Greenie, what if—"

"No more questions right now." The voice came from behind the group. Lee turned to see Major Brennan working his way to the front. "We've got to wrap this up. Work to do." He paused, longer than usual, looking intently at the faces, one by one. The group grew quiet.

"Gentlemen," the major said, "you are now in World War II. To us out here, that *two* means *two* wars. One is against the Japs; the other is against the environment. We all know that, between the two of them, some of us won't make it home. But you do have *some* control over things. If you take care of yourselves and each other, you'll find that you'll be taken care of and you won't have to go it alone. Like football, this is a team sport out here." He looked at Black Bart. "Loners don't last long." Then he turned his gaze on Lee. "Not a bright future for pilots who can't see through a little rain either."

Chapter 5

▼

The morning's flight through the storms, the meetings, along with the trips between their tent and the flight line had Lee and his tent mates burned out by the time the sun settled behind the Owen Stanley Mountains. They had no electricity to their tent, so the black night sent the new Gophers to their cots early. Lee had just told himself he'd never be able to sleep on the unforgiving canvas when he dozed off. He sank quickly into a deep sleep founded by the rhythm of a gentle rain pattering on the canvas tent. But three hours later, the peaceful escape abruptly ended.

"What the hell! Who's under my bed?"

"Holy balls!"

"Jeez! Get out of my way!"

Lee jerked upright, startled by the pandemonium. What was it—air raid? The shouts from the darkness combined with stomping, bumping movements that shook the rickety floor beneath his cot, all to the backdrop of a loud, roaring noise that was like nothing he had ever heard. When a cot banged against his with a loud thud the black hell surrounding him began to take on some meaning. He swung his feet over the side, only to find rushing water that came to his knees and threatened to capsize his cot.

The continuing yells contributed little to Lee's comprehension. The cold water had indeed done more to bring him into the present.

"Hey! Grab my pants!" shouted Sandy Sadler.

"My boots! Where the hell are my boots?" asked Robert Logan.

"Get out of my way, Bubba!" growled Black Bart.

Gradually, the shouting subsided, but the cascade of water seemed relentless. Though it defied all common sense, Lee could only guess that they had been swamped by floodwaters rushing down the mountainside. Their duffels, boots, and anything else left on the floor had been swept across to Lee's side of the tent, presumably out beneath the mosquito netting and down the hillside. Lee had experienced the ferocity of Midwestern downpours. His mother had often chuckled, clucked, and said, "Someone dumped the thunder mug." But he had never imagined that so much rain could fall with such fury that it roared like a train. It blew into the tent on the windward side; it gushed down upon them through holes in the canvas; and it threatened their very foundation as it swept through the wobbly structure.

"Hasn't anybody got a flashlight?" Bubba asked.

"Hey, you new guys! Shut up over there so we can get some sleep!"

"Yeah! Yeah! I'll get you some sleep!" bellowed Black Bart.

"Now we know why the other tents have floors that are three feet off the ground," said Lee.

"Bubba, we've got *you* to thank," groaned Black Bart. "You pissed off that sergeant, and he fixed our asses good. In the morning, you can go find my stuff."

"Just ignore him, Bubba," said Sandy Sadler. "You don't go looking for his stuff until *after* you've found mine."

Though they could barely see one another, the quintet held a short meeting and decided to surrender to the elements. There seemed to be no escape, no place they could go. Since the base was below them and the flood ran downhill, they'd probably find no respite there. Struggling in the darkness, they managed to refasten the netting. Then they stretched out on wet cots, wherever they found them, and tried to salvage some rest, if no sleep.

When the rampage finally let up it was after midnight. Lee and Sandy slipped about on the muddy floor as they tried to assess the damage. They reasoned that the end of the storm would bring an invasion of threatening insects. Sandy began to laugh softly.

"I was just thinking," Sandy said, "we trained our butts off to learn to fly and to come over here and fight Japs. And look at us. They sure didn't teach us the right things, did they?"

"I wonder," Lee replied, "if the Japs taught their pilots the right things."

He flopped back onto his cot and began taking deep, rhythmic breaths to try for the relaxation necessary for slumber. When he finally found sleep, Lee also found himself attempting to fly over, under, and around massive thunderheads that reached to 40,000 feet. He had just flown directly into a huge, boiling cloud and watched the forces of nature rip the wings off his aircraft when the morning sounds of humanity mercifully brought him awake.

A treasure hunt through the mud under the tents directly below them on the hillside found most of their belongings, although Bart still needed a boot for his right foot and Bubba's cap had apparently floated to South America. They sloshed their way down the path to breakfast and then reported to Mo on the flight line. He gathered them together on a heavily graveled patch under a large palm tree.

"Tough night, huh?" he asked with the familiar smirk. "Too bad. We have a patrol to fly in an hour. After that we'll have some time to hit up the supply people and perhaps see about better quarters. But for now, forget about all that. It's time to get serious. Until they get clearance to move us up, we'll be here on an incredibly overcrowded base. And this overcrowded base is a tempting target for the Japs. The base commander is very nervous, and I don't blame him. With all these aircraft crowded together here on the ground, we'll look like another Hickham Field on December seventh if the Japs decide to hit us. So we'll be flying patrols, sometimes twice daily for a while—to watch for the Japs and to reduce the number of planes on the ground. Now, go meet your ground crews. Then get ready to go, grab your gear, and meet me right here at 0700 hours for a quick briefing."

Lee quickly found his Number 161 with the three members of his ground crew swarming over her, topping off the fuel tanks, checking the nose gear that he had buried in the mud, and feeding belts of fifty-caliber ammunition into the nose chamber. Lee stood quietly and watched. As they finished their jobs, they came over one by one to meet their pilot.

The crew chief, Staff Sergeant "Big Ole" Anderson, came across like an easy-going but very professional guy. The huge, muscular sergeant stood several inches taller than Lee, but he slouched, as though to even the height. The visor was tilted upward on the large-billed baseball cap that was twisted off center. The smudges of grease on his broad face said he'd been busy at something.

"Ya, I checked the nose gear real good," he said, "and she's okay. I gave everything some extra lubing. She looks real good. She's all set. Now you just be sure and tell me anything goes wrong. Right?"

"Sure thing, Chief," Lee said. "Keep up the good work." Lee knew—they both knew that the crew chief had a clear-cut edge in experience, an edge for which Lee was grateful.

Next, Lee met Corporal "Mashy" Maschka, a bareheaded and bare-chested armorer who had the build of a short, sturdy oak tree, capped by thick, wavy, black hair. Mashy quickly showed himself as an energetic extrovert who frequently revised the English language.

"Hey, Lieutenant!" Mashy said. "Look at this." He scurried down from his scaffolding and held out a Colt .45 still in its holster. "I was down by the strip in the jeep, taking some tools back to the 475th. This P-47 is taking off, see? And this musta been on a wing or something. It fell off halfway down the runaway. Well, naturally I couldn't just leave it there to become a haphazard, so I tooled out there and consecrated it. Saved it from a awful death." His dark eyes flashed and he smiled triumphantly as he displayed his prize.

Private Patrick "Mac" McTern provided a startling, shy contrast. The skinny, little carrot-topped assistant mechanic's uniform consisted of khaki trousers, a khaki shirt with the sleeves rolled up tightly, and the standard khaki-colored baseball cap. Like Big Ole's, the cap's bill was creased upward to expose the underside of the bill, thus exhibiting a quasi-Brooklyn cockiness that belied his personality.

Both struck Lee as being serious about their work, but neither seemed old enough to be working on P-38s in New Guinea. He wondered if either was eighteen. Their inexperience brought home to Lee the thought that his engines might seize up or his guns might jam when he needed them most. But all he could do for the present was hope and trust that before long he would replace the hope with trust.

Within a nervous hour, Lee had sat through Mo's briefing, strapped on his chute, Mae West, inflatable dinghy and paddle, and found himself airborne on his first mission. As they climbed out to the northeast and formed up, he managed a quick study of the Dobo area. Behind him were the double southwest-to-northeast airstrips, numbered Four-East and Four-West, from which he had taken off. Joining them at an angle from the west was Strip Four-Y, the short steel-matted strip they had used in the previous day's rainstorm. Within ten miles he saw six other airstrips, the most prominent being the double strip at Borio, east of the Horanda Drome where the Gopher Squadron was based. The clearings yielded hundreds of thatched grass roofs, corrugated steel roofs, and pyramid tents, and he knew that there were probably as many more back among the trees.

The knot in his stomach told Lee that he was now in the war for which he had trained so hard. His mind raced from one aspect of his training to another. Had they overlooked anything? Would he remember everything? The cockpit began to cool down above 5,000 feet, and at 10,000 his oxygen came on. He drew several deep breaths to help him relax. He recalled Mo's final instructions.

"You're going to be nervous rookies up there, so listen for instructions, follow your flight and element leaders, and above all, stay with your wingman. And remember, every cloud has a silver lining—that really looks good when you can't shake that Zero off your tail."

Lee had been placed in the Number Four slot as Tail End Charlie of the Blue Flight under Lieutenant Gustafson. At the last position in the last flight, Lee had made his way to the very bottom of the list. Undoubtedly his consignment to hell was payback for meandering into the mud. He was to cover his element leader, Jerry Porter, who ranked next to the bottom. It struck Lee as ironic. He knew, Porter knew, and every pilot in the squadron knew that as a pilot Lee was far superior to Jerry. Perhaps it was better this way, Lee reasoned, that he protected Porter's tail rather than vice versa.

The entire 483rd Fighter Group had taken to the air for the patrol. Smaller Japanese air groups might come from any of several bases to the north and east. But a major attack would come from Rabaul at the east end of the island of New Britain and generally regarded as the largest and strongest Japanese base in the Southwest Pacific. The 126th and 127th squadrons would patrol the Vitiaz Straits between New Britain and Finschafen on the Huon Peninsula of New Guinea. The 900-mile round-trip range required for such a Japanese attack suggested that the enemy would use their Betty medium bombers escorted by the older Zero, the A6M2 model, because of its superiority in range. The Gopher Squadron had drawn the southernmost quadrant of the patrol area, theoretically in a direct line with the most likely attack route.

When they had passed the New Guinea coast by ten miles, Mo set them up in string formation with his Red Flight at 15,000 feet and White and Blue Flights following higher and behind Red Flight at 22,000 feet. Lee believed that Japanese intelligence had to have picked up on the crowded conditions at Dobodura and would set out very soon to take advantage of the situation. He knew the answers to *who, what, why,* and *where*. Only the question of *when* remained in his mind. The thought reminded him to scan below and behind and to check the morning sun more often. That's where the fighters would likely come from. A broken layer of clouds floated beneath them at 5,000 feet.

As White and Blue Flights headed north at 22,000 feet, the chill in the cockpit affirmed Lee's decision to dress warmly. But his saturated boots became, rather than covered, his Achilles heel. In several ways the center-mounted cockpit pod of the P-38 offered advantages to the pilot.

Because there was no engine in front of the pilot, visibility to the front was the best in the Air Force, and the pilot was spared the heat and fumes of conventional fighter planes. However, the limited heat piped into the cockpit from the outboard engines failed to dry Lee's wet boots. And the strong cross wind they were bucking demanded he keep his cold, damp toes on the rudder pedals for control. Lee heard a click in his headset, followed by Mo Brennan's voice.

"Gopher Mo here," came the voice. "Bandits in the basement at two o'clock. Reds, switch tanks and drop. Greenie, stay on the roof. Gus, check the attic, then come on down."

Lee tensed. The time had come. He twisted and turned, scanning as much of the morning sky above the Solomon Sea as he could. He tried to see through the glaring sun but gave it up.

"Gus here," crackled the radio. "See anything in the attic?" After a ten-second pause, Gus came back on the radio, "Switch over and drop tanks."

Lee reached down beside his seat with his left hand, felt the tank switch and turned it by feel to the main tanks. Because other P-38 crashes had been traced to mistaken tank settings, he bent over and sneaked a peek to verify. He felt a light bump as his wing tanks fluttered free.

Gus banked sharply left and started down. Allowing a few seconds between aircraft for spacing, the others followed in single file. Lee set himself up about 400 yards behind and to the right of Jerry and then eased off on his airspeed to maintain the spacing.

"Eight Betties and fifteen M-2s trying to sneak in on the deck, about a thousand angels right now," he heard Mo say, identifying the Zeros as the older model. "The Zekes are too close to the bombers again. They can't turn into us. Probably be coming right up at you, Gus."

Suddenly, Lee Marks found himself busier than at any time in his life. He checked his altimeter, his airspeed, and his spacing behind and to the right of Jerry Porter, all the while vainly searching the blue areas between the fluffy clouds below for the enemy aircraft or, for that matter, Red Flight. His mouth felt lined with sand. The large lump in his throat refused to be swallowed. Only one thing became clear—the opening in the clouds that Gus had chosen for their break-through.

With his airspeed pushing closer to 400 mph, Lee backed off more yet on the throttles. The compressibility syndrome that had killed so many P-38 pilots inched closer and closer. But he'd had no experience with the new dive flaps and this didn't seem like the time to be experimenting with them. He saw Jerry pass through the opening and disappear. In seconds Lee plummeted past the layer of clouds, and there, two miles ahead, his first combat unfolded before him. Nervously, he searched his mind for a pre-battle checklist but found nothing. But he did remember to test his fifties and his 20mm cannon with short bursts.

Flying at less than 1,000 feet, the Japanese had neutralized the Lightnings' most successful attack plan, the high speed dive from above right through the enemy formation. With little space beneath the formation and little more between the bombers and their fighter escorts, Mo's flight had been forced into a shallow diving attack from behind the fighters, blasting their way through to the bombers. Apparently the attack had worked well, for Lee could see several smoke trails leading to the sea below. Seven twin-engine Betties and a dozen Zekes remained. Caught at the slow speed of the Betties, the Zekes had no chance of catching up with Mo's flight. But they had spotted Blue Flight coming down and were climbing and turning to meet the attack. Lee doubted that the enemy would place their only escort fighters at the same low altitude as the bombers. He glanced frequently at his mirror, expecting to see single-engine silhouettes closing on Blue Flight.

The Zeros ahead of him were coming around for a head-on meeting, one that generally favored P-38s with their superior firepower. But in earlier "think times," Lee had pondered such a head-on confrontation and come up with negatives that rusted away some of the confidence he needed at the moment. His P-38 presented a much larger target. What if the pilot he faced happened to be the best shooter in the Jap Army? And if it becomes a game of chicken, which way will the Jap turn at the last moment? Or...*will* he turn? The only safe play? Shoot first and don't miss.

Following Jerry's lead, Lee began to pull out of his dive. He felt the G-force building up. When he had nearly regained level flight he knew he had recovered from the dive without the well-known black-out period. Up ahead, he saw Gus and Smokey pass through the Zekes and continue on to the Betties. One Zeke blew up. Jerry flew right at the lead Zeke. Since there was nothing more Lee could do for Jerry at the moment, he swung slightly to his right to take a deflection shot at a fighter in the rear of the formation who hadn't yet completed his turn into Blue Flight. It was a harder shot, Lee knew, but a safer one. With a little luck, he'd get his shot and be on toward the bombers before any of the others turned far enough to get at him.

Later, Lee would replay the scene over and over, still amazed at how easy it had been. He calculated his deflection, squeezed his firing button on the control yoke sending two short bursts of his fifties. He felt his heart pound and his cockpit shudder as he watched one wing break away from the Zeke sending it spinning. Lee quickly recovered, spotted Jerry and closed up on him as they flew at the bombers from behind. Lee glanced up at his rear view mirror and over both shoulders. It was still his job to make sure no enemies got them from behind.

"Greenie," Mo called, "if you're clean up there, come on down."

"Roger, Mo."

Lee picked out a Betty and dropped a little altitude so as to approach it from behind and below where only the Betty's tail gunner could get a shot at him. The gunner came into Lee's sight. Bright, little sparkles drew an arching path that passed beneath the P-38. Lee fired one long burst with his fifties and the sparkles ceased. Sighting on the fuselage, he squeezed off a second burst. Almost immediately, smoke poured from the Betty. Lee wanted to hit it one more time, but he was too close. If the bomber exploded Lee knew he would be but tiny particles scattered upon the Solomon Sea.

Putting the Lightning in a shallow dive to gain speed and evade the other bombers' guns, Lee found Jerry and angled left to rejoin him. Together they swept upward in a shallow, high speed climb, one of the aircraft's finest attributes. As they made a wide left turn to circle back, Lee saw that the choreographed techniques of both sides had all but disintegrated. The shooter-wingman pairings of the Gopher Squadron held up, however, offering the only remaining semblance of order to what otherwise had become a good old-fashioned dogfight. The once quiet mission channel on the radio had become a free-for-all, with warnings, instructions, and cheering all competing for air space. When White Flight came ripping through the Betties, the bomber formation was whittled to four. They turned, went down right on the deck, headed for Rabaul and home.

Lee followed Jerry in a wide turn back toward the remaining Zekes. He looked down and saw the Jap bombers reverse their course putting them on the same Zero-seven-eight-degree compass heading as the two Gopher pilots. Lee checked the skies at all angles and saw no Zekes nearby, certainly none showing any interest in the pair of P-38s.

"Jerry," called Lee, "Down there. Too good to pass up?"

If Jerry replied, he was preempted by other radio messages. Lee looked ahead and left to his wingman. He saw the wings of the P-38 rock several times and then start down in a shallow dive. Lee followed, dropping farther back and to Jerry's right for spacing. It would be dicey. With the Betties flying at less than a hundred feet, there would be no room for error. But if they couldn't do this right they had no business flying fighter planes. When Jerry headed for the Betty on the far left, Lee opted for the far right. As they leveled off and came in range of the gunners aboard the bombers, the two Lightnings were pushing 400 mph. Lee sighted in on the right wing root at the fuselage and fired several bursts from his fifty-caliber machine guns. While he was making hits, nothing seemed to come of them.

Off to his left came a massive explosion. Lee forced himself to ignore it. He squeezed the fifty-caliber button and raked the fuselage again. As he zoomed in on the Jap bomber, he ran out of time. He banked slightly right and fired one long burst into the craft's starboard engine. Its propeller stopped and the engine nacelle shed pieces into the air. Suddenly the Betty snapped a half-roll to the right and plunged inverted into the ocean as Lee sped past, banking into a shallow right climb away from the other bombers' range of fire. He looked ahead and to his left, to where he expected Jerry to be. Nothing. He banked sharply to his left to look back at the formation. Just as he did, he saw a flaming P-38 cartwheel into the ocean, accompanied by the barely distinguishable carcass of a Japanese Betty bomber.

Lee knew in an instant what had happened. The Japs hadn't jettisoned their bomb load, and Jerry's attack had set off the massive explosion when he was too close to escape the inevitable wall of flying debris. Lee circled slowly to watch for any sign of his wingman—his first wingman. But there could be no survivors from either of those crashes.

As Mo called for Gopher Squadron to reassemble for the trip home, Lee was glad to see ten other surviving Gophers, but he had no sooner found his spot in the formation than he began to tremble. It made no sense. The battle was over, gone, done with. But the uncontrollable shaking continued, bringing to mind one long walk home by a small boy on a cold, winter day. The boy had fallen through the ice into his favorite creek, and the trip home felt colder than the splash into the water. But this trembling seemed both cold and hot. The affliction faded only when Lee became conscious of a huge knot in his stomach.

Just like that, Jerry Porter, a veteran of perhaps four minutes of combat was gone. "His war lasted four minutes?" Lee asked aloud. "After all that hard work, sweat, and nervous strain the guy only gets four minutes?"

Lee could confirm two kills for his departed wingman, but the recollection seemed almost insulting. Four minutes?

Then Lee had to wonder if the shocking loss was his fault. He had called Jerry's attention to the unprotected bombers. Did that make it his fault? Even though Lee had made two kills in his first fight, would Mo would hold him responsible for Jerry's death? Mo had already sluffed Lee to the lowest spot in the squadron. What now?

Chapter 6

▼

"Some ways, it was a reasonably good first mission," said Major Brennan to his squadron. "We got some Betties and some Zekes." He paused, turned, and flicked a bug off the trunk of the palm tree against which he had leaned. When he turned back to face them, his face took on a determined, almost fierce expression. "But we lost. We lost a hell of a good pilot and a brand new J-model. The game is also measured by losses—our losses. We had everything in our favor, altitude, airspeed, and angles. We ran everything we had right through their escort and into the Betties, all three flights of us." He turned a steely look toward Lee. "And then these two guys decide to go down on the deck and play cat and mouse with Betties that are still loaded with bombs." He shook his head slowly.

Lee felt his face flush and his inner pressure rise. The major was treating the final attack, the effort that shot down two Betty bombers, as a piece of stupidity. Never mind that the twelve members of the squadron had totaled eleven kills and he and Porter had shot down four them. It seemed like a time to speak up.

"Excuse me, sir—"

"And Gus? Someday I'd like you to explain how you and what's his name—Smokey? How in living hell could you ram through a dozen Zeros and half-a-dozen Betties and get only *one*? How do you do that? Do you practice it?"

Lieutenant Gustafson's face appeared to change from Atabrine yellow to jungle peach. But he simply stood there in the skimpy shade of the palm tree with a hint of a grin pasted on his face. He said nothing.

Lee began to wonder if there was something else going on, something more political or least more subjective than an honest appraisal of the rookie squadron's first effort. Brennan was clearly expecting nothing but the worst from Lee and perhaps little more from Gus. Lee found himself questioning for the first time whether his months and months of difficult and challenging training had been wasted. And this was the CO who earlier had seemed to respect him so much.

"One last thing," the major began, "it is important—no, it is *vital*—that you give the intel officer the straight dope in your debriefings. I'll not stand for anyone giving kill confirmations to the wrong pilots." He stared first at Gustafson, then at Lee. "You tell the debriefing officer *exactly* what happened, nothing more, nothing less."

Lee had no doubt that he had just caught another incoming shot, but he wondered what it meant. Perhaps Gus could illuminate the matter.

"Oh, one more thing," Major Brennan said, "and then you can hit chow, take a rest, and be back on the line for our afternoon patrol at 1400 hours. Gather up your gear and meet at my place. I've found a group of three tents down here, tents with elevated floors, electricity, and some other goodies. You can move in before chow." Brennan smiled. "Do it."

The squadron mates headed up the grade toward Fungus Field. Lee waited for Lieutenant Gustafson. If there was crap going on here, he wanted to know it right up front. What would he have to do to get back on the right side of Major Brennan? But at Lee's first word, Gus glanced back over his shoulder, gave two quick shakes of his head, and split away from him.

Baffled, Lee trudged on up the hill in silence. A shower had moved in, and while Lee did not look forward to another drying out process, he had to admit that the rain felt good. If his first day at Dobodura was any indication, he would probably never be dry again.

As he walked through the steady rain, his mind tried to clear out some fog. It now appeared that Gus was also angry with him. In twenty-four hours, Lee apparently had run up an incredibly ugly scorecard. But, he reasoned, until he understood the situation there was little he could do about it. Another of his mother's ten-second lessons came to mind, "When you've got big problems and can't tell right from wrong, don't do nothing until the picture clears up." He smiled to himself. He had ignored much of his mother's advice throughout his growing years. In fact, when her face had taken on that lecture look his listening apparatus had often switched from listening to hearing. Strange, now in a war on the other side of the world he found her bits of practical wisdom surfacing regularly.

Lee recognized their tent and turned to enter. But a khaki-clad missile came hurtling from the tent, catching Lee at the knees and tumbling him backward into the slimy mud. He wrestled from under the man and struggled to his feet. It was Bubba!

"What the hell you doing, Bubba?" he yelled, shaking the gobs of slippery mud from his hands. A husky bass voice answered from the tent.

"He ain't doin' nothin. *I'm* doin' it!" shouted the awesome Sergeant Rommel. "You bastards make trouble for me, I make trouble for you. And you ain't seen nothin' yet. I'll show you *real* trouble!"

Lee blinked, looked at Bubba who was staggering clumsily to his feet, and turned to face the big man.

"I don't know what's going on here, Sergeant, but you can get out of our tent while I find out," Lee barked, aware now that the steady rain had become a downpour, dimming his vision of the big man who stood within the shadow in the tent.

"I ain't leavin' this goddamned tent for no fuckin' toy lieutenants!" Rommel shouted in a thundering voice. Then, nodding back over his shoulder toward Black Bart, he added, "And I ain't leavin' it for *that* loud-mouthed chicken-shit neither!"

Lee hesitated, wondering what to do. Then, like an explosion, the massive man was torpedoed from behind by Black Bart, and two more bodies splashed into the quagmire.

The events of the succeeding moments were too rapid, slippery, painful, and confusing for Lee to keep track. He was drawn into a mud-filled typhoon with two other men and a giant. Bodies sprawled, fists swung, curses spouted, and bodies sprawled again. Each time Lee made it to his feet, something happened, and down he went again. Then, as quickly as it began, the battle subsided.

Lee rolled from his belly to his back, sat up, and wiped the mud from his eyes. There lay Bubba and Black Bart stretched out in the mud, positioned as the other two blades of a propeller. At the hub of the human propeller stood Sergeant Rommel. He looked down at Lee and gave a peculiar, low-pitched laugh that gurgled from deep in his throat. Abruptly, he turned, stepped over Bubba, and stalked off among the tents.

"You guys all right?" Lee asked as they righted themselves and staggered over to a nearby palm tree.

"Here!" shouted Robert Logan from the tent opening. He tossed Lee a bar of soap. Taking his suggestion, the three brawlers stripped right there and showered in the New Guinea rain. Once inside the tent, they dried off the best they could and suited up with clean clothes.

"Did you shoot off your mouth again, Bubba?" Lee asked.

"No, I just—"

"You did too start it!" Barton cut in. "Didn't he, Robert?"

Robert nodded and calmly explained the events that led up to the brawl. Upon reaching the tent, Bubba had discovered that one leak in the tent roof had saturated his B-4 bag. At that moment, the sergeant happened to be passing by. Bubba called him into the tent and made a big fuss about his wet belongings. Robert paused, smiled, then continued.

"Rommel said, 'That's just a little water. Won't hurt you none. You prob'ly wet the bed every night anyway.' Bubba went a little crazy. He stuck his finger in Rommel's chest and told him he couldn't talk to an officer like that. That's when Rommel took Bubba by the seat of his pants and threw him out of the tent."

The story struck Lee right where he needed it. After all the tension of the day, he desperately needed something funny. He flopped onto his bunk, his body shaking in quiet convulsions. His salty tears stung the raw bruise on his cheekbone where someone, presumably the surly sergeant had pasted him. Despite the irritation, it felt good, so good to laugh.

"Lee? Lee, you going to talk to Major Brennan and file charges?" Bubba asked.

"Aw, come on, Bubba," said Sandy. "You don't run to the law every time somebody touches you."

"But he beat me up! And he beat them up, too!" he spewed, pointing to Lee and Bart.

"No, Bubba, no," Lee said, wiping away the tears. "He didn't beat us up. He was just trying to tell us something. If you ever get really beat up, you'll know what I mean."

"And if you don't learn to keep your mouth shut," Sandy added, "it won't be long before you find out what he means. What's with you today, anyway?"

"It's because he—" Black Bart stopped himself.

Lee recognized yet another first for the historic day. Black Bart had actually stopped himself from thrusting another of his negative opinions at the group. Why?

"Come on," said Robert Logan, "I think we'd better haul our stuff down the hill. The rain quit. It's move now or get caught by the next one."

Halfway down the hill, Lee caught on. Bubba had suddenly become so feisty because he had scored a kill in their first combat. And Bart was about to point that out when he realized that everyone in the tent but Aloysius Barton had scored that day. Lee wondered if that might quiet the troublemaker for a time.

Mo directed them to a nearby cluster of tents. He had somehow accumulated rights to three of the nicer six-man tents, each of which had a sturdy, elevated floor, regular GI bunks with springs and mattresses, electricity to a forty-watt dangling bulb, one or two pieces of homemade or scavenged furniture, and no visible holes in the canvas. Since Mo wanted the entire squadron bunking nearby, the two first lieutenants, Green and Gustafson, would move down the hill also.

"Right downtown," Sandy Sadler observed. "Actually, we'd really only need two tents for eleven guys, but this way we can divide up four, four, and three."

"Uh, Sandy," Cal Callahan said, "It's—not eleven now. It's ten. Four, *three*, and three."

Voices stopped, movement halted. Only the roar of a departing C-47 broke through the vacuum. Lee felt a numbness seep through him. Grief? Guilt? Probably both, he decided. When he retuned to the present he discovered that six of the others had separated into two groups of three and claimed their tents. He considered moving in on the group composed of Gus, Greenie, and Robert Logan, but he hesitated, reluctant to push himself in on them. The moment quickly passed and at the insistence of Bubba and Sandy, Lee found himself bunking with Bubba, Sandy, and Black Bart. Dry as it might be, the canvas pyramid would not be the peaceful home with the white picket fence, the needed sanctuary from the tensions of war.

"No, goddamn it, Bubba, that's *my* bunk!" Bart snarled. "You take one of the others."

Chapter 7

The Gopher Squadron gathered at 1300 hours beneath the familiar cluster of palm trees. Some of the pilots stood and chatted while others sprawled on their backs with their caps pulled down to shade their eyes. Lee felt a tug at one elbow and turned to find Gus motioning him off to one side for a private chat.

"I thought I should tell you before Mo does our briefing," Gus began in his articulate style, "so you won't be taken by surprise if Mo says something."

"About what?"

"That first Betty you shot up. You got her. As I climbed out and turned back I saw her pull up, stall, and go down in a flat spin. I confirmed it in debriefing."

"Hey, great! Thanks," Lee said. "That means three on my first—"

"Uh, uh," Gus cut in, "that's what I'm trying to tell you. Mo says that it was disallowed. He said he and others hit that Betty and she never went down. He says she was one of the two that got away." Gus paused to outwait a flight of old Aussie P-39s fly past on their downwind leg. "Maybe we'll get our gun cameras soon. A few of the fighter squadrons have them up and running. Then these things won't happen, at least not so often."

"I don't understand," Lee said. "It's not such a big deal. I still got two. But why would Mo do that? It would be another kill for his squadron. Is he really *that* down on me?"

"If I answered that it'd only be speculation," Gus said, removing his hat and scratching his balding head. "I think you'll have a clearer picture in a week or two. Just keep on doing what you're doing and try not to screw up." He slipped away from Lee and took a spot near Lieutenant Green as their CO stepped to the front and called for the squadron's attention.

"A few things before we talk about our afternoon mission," Mo began. He scanned the group, hesitating at Lee perhaps a moment longer than with the others. "Intel says the Betty that Marks shot up on the first pass didn't go down, so no flag for that one, Marks. On the other hand, Callahan is credited with that Zero that was a probable."

With what Lee thought might have been a light smirk in his direction Brennan drew from his cigarette and went right on. "Wingmen, do not, I repeat, do *not* slip behind and below your element leader during a fight. You're just asking for a face full of empty casings from your leader's guns. We came home with two cracked canopies this morning. I call that lucky. You suck those empties into your engines and you'll be shark bait. And from now on, when we make a pass at the Japs pick your target and *kill* him. This is not World War I dog fighting where you and the Red Baron's brother go 'round and 'round waving your scarves at each other. Things happen fast out here—three hundred-plus miles per hour. You get that Jap for two reasons: one, you likely won't get a second chance at him; and two, if you don't get him, he's going to get one of us."

Major Brennan paused for a moment. He looked at Lee and then continued.

"I want to make one thing perfectly clear. We have no room in this squadron for hotdogs.

The last hot dog pilot I had got a mustard enema."

"I heard about him," Sandy said for the benefit of his close neighbors. "He had such a big ego his mirror locked itself in the bathroom when it heard him coming."

"You have something for the group, Sadler?" the major asked.

"Uhh, no, sir."

Their leader motioned for time out while a string of mediums took off directly over them. Huge radial engines roared defiantly as they struggled to lift the heavily loaded B-25s from the Marston matting. Scuttlebutt had it that they were after Japanese shipping carrying badly needed supplies to Rabaul. With the first lull in the activity, Brennan motioned quickly for attention.

"Okay, listen up. There won't be much time for this. We take off at 1345. Flights will be the same as this morning. Marks, since you—lost your wingman—you slide up and join on Gus to make up a three-plane element. We taxi in order of flights, take off in two-ship elements. The Dobo area is especially busy right now, so we'll take a heading of zero-eight-five degrees to a few miles out and then circle to form up at 10,000 angels. Our patrol is essentially the same as this morning. You don't have much time now, so let's hit it."

The young pilots sprang into action. In fifteen minutes they had climbed aboard their aircraft and the unique sound of twenty-two throaty Allison engines heralded their call to arms. Their first take-off in pairs went well, although Lee felt awkward being a pair of one. He felt it again as he moved into Jerry Porter's position back and to the right of Gus, leaving his own Tail End Charlie spot empty. But he knew his assignment had not changed. He was still Charlie.

Lee's left engine began to sound a little rough as they reached altitude and turned on the southbound leg of their patrol area. He checked his instruments carefully, but nothing showed. He adjusted his mixture slightly and played with his combination of manifold pressure and propeller rpm, but to no avail. After some time, he convinced himself that, while the engine had not improved, he was not about to drop into the Solomon Sea. Three hours later, the Gopher Squadron turned back to Dobodura. They had done their thing, but the Japanese had not. The Gophers had seen no enemy aircraft or ships.

"It's okay," Mo said on their way in. "No action, but some good practice on procedures, and we needed that. Now when we string it out on approach, let's see better spacing. Be alert, Marks. There could be some rain back at the base."

Lee's hand snapped upward to his throat mike, but then he thought better of it. He wondered how long Brennan would keep jabbing at him. Gustafson's words came back to him, "Just keep on doing what you're doing and try not to screw up." Lee wondered if that would work. How long could he control the fire that was building within? And what if he made another mistake?

They threaded their way through local thunderheads and settled into a smooth, well-coordinated approach to Dobodura. When Lee's wheels rumbled on the steel matting, he felt himself tighten. He told himself to concentrate not only on Smokey's aircraft immediately in front of him but also on Gus up ahead to avoid another mistake on taxiway routes. Lee reached the left and right turn sequence that he had missed in the driving rain. He questioned his own competence. Now, with no rain falling, the turns were so clearly visible he wondered how he could have missed, even in bad visibility. As he taxied into his place, spun the aircraft around to face outward, and chopped the engines, he felt a surge of confidence within. He climbed down the tiny ladder and mentioned the rough sounding engine to Big Ole.

"You just hang on," the affable crew chief said, "and I'll check it right now." He climbed into the cockpit and fired up the suspicious power plant. He revved it up several times and then shut the engine down. He climbed out and down the ladder.

"You hear it?" Lee asked.

"Must be the ocean," the huge man said, shaking his head slowly.

"The ocean? How would that affect an engine?"

"Not *it*," said the crew chief. He appeared flustered, a little embarrassed as he paused. "*You*—*sir*." He turned from Lee to resume his inspection of the aircraft. Lee glanced over at his assistant mechanic, McTern. Mac simply looked upward and with his extended hands shrugged a "What can I say?"

Lee had walked about twenty paces up the path toward Fungus Field when the message finally sifted through. It was the "no place to land" syndrome. It had been discussed as far back as primary flight training, the tricks a pilot's ears can play on him when flying over vast expanses of mountains, forests, or ocean. Twenty paces later, he had conceded the point to Big Ole Anderson.

A large, new sign greeted Lee as he reached the common pathway into the tent city. A four-foot by four-foot panel of shiny aluminum, presumably a piece of wing sheeting cut in the shape of a shield, had been mounted on a new post above head height. Done in blue and gold professional quality lettering the sign read: Welcome to the home of Thunder and Lightning, 483rd Fighter Group, Fifth Air Force. Lee felt a bubble of pride surge through him.

After chow that evening, the tent quartet admired the rickety table Sandy Sadler had forged from scraps found in the area dump. Around the table sat four old metal folding chairs in various states of repair. A rack of old, badly stained red, white, and blue poker chips and a deck of cards had found their way to the tabletop.

"Okay, Guys," said Sandy, "I've done all this for you. Now, sit down and give me your money."

"But I don't play poker," said Bubba.

"You do now," said Black Bart.

Sandy's freckled grin beneath his red hair combined with his laughing eyes to quash any further negative responses, and within minutes the combat was underway.

Lee took it upon himself to help Bubba with the game, and when he could do it within the rules, to protect him from the two veterans. But Bubba quickly won four pots, and his demeanor once again assumed that surprising arrogance of the previous day's combat victor.

"I don't know what all the fuss has been about," he announced. "This really isn't that hard." He looked at Lee and added, "Your chips are going down fast, Lee. I guess I'm being a little tough on you." His Cheshire cat grin brightened his pink face, and his small, round ears seemed to stick out a little farther. "You know," he added as he swept the chips off the table for a fifth time, "I really wasn't quite honest with you guys. I did play this game one time before, back in high school."

"Shut up!" Bart snapped.

"Deal the cards," added Sandy.

When Bubba had acquired chips equal to the other three combined, the game seemed to level off with the winnings more evenly distributed. A few hands later, though still the heavy winner, Bubba had quieted down and the conversation had spread to other subjects.

"Good thing he's quieted down," observed Black Bart. "The way he was running off at the mouth he was liable to challenge Rommel again."

"As a matter of fact," spouted Bubba, "I'm going to challenge Big Mouth again. I've decided to report him."

"You *what?*" the others chorused.

"We can't let bullies like him go around beating on officers," said Bubba. "It just isn't right, and if we allow it to spread it could damage morale."

"Bubba," said Lee, "there are lots of things in this world that are wrong, but we let them go because they just *are,* that's all. Some things in life you can change. Some you can't, and you're just beating your head against a wall by trying."

"In this case," Sandy cut in with a laugh, "you'll be burying your head in the mud. I've gotta tell you, Bubba, you looked pretty good with your nose and your ears sticking out of that mud ball."

Lee and Bart joined in the laughter, but just briefly because suddenly Bubba's frustration blew the lid off.

"Piss on you, Sadler!" Bubba shouted, livid with anger. "And you guys, too! And you're a phony, Lee Marks. You don't have half the guts you pretend to have!" With the last word, Bubba flinched, that brief reaction that betrays, that tells the world the orator had overstepped and knew it.

But Lee was still too engulfed in the humor of the moment to take offense at Bubba's remarks. Bubba swept the chips and cards off the table onto the floor, whirled and took a temper-fueled dive into his bunk. Unfortunately, his momentum rolled him across the bunk and off the far side where he ended up a thrashing ball entangled in mosquito netting.

"Good shot, Bubba!" shouted Lee, roaring in laughter with the others.

"Maybe that'll cool him off," said Sandy.

"What he needs is a good fist in the chops to cool him off," countered Bart.

"I think you might be right, Bart," said Lee, "but let's let him get it somewhere else. We've got to stick together."

"Christ, Marks," said Bart, "where in the hell do you stand? You give him a rough time like that, and then you say, 'Stick together.'"

Lee felt guilt wash over him. He knew Black Bart was right. He hadn't meant to be so hard on Bubba, and he shouldn't have laughed at him. After all, Bubba had grown up in a different world. How could he know what *tough* really meant? He had probably never been in a real fight. And when his parents always carried his battles for him, how could he learn that some bad things just *are*.

No question though, the party was over. As they cleaned up the mess, turned off the dim overhead light, and settled in their bunks, the familiar patter of raindrops on the tent began again. Lee lay there, pacified for a time by the rhythm of the rain—until he began thinking about his fight with Pete Loren back in Chicago. He wondered how badly he had hurt the cocky bastard. Had Loren's father filed charges? Could they find Lee Marks over here, halfway around the world?

Chapter 8

▼

As Lee's tires cleared the matting and went silent, he tightened and focused his attention on the navigation lights of Smokey Stover's ship some two thousand feet ahead of him. The darkness into which he flew combined with the fear of losing an engine to stifle the elation he customarily felt at lift-off. Hazarding a quick glance downward at the sparsely lighted base, Lee hoped the black hole that was the New Guinea night would be lighted when he returned.

Gopher Squadron formed up as they climbed for altitude on their zero-five-eight heading. The nightly showers had apparently drifted off, and unlimited visibility had been predicted for the morning. As they climbed to their prescribed 20,000-foot altitude, the eastern sky grew lighter, and Lee found himself beginning to relax. Flying formation in the dark, with the threat of a mid-air collision but a few yards from his wingtip, demanded complete concentration. Lee wondered if he would ever grow comfortable with night flying. Perhaps someday in the future the aircraft industry would develop avionics that would remove all its risks and stresses.

Reluctantly, he followed the examples from ahead and turned off his navigation lights. He would have to concentrate on the exhaust port and the hot turbocharger on the starboard engine of Gus's Lightning in order to hold his place in the formation.

A small cluster of tiny lights far below blinked once, then went out. Lee reasoned that they were flying over the Allied base at Cape Gloucester, near the western tip of New Britain, the long quarter-moon-shaped island. Rabaul, the powerful Japanese base, lay about 350 miles to the east at the opposite end of the island.

The Gophers had been assigned to fly cover for a dozen B-25s that were after Japanese shipping headed for Rabaul. Allied conquests had finally closed a large ring around Rabaul, isolating it so as to starve it into submission or, at the least, a state of ineffectiveness. The enemy tried to sneak their transports through dangerous waters at night, hoping to avoid the Allies' efficient scouting network composed of submarines, aircraft, and coast watchers. Lee knew that at any moment the Gophers would locate the bombers and move to join them. With radio silence in effect, a preset plan called for Red and White Flights to drop down to 15,000 feet to cover the bombers while Blue Flight would remain above, flying high cover to watch for Japanese fighters.

Lee saw Mo waggle his wings and start downward with Red and White following. At the same moment, the sun broke above the eastern horizon, abruptly changing the color of Lee's world and washing him with awe at its beauty. With a surprising, smooth swiftness the black void beneath became a midnight blue Bismarck Sea. The gray sky in the east became a bright gold that blended into light blue above and behind him. New Britain suddenly changed from an irregularity in the black expanse to a gigantic, rich, green jungle island.

Gus did a waggle and turned almost due north. Lee quickly saw the reason. There, far below were unmistakable white trails, the wakes of six or eight ships. Lee could just make out the bombers as they headed for a low-level attack. Red and Blue Flights were descending beneath 10,000 feet with their protection. He jerked his attention back to business, to the eastern sky. He glanced at the golden globe, now almost complete, grateful that it was still too low in its orbit to provide high cover for enemy fighters.

Completing yet another scan of the skies above and to the east, Lee checked the action below. As the B-25s swept in over the ships, the Jap anti-aircraft guns lit up like angry fireflies. Bombs exploded everywhere, many in the ocean and some on ships. Lee's vision tracked upward and to the east. There he saw perhaps twenty-five Jap fighters diving for the bombers. Mo had seen them, too, for the eight Lightnings banked to the right and headed downward to cut off the enemy group. Red and White would be heavily outnumbered, but they had a favorable angle from which to break up the Japanese attack.

Lee's radio crackled and Gus said, "Big group coming down on you from your four o'clock, Mo. We'll try to mess 'em up."

"Roger, see them," Mo replied. "Do it right."

"Blue, switch over and drop tanks," Gus said. "Here we go." The chatter over their once quiet channel three, their mission frequency had suddenly become crowded.

Lee switched, dropped, and tested his weapons, all in rapid sequence. Smokey had moved into string formation back and to the right of Gus. Lee followed suit and set up even a larger interval between Smokey and himself so he could adequately cover both of his wingmen, should they need help. Following Gus and Smokey, he peeled to the left and started down. A sweeping left turn would bring them to a favorable angle to blast through the Zeros from above, behind, and to their left. The Japs either hadn't seen the three Lightnings or had chosen to ignore them in favor of the eight planes of Red and White Flights.

It shaped up to be a textbook attack, and Lee vowed he wouldn't waste the advantage this time. As they rapidly closed the gap he gauged the situation, determined which ones Gus and Smokey were headed for, and picked his target. It would be a deflection shot, but not the most difficult if the Jap stayed on course.

The Zero grew in size rapidly. Lee sighted the fighter within his orange ring, then adjusted slightly to put the pipper just ahead of the Zero's nose. He squeezed off several rounds with his fifties. His tracers showed he was leading by too much. A touch of right rudder set him up nearly perfectly. But before he could squeeze the button, the fighter jerked violently upward into a tight Immelman turn that Lee couldn't possibly follow. The slippery Zeke reminded Lee of trying to pick up a small glob of mercury in ninth grade science class. He charged downward through the formation, pulled out and looked around for Smokey.

Gus appeared about a thousand yards ahead, but no Smokey. Instinctively, Lee pulled up even more from his dive. The Lightning, with its broad wing and twin engine booms, was all but blind beneath, and more than one bird had gone down in combat because of a mid-air. He checked his mirror quickly for Japs, then scanned ahead to the right and left. No Smokey. He decided to tie onto Gus as they pulled up into a gentle but fast climb. He reached for his throat mike, fully expecting the crowded frequency to reject the effort. To his surprise he got through.

"Can't find Smokey," Lee said. "I'm with you, Gus."

"Roger," came Gus' reply. "A hard right should take us back for another shot."

But as they came halfway around, Lee spotted a P-38 below and to his right with two Zekes locking onto his tail. Smokey could be about there by now, he thought. He tried to advise Gus but couldn't get through, so he went down to help. Once again, his speed helped. The gap closed. He banked left to come in behind the two Japs. He raked the nearest one with his fifties and drew smoke that quickly thickened. Almost immediately, heavy flames licked back from beneath the engine cowling. As Lee slowed to try for a shot at the other Zero, his flaming victim rolled to the right and blew up.

Lee had almost lined up the remaining Zero when it abruptly turned to its left, the sharpest high-speed ninety-degree turn Lee had ever seen an aircraft execute. The pilot had apparently spotted Lee. And Lee now knew that the fabled left turn of the Zero was for real. As his speed took him past the other Lightning, Lee saw that it wasn't Smokey. It was Burner Hedman, the Tail End Charlie of White Flight.

Pulling up into a wide left climbing turn that should, or at least might, reconnect him with Gus, Lee tightened at what he saw. A Lightning up ahead, probably Gus, was making a sharp, climbing turn to its left, apparently intending to come back for another swipe at things. But the slow-turning pilot wouldn't have given away his airspeed had he known there was a Zeke below and behind him in his blind spot. Lee slid into a direct line behind the Zeke. But the gap was too large. The Jap was almost bound to get Gus before Lee could get close enough for a good shot.

Desperately, Lee lined up for a long trajectory. He fired a long burst with his fifties. If he didn't hit anything he hoped at least to distract the pilot. To his surprise, pieces flew from the light fighter plane. The pilot banked hard to the left and disappeared. Lee's training and judgment told him not to follow. He pulled up beside the other Gopher. Gus waved at him.

In a few minutes that seemed like hours, the battle was over. The B-25s had done a creditable job, sinking three ships and badly damaging two more. They were in a long, gradual climb on a course heading for Dobodura. One of the mediums had disappeared and two trailed smoke.

Mo called for the Gophers to form up on him at 10,000 angels. While they formed, he asked for a condition report. Lee felt relieved when, one by one, the pilots called in. Greenie was on one engine and Callahan had one engine overheating, soon to be shut down. But the report that sobered Lee the most was Bubba's complaint that he was bleeding badly from a head wound and the blood was running into his eyes causing vision problems.

"Anybody see Bubba?" Mo called.

"I've got him," said Sandy, "below you at 4,000."

"Stay with him," Mo directed. "You and Bubba switch to emergency channel one when you reach the coast so control knows what's coming in. Bring him up to 8,000 and get out ahead of us on a course of one-nine-five. We'll be able to keep an eye on you two that way. Bubba? You read?"

"Ahh, yes, sir. Got it," replied Bubba. There was a pause and then, "You know, it really doesn't hurt, doesn't hurt at all. How can it bleed so much?"

"See if you can come up with something for a compress," said Mo Brennan. "Try to slow it down if you can. Sandy can fly you back, but you'll need something to wipe with when you really need to see to land." There was a break, then, "Okay, Gophers, last call. Any other problems that need priority? Fuel okay?"

"We're up to 6,000, Mo," said Greenie, "but Cal and I can't keep up."

"White, stay together. We'll go on ahead," Mo said.

"Roger, Mo," said Greenie.

"Everybody else, stay off the radio. Good job, Gophers."

Lee was glad they were returning in mid-morning with clear skies. He had already learned that the weather typically got worse in late afternoon and evening. But he worried about Bubba. The green kid who couldn't even choke down Army food was now all by himself at 8,000 feet, bleeding from a head wound. Would he pass out from loss of blood? Would he pass out from the *sight* of the blood? Did he perhaps have other injuries?

The time oozed slowly by, but eventually Lee found himself on final approach to Strip 4 West. That was a break for Sandy and Bubba. The strip gave Sandy an extra 5,000 feet to get Bubba down. By landing on Strip 4 West the Gophers had a long trip on the taxiways to get to their flight line. Lee would liked to have stayed near the landing strip to see Bubba down, but they had to keep the ground traffic flowing.

Lee felt a warmth ripple through him as he parked his Lightning and his ground crew immediately swarmed over the aircraft.

"Ya, sure glad you didn't put no big holes in my airplane," said Big Ole. "Put any in theirs?" he asked as he helped Lee up from the cockpit.

Lee grinned and held up one finger. He and Big Ole made a slow trip around the aircraft, checking it for damage. It struck Lee as strange, almost weird that he had come through two intense fights without any hits on his Lightning. It could be taken as a bad omen. When he finally gets hit, will it be the big one?

Everybody stayed at the flight line. Some time later, Sandy's P-38 taxied up. Bubba's ship followed close behind with his crew chief taxiing the plane and his two assistants riding on the inboard sections of the wing. Bubba had made it. Sandy had guided him right down to the deck where Bubba's instincts took over. He had lost a lot of blood, though preliminary reports suggested the injury was a shallow scalp wound.

Half an hour later, White Flight rolled in. Both Cal and Greenie had been reduced to one engine and had obviously mastered the necessary tricks for the dreaded one-engine landing. "You know all those instructions on single engine flight?" Cal began. "They work. I won't be the least bit scared the next time. You guys ought to try it sometime," he added with a laugh.

"I suspect we will," replied the ever-serious Robert Logan.

Anxious to shed his perspiration-soaked clothing, Lee made for the tent, grabbed his shower things and fresh clothes, and headed for the improvised shower set-up. He had heard about the shower facilities the engineers rigged up for the jungle camps. But the bad stories about bitter cold water, and tanks that went empty half-way through one's shower were no deterrent. He needed this.

He stripped down and stepped gingerly into the roofless wooden construction, a large booth-like arrangement. The wooden floor could be good for a few slivers, he thought. He pulled the rope that opened the improvised wooden valve, half expecting an icy typhoon to drop on him. While it felt icy, the water fell in only a gentle sprinkle. He had wetted down, closed the sliding water valve, and proceeded to soap himself when Gus joined him.

"Thanks, Lee," the first lieutenant said as he stepped beneath the neighboring sprinkle ports. "I really blew it when I dumped so much airspeed in that turn—didn't know that Zeke was there. I—I owe you one, big time."

"Nah," Lee scoffed. "That's why we work in teams. You'll probably blow a Nip off my tail tomorrow. Did you ever find out what happened to Smokey? When I pulled up from our first pass, he was gone."

"He started to pull out with me, but then he saw someone below in real trouble so he went on down. That's why you couldn't find him. He was below you."

Lee pulled the rope to rinse himself. He shivered when the water hit him.

"If you can get in here in mid- to late-afternoon, the sun has warmed the water up there in the collection tank," said Gus. "Problem is, everybody knows that, so I just put up with the cold water treatment." He went about lathering up and then said, "How are you doing with the Mo thing? Is he getting to you?"

"Well, yeah, I guess he *is* getting to me," Lee said as he dried off. "I just don't understand it. I made one mistake. Do I get punished for the rest of my tour?"

"Tell you what, Lee. When Mo goes after somebody like that, it's for one of two reasons. Either he really has it in for you, like in my case, or he has something else in mind and he's testing you. In your case, I think it's a test."

Lee thought for a moment. "Gus, why would he have it in for you?" He finished drying off, pulled his shorts on and sat down on the rough wooden bench.

"I've tried to figure that—even asked him directly. Got nowhere. Hard to say. It's possible that, for whatever reason, he feels threatened by me. I don't know. But it's not going to change. I know that. I can feel it."

"Is it because you're close to him in the number of kills?" Lee asked.

Gus finished rinsing and began drying off his hairy body. "At first I thought that was it. But no, he wants us all to get lots of flags—good for the squadron—as long as we don't get more than he does. Tell you what, Lee. You're a damned good pilot, and you're sharp. You got what, one more and a possible today? You're credited with three, but you actually got four, maybe five, in three missions. Just be patient. I don't think it'll be too long before you'll know where you stand."

"It had better not be too long," Lee said. "I was already boiling at the thought that Mo really disliked me. But when I think he might be rubbing my nose in it just to test me—"

Chapter 9

▼

Lee had mixed feelings as Gopher Squadron patrolled the Vitiaz Strait between Finschafen and Cape Gloucester the next day. The patrol had become a respite from the previous day's frantic dogfight, but with thinking time, Lee had found himself focusing on Mo Brennan. Was he mean? Manipulative? Either or both? What was obvious to Lee was the position assignments for the day's mission. With Bubba out, Mo needed a wingman. But rather than using Lee who himself was a loner, Mo had pulled Cal out of White Flight and left both White and Blue without element leaders. Lee decided it was probably just the begin—

Thunk! Thunk! Two intrusions slammed into the cockpit pod behind Lee's seat. He felt a vibrant tingling from his scalp on down his back. Frantically he checked the mirror. Nothing! He twisted back and left. Nothing! Probably back and right side. He feinted a sharp left bank, then abruptly shifted into a hard right turn. At the same moment, he shoved the left throttle ahead full and cut the right engine back. The maneuver would either work or it would get him killed. The Lightning pulled violently to the right. He felt two more cannon shells hit somewhere aft. As the G-pressure mounted from the turn, he pushed the right throttle ahead to match the left. Then he shoved both throttles full ahead through the safety wire into war emergency power, increased his mixture, and pushed the yoke ahead for a dive.

His airspeed mounted to 350 mph. He looked over both shoulders and checked his mirror again. There were two enemy planes chasing him. Their silhouettes were unusual, streamlined as opposed to the flat-nosed Zero with its radial engine. His second look identified them as Tony fighters, the only inline, liquid-cooled fighter the Japs were known to have. Its engine he knew was a licensed version of the German Daimler Benz. Although the Tony was considerably faster than the A6M2 Zero, Lee felt relieved when he again found them in the mirror and realized he had gained a couple hundred yards on them. He knew he would widen the gap with his full throttle and shallow dive. He wished he could jink around and get behind them, but he knew he'd never survive that turn. His situation called for standard P-38 procedure, dive for speed and then make a fast, shallow climb to simply fly away from the trouble and look for a fresh opportunity.

He fingered his throat mike to call Gus and Smokey. But the dead headphones without even a trace of static told him the enemy had hit the radio mounted immediately behind his seat in the cockpit. He switched it off, knowing he would have to be pay careful visual attention to everything that went on, friendly or otherwise. When the two Tonys gave up on him he throttled back and looked the situation over. His instruments suggested that nothing else had suffered the fate of his radio. In making his escape he had flown westward and out of the battle.

As he turned back he could see tiny Japanese Army fighters and P-38s mixing it up in the distance. But from so far away, he had found a new perspective, that of a spectator.

While the battle had once again turned into a dogfight, the Gophers had, for the most part, retained their wingman partnerships. In pairs they dived through the enemy planes, pulled up to altitude and ripped through them again. The tactic employed by the RAF during the Battle of Britain and again by the Flying Tigers in China seemed to be working, even with a bunch of new pilots.

Lee saw a single Lightning coming his way about 3,000 feet below him. On its tail were three Jap fighters. He dropped his nose down into a path that would skim just above the P-38 and directly into the Tony fighters. With its nose-mounted four .50-caliber and 20mm cannon the Lightning had the advantage in a head-on fight over any fighter plane in the world.

But Lee wasn't facing just any fighter plane; he was facing three. At combined speeds of over 600 mph, however, the battle would last but a second or two. He sighted in on the center Tony, the one closest to the other P-38, angled down slightly to lead him, and fired off a long burst with his fifties. The Jap pulled up sharply to escape. Lee banked slightly to his right, and as the second Tony was about to fly into his orange ring he fired two more short bursts. He thought he had shot well, but nothing seemed to happen. Too close and too late for another try, Lee pulled up and to his left to avoid a collision. As he rocketed past the two Jap fighters he looked in the mirror. His second target Tony belatedly blew up.

The remaining Tony broke off to his right and disappeared. In his wide left circle, Lee saw the two Tonys join up and head off in the opposite direction. He was disappointed. He really thought he'd gotten that first one.

He checked all directions and then hauled his ship around to follow the P-38 he had just rescued. When at first he couldn't find it, he began to fear he'd been too late. Then, like a ghost it appeared in front of him. As he gained on the fellow Gopher, he scanned the skies and determined that someone had declared the battle over. The Japanese planes were apparently too far off to show up in his mirror. Above and to his sides, P-38s began to appear. He pulled up alongside the first Lightning. It was Mo Brennan's ship.

Through sign language Lee told Mo he had no radio. Then he drifted off to the right and dropped back to find the Blue Flight and his mandated position. As Tail End Charlie for the entire squadron, Lee could quickly do the numbers. Of the original ten, there were now nine. White Flight had lost another, but short of flying in close and checking plane numbers, Lee couldn't tell who it was.

Two of the Gophers were streaming coolant. Lee had no idea how successful the squadron had been. They had been bounced by surprise and scattered by pairs. He had spent most of those few minutes alone and far from the others. But Lee knew that, granted confirmations, his total kills would now be five, making him an ace in only four missions.

Control brought the Gophers in on Strip 4-Y, the closest to their flight line. Lee knew that if he spent the rest of his life taxiing around the left-right turn combination, he would still see his P-38 sinking in the mud at the first turn.

Big Ole confirmed Lee's analysis. The Jap had probably totaled out Lee's radio. But, it appeared that the dead radio had saved Lee's life. There were two other hits, one in the horizontal stabilizer and one in the rear portion of the right boom, just ahead of the tail. That one scared Lee a little. If it had cut his control cables, he'd have had big, big troubles.

"Oops! What's this?" Big Ole asked as he bent down into the cockpit and fingered the displaced war emergency safety wire. "You ran the engines to war emergency?"

Lee thought the look on his crew chief's face said also, "Are you trying to burn up *my* airplane?" He smiled at the big Scandinavian. "Either that or *lose* your airplane, Chief."

"How long you run her like that?"

"Only about fifteen seconds. That shouldn't have hurt the engines."

"Well, maybe not. I'll check 'em out real good."

The friendly crew chief stood on the wing shaking his head and alternately looking from the throttles to the engines to the obvious damages and back again. He seemed devastated that Lee had brought the chief's personal property home damaged. Then he began issuing instructions to Mashy and Mac. No doubt, Ole would make the craft like new in less time than it should take.

When Lee finished the debriefing, he found Mo waiting for him outside the Ops shack.

Mo's serious face set Lee on the defensive.

"Thanks for breaking up that mob," Mo said. He hesitated, then continued, "But what were you doing way out there all by yourself?"

That's it, Lee thought, looking away momentarily. That's it! He turned his flushed face toward Mo Brennan. It had gone on long enough.

"Well, anyway, thanks," Brennan said with a grin. He turned and walked off toward Ops.

Somehow Lee cooled down, and by the time he had gone through debriefing and made it back to the tent, he had concluded that Mo Brennan was indeed toying with him. And somehow, he didn't feel the same anger, just a fiery determination to outlast the major. He stretched out on his bunk, pulled the mosquito netting down, and somehow managed to doze off and escape the tensions of combat and Mo Brennan.

"You trade?"

Lee turned over in his bunk, drew a deep breath, and relaxed.

"You trade?"

There it was again.

"You trade?"

Lee opened one eye and flinched. Suddenly, the other eye popped open. There beside his tent, staring in at him through the mosquito netting was the blackest face he had ever seen. The face had wide, thick lips and large, white teeth with gaps between. A hugh flattened nose with flared nostrils twitched beneath big eyes and an immense bush of fuzzy, black hair. Close behind the squatting creature lurked another, similar enough to be a twin. Lee thought about his Colt .45, but it was hanging outside his netting on the center post.

"You trade cloths?" the man said, breaking into a warm smile as he pointed to Lee's shirt. His big eyes exuded warmth that quickly dissolved Lee's fears. He pointed again to Lee's shirt, then to his own bare chest. "You trade cloths? I have things." He pointed down to a mysterious bundle wrapped in dirty old linen that lay across his thighs. His twin moved forward into the picture, grinned a toothless grin, and nodded affirmation.

Lee looked over at his tent mates. All asleep. He turned back to his visitors, put a finger to his lips, and motioned that he would join them outside. Their smiles widened even more. Their slow, deep nods of agreement stopped just short of a bowing motion. They met Lee at the steps to the tent.

"I—Bob," the spokesman said, his smile never faltering. "He—Bill," he added, pointing to his cohort. They were both slender but muscular and wore nothing but shaggy shorts that obviously had once been G.I. khaki trousers. Bob stood about five-ten, while Bill was a couple of inches shorter. Bob laid his bundle on the step and flipped the dirty, old cloth open. "You trade?"

Lee found the array of items at first startling, then fascinating. One by one, Bob held up items and offered them to Lee. After three good-sized sweet potatoes and a bunch of small, green bananas, Bob presented a wrist watch printed in Japanese, a Japanese officer's hat, a pair of small boots, a sword, a pistol, and insignias.

"Food," Bob said, waving a sweet potato, "souvners, Jap officer souvners. You trade cloths?"

"I—well—maybe," Lee replied. He slipped into the tent and returned with the oldest of his three shirts. He held it up to Bob's chest for size.

Bob nodded enthusiastically. Without hesitation, he reached down, came up with the holstered pistol, and handed it to Lee.

Bewildered briefly by the imbalance of the trade—an old shirt for a Jap officer's pistol—Lee hesitated and then accepted the weapon, nodding agreement.

"I happy. You happy?" Bob asked. "You like these, too?" From somewhere he produced two small items that Lee had missed. In the palm of Bob's hand lay a pair of human ears, probably those of the officer to whom the other items had belonged.

"Uh—no—no," Lee said.

Bob and Bill laughed heartily as they wrapped up the collection. Bob stuffed the ears into his pocket, donned the shirt, and with Bill following started silently up the path deeper into Fungus Field.

"Hey, Lee!" came a voice from the other direction. Smokey Stover came plodding up the now dusty path. "The major wants to see you—*now!*"

Chapter 10

▼

"You wanted to see me, sir?" Lee called into Major Brennan's tent.

"Huh? Oh, yeah, Marks. Circle the field. I'll be right out."

Lee braced himself for whatever was to come. He vowed to be cautious, but not weak. If Brennan simply wanted to harass him, he'd just laugh it off. He would not let the major crumple him into a little paper ball this time.

"Come on, Marks. Let's walk on down to the flight line," Mo Brennan said as he skipped down the steps from his tent. Without waiting for an answer, he turned and stepped off, bending to light his cigarette as he walked. Lee caught up quickly and the pair walked for some distance in silence. "I thought you ought to know, Nash is fine. Even though he bled like a stuck pig, it was only a shallow cut. It just happened to be a scalp wound where we really bleed. But when he clears the hospital this afternoon, his special kitchen privileges expire."

"Does he know that?" Lee asked, determined to talk through his discomfort.

"Yeah. He knows. Don't bail him out any more, let him sink or swim. Oh, and Logan made it back. He had to land at Finschafen for repairs, but he'll be ready to go."

Lee felt relieved that Robert Logan was safe and also that this session with the major had been so light. "Anything else, sir?"

"Why, hell yes, there's more. You think I dragged you down here just to tell you about Nash? Come on." He motioned to Lee, turned and resumed his trek. Looking at Lee out of the corner of his eye, Mo said, "You don't like me very much, do you?"

"Off the record?"

"Off the record."

"Can't say I don't like you. I'm just trying to figure out what the hell you want. You're either out to nail my hide to the tree or you're trying to manipulate me into a box. I can't find a reason for either," Lee said, a little surprised at the words that had just come out.

"Ha! That's pretty good, Marks," Brennan said. "You're as sharp as I thought you were, maybe even a little tougher than I thought. No question, you're a killer in a P-38." Brennan laughed and directed Lee toward the squadron commander's own Lightning.

An enlisted man was just climbing down from armorer's scaffolding with a can of paint in one hand and two artist's brushes in the other. He turned to Mo Brennan.

"Well, what do you think of him, sir?" the man asked, wiping a smudge of gold paint from his bare chest with a thumb.

On Mo's P-38 glistened a fresh and unusual piece of nose art, a large, golden gopher wearing a pilot's helmet. The creature had fierce eyes, huge front teeth, and a forked devil-like tail. He stood tall on his haunches, and he held a Japanese plane, snapped in half, in his paws.

"Fabulous job, Corporal. Just great. Is the other side as good?"

"Well, to be honest, sir, I think it's just a bit better," the man replied with an ever-widening grin on his face. "Do you think you'll want the whole squadron done?"

"Definitely," said Mo, "but I haven't decided yet if they'll all be gophers or if we'll do like everyone else, each man for himself. Still a bottle of scotch per ship?"

"Right, sir. The good stuff if you can. It trades better."

"You're on, Corporal. I'll let you know which way we want to go."

"Great. Oh—" The corporal hesitated. "Can you use your, uh, connections to get the paint, sir? I'm running into a little trouble. Captain Mershon calls it a conflict of interest."

"Done. Good job, Corporal."

Mo turned to Lee. "What do you think of my Golden Gopher, Marks?"

"It's terrific. The guy is really good," Lee replied.

"So's the gopher. What do you think? Should we do them all the same?"

"I don't know," Lee said. "Has it ever been done before? Everyone the same?"

"Only one precedent that I know of," the major said, "but they set one hell of an example. I'm talking about the Flying Tigers." He whipped out a cigarette and lit it. "I don't have Sledge Hammer's approval yet, but I'll get it. He said I'd be marking us for the Japs, like putting a bulls-eye on the side of every ship, especially the rookies. I see it the other way around. The Japs are running out of experienced pilots. They're rushing more rookies into this mess than we are, and theirs are not well-trained. If we can keep going the way we've started, I think we'll have the upper hand psychologically. I think this guy just strengthens that upper hand. Make sense?"

It suddenly occurred to Lee that after their brusk earlier encounter, Mo was now asking for his opinion. Was this a trap? A trick question?

"I don't know the Japs yet, Major," Lee said. Then he smiled. "And the few I've met…aren't talking. But it seems like a good idea to me. Count me in."

"Okay, tell you what. You poll the rest of the guys. I won't do it unless it's unanimous."

"You won't?" Lee asked.

"Pride is a powerful thing, Lee," the major said, "but it's also a very personal thing. They have to feel good about it. Now, you give them both sides of the question so they don't feel like they were snookered into something."

"Do you really think I'm the one to do that, Major?"

"It's Mo, and yes, I do think you're the one. They've felt what you've been going through. They respected you before, and now with five flags, you've earned everyone's respect."

"Uhh, *four* flags, only four," Lee said. The mistake irritated him. There was silence. Suddenly he realized that Brennan was grinning at him, a real, warm grin.

"Five. You, uh, *did* get that first Betty. I've sent the word to your crew chief to paint it on. Come on, Ace, let's head back."

Lee felt anger tumbling and wrestling with elation within himself. Mo was suddenly treating him with respect, and he had conceded the kill of the Betty. But damn it, why the days of all that other garbage?

"You were testing me?" he asked, stopping Mo and looking directly into his blue eyes.

"Definitely."

"That's all? *Definitely?* No reasons, excuses, or anything? Just *definitely?*" Lee asked.

"Don't push your luck."

Mo Brennan was still smiling. Lee decided not to push his luck.

When they reached Mo's tent, the squadron leader paused for a moment, looked at Lee and said, "There's one other thing for now. The replacement for Porter won't be here for a few days yet, and Nash will still be out for a day or two. So two officers from Headquarters Squadron will fly with us tomorrow and maybe the next day. That is, *if* we fly."

"Oh." Lee wasn't sure what the implications were, so he waited.

"Colonel Hammer will by rank lead the squadron when he flies, so I'll move to Element Leader with Sadler on my wing. But I have to have someone good on Colonel Hammer's wing. That's you. I don't want him getting shot down on *my* watch. Understand?"

"Understand," Lee repeated. "I'd better make sure Big Ole gets my radio up in first class condition so we're not sending smoke signals."

"Good thinking. Remember, your job is to cover the colonel, nothing more."

"Barton will go where?"

"He'll take your Charlie position in Blue Flight on the wing of Captain Jackson, the Operations Officer."

"If it's all the same, I'd like you to tell him. He's going to be slightly unhappy about that."

"No," Mo said firmly, "*you* tell him. I want it out of his system *before* we fly. I rather doubt he'll ever hit a Jap plane anyway, but I don't want him so unbalanced he's crashing into our guys." He turned and headed up the steps to his tent.

Lee wanted to ask about Gus and his status, but he decided they had mended enough fences for one day. In a second thought, he concluded that his session with Mo was about to result in yet another badly damaged fence.

When Lee reached Gus' tent, he motioned for an outside consultation. He summarized his discussion with Mo, up to the part about position reassignments.

"Gus," Lee said, "could I move in with you guys? You only have three, so I wouldn't be crowding you. I've about had it with Black Bart, especially with Bart and Bubba going at it all the time."

"Not a good idea, Lee." Gus shook his head and looked at the ground. "Personally, I'd like that. But it'd be the kiss of death for you. You've finally passed Mo's test. You're going to be second in command not far down the road. You'll pass Greenie and me. And that's okay with me. You're good. You deserve to move up. But if you spend any time around me, you'll end up on the wrong end of the kiss of death. You and I understand each other. We can still do that." Gus looked into Lee's eyes and gave him a light, friendly slap on the face.

Lee hurt inside, but reluctantly he agreed and started for his own tent. He strained to pick himself up before he reached it.

"Hey, Guys!" he said enthusiastically. He went on to describe the impressive gopher on Mo's ship and the concept of a whole squadron of gophers. Sandy quickly agreed and was confident that Bubba would like the idea. After some lobbying by Sandy, Bart reluctantly came around, but he insisted Mo Brennan should pay the painter. Lee let it go so things could quiet down before he brought up the matter of squadron position changes.

After some stalling, he explained that the Headquarters people needed hours to qualify for their flight pay and that Colonel Hammer and Captain Jackson would be flying with them for a day or two. Both tent mates took the news with passive acceptance. Then, suddenly, Black Bart's wheels seemed to turn. His eyes opened wide.

"Wait a minute!" he demanded. "Where do the brass fit in—the two empty slots?"

"I don't think a major does that with the fighter group commander," Lee said. "He probably has to turn the leadership over to Colonel Hammer."

"Yeah, I suppose so," Bart said. "So then Mo flies as wingman to the colonel. Cute."

"I can't see the major as anything but a shooter," Sandy said. "Can you, Lee?"

"According to what he said," Lee said, "he'll still be a shooter."

"Wait a minute!" snapped Black Bart, shooting one of his fiercest looks at Lee. "Marks, you're dancing around like a ballerina with a hotfoot. What the hell's going on?"

"What's going on is Mo Brennan shoved me into the Red Two slot covering Colonel Hammer—"

"Hah!" Bart said in disbelief.

"And he's taking over your Red Three spot, putting you in Blue Four to fly wingman on Captain Jackson, the Ops Officer."

"You're shitting me! He's putting *me* back there in Tail End Charlie? Moving *you* up? Why you brown-nosing bastard! Of all the lowdown tricks!"

Black Bart launched from his bunk like a rocket. Lee expected the trouble and met him half way. In his temper-fueled lunge, Bart left himself wide open for a hard right to either the belly or the head. But Lee lacked the anger to take advantage so he grabbed for Bart's arms and the two locked up in a sumo-style wrestling contest, each trying to force the other off balance.

"Come on, you guys!" said Sandy Sadler as he tried to break them up. But pulling at random arms and trying to wedge himself between the combatants accomplished nothing, so he slid behind Bart and got a choking throat-hold on him from behind. Gradually, Sandy's balanced position and powerful hold around Bart's neck prevailed. Bart let go and staggered backward, yielding to Sandy's leverage.

"Now, *can* it, both of you!" Sandy shouted. "Bart, you both got assigned to cover the high-ranking brass, so what's the big deal?" He let go of Bart, spun him around, and shoved him toward his bunk. "And Lee didn't make the assignments. Damn it, Barton, you don't shoot the messenger!"

Lee's temper was finally reaching fight-stage, but Sandy's "messenger" line cooled him slightly. He sat down on the edge of his bunk, looked at Bart and shook his head slowly.

"By God, I'll shoot the suck-hole messenger," Bart said. "Marks, from now on you'd better be careful about flying in front of me."

"Now *that's* one of your threats I'll take seriously," Lee said.

"And so will *I*," added Sandy. "I'm passing *that* remark on to Major Brennan."

Chapter 11

▼

"And that's our line-up for today," said Colonel "Sledge" Hammer. "Which one's Lieutenant Marks?"

"Here, sir," Lee responded.

"Just like to know who's covering my ass. You'd better be as good as Major Brennan says you are."

The colonel was an average man in many respects, average height, average weight, average voice. But his black crewcut, his dark, steely eyes, and his challenging demeanor broke the boundaries of average. He was without doubt a stomach in, chest out, and shoulders back officer. With those eyes, Lee thought, he might take on the new A6M5 Zero and simply melt it.

At 1230 hours, the Gophers took off on a heading of three-two-zero to rendezvous with two dozen B-24 Liberators. The target was the large Jap installation at Madang on the coast, northwest of the forward Allied base at Saidor. As the Gophers climbed to 22,000 feet, Lee found himself checking the build-up of clouds against the mountains. Typically, the northeastern prevailing winds blew the day's accumulation against those Owen Stanleys and when the weather couldn't clear the mountains, it piled up, backing down the slope over Dobodura. He knew the CAVU, Ceiling And Visibility Unlimited, would not hold for the entire mission. Colonel Hammer had garnered a reputation as a fighter. He had rung up fifteen kills before being assigned to command the new 483rd Fighter Group. The word was he was a Java Man, one of the small group of pilots who had put up a valiant fight while flying obsolete aircraft against the overwhelming Japanese invasion of the Java area. His victories had come, as Mo had said in introducing their group commander, "the hard way, facing the best of the

Jap pilots. We're getting the left-overs." Lee hoped the colonel was also good at weather.

The Gophers caught up with their bombers over the rugged Finistere Mountains and throttled back to maintain their position well above and behind them. The white surf line of the southeast to northwest coast reappeared, and Lee could see the Allied base at Saidor far below. He felt the tension growing. Madang was next. It was his first high altitude escort mission, and his new position at the left wing of the squadron commander added to the pressure.

"String formation," came the colonel's voice through Lee's headset.

The directive called for Lee to swing over from his position at the colonel's left wing to his right wing. Numbers three and four would drop back to make space for him. The formation gave them the flexibility to follow single file into combat.

"Here they come, three o'clock below," Hammer said. "Switch and drop tanks."

Lee switched, dropped, and tested his guns. In the few seconds before their leader began the attack, Lee looked over the Japanese force. He thought he saw twenty-five to thirty fighters, probably 5,000 feet below and off to the right. The color of the enemy planes indicated they were Japanese Air Army, usually manned by better pilots than their Navy counterparts.

The Gophers' present angle was bad. There wouldn't be enough time to circle and come down from behind. The Japs would be into the bombers by then. So the diving attack would have to be at a downward, front-quarter angle. Hits would be difficult, but the twelve Lightnings had a good chance of breaking up the Jap formation and spoiling their attack. If the enemy pilots were inexperienced they might turn up to meet the Gophers, thereby negating their own attack and giving the Lightnings their favorable head-on approach.

Colonel Hammer banked and started down. Lee waited briefly, then followed. He planned to leave a sizeable gap between his leader and himself to maintain a better picture of things and to prevent the enemy from getting on both of their tails at once. He could see the colonel firing at the lead Zero. Lee sighted on the leader's right wingman. Hammer's target caught fire and rolled to its left into a fatal dive, but the enemy fighters held their course toward the bombers. They were not turning up into the Gophers.

Lee searched for the right distance to lead his target. His tracers told him he was too far out front. But if he held his position, the Jap should fly into his line of fire. He fired two more solid bursts but saw no signs of damage. He gave it up, flew through the enemy, and searched for his leader. Sledge Hammer had turned into a shallow climb to the right to get behind the Japs for another run at them. It seemed like a good play to Lee, but there wouldn't be time for the whole squadron to follow. They would be getting too close to the Liberators.

"White and Blue," he heard Hammer's voice, "break left and come around the other side."

"Roger."

Good move, Lee thought. He swiveled about to assess the situation. He caught a glimpse of Mo back and to his right. But in that search, Lee discovered something else. While the lead Zeros continued for the B-24s, several had broken from the rear of their formation. With their superior turning capabilities, they were succeeding in cutting in on the Red Flight's wide circle.

He pressed his throat mike switch. "They're cutting in on us, Red," he called. "Two after you, Red One. I'm on them."

"Get 'em off me, Marks!"

One more quick glance told Lee the two sides had set up an alternate follow-the-leader pattern almost as though it had been choreographed. It seemed as though every Gopher who had a Jap in front of him also had one on his tail. Lee tried to ignore the one working in behind him to concentrate on the two after the colonel.

"Red One," Lee called. "Take 'em down and left."

"Roger."

As the Japs followed Colonel Hammer's move, it brought them into Lee's line. He put several rounds from his 20mm into the nearest one. It pulled up into a stall and fell off in a flat tailspin.

"Got one," Lee called. "Now the other."

"Don't talk about it—do it!" barked the colonel.

Lee had almost sighted in on the remaining Zero when it abruptly broke off in a sharp left turn. Turning with the Jap was out of the question. Lee followed his leader as they climbed for altitude. Temporarily clear of enemy planes, Lee surveyed the situation as Red Flight regained their altitude.

It had turned into a real donnybrook with planes from both sides turning, firing, diving, and climbing again. And the mess had moved close to the flight of bombers. But only four or five of the Zeros were still after the bombers. Each bomber had five machine gun positions, and they could expect to hold their own with those odds.

Suddenly, the enemy planes broke off and headed toward the ocean, forming up as they went. Lee soon realized why as the enemy anti-aircraft batteries opened up. The Lightnings pulled off and climbed to the seaward side to reset their protective cover. The Liberators had split into two groups among the ugly, explosions of flak. One group dropped its bomb loads on the airfields and the other aimed for the shipping in the harbor. From 20,000 feet Lee couldn't be sure of the damage inflicted, but the carpet of explosions told him it had to be substantial.

The bombers made their turns and started home. Gopher Squadron followed above on the seaward side, with all eyes watching for the Japanese Air Army to return. Two B-24s had gone down in the barrage of flak. Two others trailed smoke and had feathered an engine. One Gopher Lightning trailed coolant, but all twelve had made it back into formation.

Once past Saidor and back in a safer zone, Colonel Hammer called for a status check. One by one, the pilots reported in.

"Red Two," Lee said. "Okay."

"Red Three," followed Mo. "Okay."

"Red Four," came Sandy's voice. "I've got a prop that wants to run away."

When the calls were finished, it was clear that two Gophers had serious mechanical problems and two others had minor difficulties. Colonel Hammer sent the four home with the bombers and called for the remaining eight to move up and form new Red and White Flights.

"Okay, Red and White," Colonel Hammer said. "We're going duck hunting."

Having lost their bases at Lae, Finschafen, and Saidor, an estimated 8,000 Japanese soldiers of the Eighteenth Army had been forced inland, taking to the jungles and mountains. The only avenue by which they might rejoin the war required a trek of well over a hundred miles through nearly impassable jungles to Madang. Intelligence had predicted that nearly half of the enemy troops would die of disease or starvation and that few would ever reach their goal. The Japanese were attempting to supply them by using small boats, barges, and submarines.

Colonel Hammer flew a steep descent. He seemed to be in a hurry to get down. Lee's ears had never been particularly sensitive to changes in air pressure, but the constant, sharp pain he felt became tortuous. He wondered if any of the others were suffer—

"Uncle!" came a voice over the radio. "Uncle, I give up! I'll tell you anything you want to know," said the voice. It sounded like Burner Hedman, but Lee would never tell.

Without an acknowledgement, their leader altered the descent to a slower, more gradual angle. After a minute or two on the deck, Lee felt the pain ease up. They had dropped back into string formation.

"Mouth of a river up ahead. They'll be on the shady side. Harder to see."

About fifty feet above the water, Colonel Hammer slowed, banked right, dropped lower still, and started up the river. Lee could see Hammer's tracers raking through the overgrowth along the left bank, so he aligned himself similarly. He saw nothing.

"Did I draw any fire, Marks?" the leader asked.

"Don't see any," Lee replied.

"We'll go in until the trees touch."

Up ahead, Lee could see the point at which the growth on the two sides seemed to come together. Though they had cut their airspeed to 250 mph, that point approached all too rapidly. Lee saw Hammer fire again, then pull up to zoom out of the channel. Lee was almost to the pull-up point when he heard slugs slam into his Lightning. As he climbed up over the trees, he scanned his instruments and did a visual exterior check.

"Mo, did you see that?" Lee called. "I took some hits in that last stretch."

"I'm on them," Mo said.

"Everybody make one pass, then join up," ordered the colonel. "We're not equipped for that job. Let's go home."

The directive surprised Lee. He had supposed that Colonel Sledge Hammer was an aggressive pit bull who would never let go. But the decision did nothing to lessen his confidence in the leader's judgment. The P-38s could only fire blindly into the thick jungle growth. The Jap soldiers could hear and see the fighters coming. They had every advantage. The answer, he knew, would be low-level bombing or napalm.

Lee followed the colonel in at Dobo an hour later, relieved that the nearest thunderheads were still a mile away. As he looked over the damage with Big Ole, Colonel Hammer walked past.

"Good job," the colonel said with a slight wave, never breaking stride.

When the Gophers had all cleared the debriefing, they had a clearer picture of the mission. The wounded birds had all made it back safely. Confirmed kills went to:

Hammer—1	Green—1	Gustafson—0
Marks—1	Logan—0	Stover—1
Brennan—1	Callahan—0	Jackson—1
Sadler—0	Hedman—1	Barton—0

"That, Gentlemen," Colonel Hammer said looking at the scoresheet, "is the nature of the beast. Nobody got more than one. But we did what we were hired to do. We broke up the attack. The only big brothers we lost were to flak. We'll send an F-5 recon over at first light so we can get some photos and assess the damage." He turned to Major Brennan, "Mo, I'm impressed with this bunch of rookies you have. Yeah, do the gopher thing if you want—after tomorrow. If I should fly with you tomorrow, I don't want to be the only non-gopher and get all those Japs down on *me.*" He turned and left the Ops area.

Lee and Gus walked slowly up the path toward the tent city. They discussed the mission, the things they might have done differently, better or worse. They stopped for a moment at the Fungus Field signpost. A rough, homemade sign had been added carelessly to the post. Someone had sketched the top half of a bald head with two large eyes peering over a horizontal line that represented a wall. To each side of the face was a set of fingers that appeared to be gripping the top of the wall. Crude printing said: KILROY WAS HERE.

The curious but humorous phenomenon had swept the world in but months, and apparently the mysterious Kilroy delighted most in posting his message in unpredictable places. Scuttlebutt had it that a pilot from a neighboring bomb group had been about to take his seat on the wooden outdoor latrine when he happened to glance down through the hole. There, looking up at him was the familiar Kilroy face.

As Lee and Gus shared a laugh at the new addition, Black Bart stomped past.

"Smart move, Suckhole," he said to Lee. "But you'll get yours."

"Man," Gus gave a shake of his head, "I hope he has an accident. Maybe shoots a Jap plane one of these days."

Chapter 12

▼

"Changed my mind! I don't give a damn what the rest of you do! I'm not having a stupid goddamned gopher painted on my ship just to be like the rest of you!" roared Black Bart.

Lee had called the squadron mates together down on the flight line right after early morning chow. He had presented Mo Brennan's suggestion that they all use the golden gopher for nose art. Though the project seemed somewhat silly, he thought it might provide the guys with some fun and strengthen their comradery. He had ridden the neutral fence well, getting all of their opinions without stating his own. And when Black Bart stepped up with his venomous veto, Lee never had to take a stand.

"Come on, Barton," Gus said. "Quit pouting. Maybe if you changed your attitude you'd start hitting some Japs."

"What a chicken shit loner," Burner Hedman said. "Why don't you put in for a transfer?"

Bart made no response. Lee knew that Bart was afraid of the burly lumberjack

"Nobody else will take him," added Sandy Sadler.

"Okay, okay," Lee cut in. "Let's not have our own war over this. It was just an idea. Subject closed. I'll tell the major we prefer to choose our own nose art. You know, he *is* paying the painter for the whole squadron, though. That is, *if* the corporal says your requests are reasonable. For really elaborate stuff the great master painter wants an extra bottle of scotch."

"Man, with all the scotch he's going to have, he could buy Fort Knox," Callahan said.

"No question about it," Sandy added, "he's one of the local bankers. If you need currency, that's where you go. Just don't drop the bottle."

I hear gin is a hot trading item, too," said Burner Hedman. "Easier to get. Of course, I'm sure it won't buy what scotch will buy."

"Hey," said Cal, "it's past 0600 hours. I thought Colonel Hammer and Major Brennan would be here to brief us.

"There's no mission today," said Big Ole as he approached the group. "I just come past Ops. They said the mission's been scrubbed." He went on toward Lee's Number 161.

Nobody mentioned it, but Lee could feel the tension drain from the group. Even Bart looked a tad more friendly. Lee caught Greenie as he started to leave the group.

"Greenie, I need some help." He pulled the Japanese pistol from his shoulder holster. "Any idea where I can find some shells for this?" Lee asked. "I think it's nine millimeter."

Several Gophers gathered around.

"I traded with a native called Bob," Lee said. "Isn't that kind of funny? He called himself Bob and his buddy was Bill. Bob and Bill? Out here in the New Guinea jungle?"

"Your first brush with the Fuzzy Wuzzies, huh," Greenie said. "That Bob's a real entrepreneur. He ought to be selling used cars. Bill just follows him around like he's knocked out by the whole process. Actually, I think Bill is knocked out on betelnut. They come into camp every few days. Beyond Bob's dealing, they're really nice guys. What did the weapon cost you?"

"My oldest shirt," Lee replied.

"Hey, not bad," Greenie said, tossing the pistol from hand to hand to get the feel of it.

"I was surprised that they spoke English. How did they get American names?"

The rest of the group eyed the pistol with envy, but they listened intently to Greenie.

"Bob, like a lot of them, was taught by missionaries. Bill apparently flunked English. We don't know if the missionaries gave them the names or if they just picked names they liked from the first troops they met. Wait till you meet George and Ethyl."

"George and Ethyl?" Smokey Stover asked. "Ethyl—a woman?"

"Oh, no," Greenie corrected. "Ethyl's a man, a *big* man, and very proud of his name. He just doesn't know Ethyl's a woman's name." He paused. "I'm not going to tell him, and I'd suggest that you don't tell him, either. Now, Lee, that cannon of yours. Sergeant Ainsley over in Transportation has piled up a good collection of weapons. He'll probably have the right ammo."

"Hey, great!" Lee said. "I hope I can find some. I'd much rather carry this than that heavy forty-five we're issued."

"You try to get into your ship with this gun strapped on, and I'll have Big Ole castrate you," Greenie said, tossing the weapon back to Lee. "You get caught in Jap territory carrying that thing, and that's just *one* of the things that'll happen to you."

Apparently Lee wasn't the only one who had not thought ahead. The group went silent. Their faces screwed up when Lee added the bit about the Jap officer's ears. Soberly, the men drifted down the flight line toward their aircraft.

"Thanks, Greenie," Lee said. "I'd never have thought of that."

"I probably wouldn't have either," Greenie replied. "When I was finding my way back through the jungle, I came across a small Japanese camp one night. And I saw what they were doing to an Aussie prisoner. Believe me, you don't want to know. I can't possibly live long enough to forget that night."

When Lee reached his Number 161, Mac was carefully smoothing the edges of the aluminum patches to cover the shell holes from the previous mission.

"That corporal, the painter, was here looking for you," Mac said. "Oh, there he comes now."

The corporal turned out to be Corporal Jones.

"Major Brennan said that you'd have the answer on the Gopher thing?"

"Great idea, Jones," said Lee, "but they didn't all buy into it. So it'll be every man for himself. Sorry about that."

"Oh, don't be sorry. I'm an artist, not a copyist. I was dreading having to do twenty-two more gophers—exactly alike. Have you decided on what you want? Major Brennan said you come first."

"Not really. I don't have a college mascot that would be good. Nobody knows what a champion looks like. I don't have a wife or special girl friend." Lee paused. "I don't even have a dog."

"Oh, that's okay," said Corporal Jones enthusiastically. "Those are all over-used and boring, anyway. We'll come up with a good one." He thought for a moment. "Are you smart?"

Lee nodded self-consciously.

"Aggressive?"

Another nod.

"A good shot?"

Lee held up five fingers.

"Trust me?" the corporal asked.

"I—yeah, I think I do," Lee said.

"Okay, you go do whatever second lieutenants do when they're not flying P-38s, and in a couple of hours we'll have something. Okay?"

"Okay."

On his way back toward Fungus Field, Lee wondered about his judgment. Maybe Corporal Jones only meant that he'd have an *idea* for Lee's approval. No, Lee didn't really believe that. Perhaps he had just made one of his dumber mistakes.

As he passed the Ops shack, Mo Brennan called to him. He found the major sitting in a corner with a cup of coffee in one hand and the perpetual cigarette in the other.

"They didn't go with the Gopher idea, did they?" the major asked.

"Sorry. No."

"Let me guess. You all voted for it but Barton."

"How—I didn't say that," Lee responded quickly.

"Of course not. But I see real squadron pride, the kind we have to have, building here, building quickly. And that's good! But we have one guy with personal problems that interfere, and that's Barton." He looked up at Lee. "Am I wrong?"

"Sir, I really shouldn't—"

"Of course you shouldn't get into personalities. But I can. Am I wrong?"

Lee smiled and shook his head.

"Okay, my job and your job—to bring him around, wise him up."

"Whoa!" Lee said. "Black Bart hates my guts. I'm the last one who could hope to straighten him out. And moving me up to Red Flight yesterday didn't help things. With all due respect, sir, he's *your* job."

"Uh—yeah, you're right, Marks. Just don't knuckle under to the bastard. Okay?"

"Never have so far," Lee said.

"Here, sit down," Major Brennan said, kicking a folding wooden chair out from under the long table. "Coffee? Got a pot brewing over there." He nodded to the far corner of the open-sided Ops shack.

"If I do more than two cups of that stuff, it'll eat my guts out," Lee said with a laugh. "So the mission was scrubbed?"

"Scrubbed, but we're on one-hour-alert starting at 1200 hours. Unless we grab some more Jap bases to the west, we'll be so crowded here we'll be drawing straws for permission to fly," Mo said. "And that doesn't fit my plans at all."

"Excuse me—your plans?"

"Uhhh, yeah." Mo took a sip of his coffee, but his eyes peered intensely over the rim of the cup at Lee.

"You're from Chicago?"

"South Side, all my life," Lee said.

"I'm from Minneapolis. Great place. Graduated from the University of Minnesota in thirty-nine. My father owns a sizeable foundry in Minneapolis."

"So you'll be going into the foundry business when you go home?" Lee asked.

"Probably, but that's just a means to an end." Mo looked past Lee as though off in another world. "I'm really headed for politics. Hell, Marks, you're looking at the future mayor of Minneapolis. And I might go on from there to Washington. What are your plans?"

"Don't have any," Lee said. "The first thing is to get home in one piece. I'm sure not planning on being elected to anything. Nobody who is anybody knows me."

"Ah, but they could, you know. You need to think ahead. Always think ahead. You've got a chance to win thousands, maybe millions of votes in the next few months. Think about that. Most of the guys over here are fighting a war and trying to survive it. And that's good. But the bright ones are doing those two things *and* looking for ways to make this damned war work for them instead of against them. Think about that."

"Yeah, I will." Lee felt uncomfortable with the direction Mo was headed.

"This world is all about reputation, about image," Mo said. He leaned forward on the tabletop, lowered his voice, and glanced around as though to insure their privacy. "You get paid to kill Japs, right?"

"Well, yeah."

"Okay. You kill enough Japs and you go home with a big reputation. Accolades in the news media—maybe even a statue in the park. Why not cash in on it? You have to kill Japs anyway."

Like all of the pilots, Lee had heard of Bong, McGuire, and the other multiple aces in the Fifth Air Force. But it had never occurred to him that their notoriety might be spread beyond the pilots in New Guinea. He wondered if the leading ace Dick Bong had visions of statues in his mind when he shot at Japs. Somehow Lee doubted it. Still, Mo Brennan had a point. As long as he was stuck in this dangerous occupation, why not do the best possible job?

"I guess you're off to a good start," Lee said. "You're almost a triple ace."

"And I'm going to stay alive to become a triple—and more." His face, his eyes radiated an intensity that was new to Lee. "I want to catch Bong and McGuire. I want forty, fifty, maybe sixty kills." A devilish grin broke on his face. "And you should, too."

"I guess so," Lee said. "I just never thought of it like that."

"It's time, my friend. It's time. You're already up to six, averaging one a mission. That's almost a record in itself. If you're determined, careful, and smart, you can get to forty or fifty flags, especially if we work together. By the way, Sledge was very impressed with the way you covered him yesterday. So we've got him in our corner. You know, the better Gopher Squadron does, the better his brand new 483rd Fighter Group looks. He thinks we can catch the 475th Satan's Angels. That's asking a lot. But he *really* wants to."

It warmed Lee to be recognized. What a change in only two days. And Mo Brennan's slant on their air war did make sense, in fact his concept fired a strange, new excitement within Lee. But he needed some time to digest this portion before biting into more.

"I—I guess I'd better get back down to the flight line and make sure everything's getting done," he said, rising to leave. "I don't have the slightest notion of what Jones is painting on my ship."

"Hey, Killer, if I trust him, you trust him. Oh, by the way," Mo said, "I'm moving you into the element leader slot in Red Flight. With the two of us in the shooter spots, we can really run up the scoreboard. You pick your wingman."

"Oh, I'll want to keep Sandy Sadler there, if that's okay."

"Fine." Mo said. "I'm going to keep Bubba for a while. The kid just might work out." He paused, then looked up at Lee. "Now, this conversation is just between us, right?"

"Well, yes, of course."

"Good, and remember, thou shalt have no other gods before your CO."

Chapter 13

▼

"Hey, here he comes," said Sandy. "Doesn't look too bad, either."

"Bubba, welcome home!" Lee said as the gangly tent mate negotiated the three rough wooden steps up to the tent. "We hoped you'd make it last night. Are the hospital bunks better than ours?" Lee had vowed to resume his previous role as Bubba's protector. He hoped Bubba had gotten over his anger.

"Hi, Guys, I'm back," Bubba said modestly. A heavy white bandage wrapped around his head like a topless turban. Pointing to the bandage, he said, "The people in the hospital called me the king—because of my crown." He turned on his boyish grin. "If I get this big thing off today and the helmet doesn't bother, Captain Talbot, the flight surgeon, says I can fly tomorrow."

"Hell! What do you mean, 'King?'" Bart thundered.

Lee tensed, ready to jump into the impending battle.

"You're no king," Bart repeated, "but you *are* the first new medal winner in the whole 483rd Fighter Group since the group was formed. Did you know that?"

Bubba looked confused, turned to Lee, who simply shrugged.

"Hell yes," Sandy added, "the group's first medal winner—the purple heart!"

"Golly, that's right," Bubba said. "I wonder how soon I'll get it."

"Oh, they wait a long time," Black Bart said. "They figure if they wait long enough you'll get killed. Save them the trouble and the cost."

Lee almost went after Bart on that one, but Bart's tone was friendly and he laughed as he said it.

"Uh, Lee?" Bubba motioned to the door of the tent. When the two Gophers had left the others behind, Bubba said, "I just wanted you to know I'm not mad at you any more. I got to do some thinking over in the hospital tent. This came pretty close," he said, pointing to his turban. "If I'd have gotten killed, you would always believe that I died hating you. That would be awful to go through life believing something like that when it isn't true. I'm sorry I yelled at you."

"Oh, that's okay, Bubba. I knew you weren't really mad at me, just mad."

"You've done more for me along the way than all of the others put together," Bubba said. "In fact, time and time again you defended me against the others. Remember when that old drill sergeant stuck me with the nickname, Bubbles?"

Lee smiled. He remembered it well.

"And the name stuck for a couple of days. I'd still have it if you hadn't stepped in and used Bubba thirty or forty times a day until they forgot about Bubbles. I owe you for that."

"Glad I could help. Tell you what, Bubba. Mo Brennan has changed some of the flight assignments around. But he wants to give you more time as his wingman, likes what he's seen."

"Really? How come he didn't choose you? You're better than I am."

"He switched me with Barton, said he wanted *you* for wingman. Now, if you owe *anybody,* go out there and cover Mo Brennan's butt. And *no* more food problems, okay?"

"You've got it! Thanks, Lee."

As they returned to the tent, Bubba's gratitude mixed with his enthusiasm, and a chemical reaction erupted, "Guess what? Major Brennan wants me back as his wingman!"

Sandy raised an eyebrow and looked at Lee. Lee tried not to look at Barton, but it didn't matter.

"So if you're in the Number Two slot, where does Marks go?" asked Black Bart.

"Oh, he'll be in your old slot," replied Bubba.

"In *my* slot?" Bart came up off his bunk and started for Lee. "Why you brown-nosing bastard. The final low blow!"

Bubba stood frozen to his spot on the wooden floor. His expression ranked somewhere between utter confusion and horror. But Sandy jumped in front of Black Bart.

"This is getting old, Bart!" Sandy shouted. "If you've got a bitch, take it to the major! Lee had nothing to do with this."

"Yeah, I'll bet!" Black Bart stomped out of the tent, jumped the three steps to the ground and struck out with giant strides down the dusty path toward Mo Brennan's tent.

"Thanks, Sandy," Lee said. "I don't know how much longer I can hold it in. I thought that was going to be the one."

"*Are* you brown-nosing with Mo Brennan?" Sandy asked, his freckled face as serious as Lee had ever seen it.

"That," Lee replied, "depends on your definition of brown-nosing. When my commanding officer says, 'Come in, sit down, and listen,' I do that. I come in, I sit down, and I listen. What would you do? Tell him to go to hell?"

Sandy broke into his characteristic grin. "Thought I'd ask," he said. "But I want you to know, I'm not going to play referee forever. One of these days, when that ornery bastard starts for you, I'm heading for the basement." He looked down at the ramshackle floor.

"The base—?" Bubba stifled his question.

"Sandy, try to pick one of my bad days, will you? When I'm inclined to laugh at Bart, I'm in no mood to fight. And by the time I get mad, I'm liable to get my butt kicked." He turned to Bubba. "Come on, Sheik. Let's go down to the flight line and see if we can find Corporal Jones. He's waiting for your order on nose art."

Bubba's excitement reached the red zone when he started down the line of P-38s.

Major Brennan's Golden Gopher—Sandy Sadler's freckled, but sexy Little Orphan Annie—Black Bart's one-eyed pirate—Gus's Goose, a sexy goose with tiger-like saber teeth—Greenie's Brownie, a cute little brown elf with a lightning bolt ray gun—and Lee's The Marksman, a Robin Hood-like character with drawn bow.

"Wow, Lee!" Bubba yipped. "How did you guys think of all these good ideas?"

"Tell you, Bubba," Lee said seriously, "We thought, and thought, and thought some more. And then we told Corporal Jones, 'Do whatever you think is best.' That is, all but Bart. And I have to admit, he sure picked an appropriate figure." They studied the patch-eyed pirate with a saber in one hand and an old flintlock pistol in the other.

"The pirate looks friendlier than Bart," Bubba observed.

* * * *

For three successive days, Gopher Squadron flew the familiar patrol over the Solomon Sea, off the southwest tip of New Britain. The first two days were busts—nothing except the challenge of getting home in hellish weather, something three members of Greenie's flight barely managed on the second patrol.

The fourth member, Cal Callahan, had aborted earlier with an electrical problem. He never made base. Army Air Force PBY flying boats were out patrolling the area, looking for Cal, but the entire squadron quieted under a blanket of apprehension.

The statement, "The weather takes as many of us as the Japs do," loomed larger and larger in Lee's consciousness. In some ways, he felt the tension of bad-weather-flying was worse than that of combat. Combat was usually over in minutes. A flight home in horrendous weather took forever. The constant strain of trying to see through a rain-spattered windshield while trying to let down through the storm clouds, all the while expecting a giant mountain to spring up suddenly, took its toll.

On the third day they tangled with Japanese Val dive-bombers that were escorted by the newer A6M5 Zeros, and Lee discovered that the M5 was indeed much faster than its predecessor, the A6M2. Lee got a Val on his first pass. Then a miscalculation got him into serious trouble. But solid, reliable Sandy was there to blow the Zero off his tail. For the first time, Lee actually felt the immense gratitude so common after a pilot's salvation by a wingman. And with each such occurrence, the spirit of teamwork and camaraderie within Gopher Squadron grew stronger.

Flying back to Dobodura, Lee spotted a Japanese Nakajima "Rufe" single-pontoon reconnaissance plane lumbering along just above the surface of the sea. The Rufe was a converted Zero, but the gigantic pontoon beneath it had changed a stinging bee into a clumsy turtle. Mo sent Lee and Sandy to handle the matter. On the way down from 15,000 feet, Lee handed off the first shot to Sandy who promptly dispatched the Rufe from behind. The scout plane touched the water, did one gigantic flip, and landed on its back in the ocean. Lee had added only one flag in three missions and was dealing with frustration, but the good feeling that came with giving that kill to Sandy eased his anxiety.

The Gophers joined the chow line that evening with more interest than usual. The word was out that they were actually going to have ice cream for dessert. The betting was evenly split between ice cream and mere rumor. Lee leaned to the negative, wondering where they could have gotten the deluxe treat, how they'd kept it frozen in transit, and how an ongoing menu that offered little but survival nutrition could suddenly sprout anything that good. He had almost reached the serving station when Bubba, who had already gone through the line, stopped and shoved his food in front of Lee.

"God-darn it!" Bubba spouted. "Look at this! We finally get something good like ice cream, and what do they do? Just like everything else, they dump it in the god-darned gravy!" The crowd, particularly those who knew of Bubba's mess hall history exploded in laughter. Lee's own enjoyment curve flattened a little. Bubba had done well with the chow for several days. Lee hoped he wasn't seeing the prelude to a relapse.

After chow that evening, the cowboy movie starring Bob Steele as *Billy the Kid in Texas* was scheduled in the amphitheater, a large, bowl-like product of G.I. ingenuity. The engineers had combined with volunteer help to take advantage of a steep, concave hillside. They had first dug large drainage ditches that encircled the facility above the bowl and down both sides to divert run-off water as well as provide emergency trenches in case of air raids. On the hillside, long benches made of tree trunks were set in horizontal rows from top to bottom. In the level space at the bottom they had erected a large stage, over which a huge movie screen could be mounted and unrolled. Loudspeakers hung from poles on either side of the stage.

Smudge pots on poles combined with the heavy blanket of cigar and cigarette smoke to ward off some of the mosquitoes, but the theater-goers all sprinkled on extra heavy doses of DDT powder. Even many of the non-smokers lit up in self-defense at movie time. Lee sometimes felt that, between the layers of protective powder and the Atabrine that turned their skin so yellow, they had ceased to be human beings and had become weird-smelling, yellow creatures from another planet.

The night's movie got off to its customary shaky start. Three minutes into the film, the images on the screen began to flutter and the projector ground to a halt. The actors' voices became garbled as they slowed and sank in pitch. It made Lee think of a drowning man and his last words. A joker in the front row stood and waved a KILROY WAS HERE. But once past the opening pitfall, the movie rolled smoothly. Lee and the others enjoyed it. The action held their attention and the overall experience gave them a badly needed taste of home. As they filed out of the amphitheater Gus joined Lee.

"I guess you had your recruitment meeting with Mo," Gus said.

"Well," Lee hesitated, "we did have a little talk the other day. Recruitment?"

"Yeah, the speech where he recruits you to be his special partner," Gus said, glancing about as though searching for someone, "the one where he talks about his political plans and how the two of you can go home heroes and cash in on it after the war."

"You—" Lee locked up temporarily. "You were given the same talk?"

"I'd call it a pitch, myself."

"Okay, Gus, I have to believe you. You've never been anything but honest with me," Lee said. They walked slowly down the crowded path. "What happened?"

"Not sure," Gus replied, "but I think Mo decided he couldn't trust me to keep my mouth shut. I said something once to one of the others. Mo picked up on it and decided I had breached a confidence. He still uses me to best advantage for my experience, but really I'm on his shit list—oops!" Gus gave a light, forward push on Lee's back and then stalled to drop farther back into the line of G.I. theater-goers.

Lee continued on in the slow-moving queue and looked about, confused by his friend's strange behavior until he came to the next intersection of pathways. Off to one side stood Mo Brennan, chatting with Colonel Sledge Hammer. Mo gave Lee a nod and a casual wave with his cigarette hand.

Chapter 14

Lee had nearly finished shoveling dirt over his droppings in the temporary latrine trench when he heard the familiar voice behind him.

"Got to hand it to you, Marks," said Black Bart as he squatted over the trench, "you worked it out nice, getting Brennan to cover your ass. Did you rehearse the lines together?"

"I don't know what you're talking about, Bart," Lee said as he turned to leave, "but then, you don't either."

"I'm talking about Porter's replacement, this guy Forbes who's due in today. Brennan says he's to take over Element Leader in Blue Flight. That leaves me still back in Tail End Charlie." Bart glared at Lee. "I suppose you had nothing to do with that."

"For once you're right," Lee said as he walked away.

"Yeah, just run away, Chicken Shit."

Lee stopped. He felt the heat rush to his face. Bart's name calling took him back 14,000 miles and ten years to his boyhood in South Chicago. In those days the two words from Bart ranked with "Fuck you," and they were fighting words. He spun around, ready to dump Barton into his own trench. But he thought for a moment, then turned and walked away. He knew that someday the conflict would come to blows, but he vowed he wouldn't let it happen over "Chicken Shit." He knew, though, that each time he turned away from battle, Black Bart became more convinced that Lee was afraid of him, and that meant the provocations would increase. Could there be a peaceful way to end the territorial challenge of the raging lion?

At the flight line, Lee found Sandy waiting for him. Above his toothy grin, Sandy's freckles seemed to glow in the bright morning sun.

"What did Mo say, Lee?" Sandy asked with boyish enthusiasm.

Lee smiled and nodded. They headed down the line toward their Lightnings.

"Mo said we could take an hour to try them out, but he said to stay off the radio as much as possible," Lee offered. "No point in telling any Japs in the area what we're doing. Before we take off, let's jot down a list of what we want to do. Then we can signal with just a waggle here and there."

Half an hour later, Lee and Sandy had completed pre-flight checks, taxied to Strip 4-West, and were lifting from the compacted ground. With Sandy behind and to his right, Lee took a heading of zero-seven-seven degrees toward the Solomon coast. They continued their climb to 22,000 feet to begin their experiments.

In hangar-flying sessions with more experienced pilots from other squadrons, Lee had picked up some tricks peculiar to the Lightning that deserved to be tested. Lee had suggested to Mo that the Gophers were not using the P-38's capabilities to full advantage, a shortcoming that would inevitably cost lives in the near future.

First, he and Sandy would try the new dive flaps. Taking steep-angle dives to various speeds and altitudes, they quickly came to admire the new equipment. In their final dive from high altitude, Lee pressed his speed to well over 400 mph, to the point where he began to feel compressibility buffeting. He touched the control button on the yoke. The flaps opened and slowly but smoothly the nose began to pull up, even with no movement of the elevator.

The two pilots leveled off at 12,000 feet and Lee signaled for another dive. It worked as he had expected. At 5,000 feet he applied the dive flaps, and with the heavier air at low altitude, the nose swiftly pulled up into a climb. Lee had found a new excitement that further tightened his bond to his P-38, The Marksman.

Following their plan, Sandy then assumed the position of the chaser, as though trying to shoot Lee down. Lee experimented with several turning maneuvers using his regular Fowler flaps or his diving flaps in combination with what he called "splitting the engines." In a sharp right turn at moderate to slow speed he would suddenly pull his Fowler flaps to twenty degrees, pull the right throttle way back, and shove the left throttle ahead to full. The 17,000-pound fighter whipped around like a toy on a string, and Sandy, relying on conventional techniques, slid on past. Even though Sandy knew the move was coming, it was impossible for him to stay close to Lee. In a high-speed turn, Lee combined his new diving flaps with the splitting process and found similar success. It seemed as though some invisible giant had grasped the nose and jerked it around the corner.

They played cat-and-mouse with Sandy taking his turns as the trickster for some time before returning to base. Lee felt the elation of a first solo flight. The new turns gave his powerful, big Lightning maneuverability never dreamed of back in advanced training. He felt a chill, however, when he considered the number of P-38 pilots who had been lost because of inadequate training or because their earlier models lacked the diving flaps. He couldn't wait to tell the older pilots how grateful he was for their suggestions, and he was anxious to pass the results on to Mo Brennan.

Lee had just completed his post-flight checks when he noticed a gathering of Gophers down the line. Together with Sandy he walked down to a previously empty parking slot. There sat a Lightning with different markings. A group of the Gophers had gathered around its pilot.

Charles "Chub" Forbes, the replacement for Jerry Porter, had just flown in from Finschafen and was meeting his new squadron mates. The name, "Chub," was indeed short for "Chubby," the newcomer explained with a wry grin. He was a short, slight man, far closer to skinny than to chubby. He had straight brown hair and a thin, face with the darting eyes of a hawk. Chub was an experienced pilot with three kills, and Mo had somehow acquired him from the Forty-ninth Fighter Group. Hearing that explanation, Lee looked around and spotted Black Bart off in the distance, heading for Fungus Field. Lee felt a brief touch of sympathy wash through him. It appeared that the Gophers had acquired yet another pilot with skills superior to those of Aloysius Barton.

The throaty roar of twin Wright Cyclone radial engines drowned out any further conversation, and Lee looked up to see their Golden Goose parking in its revetment. The engines had no sooner stopped than the improvised side door opened and Cal Callahan jumped to the ground. He trotted toward the group. Sandy met him halfway with a businesslike handshake.

"Damn, Cal. Bad timing," Sandy said seriously. "Your replacement just flew in," he added, pointing to Chub Forbes. "What'd you come back for?" Then the freckled jester broke into his trademark smile, hugged his good friend, and shared his relief with the others.

Lee found Mo Brennan with his customary cigarette and coffee cup in the Ops shack. Mo waved him to the coffee, but when Lee got to the corner set-up he found no available cups.

"You look bright this morning," Mo said as Lee sat down across the table from him. "You met Chub Forbes, huh?"

"Uh, yes, but Chub's not what put the grin on my face."

Expressionless, Mo simply took a drag, leaned back in his chair, and forcefully exhaled.

"We tried out several moves, Mo, and they work. They really work!" Lee paused. "Of course, I'm not saying we should make it a practice to turn left with Zeros. But when we need a sharp turn to get at one, or if we've got one on our tail and we don't have speed or altitude going for us, there are ways to get it done."

Lee went on to explain the experiments he and Sandy had run using the split engine principle, making the sharp turn at slow speeds by deploying the regular flaps and the similar maneuver at high speeds using the dive flaps.

"We didn't try to rip the wings off," Lee said, "but I can tell you that on the edge of compressibility, the dive flaps bring the nose right up. Hardly need any elevator."

"Sounds great," Mo said, "especially for tractor jockeys like me. It sounds like my kind of flying."

"Excuse me?"

"There are birds and there are drivers," Mo replied. "Guys like Bong, McGuire…and *you* are birds. You guys have feelings, the touch, built right into you, I don't know, maybe in the seat of your pants? The rest of us move levers this way and that way because that's what we were taught to do. This stuff you're onto sounds like lever pulling to me. But it sounds good. Tell you what. I want you to take us all, the whole squadron, through these moves in the morning—if we're not scheduled. I want each of us to know how it works, what we can do, and what we can't do. Okay, Teach?"

"You're on," Lee said confidently.

"Tell you what," Mo said with a glance at his watch. "It's chow time. Go get fed, then come on back. We can go over some other things."

"Things?"

"Oh, nothing too serious. Now, go on," Mo said with a wave-off.

Lee almost suggested that Mo go with him to chow, but reticence won out. When he got to the mess tent and saw Black Bart there he was glad he hadn't asked his CO to eat with him. As he stepped up to be served, the crescendo of an approaching roar reached a peak immediately overhead. Everything in the kitchen rattled, and a stack of tin cups toppled off a shelf. The B-24s were taking were taking off on a mission. The cooks swore and looked upward with contempt.

"Another one! How many of those damned things they got out there anyway?" one demanded.

"Relax, Cooby. That's just the beginning. Lots more to come!" another answered as he slopped Lee's portion onto his tray.

"Shit on the shingle—again?" Lee moaned under his breath when he glanced down at the offering. He looked up at the face of the server. No guilt there—not even a hint of an apology. Lee sat alone, bolted the creamed dried beef on toast, and set out for his meeting with Mo.

"Did things come out all right at the latrine this morning?" Mo asked Lee when they had resettled in the corner of the Ops shack.

"Huh? How did you hear about that?"

"Frankly, I thought it was kind of funny. I can just see Barton straddling the trench with crap coming out of both ends," Mo replied with a laugh. "I could hang him out to dry, but I'd rather wait. He might grow up. And if he doesn't," he smiled, "he'll hang himself."

"Where did the '24's go today?" Lee asked, trying for a subject more comfortable.

"We got a hot tip that the enemy has a convoy heading for Wewak, probably supplies and reinforcements. We were just arguing about that," he went on, nodding his head toward the group of officers standing at huge map. "We think that the B-25s and our P-38s would do better at low level than the heavies up high on a harbor attack, but then…."

As the conversation went on, Lee felt himself relaxing. Mo Brennan's casual manner and ever-present smile made it easier. Along with some football talk, they exchanged more on their personal histories. It came out that Mo had been an only child, the son of the successful businessman to whom Mo referred as "the old man." Lee found himself grappling with what he was learning. He had long held a couple of stereotypes that were now being tested.

To him an "only child" was usually a spoiled child. A son of a wealthy family was inevitably soft. Therefore, the only child son of a wealthy family must be spoiled and soft. Lee had come to associate "tough" with "poor." Yet here was Mo Brennan.

Lee inquired about the family foundry. Mo explained that his father's foundry had provided certain castings for Midwest tractor and implement manufacturers before the war.

"Now," Mo added, "they're up to their necks in government contracts. I really don't know much about what they're manufacturing, and it really won't matter until I get home. By then, we'll probably be retooling for civilian business again. The old man's a real wheeling dealer," Mo went on.

Lee smiled, then wondered if he should have.

"He took the tiny shop my grandfather left him and turned it into a five-hundred-man operation in twenty years. I know it sounds boastful, but there isn't much about the business that the old man doesn't know. Like I said yesterday, I'll go back to the foundry as a means to an end. I'd be rather stupid not to start at the top with all that power. To do anything else would be like enlisting in the infantry when I had the opportunity for a commission in the Air Force."

"I guess so," said Lee. "But it seems to me that in war, except for rank and pay, it's all the same over here, isn't it?"

"Uh, uh. Not at all," replied Mo. "Our pilots were picked to fight an intelligent, strategic war. We have wide latitude for movement, and each of us packs enough punch to really hurt the enemy. You or I can take out fifty men in one strafing run. Those poor doggies down in the jungle have no leeway. They're not allowed to think. They crawl straight ahead into the jungle, shooting the enemy one at a time *if* they don't get blown up first."

Lee nodded thoughtfully. He had never thought of himself as a super weapon, just a man like all of the others sent over to fight a war he hadn't asked for. Mo was watching him and smiling, that smile that seemed to say he knew what was coming next, the smile he had shown when he made the latrine remark earlier.

"Professor Steinmetz used to tell us," Lee offered, "that even though wars are fought over ideological differences and economic confrontations, they are ultimately won by capturing and holding land. Gopher Squadron can't do that."

"You're right, Lee," Mo said, "but in this kind of twentieth-century war, they can't capture much of anything without us." He paused and looked intently at Lee. "Are you a competitor—or a killer?"

Stymied by the question, Lee said, "I'm not sure, not sure what you mean."

"Out here we have three kinds of pilots, the competitors, the killers, and the rest, who, I might add, don't contribute a hell of a lot to our war effort. Now, take me. I'm a *competitor*. I don't particularly like *killing*, but I *do* like *winning*. I like that feeling that comes with hitting what I aim at, with outsmarting or outflying a Jap. I like that." He paused to light another cigarette. "Some pilots are real killers. They came out here to kill Japs, and that's what they're going to do. Then there are the others, the 'Do Littles,' pardon the pun. I guess even they do serve a purpose, in fact, two purposes. One, they're up there around my plane and that counts statistically. A Jap's not as anxious to attack, even out of the sun, if the numbers are with us. And two, looking up and seeing the sky full of P-38s is very comforting to those doggies down below in the mud." Mo looked at his watch and got up from the table. "My friend—*you* are a *killer*—no doubt about it." He looked seriously at Lee for a moment and then walked away.

Lee sat there for a moment trying to digest it all. Then he left the Ops shack and headed for Fungus Field. As he walked, he replayed Mo's little speech. A killer? Lee Marks a killer? It sounded terrible. His mother would have died, had she heard that. But so far, Mo Brennan had yet to be wrong. In but a few missions, Lee had downed seven, possibly eight enemy planes. He could have been riding on luck, skill, or perhaps a killer instinct. Killer?

Chapter 15

▼

Lee popped awake early the next morning despite the sleep-inducing rhythm of the pattering rain. Even as his eyes opened, his mind raced through preparations for his presentation to the squadron. He hadn't spoken to a group since college days. How would he react if Black Bart started to harrass him? The thought washed aside any last comfort in his bunk so he jumped up and scrambled into his clothes.

The air smelled fresh and invigorating as he made his way through the rain shower down the muddy path to the mess tent. It seemed as though the rain washed other less desirable smells from the air, smells like the dank, musty jungle and the occasional wafts of repugnance blown into camp from the nearest latrines. But more important, a steady rain grounded the mosquitoes. The thought reminded Lee that he hadn't powdered up with DDT before leaving the tent. He walked faster.

He rushed through his powdered eggs and toast, waved to the cooks, refilled his GI cup with coffee, washed his kit, and headed for the Ops shack. The rain had stopped and the eastern sky offered promise that the sun would rise again. An hour later, the rest of the Gophers came straggling in, obviously less than thrilled with the mandatory morning meeting. Lee watched Mo for the signal to begin, but the CO seemed to be focused elsewhere. Finally, Lee decided to launch the lecture. He stepped to the front and raised his hands. With the group's energy registering in minus figures, silence came quickly.

"I'm no speech maker," Lee began, "but Sandy and I have worked on some moves that the major thought we ought to share with you guys. I picked up the ideas from a couple of guys in the 475th, and we went up yesterday to try them—"

"Marks," Mo Brennan cut in, "let's have Sadler tell them about it."

Lee looked from Mo Brennan to Sandy Sadler and back again to Mo. He hoped his face didn't show the disbelief that was rapidly turning to embarrassment. Mo offered no explanation. He simply looked at Lee as though waiting for his suggestion to be carried through.

"Uh—sure. Sandy?"

Sandy's freckles blended in with his reddened face, but he struggled up from his chair. After a long hesitation, he began.

"This is probably the first time the class clown has been caught with nothing to say." The sleepy group came to life and briefly laughed. Sandy stumbled his way through an introduction to the topic and began to explain the experience using the dive flaps to control power dive speed and enable a pullout, thus escaping the dreaded compressibility.

Lee heard little of Sandy's presentation. His embarrassment had turned to anger. He looked long at Mo. The leader seemed engrossed in Sandy's words, yet his perpetual smile seemed a little more pronounced than usual. After wrestling with it, Lee decided to ignore the affront and he convinced himself not to overreact. Maybe Mo only wanted to give Sandy some of the credit, plus a little experience as a leader. Certainly there could be no harm in either. By the time Sandy finished the last maneuver, the sharp turn at slow speeds, Lee's mind had rejoined the group.

The squadron fully came to life in the question-answer follow-up. Some of the questions were directed at Lee, and by the time the meeting concluded, he had forgotten his anger, except for the tiny elf in the back of his brain who kept asking, "Why?"

"I caution you," Mo Brennan said as he took over the meeting, "most of us aren't the flyers that Marks and Sadler are. I don't think combat is the place to experiment too much with new tricks. Do you agree with that, Marks?"

"I guess I'd say, be careful at first. The biggest danger would be if you try to haul the nose around too fast. You could pull yourself right into a stall. Could they have some practice time today?" he asked Mo.

"You'll all get some practice time, I promise you," said Mo. "This stuff is pretty good—could get a lot of Japs and save some lives. But not today." He pulled a cigarette from his shirt pocket, jammed it between his lips and lit up. "We're going into Madang Harbor with the B-25's this morning—0800 hours. We'll fly high cover until they've done their job and are on the way home. Then we go in low to raise some hell. Flight positions the same, except Hedman takes Element Leader in White Flight with Callahan as wingman, and Forbes takes

Element Leader in Blue. Barton, you cover him. We'll be armed with armor piercing stuff, no tracers, so don't be wasting time looking for your tracers. It's about time you yardbirds cut your dependency on them anyway. When you miss your target, the tracers tip the Japs off that you're behind them, and *that* can get you killed. That's all. See you at 0730."

"How did I do, Lee?" Sandy asked as they started back to their tent.

"I'm certainly no speech coach, Sandy, but I thought you did great."

"Lee, why did the major do that, take it from you and dump it on me at the last minute?"

"Don't know. I can tell you Mo Brennan has a reason for everything he does. He has his reasons all right, but he's seldom going to tell us what they are," Lee said. "Sandy, the guy who figures out how to read him will be sitting at the right hand of God."

Lee's Marksman cleared the Dobodura Strip 4-Y at 0804 hours and climbed out on a heading of three-five-five toward Nadzab. They were to pick up the mediums over the Markham River Valley north of Nadzab. From there they would circle around and come in at Madang from the north. The B-25s on this mission were the later-model solid-nosed ships with an arsenal of forward-firing cannons and machine guns. They would go in low this time using skip bombing on the ships along with the heavy strafing.

The U.S. air powers had developed skip bombing into a formidable technique to sink enemy shipping. Instead of trying to hit a tiny target from high altitude, the medium bombers went in just above the water. At a prescribed distance, altitude, and speed, the crew would drop a delayed-fuse bomb that would literally skip off the water's surface like a flat stone. If timed properly, the bomb would skip horizontally into the vulnerable side of the ship at water level and penetrate the ship's hull before exploding.

Lee felt relieved that the B-25s, and not the P-38s, were employing the delicate technique. The procedure had produced great results, but it was wrought with risks as well. If dropped incorrectly, the bomb might simply plummet into the water and kill lots of fish. Or it might bounce too high and become a threat to the aircraft. And there were stories of crews loading the wrong bombs onto the aircraft, bombs with no delay-action fuses, bombs that exploded upon contact with the water—only thirty feet beneath the aircraft. Then too, while the bombers were flying directly toward the side of a Japanese ship, the enemy gunners were not sitting around sipping saki. With an aircraft flying directly at a heavy machine gun emplacement in a frontal attack, angular deflection shots by the gunners were not necessary. It was a head-to-head battle, straight-on shooting.

The bombers hoped to knock out the gun emplacements before the Jap gunners could sight in on them.

By the time the bombers had circled to the north of the Madang installation and were heading south at low altitude toward the harbor, Mo had strategically placed the Gopher Squadron. White and Blue Flights followed above and behind the bombers at 10,000 feet, while Red Flight provided high cover at 20,000 feet from the southeast, well-hidden in the bright sun.

Lee could see the entire harbor and neighboring facilities from that altitude, and he quickly counted over a dozen ships in the harbor. Some were in close to the shoreline, obviously to unload supplies, and he guessed that the others were anchored in the harbor waiting their turns to unload. He rotated his focus among the bombers, their targets far below, and the bright sun high and behind him. While Red Flight was well hidden in the sun, there was that possibility that enemy planes might also be hiding above them. Mo apparently assumed that Red Flight was currently the highest in the food chain. If he was wrong, the flight would be extremely vulnerable to attack from above and behind. Lee felt himself tightening. That "if" in the strategy bothered him immensely.

Far below, the bombers headed toward the harbor at tree top level. Puffs of anti-aircraft bursts dotted the sky. Lee couldn't see what had to be thousands of tracer bullets accompanying the ack-ack, but he knew they were there. Fortunately the bombers were beneath the dangerous flak. Most of it seemed to be exploding at altitudes somewhere between the bombers and White and Blue Flights.

Lee knew enemy fighters had to be in the vicinity. They were overdue. It was inconceivable that the Japs would meet this attack with only anti-aircraft fire. Then he spotted them. At nine o'clock and at an altitude perhaps three thousand feet above his own, Lee saw a dozen or more enemy fighters headed toward his three flight mates and himself.

"Reds," came Mo's voice. "Bandits nine o'clock low. Switch 'em and drop 'em."

"You mean nine o'clock *high?*" Lee asked quickly. He switched to his main tanks, dropped his belly tanks, and waited for Mo to correct his error.

But Mo's P-38 peeled to the left and started down, followed shortly thereafter by Bubba. Lee hesitated. Mo was giving up their altitude to the oncoming Zeros. He must not have seen them. Those enemy fighters below were the province of White and Blue Flights. Red Flight's task was to protect against enemies attacking the fighters or bombers below from higher altitudes. When Lee dared delay no longer, he rolled left and started down with Sandy following. Once in the dive he spotted the targets Mo had in mind, and they were indeed inviting targets. The Zeros were coming out over the harbor at about 7,000 feet. Obviously, they planned to turn down into the B-25s and catch them before they reached the ships.

The predictable S-turn Mo had begun as they headed down at a moderate angle would bring them in on the Jap fighters from above and behind. The Lightnings hurtled downward through 10,000 feet. The airspeed indicator crept up and over 400 mph. Lee contemplated using his dive flaps, but he feared they would force him up and out of his dive much too soon. Instead he eased the throttles back to compensate. Although their target Zeros had also started downward, the Lightnings closed the gap quickly. Lee saw Mo lead Bubba to the left, so he took Sandy to the right and picked his targets. He knew without searching for them that the upper flight of enemy fighters was also descending to enter the fray, but they couldn't possibly catch Red Flight until after the initial contact. Lee saw Mo flame one fighter. Bubba blew its neighbor up, and Mo followed with a second kill.

Lee sighted on his target. At 400 yards he fired a short burst and wished for his tracers. Concentrating harder, he fired again and the Zeke flipped over into a dive that took him below into Lee's blind spot. Lee banked right and caught a second Jap in his sight. A quick reflex burst was all he had time for. A few pieces of the Zero flew back in the slipstream, but he continued straight ahead showing no signs of distress. Lee felt angry, frustrated with himself. He had hit both Zekes and gotten neither. He was grateful that Mo couldn't have seen his misses.

As Lee flashed through what was left of the Japanese formation, he spotted Mo and Bubba. He banked left and followed them in a sweeping climb to the left. Lee could see the B-25 Mitchells racing at wave-top altitude through the gathering of ships. Explosions popped and puffed everywhere, but there was no time to keep score. Lee checked for the second group of Jap fighters. They were headed for White and Blue Flights, and with their altitude and speed advantages, they seemed to hold the cards.

Suddenly, it occurred to Lee that the other two flights had not seen the threat from above.

If they maintained their present course, they would be ducks in a barrel. He reached quickly for his throat mike.

"Lee here. White and Blue, see the bandits coming down at your two o'clock?"

"See them," came Greenie's voice. "Playing possum."

Lee and Sandy joined up with Mo and Bubba. If they maintained their climbing left turn, they might have deflection shots at the upper attacking group at about the time they met the other two flights of Lightnings. That seemed to be Mo's intention. But Lee dropped his right wing for a look below. The six Zeros that survived Red's first attack were heading down after the bombers. Lee looked over his right shoulder to find Sandy where he belonged. With a couple of warning waggles to Sandy, Lee dropped off to his right and started down.

"Lee here—unfinished work down below—six of them," Lee called. Any answer he might have expected was lost in the ensuing jabber over the mission frequency.

At 7,000 feet, Lee dropped the nose into a steeper dive toward the water below. The airspeed climbed rapidly, but Lee had gained confidence the previous day in his dive flaps. And the duo needed to get down on the deck quickly. The Zekes were getting dangerously close to the Mitchell bombers. At 3,000 feet, Lee deployed the dive flaps. Up came the nose a little too quickly. He closed the flaps and put his Marksman back into a shallow dive that was bringing him to the enemy fighters from above and behind with a decided airspeed advantage. If the Japs had seen Lee and Sandy, they made no changes to show it.

Lee hoped the Jap pilots were inexperienced and blindly determined to follow orders to get the bombers. With inadequate altitude below the formation to allow the two Lightnings to dive through the group and recover, Lee dumped airspeed to stay behind the enemy group a little longer so as to pick them off one by one. Sandy slid up on Lee's right side, then apparently figured it out and reduced airspeed. Lee hoped he hadn't led Sandy into a fatal mistake. Abandoning airspeed in a fight often bought a one-way ticket to the hereafter. He checked over both shoulders, then the mirror. Clean.

The two P-38s caught the six enemy fighters before they could reach the bombers. Lee and Sandy opened up simultaneously. Lee's target lost a third of his left wing and tumbled in corkscrew fashion toward the bay below. Lee angled slightly left and fired again. The Zeke began to trail smoke. Just as Lee locked on for a second try, the Jap blew up. A pattern of debris spread open before Lee, a pattern too large to avoid. He pulled up to miss the stricken Zero and ducked his head involuntarily as several bits of aluminum and steel slammed into the Lightning. As he emerged from the barrage of shrapnel, he scoffed at himself for ducking.

Suddenly his left propeller ran away, its rpm increasing uncontrollably. Relying on his training drills, he pulled both throttles back and quickly shut the left engine down. Then he feathered its propeller while compensating with his ailerons to keep from flipping over. Immediately he shoved the right throttle ahead to sixty inches of manifold pressure to regain lost airspeed and control. Lee ran through the sequence in about three seconds, and he was glad he had drilled overtime on the procedure. The conversion from two engines to one was perhaps the most dangerous experience one could have in the Lightning, especially on take-off. Many pilots had been caught unprepared and before they could take the necessary steps, the remaining engine had flipped the airplane upside down and plunged it into the ground.

With the emergency under control, Lee swiveled his head around to assess the external picture. Sandy was hanging well back off Lee's right wing, precisely where he belonged. The remaining Zeros had finally broken off their chase of the bombers and disappeared. That bothered Lee.

"Sandy, where did they go?" Lee called.

"They did a one-eighty," came the reply. "I'm watching them. Still going. I think we're clear for now, but I'll be here."

Lee tried restarting the left engine using different propeller settings, but it became apparent that he would not be able to control that prop, so he shut the left side down again and resigned himself to making the trip home on one engine.

"Sandy, hook up with Mo. I'll join the big brothers and let them cover *me* this time."

Although the empty B-25s sizzled right along, Lee had little trouble keeping up with them on a single engine. He picked a spot to the right of the outside right bomber. The bomber's co-pilot saw Lee's difficulty and gave him a thumbs up wave. The bombers set up for an approach at Nadzab, but Lee felt confident he could make it to Dobodura.

In just under a hour he turned final to Strip 4-Y. He quickly replayed the rules for single-engine landings, most aware that once below 500 feet he was committed to landing. There would be no going around for a second attempt.

Among the thrills and satisfactions that get into a pilot's blood and add to his addiction is the thrill of take-off. Perhaps second would rank the satisfaction of a perfect landing, especially with a large audience on the ground. Lee greased his single-engine P-38 in as smoothly as he ever had under normal conditions. He smiled to himself, then wondered if he could ever again match the performance on one engine. But taxiing the ship on one engine became a more difficult task. Lee stood on the right rudder pedal and brake, jockeying the right throttle in bursts. Finally a blunt-nosed tractor came to the rescue and towed him home. By the time he reached his spot on the flight line, Lee felt he had earned his pay. As he climbed from the cockpit, he realized he was soaking wet.

"Ya, we got some patching to do," said Big Ole. "But that prop, that'll take some time. And we better check the radiator and everything else. Lee hung around waiting for the others to return. He counted nine birds as they made the sharp right turn in the taxiway that brought them to their flight line. Two missing. He tensed. His mouth dried up. Even a couple of cups from the drinking tank barely helped. With all the Gophers in their respective slots, he could tell they were missing Robert Logan from White and Smokey Stover from Blue. He saw Mo heading his way. "They're all right," Mo said, motioning to the two empty parking slots. "Robert was leaking fuel and headed for the closest place, Saidor. Smokey lost an engine. He stayed with us till Nadzab. I think they both got down okay. We'll check into it after debriefing. We can send the Goose after them tomorrow if they can't fly home."

"Mo," Lee said, "I'm sorry. I blew it. I assumed you were going after the same group that I saw and just misspoke. It didn't occur to me that you hadn't seen them until too late."

Without even a glance toward Lee, Mo said, "I saw them."

"You—did?" Lee walked along silently.

"What you really want to say is I took Red Flight after the wrong targets, isn't it?"

"Well, no."

"Come on, Killer." Mo stopped and looked directly at Lee. "You think I screwed up. Why don't you say it?" He grinned as he waited for the answer that didn't come. "All right, tell me this. How many did you get today? Two?"

"Two, and a couple of possibles."

"And Sandy?" Mo resumed the walk, and Lee fell in stride with him.

"Not sure, two, maybe three," Lee said.

"Okay," Mo said through his grin, "do a little math for Red Flight. I got three, Bubba got two, you got two, and Sandy got three. That's ten by our flight alone. Not too bad for a few minutes work, is it? That, Killer, is called recognizing an opportunity and making the most of it."

Lee motioned to two of the heavily damaged Blue Flight ships as they walked past.

"White and Blue got hit pretty hard. I wonder if they'd agree with you," Lee said.

"Doesn't really matter."

Chapter 16

Bam!...Bam!...Bam! The warning shots came from the anti-aircraft installation at the north edge of the blacked-out Dobodura base. Everyone understood the announcement that Washing Machine Charlie, aka Bedcheck Charlie or Piss Call Paul, as he was named by some of Lee's neighbors, had returned for a nocturnal visit. But his timing, arriving overhead for his harassing bombing attack an hour after midnight, blanketed all GI humor.

"Damn!" Lee sputtered as he rolled into one of the trenches on their side of the camp, only to find himself in a natural tub lined with New Guinea mud.

"Kind of the shits, isn't it?" remarked the body next to him. "We'd gotten to where we just turned over and ignored the bastard. But lately, his aim has gotten better. Seems like the shit head always comes after a rain when the foxholes and trenches are muddier than hell."

Lee could hear the unsynchronized twin engines of the Japanese Betty bomber as it approached. A deliberate, irritating pulsation was set up by the clashing of the unmatched engine rhythms. The tempo of the ack-ack increased rapidly as the agitant flew closer. Lee could hear bomb bursts walking toward Fungus Field. From the sounds, he tried to visualize where the bombs were striking. It seemed they were closer to the support installations and were missing the flight lines. Then, almost suddenly, the event ended. The bombs and the ack-ack stopped, and the Betty turned eastward and faded into the black.

"One consolation," said the voice next to Lee as they climbed from the hole, "Paul doesn't live long."

"Meaning?" Lee asked.

"Meaning, how would you like to do all your missions and find your way through this goddamned weather at night? How long do you think *you'd* stay alive? Kind of gives new meaning to "music under the stars," though, doesn't it?"

After a time, essential lights came back on. Those who came out of the mud in the worst shape made for the showers. Others wiped off the best they could and tried to get back to sleep. It was the first such experience for the new Gophers. Lee judged that, from the Japanese point of view, the mission had to be called a success, whether they had hit anything or not. He also decided that in the future he wouldn't be so quick to dive into a muddy hole. He would simply get close to the hole and decide whether to or when to by the sounds of the approaching bombs.

As the earlier foxholes had presented drainage problems resulting in mud and an increased mosquito threat, slots were cut in from one to the next to improve drainage. The alterations were changing the face of the camp's perimeter from separate holes to connected holes and eventually to trenches that served as drainage ditches as well. Ditching was not a pleasant experience, but if Charlie dropped his eggs close it beat the alternative.

Lee awoke to the sounds of another squabble between Bart and Bubba, something about how close the bombs did or did not come to their tent. It occurred to Lee that Bart seized every opportunity to do battle with naive and innocent Bubba because in arguing with Bubba, Bart would be right about half the time. Where else could he get those odds?

As they walked down the hill to chow, Lee could hear the engineers' bulldozers already at work filling bomb craters. Oldtimers said that the Japanese seldom bothered with the task and were believed to have a much higher malaria rate. The bomb craters filled with water and became prime breeding places for mosquitoes. After the first horrible months in eastern New Guinea where the disability rate attributed to the environment equaled or surpassed the casualties inflicted by the enemy, the Americans and Australians had learned something. Eliminating the breeding places, along with the regular use of Atabrine tablets and DDT powder, had greatly reduced the number of malaria victims. Changes in the GI diet, including the frequent inclusion of cheese along with better water treatment, appeared to winning the battle with dysentery.

Lee found himself sitting with Bubba, Cal, and Burner Hedman at chow. Out of the corner of his eye, Lee watched as Bubba bolted the morning offerings down. A touch of the old Bubba still showed when he picked the weevils from the toast. He attacked each grub with a quick pinching motion as though it were a live and dangerous creature. While Bubba was clearly very proud of his adjustment, Lee did detect a slight flinch with each pinch.

"Boy, I thought we really banged them," Bubba was saying, "especially Red Flight."

Lee glared at Bubba, but his naïve, young friend missed the message.

"So you guys in Red Flight are pretty good, huh?" Burner asked in his powerful, deep voice. Everything about Burner Hedman reflected his background as a lumberjack. His sturdy, coarse face, his shaggy, unruly hair, his massive shoulders and chest, and the pair of hands the size of bombs, bombs looking for a place to land.

Lee kicked under the table at Bubba's shin. Unfortunately, Cal jerked back, then glared across the table at Lee.

"Yes," Bubba replied with only a modicum of modesty, "I guess we really *are* pretty good. Of course, when you have two shooters like Lee and the major that helps a lot." Bubba looked to Lee with pride glowing on his face.

Lee rolled his eyes and slowly shook his head.

"They're still fussing over a couple of confirmations on yesterday's mission," Bubba said, "but it looks like the squadron got seventeen. Thirteen of those were Red Flight's."

"Bubba," Lee said, glaring across the table.

"Let me tell you something, Hot Shot," Hedman said, looking from Bubba to Lee. "You guys leave your high cover—leave us exposed again like you did yesterday—you'd better start looking over your shoulders more often."

"Why, we didn't—"

"Shut up, Bubba!" Lee snapped. "He's got a point. Listen to him."

Bubba's face showed the hurt Lee had seen only days earlier. He hoped it would stop there, that he wouldn't have to deal with Bubba's adolescent anger again. As Bubba's face reddened it seemed his white hair got whiter. He jumped up, picked up his utensils and left.

"Don't make too much of it, Burner," Lee said. "I don't think the major saw the high group of Zeros."

"You did."

"I did, and I didn't communicate very well. That was my fault." Surprised at his own defense of Mo Brennan, Lee thought it best to drop the subject. He liked and respected Burner Hedman, and he had sensed that the feelings were reciprocal. He didn't want to jeopardize the relationship further. He picked up his things and left.

Later that morning, a bucket-busting shower cleared and Mo gave the Gophers whose P-38s were sound the clearance to go aloft and play tag in pairs to familiarize themselves with the various flap and split-engine maneuvers. Lee's Marksman was among the Lightnings still grounded for repairs.

"You look here!" Big Ole said. "Just look here! We fished these pieces of Japanese airplane out of her!"

There on an old metal sheet lay eleven jagged pieces of steel and aluminum.

"No wonder I ducked when I ran into them," Lee laughed.

"Ya, you laugh," Big Ole said seriously. "But you going to miss the next eleven?" He drew his index finger across his throat like a knife. "Too close! Too damned close!"

While the Gophers practiced their one-on-one experiments over the Solomon Sea, Robert Logan and Smokey Stover landed their Lightnings within minutes of each other. Both pilots were fine, and both aircraft had been quickly repaired by line mechanics at Saidor and Nadzab. But the propellers had hardly stopped turning when Sergeant Worley and the combined ground crews swarmed over the two P-38s.

A convivial Mo Brennan called the squadron together in the Ops shack that afternoon for a buzz session. He began the meeting by conducting a discussion on the new flap/split-engine techniques for dives and sharp turns. Excitement bubbled as the Gophers compared experiences and shared related suggestions.

Several times the group became hung up on a point and turned to Lee for an opinion. Lee felt warmed by the respect. Apparently Mo's earlier comment rating Lee and Sandy as superior pilots had stuck. Then it crossed Lee's mind that perhaps his incredibly quick accumulation of nine kills had something to do with it. In the Gopher Squadron, only Mo with eighteen flags, Gus with twelve, and Greenie with ten had shot down more.

"Okay!" Mo called to quell a spontaneous burst of enthusiasm. "You are now licensed to get your fancy flaps working. But be careful. A stalled P-38 is a dead P-38. Remember, sticks and stones can break my bones…but look what that Zero just did to me." He paused for effect. "Now, I want to take a look at the overall picture of this new squadron.

"It's pretty obvious to you, to me, and to everyone in Command that we've done well—very, very well. What does that mean? To Command it means that they can count on us, that they can give this brand new squadron a job and it'll by God get done!" He paused, smiled, and lowered his voice, "It also means that those people who have been raving about the 475th Fighter Group, particularly the 431st Squadron, are beginning to notice our Gophers. In fact, the colonel tells me to get some info ready for a propaganda spread. They want some fresh stuff to help sell bonds back home."

A chorus of cheers, yelps, and hoots answered Mo's statement. He stood there smiling, letting the Gophers relish in the moment. Finally, he motioned for quiet and continued.

"Now, so you can get your ships properly decorated with flags during our down time, here are the confirmed kill numbers they have on Gopher Squadron. Of the total of 76 scores by the 483rd Fighter Group, 35 have been added by you new pilots in the month-plus that you've been here. Gentlemen, we don't have many yard birds left here."

When their reaction died down, he began to read off the numbers. "RED FLIGHT, Brennan—eighteen, Nash—four, Marks—nine, Sadler—five. WHITE FLIGHT, Greene—ten, Logan—two, Hedman—three, Callahan—two. BLUE FLIGHT, Gustafson—twelve, Stover—four, Forbes—four, and Porter—2 before we lost him."

Mo hesitated, reached behind him to pick something up, and while keeping the object hidden, he moved toward Black Bart. "And Barton—one," he said as he pulled the object out front and handed it to Bart. It was a crude but unmistakable model of a Japanese Zero.

Bart looked at it, blinked, and sat there as though paralyzed. The group exploded in laughter and then suddenly stopped, leaving the shack locked in silence.

Lee had laughed, too. But he stopped with the others. As much as he disliked Black Bart, who seemed to work at being obnoxious, he felt sorry for the "Devil's Catalyst," as Robert Logan had once labeled Bart. Yet, Lee was puzzled. If he felt sorry for Bart, he should feel anger or at least resentment toward Mo for pulling such a stunt. He didn't. Mo stood a few feet from Barton, simply looking at him with a rarely seen blank face.

Black Bart suddenly jumped up as though shocked out of a coma. He held the model up with both hands in front of himself. With a single, fierce snap he broke the wooden model in half and carelessly tossed both halves back over his shoulders. Then he plopped back down again. He bit his lower lip, folded his arms, and glared at Mo.

Mo let the silence hold for several seconds. His gaze moved slowly about the shack, from one Gopher to the next and back to Black Bart. Finally, the trademark grin reappeared on Mo's face.

"I'd give a penny for your thoughts, Barton, but mine are worth a hell of a lot more. But I have to tell you, that kill wasn't confirmed," Mo said. "We'll have to disallow it." Still staring at Barton, he went on. "Now, that was kind of a dirty trick, Barton, and I think every man here is a little sorry he laughed. Right?"

"Right," chorused the group, grateful for the opportunity to endorse the one-word apology.

Bart sat there fuming. For the first time in Lee's memory, an angry Black Bart looked at no one. He stared alternately at the dirt floor and the thatched roof, but his eyes met no others.

"You're wondering why this dirty son-of-a-bitch did that," Mo went on. "I'm going to tell you. Every man here but Second Lieutenant Barton has shot down at least one Jap plane." Mo looked around. "Can any of you tell us you made a kill while in a fit of rage?"

Heads slowly shook the negative reply.

"Okay, Barton, here it is, short and simple. Everybody's at fault but you. You get up in the morning mad. You go through the day mad. You go to bed at night mad. You seem to be mad at one or another of us all the time. You can't fight Jap Zeros in that condition. You keep trying and you're going to get yourself killed—and maybe some of your squadron mates, too. That kind of anger makes a pilot over anxious. He shoots too soon, from too far, and much too carelessly. You're so damned mad at the world there's not an ounce of patience left in you. And a fighter pilot, no matter how aggressive, needs to use patience. Now, I'm hoping that when you snapped that wooden Zero in half and tossed it over your shoulder you threw at least ninety-five percent of that anger with it."

Mo paused, took a deep breath, glanced around at the others, and turned back to Bart.

"In fact, I'm betting on it, and I don't like to lose bets." Mo scanned the group again. "And to the rest of you I'm saying this guy's going to make some changes. Don't take any shit from him. But I don't want to hear that you gave him any shit either. Do you follow me?"

As the meeting broke up, Mo pulled Lee aside and asked, "Lee, couldn't you help Barton with his gunnery?"

"Sure can," Lee said, "when his attitude changes. I happen to think you were right. I'd bet he's shooting too soon from too far out. I also suspect that when he gets ready to press the trigger he quits flying the plane."

"All right," said Mo, "Step in there as soon as you think he's ready. If I don't see progress in the next week or two, he's out of here. This squadron is on a roll. We can't afford to drag an anchor like Barton along with us. And it's not fair to Forbes. How'd *you* like to have Barton covering your ass?"

He turned away from Lee "Oh, Hedman, walk over to mess with me, will you? I've got something I want to see you about."

Lee couldn't stop the tiny bolt of jealousy that zipped through him. Mo Brennan seemed to be playing him like a concertina, pushing the correct buttons when he needed something. Then, about the time Lee began to feel he was in the right key, the major called someone else's tune.

Chapter 17

The calendar dates on the duty board rolled on into February and the action began to slow. The enemy seemed to have switched to a defensive mode. Their Air Army units had taken one beating after another, with many of their most experienced pilots lost in the process. The Japanese Navy had lost command of the southwest Pacific waters and had pulled many of their land-based aircraft to refill empty aircraft carriers. Intelligence confirmed that the Japanese were consolidating their air forces at Rabaul, Madang, and Hollandia. The latter was a huge coastal complex 350 miles west of Madang. When attacked at Rabaul and Madang, the Jap fighters still swarmed with the fury of angry bees. But Japanese air attacks against the Americans and Australians seemed to have been reduced to the nocturnal forays by Washing Machine Charlie. Unfortunately the night-time intrusions increased to near daily frequency and improved efficiency.

Fifth Air Force desperately needed an airplane with the capability of searching out enemy aircraft at night. The word was out that a new twin-engine night fighter, the Northrop P-61 Black Widow, would be coming. While it had cleared its final tests, delivery in sufficient numbers with adequately trained crews was still a few months away. Command had been working for some time on the P-38-M, a stop-gap night fighter about which Colonel Sledge Hammer had said, "…a jury-rigged half-breed bastard at best, but what else do we have?"

Engineers had modified a new L-model, most noted for its more powerful engines, by moving the radio gear from behind the pilot's seat into the nose along with the newly added radar. Then they crammed a second seat and the necessary radar controls into the small area behind the pilot. To increase the headroom for the radar operator, they constructed a plexiglass bubble that rose above the pilot's cockpit. Scuttlebutt had it that the station was ideal for a radar operator who was a midget. But with its power, speed, range, and twin-engine safety, the P-38 was without question the most appropriate choice for a temporary night fighter.

Lee lay on his bunk just after dawn contemplating the Washing Machine Charlie problem. He had heard about the new P-38-M and wondered if it would really work, if the new airborne radar was really that good. They had lost sleep four nights in a row, and Charlie was inspiring more epithets than jokes.

Then something flipped his thoughts from Charlie and Dobodura far across the Pacific to Chicago, to his mother. It was February 14th and he wished he had sent a valentine. Of course, he would have had to mail it at Christmas time. And at Christmas time he was back in the States preparing to ship overseas. He smiled at the twist created by the GI time machine.

"You trade cloths?" came a deep, crisp voice behind him. He rolled over to find Bob and Bill once more grinning in at him through the mosquito netting. "You trade cloths?" Bob repeated. In addition to his threadbare khaki shorts, he wore Lee's old shirt—minus its sleeves. Lee pondered the amputations. But when Bob stood up to move to the front of the tent, Lee saw the answer. Hanging from Bob's G.I. web belt on each side was a bulging khaki sleeve with the cuff tied shut at the bottom to form a deep holster. As Lee moved to the front steps of the tent, he smiled to himself, wondering what surprises Bob had down his sleeves.

"Good shirt," Bob said, gesturing to Lee's old garment. "You have red cloth?"

"Red cloth?"

"Red cloth—holes." Bob spread his arms wide indicating something very large. Bill simply stood behind his fuzzy-headed partner, grinning and nodding his immense bird nest.

"You don't know what he's after, do you?"

Lee looked up. It was Lieutenant Nelson from a neighboring tent.

"He's got me," Lee confessed.

"He wants target silk. You know, red silk tow targets? They love the stuff. They make shirts, dresses, and jock straps out of it." The officer laughed and went on down the path.

"No have—" Lee caught himself. "I don't have any target silk, but I'll see if I can find some," he said slowly, enunciating as though he were speaking at Soldier Field.

"You prob'ly find some," Bob said reassuringly. "What you got?"

Lee thought for a moment. He really had nothing to trade, nothing but the bare essentials in clothing. He realized for the first time since landing in New

Guinea that if measured by personal possessions, Lee Marks was a pauper. All his worldly possessions hardly filled one B-4 bag.

Bob dug down in one of the sleeves. Out came a pearl-handled Japanese dagger followed by a handful of cartridges from the opposite sleeve. He laid the booty on the step and reached once again into one of his deep pockets. A pair of Japanese-issue field glasses joined the display. Bob tilted his head to one side and then the other, looking at Lee's face as though searching for a reaction. Lee shrugged and picked up one of the cartridges. He was almost certain the cartridges were the nine-millimeter shells he needed for the Jap pistol. Indeed, they might even be the shells that came from the pistol that had belonged to the earless officer. He was about to head into the tent to get the pistol when he heard a voice from behind him.

"I'll give you a nice shirt for those," Bart said, motioning to the cartridges. He held out a khaki shirt that was considerably newer than the mutilation that Bob wore.

"You good deal," Bob said. He quickly swept up the ammunition and exchanged it for the shirt.

Lee turned a hard look at Black Bart who smiled triumphantly and reentered the tent clutching his miniature trophies. Trying not to show his disappointment, Lee headed for his duffel. He rummaged around and finally came up with the small object of his search. He stepped back outside and held up his prized jackknife. Slowly and deliberately he opened the four blades and tools and held it out to Bob. Then he reached for the field glasses.

"Already have dickknife," Bob said. "Don't need dickknife."

"Sorry," Lee said. "Don't have anything else to trade right now." He retrieved his knife and turned to leave the visiting traders. "Maybe some day I'll find some red cloth—holes." He turned and sat down on the edge of his bunk. Like ghosts, the Fuzzies disappeared.

"Okay, Bart," Lee said. "That was cute. What do you want for the cartridges?"

"You can't afford to buy these," said Bart. The grin on his face said more than the words.

"So be it," Lee said. "But don't hurt yourself. They're loaded."

Sandy had quietly watched the brief episode. He sat on his bunk, staring at Bart, slowly shaking his head. Then he nodded at Lee and looked to the door.

"Come on, Lee," he said. "He thinks they're suppositories. Maybe they'll help."

The pair headed down to the flight line. As they passed the Ops shack, Lee motioned for Sandy to hold up for a minute. He spotted Mo back in his favorite corner talking with Burner Hedman. As he started toward the pair, Hedman leaned back and laughed loudly, slapping a giant paw on the table.

Lee waited a few steps away to be recognized. Mo looked up at him but went right on with what he was saying. Lee hoped for a break in their conversation. He only wanted a quick answer to a short question. As the duo continued on with their conversation, Mo looked up at Lee two more times. Lee wagged a finger, indicated a number one with his index finger, and then pointed to himself.

"I'm busy right now, Marks," Mo said. "See me another time."

Lee felt the frustration and embarrassment rush to his face. He wheeled and left.

"What's with that guy, Sandy?" he asked as the pair walked toward the flight line.

"Damned if I know," Sandy replied. "For a couple of days you seemed to be the object of his affection. That made good sense. You'd even make a good exec for the squadron. Then he spent two or three gab sessions with me. Now it's Burner. It won't surprise me if he picks Black Bart next."

"Funny," Lee said, "when he's talking with you he can make you feel so good, so much like you're an important part of things. About the time you start believing it...."

"Well, just remember, he may be the CO, but you and I have done well. He needs us, too."

The Gopher flight line buzzed with activity. Ground crews, tank trucks and their drivers hustled about, dodging one another as though choreographed. Atop the scaffolding at the nose of each Lightning worked an armorer, carefully loading the belts of fifty-caliber machine gun and twenty-millimeter cannon cartridges. Bubba's crew chief sat straddling the right boom of Bubba's Lightning as though on a horse. Apparently he was working on the turbocharger.

"What happened?" Lee asked Big Ole. "You guys get your butts chewed for something?"

"Na-a-w," Big Ole said with a chuckle, "told to get you ready to go by 1200 hours."

Lee and Sandy looked at each other and shrugged.

"Hey, Lieutenant!" Corporal Mashka called from the scaffolding at Lee's ship. "Did you hear what happened over at the 127th?"

"Nothing bad I hope," Lee replied.

"Couldn't get much worse. Some stupe retracted the gear on Captain Robesky's plane. Had the nose blocked up, working on the nose gear. Tail dropped and buckled both booms—totaled her out!" He illustrated with his hands. "You need another mechanic? I know where you can get one! 'Course you might have to dig him out of a latrine!"

The crew laughed. Lee and Sandy struggled to control their impulses and only smile. That was one fine and expensive piece of airplane ruined. Not exactly a laughing matter.

"Should we go see that?" asked Sandy.

Lee hesitated. "Yes—and no," he replied. "Not till we find out what's going on here."

At 0130 that afternoon, the Gophers were wrapping up their preflight briefing in the Ops shack. Before them hung a large map showing the New Guinea coastline from the U.S. base at Finschafen on the point of the Huon Peninsula west to the Jap stronghold at Madang. Colonel Hammer explained that when the Allies captured Nadzab and Lae to add to their previous conquests at Finschafen and Saidor, they had in effect gained control most of the perimeter of the arrowhead-shaped Huon Peninsula.

Reports were indicating an increase in barge and small boat traffic along the coast between Finschafen and Saidor, obvious attempts to keep the Japanese Eighteenth Army alive. With the Japanese Air Army showing a studied reluctance to come out and fight, the punch of the 483rd Fighter Group would be turned for a time against enemy ships and barges along the coast. It looked like the Gophers would spend some time duck hunting.

"Can't get any Zeros shooting at rowboats," the familiar voice of Barton grumbled.

"Until you can *hit* a zero," said Sandy, "you'd better practice on rowboats."

"A couple of flight position changes for today," Major Brennan began, "Hedman will take the Red Three spot. Forbes moves up to White Three, and Marks will move back to Blue Three." He looked directly at Lee as though daring him to question the order.

Lee turned and saw Sandy looking directly at him, shaking his head ever so slightly. The change meant that Lee was back to within one step of where he had begun as the last Tail End Charlie. Discouraging as the switch was to Lee, it came as no surprise. The worst of it, Lee was exchanging Sandy as a wingman for Black Bart. The ornery, angry antagonist would be flying behind him. He thought back to Bart's recent threat relating to exactly such a situation, a sobering thought.

By 0230 the Gopher squadron was over Finschafen at 10,000 feet and letting down. Lee's attention fell to the strange-looking network of roads below. At 5,000 feet he could tell that the roads were an unusual gray color. He had heard of the phenomenon. In an effort to combat the muddy conditions the engineers had harvested and ground up coral to spread on the roads. According to scuttlebutt the Finschafen troops now had muddy roads that were gray.

As they continued their descent, Lee began searching the coastline for rivers, streams, tiny cuts, or coves in which the Japs might hide barges and small boats. Since the top priority of camouflage was to conceal installations and equipment from over-flying aircraft, the Gophers' best chance for spotting targets came with flying extremely low. The angles of vision changed and opened up side views as well as overhead views. They had reached the Vitiaz Strait and were cruising parallel to the coastline at 2,000 feet when Mo called.

"Mo here," crackled Lee's headphones. "Gus, go down here and cover the next twenty-five miles."

"Roger," said Gus. "Blue, string 'em out, space 'em out."

Lee gave one last thorough look at the skies above and to all sides of them. Then he backed off on his airspeed and pulled wider to the right to give Smokey the slot behind and to the right of the flight leader. He knew that Barton would be pulling in almost directly behind him as they adjusted their echelon formation to single file for strafing. He wanted to believe that Bart's threat had been simply angry words without intent. But if he really was crazy angry, a single-file strafing run would be the ideal place to have a friendly fire accident. Bart was the last man in the string—nobody behind him to observe what had happened. Lee wondered if Mo had placed Lee in the Blue Three position to test Bart. As they stretched the gaps beyond 500 yards between planes, Lee told himself that Mo had put him in the Blue Three spot to teach Bart through example. But he wished he had heard Mo say those words.

Up ahead he thought he saw Gus firing, tracking through the water and into the foliage.

"Blue!" shouted Gus. "That point in the jungle that sticks up higher than the rest. That's *not* a tree. Go for it!"

Smokey's fire trail ripped into the area of the high point. As Lee approached closer he slowed to 250 mph and studied the area at water level below the high point. Suddenly the vague, shapeless jungle became a ship, a small ship perhaps the size of a U.S. Coast Guard cutter! He banked slightly right to line up.

"Blue," Lee called, "that's a ship—cutter-sized ship!"

Lee went in right over the wave tops, raking the ship at deck level with his fifties and the cannon. The cockpit pod vibrated with each burst, sealing its complaint with the smell of cordite. Tracers made their way toward him. And with the tracers he knew there had to be heavier stuff. His first goal was to knock out as many of the ship's defenses as possible. He felt he was right on target, but the target still lacked definition because of the camouflage netting. Just before he pulled up, he saw a small explosion that sent a burst of gray smoke upward. A glance in the mirror picked up Bart. The nose of his Lightning showed the twinkling signs that he was firing.

Lee shoved the throttles ahead to the wire and pulled up as sharply as he could without losing valuable air speed.

Playing follow-the-leader, Lee climbed out and began a sweeping left turn to come around for another pass. As he looked down, the gray smoke from his hits had changed to a billowing black plume that grew wider and wider as it surged upward, sure signs of a burning fuel tank. By the time Gus and Smokey had finished their second pass, the ship burned furiously. The flames had burned or melted much of the camouflage netting, and it began to collapse, revealing the outlines of three barges tied to shore in front of the burning ship.

As Lee sighted in and began firing at the first barge, he saw several twinkling sources of return fire. He felt his ship take some hits and it distracted him for a moment. Gathering his concentration he aimed maximum fire at the second barge and then the third. The twinklings stopped. He banked left early to avoid flying directly over the burning ship. Just as he passed it he felt an enormous concussion. His Lightning seemed to hop to the left about twenty yards.

Before he could turn far enough to get a glimpse of the ship, he could guess what had happened. The fire had reached the ship's magazine. Although he had little knowledge of ships, he knew that this one had finished its war. His mirror told him that Bart had reacted well. He had pulled up and out short of the exploding ship. While Lee had felt the concussion, Bart would have flown into the inevitable shrapnel from the explosion. Had it exploded a second or two earlier that would have been Lee's fate. He hoped the bulk of the shrapnel had scattered and fallen before Bart came close enough to catch it. His mouth suddenly became dry; his body became damp. But his conscience seemed to smile at him. Here he was, concerned for Bart's welfare. Moments before, he had been thinking of what Bart might do to him.

"Gus here. One more pass at the barges and we'd better move on. Places to go and people to see. Make this a good one."

Blue Flight made a good pass. As they pulled up and circled to seaward they could see one barge burning and another already settling low in the water. The scene proved to the young pilots in Blue Flight what their concentrated firepower could do to ships and barges. Gus took them up to 1,000 feet and they headed to the northwest looking for more ducks along the coast of the Huon Peninsula. On impulse, Lee reached for his throat mike.

"Bart, did you get through that explosion okay?"

"Yeah," responded Black Bart, "but I missed one target, a special one."

Lee turned to look over his right shoulder. He couldn't be certain—Bart was too far away. But he'd bet that Bart was watching him closely.

Blue Flight continued to the northwest. Twice they went down to investigate openings in the coastline where creeks or small rivers flowed into the Bismarck Sea. But they saw nothing to shoot at and they drew no enemy fire. If there were Japanese boats hidden in the overgrowth, they had to be small ones.

"Blue, let's head for the barn. Form up fingertip."

As they headed straight south they climbed to 16,000 feet to clear the unfriendly Finnistere Mountains. Their course took them midway between the big Allied bases at Finschafen and Lae and across the Huon Gulf to Dobodura. To their right, Lee could see massive, ugly afternoon storm cells building up against the Owen Stanleys and spilling back toward their base. They would be no threat to Blue Flight, but Lee wondered if the other two flights were far behind them. He considered putting out a call when he heard Gus.

"Gopher Gus to Red and White. Big weather closing in toward home. Suggest you not dally."

"Mo here. Roger."

"Greenie. That's a Roger."

With a squadron of P-47 Thunderbolts already in the process of landing, Blue Flight had to circle for a time before landing. When Lee pushed his landing gear lever down, the landing gear light remained off. He raised and lowered the lever again. He could hear and feel gear mechanisms working, but he couldn't be sure all three were down and locked. He aborted on his final approach to go around again. On his second downwind pass, control notified him that things looked okay. At that same moment, the light came on. By the time Lee had gingerly touched down, the other two flights were entering the landing pattern.

Lee and Big Ole were examining the wheel wells for damage when Mo Brennan walked up to them. He lit a cigarette and squinted as the initial burst of smoke wafted into his face.

"How the hell did you miss them?" he demanded of Lee.

"Miss what?"

"Miss *what?*" Mo parroted. "Miss those four patrol boats out in open water in *your* sector! We sank them on the way home. Why the hell didn't you?" Without waiting for an answer, the major stomped off toward the Ops shack.

Chapter 18

▼

"No bull now, Sandy! Where did Red Flight find those patrol boats? In our sector?"

"Hey, calm down, Lee," Sandy replied. "You know there aren't any sharp lines drawn on the water."

"Sandy?" Lea repeated, glancing up at his friend and then refocusing on the dark pathway they walked.

"Well," Sandy began, "I can't say for sure, but it seemed to me like it might have been about ten miles north of your assigned sector. We had gone way beyond that point and were headed back home when we spotted them."

"How far from shore were they?" Lee asked.

"Couple of miles." Sandy hesitated. "You know, Lee, we're probably waking everybody up. Maybe we should hold this discussion until we get to the mess tent."

"And you guys didn't see them on your way north?"

"No."

"So," Lee said, "they probably came out from shore after Red and White flew past."

"Probably," replied Sandy.

"So nobody's to blame. Why are *we* catching the flak?"

"Okay, okay," said Sandy. "So his accusation was unfair. What's the big deal? It isn't as though this was the first time. He's been doing this to you almost since we got here."

"The big deal, Sandy, is…." Lee thought for a moment. "Well, I'll let you know what the big deal is. And I'll let you know if I was right or wrong."

Lee and Sandy hit the mess at 0400 hours for what Lee had come to call "midnight breakfast," the prelude to early missions. The heavy, slightly rubbery pancakes tasted good.

The Gopher Squadron had been pulled off the duck hunting schedule to escort a dozen B-25s to Kavieng, the Japanese stronghold on the north tip of New Ireland, the island just east of New Britain. Kavieng alone was considered tough duty, but to get there the Gophers would have to fly much too close to Rabaul. In an effort to neutralize that Japanese hornets' nest, however, a large bomber force from Guadalcanal in the Solomons was to attack Rabaul in a coordinated effort. If the plan worked, the Japs at Rabaul would be too busy defending themselves against the B-24s and their escorts from the Solomons to pay much attention to the Kavieng strike.

"You know, Lee," Sandy was saying, "these big, super-coordinated plans make me nervous. When the big brass plan these things, it's all done with the assumption that all will go according to plan. You and I have already learned that in this war, in this god awful climate, not too many things go according to plan. If those big boys from Henderson Field don't show up on time, they'll leave us dangling out there like dog meat, a dozen mediums with only a dozen escorts against a hundred Zeros."

"I've made up my mind. I'm going to challenge him on it," Lee said.

"You—" Sandy stopped the huge bite of pancake halfway to his mouth.

"I'm going to," Lee repeated. "If I'm wrong, so what? He moves me back to Tail End Charlie where I can cover Black Bart's ass? He won't transfer me—can't afford to ground me."

"You know, sometimes you piss me off," Sandy said.

"What? That I'm going to challenge him?"

"No, that you weren't listening to a word I said."

"Sorry, Sandy. You of all people deserve better than that." Lee looked at his watch. Sandy reacted by checking his own. The two gobbled their remaining breakfast and headed for the flight line. Big Ole, Mashy, and Mac were already busy on Lee's Marksman.

"I replaced that bulb," said Big Ole, "and I checked the circuit breaker. Everything seems okay," he said as he strapped Lee into the cockpit.

"Good, Ole. At least I've had a warning. I'll watch and listen to the gear carefully today."

"You just be sure you come back, you hear?" Big Ole shouted as he turned to dismount from the wing.

Lee lifted off into the darkness at 0445 and cut a sharp corner to reduce the catch-up time. He listened carefully to his landing gear retract. It sounded normal. The light went off right on schedule. He saw Bart's navigation lights behind him. It seemed that Mo was taking the squadron to altitude a bit faster than usual making the catch-up difficult for Lee and Bart. The thought inspired another touch of Black Bart paranoia that Lee quickly willed away. He and Bart finally caught up with the squadron at 12,000 feet where he switched off his navigation lights.

The eastern horizon glowed with the promise of the day. As he looked into the lighter sky, Lee was glad that, because of the coordinated attack plan, the Gophers could cruise this trip at 24,000 feet rather than at wave-top altitude. If things were on schedule, the attack on Rabaul was already underway and the Japanese were very busy. If not.... He searched the eastern skies for enemy fighters. To add to the deception, the Gopher Squadron flew on a heading of zero-two-eight, keeping far to the left of a bee-line track for Kavieng. The hope was that Japanese ground observers would assume the Gophers were headed to the north for the Admiralties island group and not see them as a threat to either Rabaul or Kavieng. Half an hour out over the Bismarck Sea they would turn due east toward Kavieng.

Suddenly, Lee saw Bubba waggle his wings several times, break formation, and drop away to their left, disappearing below and behind them. Aborting a mission was standard procedure when mechanical difficulties arose, but it concerned Lee more than usual because this time it was Bubba. He hoped that Bubba would be able to make—

"Marks," came the single word to break their radio silence.

Lee studied Mo's Lightning far ahead and to his left. The wings waggled. He could only conclude that for whatever reason Mo wanted him to assume Bubba's place as his wingman. Lee eased the throttles ahead, swung out to clear, and slid up on Mo's left. He saw Mo's nod of approval so he dropped back into the Number Two position behind and to Mo's left.

Soon, Mo sent another silent signal and turned his squadron to the new heading of zero-eight-five, nearly straight east. They headed directly into a brilliant rising sun that seemed a darker red-orange, like a giant warning sign that said: "JAPANESE TERRITORY, KEEP OUT!" Lee wished their attack could hit Kavieng from the east with the sun at their backs, but they dared not risk a crossing over either Rabaul or Kavieng to gain that advantage.

They overtook the B-25 Mitchell bombers flying below them at about 15,000 feet. Lee watched his leader carefully as they throttled back to hold with the slower bombers. For whatever reasons, the bombers had been armed and fused for high altitude release on the mission. To Lee that meant that any battles with Jap fighters would likely occur between 14,000 and 20,000 feet. And that meant that his Lightning would react to the controls slower than at lower altitudes. As they drew closer to Kavieng, Lee found himself playing and replaying thoughts of combat, the *do's* and the *don'ts* that would have to come instinctively once the battle began.

The narrow island of New Ireland came into view, and the harbor at Kavieng began to take shape. It was smaller and more compact than the enormous, rambling complex of six bases at Rabaul. Slightly to the right, Lee could see the northeastern tip of New Britain—Rabaul. As they drew closer, he could see columns of smoke rising over the dreaded stronghold.

"Little Brothers," came a strange voice in Lee's headphones. "The cat's out of the bag. We've got bogies, about twenty of them, coming up at twelve o'clock level."

"Roger," said Mo. "See them. Anybody see any others?" There was no response. "Gus, come with us. Greenie, stay up. Red and Blue, switch 'em and drop 'em. String it out."

Lee had just switched tanks, dropped his belly tanks, and moved over to Mo's right wing when the CO started down. It appeared that the diving Lightnings would meet the climbing fighters at about 17,000 feet and perhaps two miles in front of the bombers. Lee knew that was cutting it close, at least from the bomber crews' perspective, but if the seven Lightnings managed to shoot well, they could reduce the enemy formation of Oscars and perhaps break it up. The cockpit vibrated as Lee tested his weapons.

Mo's P-38 hurtled toward the Japanese lead aircraft, so Lee picked the Oscar to the Jap leader's left. The two lead flights of enemies continued directly toward the bombers, but two rear flights broke formation and rose to meet the Lightnings. Still more than 2,000 yards away, they were firing at Mo and Lee, their tracers falling short. Lee hoped that meant inexperienced enemy pilots. But the gap narrowed incredibly fast, and he had to fight to avoid being distracted from his own target.

Lee and Mo fired simultaneously. Mo's lead Oscar caught fire and rolled into a vertical dive toward the sea far below. Lee's target seemed immune to his fifties, but when he touched off his third burst, the Oscar shed most of its tail assembly. It slid into a flat spin that could lead to only one conclusion. As Mo and Lee blasted through the formation, two of the remaining Oscars fired at them but were much too late.

The designated radio channel was once again filled with warnings, victory cries, and calls for help. Lee followed Mo in a sweeping, climbing left turn for a second pass. Over his shoulder, Lee glimpsed several trails of smoke leading to the ocean, but he dared not take the time to try to identify the sources of the trails. Hedman and Sandy had apparently split off in another direction, and Lee concentrated on staying with his leader.

Suddenly, tracers appeared out of nowhere angling downward past Lee's nose, missing by perhaps ten yards. A normal reaction would be to turn sharply to the left. Not a good idea against the agile Japanese fighters. In one motion, Lee pushed the nose down, banked sharply right, cut the right throttle, accelerated the left, and touched the button for his dive flaps. As the nose whipped around to the right, he looked over his left shoulder and saw the Oscar flash past. Lee reversed the process and quickly brought his bird back to his original course.

He looked for Mo and found him about 1,500 yards ahead and above. The Oscar that had overshot Lee had joined another and the two were closing in on Mo from behind and below.

"Mo," Lee called. "Two behind and below you! Break right and down!"

If his message had gotten through, Mo would lead them in a right turn, setting them up for Lee. If Mo didn't respond, Lee might pull off a couple of long shots, but not with good odds. After what seemed like forever, Mo suddenly turned sharply to his right and downward. The nimble Oscars followed.

Lee steadied on the lead Oscar, led it to allow for the deflection angle, and fired two short bursts. While he thought he had hit the lead fighter hard, he couldn't be sure. The second Jap fighter drifted into his line of sight. But before he could fire, he found himself transfixed by one of the absurd anomalies of war. The lead Oscar suddenly pulled up sharply. The hapless pilot of the second fighter was left with no time, no options, and no future. He flew directly into his comrade, and the two dropped toward the Bismarck Sea in a giant fireball.

"Good shooting, Lee!" shouted Mo. "Goddamned good shooting!"

Lee doubted that Mo had seen what really had happened. But the compliments warmed him nevertheless. The duo climbed to recapture lost altitude and as they circled to search out more Oscars, Lee had time to survey the situation. The Mitchells were dropping their loads over Kavieng harbor and were being harassed by heavy flak. Off to the right, Lee saw Lightnings and Oscars climbing, turning, and diving in the distance.

"I'm right on you, Mo," Lee called. "You pick 'em."

Mo banked right and the pair of Lightnings headed for two Oscars that seemed intent on erasing a Gopher Lightning from behind. With an altitude advantage that quickly converted to speed Mo and Lee closed rapidly on the Jap fighters. Mo flamed the first. But before Lee could get lined up on the second, the Oscar turned sharply to his left and headed for home. The rest of his fellow pilots had apparently reached the same decision. Mo and Lee chased them for a couple of miles, but once satisfied that the remaining seven or eight Oscars posed no threat to the bombers, Mo did a climbing one-eighty to collect his Gophers.

"Who's that up ahead of us?" Mo called.

Lee saw two Lightnings far ahead and below, one perhaps three miles behind the other. Both were smoking heavily. The farthest P-38 trailed white coolant from one engine and black smoke from the other. As Lee watched, a parachute opened up behind and below the stricken fighter.

"I think that's Robert in the chute," came Greenie's voice. "And the one following is Cal. They ended up with about six on their tails as they came through on the first pass."

"Greenie," called Mo. "Take Chub and cover them. Call it in."

"Roger."

About the time the remaining two ships in White Flight broke formation, Lee saw another parachute blossom below. It appeared that Cal had held on so as to bail out close to Robert. Good thinking. Lee wished he were going down for a look, but he knew he could do nothing that Greenie and Chub couldn't do.

If both pilots made it down and got into their one-man dinghies successfully they would have a good chance at survival. Lee made their position to be about thirty miles off the northwest shore of New Britain, close to the half-way mark of the concave, quarter-moon-shaped island. On the dark side, the prevailing currents would inevitably take the two flyers to that shoreline unless Air-Sea Rescue could get to them first. On the bright side, there were only light concentrations of enemy troops along that shore. Lee hoped that the Navy had a submarine close by.

The bombers had fared a little worse. Lee's count found two missing and two more trailing smoke. The formation was poking along at about 150 mph covering their damaged comrades. Mo sent the three remaining ships of Blue Flight to escort the two crippled Mitchells back as far as the Huon Peninsula and friendly skies. The remaining bombers, with Red Flight flying cover, could then make better time on their return to Nadzab.

Loafing along at 200 mph Lee felt bored. The trip would take forever. Then it occurred to him that the bombers probably carried wounded, bleeding crewmen for whom the return trip was taking longer than forever.

When the friendly coast of the Huon Peninsula loomed before them, Red Flight broke off and headed south to Dobodura. Lee hoped they would soon get their orders to move north to a forward base, a move that could save them as much as two hours per mission. Gus had speculated that the Gophers were being held back and given the longer flights because of their range and the fact that the Gophers had less flight time on their ships than many of the others.

The Americans now held numerous bases closer to the action by seventy-five to a hundred-seventy-five miles, including Wau, Tsili Tsili, Salamaua, Lae, Fincschafen, Nadzab, and Saidor. In addition, they had carved out a strip for emergencies at Gusap, well up the Markham River and only fifty miles inland from the big Japanese coastal base at Madang. Cementing the Americans' control of the Huon Gulf and the Vitiaz Straits were their acquisitions at Cape Gloucester and Arawe on the eastern end of New Britain. Dobodura had indeed become a rear base.

Lee listened intently as his gear went down. The light came on as it should. But he felt a little flutter in his stomach as he flared out for touchdown, not absolutely certain he had three legs down and locked. He found himself hoping the bad gear would be his nose gear and not one of his mains. The fears went wasting, for the heavy ship settled in smoothly on the surprisingly dusty strip. If he flew a thousand missions out of New Guinea, Lee knew he would never understand how deep, sloppy mud could become dust in but a few hours.

"Marks, park in the Red Two slot," came the curt radio message.

"Roger. Red Two slot," Lee acknowledged.

As he followed the order, he realized that Bubba's ship was nowhere to be seen. He felt a leaden lump develop in his gut. Bubba didn't make it back? Maybe he landed at one of the closer bases. That had to be it. It had to be! Good flyer that he was, Bubba lacked the natural resources to deal with a bail-out, or a crash-landing. Lee could envision the naïve, white-haired kid just sitting there in his cockpit paralyzed by fear while his Lightning sank beneath the waves.

Chapter 19

Lee stumbled awkwardly down the little ladder from his P-38 and joined a somber group of Gophers. Quiet questions, almost whispers, passed from one pilot to the next. Only questions—nobody had any answers. They seemed to be in shock, too bound up in pain to even speculate on the welfare of Bubba, Robert, and Cal. Three of them down? It just couldn't happen.

Lee felt someone grab his elbow from behind. It was Major Brennan.

"Marks," he said, "I want to see you as soon as you've debriefed. Come up to my tent. Got it?"

"Got it."

As the major strode off, Lee wondered what was scratching his crankshaft this time. In spite of a job well done, Lee sensed he was about to catch hell again. For a moment, the tension lifted him a little, but as he thought about the net of criticism Mo Brennan kept setting for him, he sank back into the cesspool with the rest of the young pilots. It was Gus who finally broke the spell. He stepped to the front of the group and raised a hand.

"Okay, Gophers, listen up!" Gus paused and looked about the group. "I've got a couple of things to say, and then you're on your own. I don't think you've any idea how damned lucky you yard birds have been to this point. You came into this scene a little over a month ago. You've piled up a record of kills that everybody in the Fifth Fighter Command is talking about. And in the process, only one loss. Only *one?* We're talking what? A forty to one kill ratio? Did you really expect that to go on indefinitely? You've been in dreamland, Punks. Get real! This is not a board game you're playing here."

Gus's diatribe certainly didn't fit what the sullen Gophers thought they needed. But as Lee processed the message from Gus, he sensed that the others were sliding onto a similar track.

"Now I for one," Gus continued, "don't want to find myself in a mess like we got into today if all I have for wingmen is a bunch of snot-nosed kids with their heads buried in their hankies. Wingmen like that get you killed!" He stomped off toward Ops.

"He's got that right," added Greenie. "I'm not giving up on those three yet, but the odds are that they didn't all make it. We can only do what we can do and learn to forget what we can't do." He turned to catch up with Gus.

"When did *they* get so goddamned smart?" Bart spouted.

"You dumb shit," said Hedman. "You forgetting that Greenie's already been there? He bailed out and clawed his way through the jungle for a week to get home. And what do you think was on Gus's mind all that time? Yeah, I'd say they've been there."

The discussion withered instantly and fell to the sun-baked mud. The group broke up as singles, pairs, and threesomes began making their way toward Ops for debriefing. Lee hadn't given much thought to the medicinal booze that Doc Talbot dispensed after each mission. Once or twice he had even passed it by. But this time he bolted it down and wished for more.

When he finished giving his version of the mission to the intelligence officer, a blond-headed first lieutenant from Rockford, Illinois, Lee hesitated for a moment.

"No," said the lieutenant, "no word yet on the missing pilots. Next."

Lee stood leaning against a corner post at the front of the open-sided Ops shack for a few minutes. He watched the pilots come and go. He looked back to Mo Brennan's customary corner, now occupied by strangers. That was fine with Lee. He wasn't at all anxious to meet with Napoleon. But he wondered where he had gone wrong. His first experiences with the major had seemingly brought substantial respect. Then it was down the ladder, up the ladder, then down again, like a yo-yo on a string—with someone waiting to snip the string.

Having just run his total to twelve Japanese planes shot down, Lee searched for the exhilaration he should be feeling. But in the muck of distress over his downed mates and the tension of a forthcoming session with his CO, he gave up the search. Finally, with two resolutions made, he started for Mo Brennan's tent. He would stand up and be strong, but he would try his damnedest to remain cool and respectful to avoid unduly stirring the pot.

Lee was but a few yards from Mo Brennan's tent when Mo strode out toward him. He had a small canvas bag slung over a shoulder. The usual cigarette dangled from one hand.

"Come on," Mo said curtly as he turned onto the path toward the amphitheater and strode off at a pace that challenged Lee to catch up.

By the time Lee caught up with his CO he had decided to table his planned attack, at least long enough to learn what Mo had in mind. But he determined that at the first sign of yet another castigation he would rise up. The pair walked in silence around the top ridge to the rear center overlooking the entertainment bowl. Then Mo led the way back along a narrow footpath toward a cluster of palm trees on the edge of the jungle. Mo stopped abruptly, raised both hands above his head, and stood for a moment looking directly up at the palm leaves waving in the breeze.

"Yes…good," Mo said. "Nice breeze here. No people, no mosquitoes. We can talk."

He motioned Lee to one of two palm stumps. As Lee sat down, Mo opened the canvas bag, brought out two tin cups and a bottle of Scotch. He sloshed each cup to half-full, handed one to Lee, then plopped down on the other stump. Looking at Lee, he raised his cup in a toast gesture, and gulped a large swallow.

"Okay," he said, "the world makes sense again. What's on your mind?"

"I think you know what's on my mind."

"Yeah, I suppose I do. You're tired of being treated like a corralled pogo stick. Right?"

"I guess that's one way to put it," Lee said, pausing for a swallow of Scotch. "I'd thought of it more like a carousel with nails on the saddles."

Mo laughed. "Well, Killer, you can relax. That's over. You passed." He watched for Lee's reaction. "Remember, the grass is always greener where the shit lands."

"I passed? You mean all that crud was to test me again? Test me for *what?* Patience? Courage? Stupidity?"

"All of the above," Mo said. "In a nut shell, I need an exec, an assistant leader, unofficial of course, to help me run this group, in the air and on the ground. I'm doing fine as far as the Army is concerned. But, as you might recall, I'm thinking beyond that. I'm looking to get as much out of this duty as I can. And I want the same for you. Still listening?" He took another big slug from the tin cup.

Lee took a swallow, a big one, then gulped a second swallow, hoping to wash his anger far enough away that he could deal with this situation. Then he bought some time by quietly staring off into the distance. Finally, he had resolved to play along with his CO, but he would make no commitments that he might regret should the carousel start up again.

"I guess I want what you want, success here that will help out later. But I have no idea what kinds of success I need or what my later needs will be. You have that all planned out. I don't." Lee watched a foursome set up for a card game on the stage far below.

"Hell, you've got time to plan out the *later* part while you're here, pretty good idea, in fact," Mo said. "So set that aside for the moment. Think about what you'd like to take back with you to Chicago, or wherever, that would help you to reach just about any goals you might set."

Lee took another swallow. He'd never liked Scotch, but it was beginning to slide down quite smoothly.

"I, uh, don't—"

"Oh, come on, Killer," Mo cut in. "Sure you know. It's the same three things we all want to take back with us."

"It is? Three things?" Lee wondered if the whiskey had dulled his brain. Or perhaps Mo Brennan simply lived on some radically different plane of life, an existence that Lee Marks could not even fathom, let alone reach.

"Sure it is. First, you want to go home alive and in one piece. Second, you want to go home a hero, with lots of kills, medals, and rank. And third, you want to go home with a solid network of connections made with influential people. And what do these three things bring you when you get home?" Mo looked Lee right in the eyes. "Respect, my friend, respect. And you take that respect and use it to reach your goals, fame, fortune, whatever the hell they are. Make sense?"

Lee nodded. Yes, when Mo Brennan actually talked to him instead of shooting barbs at him, he made a lot of sense.

"I wonder," Lee said, "I wonder how many of our guys have thought all that through?"

"Only the few who are high-ranking career officers," Mo said. "Few of the war-time rats like you and me have thought that far ahead. But tell me the plan doesn't make sense."

Mo poured refills for Lee and himself. Lee noticed that Mo's cup was filled to the rim.

"Yes," Lee replied. "It does make sense, a lot of sense. I guess I've always focused on the immediate challenge without looking far enough ahead."

"Exactly—big picture, little picture." Mo looked off at the airstrips that spread below them. "Okay, this ought to get you started in the right direction, toward the big picture. You're still below the zone, with only a month in action, but I've put you in for promotion to First Lieutenant. I know Sledge will back me on it, so I think you can count on it."

"Whew, thanks!" Lee said. He had read of "bolts out of the blue," and he had heard of them, but this— He recalled his earlier plan for this confrontation with Mo and silently chided himself. "But, you've already got two first lieutenants."

"Oh, don't worry. They won't be in your way," Mo responded. "We need to get you to captain as soon as possible. Need a little more of this?" he asked, waving the bottle.

"God, I'd like to," said Lee, "but I'm flying now. I think I'd better try to get my gear back down."

"I'm not sure about something," Mo said. He fumbled for a cigarette and dropped his lighter as he tried to light up. He snapped it up on the first bounce, lit up, and took a long drag. "I haven't decided whether to fly you on my wing, put you in as element leader, or leave you back in the other flights to be a teacher. What do you think?"

Lee thought his squadron commander was drunk, but he said, "Let's take it backwards. Who am I going to teach? Black Bart? I could help him a lot if he could admit that he needs help. Personally, I think hell will freeze over first." Lee paused for a moment to watch Mo's eyes. It seemed like he was still short of blotto. "So then, your wingman or element leader. It depends, I guess, on what you want. If you want me there to cover your ass, make sure you don't get blind-sided, then wingman would be the choice. If you want me to feed as many Jap pilots to the sharks as possible, I should fly the number three slot."

"Good. Good logic. Let's fly you as my wingman for now. We'll wait a bit and see if Bubba gets back. Then we can put you where you can do the most good for our little corporation. Up front with me on something?"

"Sure. What is it?" Lee asked.

"Barton. I'm not sure that he can learn anything even *if* we could change his lousy, fucking attitude. He reminds me of a guy back in primary, Crandon was his name. He flew so badly that he must have gotten his wings by default. I think the instructor passed him rather than get into the same plane with him." Mo laughed, a good, hard belly laugh like Lee hadn't seen. "Crandon was so bad," Mo went on, "so bad in his first ten landings the instructors all put in for transfers to submarines." Mo looked Lee in the eye. "Realistically, do you think you can help him?"

"Realistically, I doubt it. But I'm willing to try *if* he is."

"Good enough," Mo said. "Let's give it more time. Hey, right now, it's chow time."

When Mo stood and walked steadily down the path toward Fungus Field, Lee realized his leader could still walk his way through a substantial buzz. Would he try to fly his way through one?

CHAPTER 20

▼

"It's a first class thunder boomer," Lee said as he and Mo Brennan stood just inside the mess after chow, waiting for the deluge to let up.

"Damn, I hope we live long enough to see June and July," said Mo. "They're probably the only months out here that are close to being suitable for fly—"

Zzzooooooommm! A pair of powerful Wright Cyclone radial engines skimmed overhead at little more than treetop altitude. Lee and Mo snapped their heads to the right as though watching a tennis match when the B-25, barely visible in the rain, flashed past.

"Holy Cow!" someone shouted.

"Je—sus Christ!"

"Duck your heads!"

A loud crash of pots and pans came from the kitchen, followed by more epithets.

"Man, is he low!" exclaimed Lee. "Think he'll make it in?"

"Yeah, he'll make it in," Mo said.

"You sound rather confident."

"I am," said Mo. "That's Marv flying our Goose, and he can smell a flat patch of land in the middle of a typhoon. He went down to Lae for some goodies we need. Then we got word that the Navy had brought a couple of guys into Finschafen. So the colonel told him to go on over and see if any were our guys."

In minutes, Mo had commandeered the headquarters jeep and had the pair on their way to the flight line. When they reached the revetment assigned to the Golden Goose, Mo backed into a position that reduced the exposure of the jeep's open sides to the rain. He lit up a cigarette.

While Mo had sounded as calm as an evening rose, Lee sensed tension there. And the longer they waited, the less Mo talked. Maybe Marv hadn't made it in. He had been headed in the general direction of his downwind leg when he buzzed the camp. That meant that somewhere out in that downpour he had to turn a hundred and eighty degrees at an altitude of perhaps a hundred feet and then locate and line up on the runway when coming back. No small task on a sunny day, let alone in the middle of a tropical thunderstorm.

Mo had just chain-lit his fourth cigarette when they heard the unmistakable sounds of the Golden Goose taxiing their way. Marv deftly taxied up before the revetment, locked one brake and spun the Goose around, ready to be backed into her home, a high, circular berm of soil. Mo drove the jeep close to the craft's improvised main door.

The door opened and out jumped Bubba, followed by the ship's co-pilot, the gunner, and Marv Harper, the pilot. Mo waved them to the jeep and with no hesitation they piled on. Three of them somehow squeezed into the two-man back seat, and diminutive Marv launched himself onto Lee's lap. Mo snapped the vehicle into low gear and took off for the Ops shack. The tiny four-cylinder engine screamed in protest, but Mo showed no mercy until he slid to a stop at his destination. The six jumped and slid from the jeep. The gunner, an enlisted man, took off for his world, and the remaining five scampered into the Ops shack.

While Bubba talked with the blond-headed lieutenant, Mo and the two pilots huddled in another area with Colonel Hammer. Finally, Bubba stood and came Lee's way.

"I can't tell you how glad I am to see you," said Lee, shaking his young friend's hand.

"I'm glad to see me here, too! Lee, you won't believe it. I did it—I really did it!"

"Did what, Bubba?"

"I really did it. I'll bet nobody in the squadron thought I could—but I did it!"

Lee said nothing, for it seemed nothing he could say at the moment would affect Bubba. Whatever Bubba did would come out eventually.

"I brought her down—"

"Wait a minute, Bubba," Lee cut in. "Start at the beginning, will you? I saw you abort. Then what happened?"

"Well, it all started when the cooling vent on my right-side engine jammed. The temp started going up and nothing I tried seemed to do any good. That's when I decided I'd better head for land." With each word, Bubba's tempo increased. He seemed to have found a bottomless tank of adrenalin. "But I hadn't gone five minutes before I had to shut the engine down or burn it up. I'm really getting pretty good on the two-to-one transition, Lee. Ten minutes after I shut it down, the other engine started getting rough, then quit."

"Where were you at that point?" Lee asked.

"I was south of the Straits over the Solomon, but at only 5,000 feet, no way I could go anywhere. I was afraid that by the time I got opened up to bail out I might be too low. So I just said, 'Bubba, what do you do best?' And Bubba answered, 'I fly P-38's.' So I said—"

"Easy! Easy, Bubba, slow down!"

"Huh? Oh, yeah. So I said, 'Put this thing on the water. Set her down like a ball of cotton.' And you know what? That's just what I did. I greased her in so smooth, I hardly got her tail wet."

Lee remembered his vision of Bubba in such a situation, sitting in the cockpit of a sinking Lightning, too paralyzed by fear to get out. Obviously, he had been wro—

"And then I came apart, Lee. I came completely apart. It makes no sense. I can't believe it yet!"

Lee motioned again with his hands to try to slow the tempo.

"Lee, I switched from two engines to one. I lost my other engine, but I kept perfect control of her. I brought her down to the water and set her in perfectly." Bubba looked at Lee. "And then, you know what?"

"What?" Lee studied the red face that almost glowed beneath the white hair.

"I panicked. I went completely brain dead. I lost it. I sat there in the cockpit, still strapped in, cockpit glass still all closed. I sat there—seemed like hours. She started going down, and I just sat there. I said, 'Bubba, get out.' Bubba said, 'Right, get out.' But I just sat there."

"Obviously, at some point you made a move."

"Yeah. You know what did it? When the cold water started filling the cockpit, it kind of woke me up. Then I had to really scramble to get opened up, unhooked, and out of there. But I did it! I really did it! I got my Mae West and my raft blown up. I even remembered how to get into the raft."

"That's great, Bubba." Lee said. "I knew you'd handle an emergency all right. They must have picked you up rather quickly, huh?"

"Oh, I'm not done yet, Lee. I'm just getting started."

"You're just getting started?"

"Yeah. See, I'm floating along in my little raft, wondering what I should do that I hadn't already done. Lee, did you ever get that feeling that someone's right behind you, even when you hadn't heard or seen anything of them?"

"Well, yes, I guess I have."

"I got this feeling, this feeling that I wasn't alone," Bubba said. His eyes opened wider as he continued. "I started looking around. I wasn't—wasn't alone! Right there behind me, maybe ten yards behind me…a periscope! A submarine periscope! They're just sitting down there watching. I'll bet they were watching me when I pissed over the side of the raft!"

"That's good, Bubba. I'll bet they got some laughs out of that. Did they give you a good ribbing when they picked you up?"

"No."

"No?" Lee said. "I can't believe a bunch of our sailors would let that one go past."

"Oh, but they weren't *our* sailors," Bubba said. "It was a Jap sub. Lee, it was a goddamned Jap sub!"

Lee flinched. He believed the part about the Jap sub because it was Bubba telling the story. It would be beyond Bubba to make up a tale like that. But in nearly a year together, he had never heard the innocent towhead swear.

"Then what happened?" Lee asked. It had to be the most exciting story Lee had heard since he enlisted.

"Well, they watched me. Then the periscope would turn a three-sixty. Then they'd watch me some more. Then another three-sixty. And then, then I really got scared. The periscope started coming up out of the water, up to three feet, five feet, eight feet. I paddled like hell to get away from those bastards."

Lee felt himself tensing up.

"The conning tower came up out of the water, and they stopped there. Pretty soon I heard jabbering from the sub, and I looked. Two guys were up there on the conning tower looking at me and motioning for me to come to them. I just kept paddling. Didn't seem like I was moving an inch, but I kept paddling. They shouted at me in Japanese and pointed a machine gun at me, but I just kept on paddling. They fired a few rounds into the water. Then, the strangest thing…."

"Oh?" Lee knew there could be nothing stranger than what he'd just heard.

"Yeah. The two guys start shouting something different. They disappear, and I hear the hatch slam. The sub starts down, I mean really fast. The suction pulls me right over there. I thought I was going down with them for a minute. But they disappeared, periscope and all. When the water stopped bubbling so I could hear, I found out why those rotten shit heads had run the way they did. I heard boats coming fast, slapping against the waves. I turned around and there came three of our PT boats."

"Wow! Saved at last!" Lee exclaimed. He could think of no one more deserving of that salvation, unless Bubba's newfound profanity was to become a habit.

"When they pulled me aboard they said they'd just gotten a glimpse of the sub when she went down. They said they didn't have anything to use on the sub, but they called the position in right away. They took me into Finschafen. Really nice guys. Seemed like they'd do just about anything for me. Really nice guys."

"Bubba," Lee said, "I think I can stop worrying about you. I think you became a man today, a real mature pilot who can take care of himself. Now, of the whole escapade, what was the most scary?"

"Oh, hell, that's easy," Bubba said, "the ride home in the storm with Marv. I thought I'd shit my pants. A storm is a hell of a lot more scary when you're riding with someone else."

"I think I'd agree with that. When you came in downwind you just about creased our scalps. Mo calls that good flying. I call it Russian Roulette. Now what, Bubba?"

"I'm going to get something to eat. Then I'm going to bed. And you guys had better keep your damned mouths shut so I can sleep. I am damned, fucking tired."

Lee cupped his hands over his ears, but Bubba didn't catch it. He had turned and struck out in the rain for the mess tent. Lee doubted that Bubba's system would slow down in time for sleep that night.

Chapter 21

Lieutenant Lee Marks bounced into the world with renewed energy the next morning. While the possible loss of Robert and Cal still burned deep in his gut, his forthcoming promotion, Bubba's safe return, and the new relationship with Mo Brennan had combined to wash away some of his negative garbage. Even the mess tent smelled better as he approached.

After chow, he rushed over to Ops to get the latest word on the search for his squadron mates. One of the Fifth Air Force PBY Catalinas had searched the appropriate sectors of the south Bismarck Sea until dark the previous day. In addition, a PT boat squadron had been active in the area and had been alerted to search for the missing pilots. No positive reports had come through, but Lee learned that the search would resume at dawn. There was always the chance that the two had made it safely ashore on New Britain. Though their most likely landing point was in Japanese-held territory, they wouldn't be the first to successfully hide in the enemy's jungle and manage a signal to passing vehicles. Downed pilots had been rescued from hostile shores by PBY Catalinas, PT boats, submarines, and even an occasional small surface ship.

As Lee walked down to the flight line, Bubba fell in beside him. Bubba's speech had slowed only a trifle; he still rattled on in a rapid-fire mode. More than that, Lee couldn't help but notice the difference in Bubba's gait. Where he had previously slid along like a hunch-backed gook, he now stood tall and straight and walked with a slight swagger. And more remarkable, the slender pilot with the boyish face of a sixteen-year-old rattled off his pent-up pieces of profanity even more frequently than during the previous evening's story-telling session.

Lee smiled and shook his head. He wondered if he was seeing a complete personality change or some temporary hybrid that had resulted from a shocking, fearful experience.

"You know, Bubba," Lee said, "if you keep swearing like this I'm going to have to write your mother."

"No shit? You'd do that?" Bubba asked. Then he grinned. "No you wouldn't."

"Well, my friend, we're going to have to do something to find my old friend, the one we all know and like so much."

"Hell, don't even look for him. He's gone," Bubba said. "Come on over here for a minute." He motioned to a collection of fifty-five-gallon drums standing on end in the sand. He turned his back to one and using his hands, sprang up to take a seat on top.

Lee clamored up on a neighboring drum and turned, curious to know more about this Bubba Nash, this character he didn't know and never would have dreamed he'd ever meet.

"Lee, seems like I've got to talk to you about this. You've always been my friend, sometimes the only friend I had. In our last little chat," Bubba paused, "I wanted to tell you something else, but I just couldn't make myself do it. Scared, I guess."

"What on earth would you be scared to tell *me?*" Lee asked.

"I was scared to tell you just how goddamned scared I was! Lee, all my life I've been scared, at least as far back as I can remember. Authority figures? Whoof! I was almost too scared to try to do what they told me to do. But I was more scared not to."

"I think we can all identify with that, Bubba," Lee said.

"No, I'm talking really scared, petrified scared," Bubba corrected. "I'm talking scared shitless. That's right. Most of my life I've been that scared."

"Aww, Bubba, if you were that scared, how did you get this far?" Lee asked. "You know, we're all scared, even Black Bart. That's part of the reason he acts the way he does."

"Yeah, you guys are scared, nervous-like before a mission. But once you get into action you push the fear away and do your thing." Bubba paused and contemplated the rising sun for a moment as though it was also a member of his audience. "But me? I've been petrified before the missions, scared to death all through them, and not a hell of a lot better until long after we've landed and been debriefed."

"Whew! I never would have guessed it. You carried on so well. How could you do that?"

"Two things, I think," Bubba replied. "Most important, I wore that P-38. I had a lot of faith in it. And second, I had all you guys wrapped around me like a cocoon. Without all that support I'd have died on the first take-off."

"Okay, Bubba," Lee said. "I understand better who you were. Who are you now?"

"I'm not sure yet. But that experience yesterday changed me. Lee, I brought that damned plane down dead-stick from 5,000 feet and landed on the water, got out and did all the things you're supposed to do. And I said, 'Go to hell,' to a Japanese submarine. Actually," he paused and turned on a huge grin, "I handled myself pretty damned well. Wouldn't you say?"

"I'd say you couldn't have done things any better, Bubba."

"But you know something?"

"What?"

"Bad and scary as it was, it was the best goddamned thing that could have happened to me. It's like I dumped half of my fears in the ocean when my ship went down and the other half when that Jap sub ran away." He looked at Lee. "Could that happen? I mean that I came out of yesterday a new man—can that *really* happen?"

"It's looking like it did happen, Bubba. I guess," Lee paused, "it did happen."

"You hesitate," Bubba said. "What's wrong?"

"I'm just hoping you don't go to the other extreme and become fearless."

"Hell, what's wrong with being fearless? Isn't that the whole idea?"

"No, no, no, Bubba. Most of us have fears. That makes us sharper. But fearless pilots become reckless pilots, and reckless pilots become dead pilots. They're easy meat for a bunch of Zeros—that is, if the New Guinea weather doesn't get them first."

Lee could see that Bubba was considering the statement. Good. But the new Bubba would certainly bear watching in the days to come. It might be better for Red Flight if Lee settled into the Number Three slot. That way he would be directly behind Bubba, at least until the flight got split up into pairs for action.

"How about we head back up to Ops, Lee?" Bubba asked. "I've got to see about getting a new ship. And by God if they try to charge me for the old one, I'll tell 'em to send the fucking bill to you."

As the duo walked along the crunchy pathway, Lee wondered if he should share the development with Mo. Could he trust Mo to be discreet and not betray him? It might be time to test Mo. He smiled at the reversal and the decision was made. Actually, Mo or any pilot deserved to know who his wingman really was. His life depended on that wingman.

At the Ops shack, Mo met Bubba with good news. To get him back into the air, they were drawing off one of the four P-38Js from Headquarters Squadron. The time lag in replacing that ship was less critical to Headquarters Squadron because they flew less often.

"Hey, that's great!" Bubba exclaimed, almost jumping up and down at the plan. Then he straightened up noticeably and pulled his shoulders back. "Yeah," he continued in his deepest voice, "Damned good way to handle the situation. I'll get my ground crew on it right away, check it from ass to nose."

The new Bubba strode purposefully from the Ops shack, and Lee rolled his eyes. He looked over at his leader to see Mo light a cigarette, pull his cap off with the cigarette hand and scratch his head with the other. He squinted through the smoke at Lee, smiled, and shrugged his shoulders.

"I guess I'd better not wait on this," Lee said. He led Mo to a quiet corner of the shack and proceeded with the Bubba story. When he finished, Mo simply exhaled and smiled.

"It do happen, Killer. It do happen. But it bears watching. I agree, we should put you right behind him where you can watch him. I'm going to see if they can jury-rig a huge goddamned mirror on my ship so I can watch him, too." With his hands he outlined something three feet by three feet, and they both laughed.

Colonel Hammer walked up, plunked his coffee on a nearby table, and motioned for them to get some coffee and join him. Lee managed to find a spare cup this time. He had no idea where this discussion was headed, so he poached a bit of Bubba's bravado as he sat down.

"Marks," Colonel Hammer began, "I've got to tell you you've done one hell of a job. One month—twelve Jap planes. That's unheard of! Think you can keep it up?"

The politically correct answer to the question called for more of Bubba's bravado than Lee could borrow.

"Seriously, sir, I rather doubt it," he said, "but if I don't, it won't be for lack of effort."

"Hah!" Colonel Hammer barked, turning to Mo with a big grin. "He handles himself well on the ground, too, doesn't he?"

Lee had come to see Colonel Sledge Hammer, with his salt and pepper crewcut, chiseled face, steely eyes, and no-nonsense personality as a small but powerful bear. It was good to see papa bear smile.

"I told you so," Mo said. "Command potential there."

"Yeah, you did, Mo. I think he can help us a lot. Did you mention the promotion to him?"

Mo simply nodded, and Lee nodded his confirmation.

"Good, Marks—it's Lee, isn't it?"

"Right, sir," Lee replied.

"Mo," the colonel asked, "can Lee keep his mouth zipped?"

"I don't know, Sledge," Mo said quickly. "Ask him."

"You know what I mean?" the colonel asked, looking directly at Lee with a cold, penetrating stare.

"I think I do, sir."

"Yes, I think you do. Be very sure that you do. Understand?"

"What he's telling you," said Mo, "is that we're going to start involving you in a few things around here, but we have to know that we can…depend on you."

"Okay," Lee responded, more casually than he'd intended.

"For starters," Colonel Sledge Hammer said, "we've put you in for promotion, with a rush on it. Second, we've put you in for your first medal, and we hope not the *last* one, the Air Medal. With the record you've set for one month, I really don't think there's a chance of it being denied."

"Thank you, sir!" Lee tried to turn off his smile as he looked at Mo, but he couldn't.

"So far, there are just a handful of medals split among three pilots in the 125th, Greenie, Gus, and myself," said Mo. "We need to spread it around for PR purposes, and you've given us our start." He looked over at the colonel and got a nod in return. "And unless you screw up…or go and get yourself killed…we'd like to hang captain's bars on you within two or three months. That's way ahead of the customary time frame, bumping you ahead of the zone, but with your past and future accomplishments, we think it'll fly. And I need an unofficial exec—now."

"But what about Greenie and Gus?" Lee asked.

"And the next thing," said the colonel, "we want you to take on some leadership in our upcoming move."

"We're—moving?"

"Moving up to Nadzab," Mo said, "but not until tomorrow."

"Tomorrow?" Lee felt like he had been dropped from a moving plane—without a parachute. "You mean *tomorrow?* Like the day after *today?* The *whole* fighter group?"

Colonel Hammer and Mo both laughed and nodded.

"Here," Mo said, handing Lee a five by eight card on which had been typed a list. "We've divided up the duties. These are yours. You shouldn't have any trouble with them."

Lee blinked, took the card and studied it. It seemed to a basic checklist of duties to pass on to the pilots and enlisted men, nothing complicated, unless they objected to taking orders from a second lieutenant. After scanning the list, he looked at Mo.

"No," said Mo before Lee could even ask the question. "That won't be a problem. You tell them that you're just the messenger and follow-up man, that the orders came from me."

"No problem," said Lee. "Consider it done. What time tomorrow?"

"Our target is 1400 hours," the colonel said. "We want everything packed up and checked off, ready to go by 1200 hours. Then the men can chow down and get their own gear packed up and down to the flight line in time to load and fly."

"They'll ask me how everything's going to work, how it's to be done," said Lee.

"And Mo will tell them all about it," Colonel Hammer said. "Your job is to get them rolling on the preparations. I can tell you this much, though. Pilots will fly their aircraft up. Personal gear goes on the Goose. Office gear, special equipment, and some tools go on a Gooney, along with the crew chiefs. Ah, Mo, you'll need to get that special equipment sealed up. All the heavy stuff and vehicles will be driven to the coast and shipped on an LST to Lae, then driven on up to Nadzab from there. It's only about forty miles up the Markham River."

"That it?" Lee asked.

"All for now," Colonel Hammer said. "Go with it."

As Lee got up to leave he was startled to find Mo accompanying him.

"Wow," Lee said softly, "when things happen around here they really happen."

"Okay, Killer, this is your last chance to wrap up any personal business here at Dobo. What do you need?"

"I don't really need anything. Not really," Lee said.

"So if you *wanted* something that wasn't really a need, what would it be?" Mo asked, a hint of a grin appearing.

"Well—this native, a guy called Bob, has some nice souvenirs. But I don't have anything to trade him. He wants red tow target silk. I haven't the slightest idea how one gets a hold of used tow targets, have you?"

"No, I don't," Mo replied, "but I'll bet we can come up with a *new* one."

"You're kidding!"

"Come on, Killer, I'll show you how you do that."

He turned off on a different path and motioned for Lee to follow. The path wound through a cluster of palm trees and led to an isolated clearing that held three short rows of huge, wooden crates, each about four feet wide, eight feet long, and six feet high. Mo led the way to a crate. While he dug in his pocket for a key, Lee noticed the placard on the door that read:

NO UNAUTHORIZED ADMITTANCE
SIGNED—*Colonel Rayburn Hammer*

Mo opened the large, sturdy padlock, glanced in both directions, then pulled the squeaky door-like side of the container open.

"Go on," Mo said, "take a look."

Lee stepped closer, fascinated. At his right stood stacks of wooden and cardboard cases, perhaps two dozen marked with a variety of labels: Vodka, Gin, Scotch, Bourbon. To the left hung a variety of Japanese swords, rifles, a couple of light machine guns, several flags, and several complete Japanese officers' uniforms. In a huge pile beneath the longer hanging items, Lee saw enemy helmets, canteens, pistols and holsters, ammo pouches, belts, and several cases of saki.

"Oh, my God!" Lee exclaimed.

"Welcome to the bank," Mo said with a big smile. "This—is New Guinea currency, better than money. There are only three people who have access to this, Colonel Hammer, myself, and Staff Sergeant Jernigan. You will be the fourth. Can you handle that?"

"Well, of course."

"There are just a few rules that go with this operation, so listen up," Mo said. He reached into his shirt pocket for a cigarette." You can see that some of the items are marked with our personal tags. Those are off limits. The other stuff is what we call corporate property. It can be used for the benefit of the fighter group personnel, or it can be used judiciously for our own personal comforts." He patted his shirt pocket. "I have the inventory list. Most important: nothing leaves here without being cleared with me first, and this door is never opened if there's anyone else around. Obviously, you don't go trotting down the path carrying a case of bourbon."

"But what did you use to trade for all this stuff?"

Mo said, "Sledge and I have a source in Townsville where we buy the booze—cheap. Of course, since we put our own money into the booze we have to feel we're getting our money's worth in subsequent trades."

"What did you use with the natives—for the Jap stuff?"

Mo laughed. "We have a rigid policy in place that we absolutely *must* adhere to. Goes like this. If an object isn't critical to the war effort and isn't nailed down...."

Mo's humorous pronouncement told Lee something else as well. He had indeed been accepted into his two superior officers' confidence. He would have to carefully guard that trust.

"Now," Mo began seriously, "we don't have much time, and we have a lot to do. You'll have to help…a lot."

"I'm in, Mo. How do we ship this stuff, especially the booze?"

"They'll load these crates onto trucks that drive onto the LSTs. If you'll notice, the bottom item on your list says, 'Button up the box.' You any good with a hammer and nails?"

"I helped a neighbor build several garages one summer."

"Good," Mo said. "Scrounge up a hammer and some hefty nails. Restack the booze no higher than necessary, all on the floor if possible. Then secure things and nail it up tight. But remember, it'll get bounced around quite a bit before we're done. Here's the key. Now, *your* pending business. You take two bourbons and a gin over to Sergeant Garner at Fighter Group Supply. Give him this." Mo scribbled out a cryptic note and signed it. "Better scrounge up an old blanket, sheet, or something for a cover now that you're in the corporation."

"But even if I get the tow target, I can't be sure the natives will show up."

"Oh, they'll show up all right. They know everything we're doing. And when we're about to move, they can smell it. They'll show up."

By 0900 hours, Lee had dealt with Sergeant Garner and trudged up the pathway to Fungus Field with his new red silk tow target carefully bundled in an old blanket. The ease with which the Garner transaction had gone astounded Lee. He had simply walked into the supply tent with his three bottles wrapped in the blanket, introduced himself, handed the note and the bundle to the sergeant, and within two minutes walked out with a larger bundle that didn't clink. Fortunately, his tent mates were all out. Lee packed up his few things, then slid his valuable bundle well back under his bunk, and headed back down the trail toward camp. Whether he had connected with Bob or not, it was time to get on with the other duties Mo had assigned.

First, he spread the word on the forthcoming move to all the Gopher pilots and ground crew. In each case he passed on the appropriate instructions for preparation. To Lee's surprise, he got no negative reactions, not even from Greenie, Gus, or Black Bart. It seemed as though they were all excited at the prospect of moving. He pondered that at noon as he ate. He felt that same excitement, but why? After all, they were moving closer to the combat, and they would have to set up camp and learn all the new facets of camp survival all over again. And while Fungus Field was no Ritz Hotel, it might be better than what lay ahead. Yet he could sense the feeling all around him at chow. A new, light but steady buzz, like a friendly electric hum, seemed to hover just above the tables. Then Lee heard the answer to his question from a nearby officer.

"Damn glad we're finally moving," the captain said. "Something to break the boredom."

"Boredom," Lee said softly to himself, "of course." There was often as much waiting as working, especially for the ground pounders, the ground support people. Once their routine work was finished, they had little to do but wait for the cycle to repeat itself. He rechecked his list. Except for the follow-up the next morning, he had finished everything but the corporate crate.

Lee's luck seemed to be holding. When he returned to the tent, it was still empty. Good. Maybe the move thing was keeping his tent mates down on the flight line.

"You trade?"

Lee knew the voice. Just as Mo had predicted, Bob was there with a large collection bundled up in his old cloth. His eyes grew larger and his grin broadened as Lee pulled the target out a foot at a time. By the time Lee had spread the whole target out, Bob bounced from one side to the other, fingering the red silk, holding it up for silent Bill to see.

"You good trade," he said. "No holes?" Winding the end of the target around his mid-section, he added, "Bob rich man—rich man!" Then he reached down and pulled his dirty old cloth open. There lay by far the largest offering he had presented. In addition to three swords, there were four rifles, a pistol, two field glasses, and countless other smaller trophies.

"Good trade, Bob," Lee said. "Help me get this stuff wrapped up before someone comes along."

"You don't like old Coconut Face much do you?" Bob asked as they worked

"Coconut Face?"

"That one traded shirt for bullets." He distorted his face to an unpleasant portrait.

"He's not nice man," Lee said as he wrapped the blanket tightly around his loot.

"Short way to big box?" Bob said.

"Big box?"

"Big box where major boss keep stuff. Come, I show you."

Bob led Lee down a quiet, isolated path, one Lee had never bothered to explore. At one intersection, Bob paused and pointed the direction to Lee.

"Good luck," Bob said, grinning and lightly slapping Lee's butt. "You keep war going long time, okay? Good war. Specially good war." With that he turned and trotted back up the path.

Lee set about reloading the huge crate. With the cases of booze set evenly on the floor, he packed the souvenirs around the edges to cushion the load and help keep it in place. Then he tagged one sword, a rifle, and one field glass for himself, locked the crate and left to find a hammer and nails. He returned shortly and drove sixteen-penny nails through the door into the box where ever there seemed to be room for them. Last, he tacked two large signs on the crate that read:

FRAGILE!
AIRCRAFT INSTRUMENTS
HANDLE WITH CARE

After chow that evening, the officers of the 483rd Fighter Group decided to have a little going away party in the mess tent. From somewhere a mixed case of bourbon and gin appeared. Lee noted that the case didn't match those he had recently handled, so he reasoned that someone else had a system going also. One pilot from the 126th Squadron brought his portable phonograph and the few records he had managed to preserve. The big band offerings were worn and scratchy, but Lee reasoned so was the party and there were no complaints...on anything. The New Bubba seemed determined to wash away the last bonds of fear. He quickly went from interesting—to fascinating—to funny—to flopped out dead drunk in one corner of the tent, oblivious to the hoots and hollers of the party.

The scratchy phonograph gave way to a powerful radio someone from Ops produced, so they found themselves listening to better sounding American dance band music, albeit sandwiched among the sultry propaganda pitches by Tokyo Rose. Some listened. Others completely ignored her. Then there were those who responded angrily.

"That yellow bitch!" one pilot said.

"I'd like to kick her ass from Tokyo to San Quentin!"

"I'd like to catch her in the outhouse with a five hundred pounder!"

"Hell, I'd even bomb her grandmother's shithouse if I could find it," added Burner Hedman.

"Hey! Quiet down!" someone shouted

"Listen up!"

In seconds, the boisterous celebration had closed to a whisper. The radio volume was turned up.

"....and to Major Brandon and his newly formed 125th Squadron at Dobodura, New Guinea...you were *so* fortunate yesterday to have lost only Lieutenants Logan and Callahan. But do come back again so we can get acquainted with the rest of your group."

Chapter 22

At 0930 the next morning, Lee stopped his scurrying about the flight line for a moment to watch the activities. He was impressed. Early that morning, pilots, ground crews, and other support personnel had begun hustling about like ants, each with a job to do and each intent on getting the job done. He plopped his sweaty body down, leaned back against a palm tree, and took a long swig of water from his canteen. Soon, however, he dragged himself up again and headed for his next task.

Contrary to the cooperation shown by the men, however, the weather gods were taking a firm stand against the 483rd Fighter Group's move from Dobodura to Nadzab. By mid-morning the temperature had risen close to one hundred degrees with the humidity pushing one hundred percent. A cluster of ominous clouds had grown steadily since sunrise, and it showed no signs of retreat. Every man on the line had stripped to saturated khakis or shorts and a knife-edged temper. They weren't against the move, nor did they resent the work it entailed. But they did believe they deserved a break in the weather.

Lee had stopped for a moment's rest when Greenie approached.

"You know, don't you, that the major doesn't like to have his executive officer resting while the men work," Greenie said, "especially right after a promotion."

Greenie's jab disappointed Lee, but it didn't surprise him.

"Thanks, Greenie, I'll tell the exec if he should happen to come along here," Lee said.

"Don't give me that," Greenie said. "You're his exec now, and as soon as he can justify another promotion, you'll outrank Gus and me. And that'll be that."

"Not sure you're right about that," Lee responded. "After all, you got your promotion."

"Like hell I did."

Lee felt like he had been blind-sided by a truck.

"Are you saying you *didn't* get captain?" he asked.

"Are you saying I *did?*"

"Well—he didn't exactly say it, but—"

"If you want to survive out here, Lee, you'd better insist that the major *exactly say things.* And he passed Gus by, too. Did you ever read *Faust?*" Greenie turned and headed for his ship, leaving Lee to ponder the question.

Lee thought for a moment about the implications of Greenie's statement, but he couldn't recall enough about *Faust* to decode the message. His best recollection was of someone making a deal with the devil. He clamored to his feet and started down the line to see how the ground crews were doing at dismantling their scaffolds. The literary puzzle could come later.

"Lee! Lee!" It was Bubba, hurrying to catch up. When Lee looked into his friend's eyes he expected him to bleed to death. His hair, customarily well placed, pointed in every direction like bent straws in a broom. His skin sported a pallor that suggested anemia. And as he drew closer, Lee knew Bubba had recently puked.

"Well, Bubba, welcome to the brave new world!" Lee said, smiling at his protégé. "Is this truly a better world than the old one?"

"Okay, okay," groused Bubba. "Please, I need your help."

"I don't do hangovers," Lee chided.

"Oh, come on, Lee," said Bubba, "I need to find that Jones guy to do the nose art on my new ship before we leave."

"Ohhh, Bubba," Lee said, "we don't have time to mess with that now. By the time you find him and get him up here, we'll be starting engines."

"I won't hold us up," Bubba insisted. "If it isn't done, I'll just leave when I have to. But at least, can I have a chance? Tell me where to find him?

"Okay. He's Corporal Jones. He's down the line with one of the bomb groups. I don't remember which. But he won't even have a scaffold. They're all torn apart for shipping."

"Thanks, Lee!" Bubba said as he headed down the line, half-trotting and half-walking.

Lee rejoined his ground crew in time to help Big Ole and Mashy lift the heavy bundles of scaffolding pipes up into a canvas covered army truck. Little Mac stood by helplessly. The weight of the pipes and the height of the truck bed combined to severely challenge a small worker such as little Mac.

"Lieutenant," said Mashy, "do me a big favor?"

"If I can," Lee responded.

"Could you finagle some excuse for me to go with Big Ole in the Gooneybird?"

"You'd rather get to Nadzab sooner so you can get in on more work?"

"Well, I hadn't exactly thought about it that way, sir," said Mashy. "I just don't want to ride that slow LST for twenty-four hours. You know what LST stands for, don't you?"

"I think it's Landing Ship—Tank," Lee said.

"Oh, no. It's Long Slow Target. I just hope they use some of them mirage balloons."

Lee winked at Big Ole. As usual, Ole's large-billed baseball cap was twisted off center and his face sported several grease smudges. Big Ole just looked at Lee, but his eyes said, "No."

"Tell you what, Mashy. I'll think about it, but don't get your hopes up. Okay?"

A few minutes later, Big Ole caught Lee off to one side and explained his reasoning.

"We need both them guys to watch our stuff on the ship. If we don't, it'll get stolen for sure. I guarantee it," the big crew chief said.

Lee passed the logic on to Mashy and stressed the importance of guarding their equipment and tools.

"Yeah, that's what the Chief said, too," Mashy responded. "I'll just have to find me a barf bucket, I guess. I bet I'll lose ten pounds from Buna to Lae." He turned his dark eyes and pathetic look into a last ditch appeal.

"Sorry, Mashy," Lee said. "Tell you what. We'll weigh you now and again at Nadzab. For every pound more than five that you lose, I'll give *you* five bucks. For every pound less than five that you lose, you give *me* five bucks."

"How irrigant do you think I am?" Mashy said with a laugh. "Are you sure you wouldn't like to join us on this wonderful cruise? The casino will be rumbling and I'm told the quizzing is excellent."

"I hope you win a bundle," said Lee with a smile, "but you be sure one of you is around those trucks *at all times.*"

Lee worked his way down the line, checking off items as they were loaded. When he got to Gus he felt compelled to mention the promotion business, to try to explain something—he wasn't even sure what.

"Hey, Lee," Gus said reassuringly, "you remember? I predicted this. It's okay. It's the way Major Brennan works, and I've known that for five months now. And it isn't all bad. He gets a lot more done *his* way than anyone could doing things the *right* way."

"Just the same, Gus," said Lee, "I'll tell you this—and you can count on it—I won't accept captain's bars unless you have yours."

"I guess that doesn't surprise me." Gus smiled and shook Lee's hand. "Does that go for Greenie, too?"

"Not as willingly, but yes."

"I'll tell him. It'll help him get past this," Gus said.

The rest of the packing and loading went smoothly, and at 0145, the trucks left for the coast, the Gophers started their engines, and the thunder, lightning, and rain exploded with the ferocity of an artillery battle. The squadron taxied single-file to where Mo was about to turn onto the active runway. At that point, the torrent increased and the visibility decreased. Lee could barely make out Mo's ship only two spots ahead of him in line. He heard Mo on the radio to control asking for info on the weather. Unless they could be assured of better weather ahead, they couldn't take off. They would never find their way back down again.

As Lee sat waiting in the steamy cockpit, he watched the engine temperature gauges. Idling endlessly on such a hot, humid day presented the challenge of keeping the engines from overheating. After ten minutes, the rain let up. Control promised broken clouds and scattered storm cells ahead, with good visibility at Finschafen as an alternate, so Mo gave the order.

They formed up at 10,000 feet and headed for the coast where the clouds were less thick. Once over the coast, they turned left to a heading of three-one-zero, parallel to the coast. As they drew closer to the north coast of the Huon Gulf, Mo took them down to 5,000 feet and turned almost due west to find the mouth of the Markham River. It was turning into one of the longest short flights Lee had ever made. And the weather ahead appeared to be even thicker than that they had left behind.

With Mo in the lead, they tried several times to get through apparent openings in the front, only to find themselves boxed in by the ugly, black cloud formations. Finally, they dropped down on the deck and sneaked up the Markham River Valley at 700 feet, frequently bumped about by the turbulence above them. The rain was spotty, a light drizzle here and a deluge there. Lee felt a tension headache building. Mo ordered a change in radio frequency.

"Nadzab Control, this is Gopher Leader," came over Lee's radio. "I have ten birds coming in from the south at seven hundred angels. We need a nest."

"Gopher Leader, we have you on radar," came the reply. "You are on line and cleared for straight-in approach. We have PSP matting down, but it's soupy on top. You'll follow a jeep left at the end of the runway."

"Roger, Nadzab Control. Gophers, string it out. Drop back as far as you can and still see the bird in front of you. You heard him. It's soupy. Keep your nose wheel up off the mats as long as you can."

It was a blind "follow the leader" game. It would work if no one screwed up. Lee followed Bubba move for move, noting the exact spot where he set his Lightning on the perforated steel matting.

He saw the splashing rooster tails of water from Bubba's wheels stop, but it didn't register. Suddenly he realized that Bubba had stopped almost dead center in the runway. Lee's judgment quickly ruled out any possibility of setting down early and stopping before he reached Bubba. Was there room to go in over Bubba, set down, and stop in front of him? With such poor visibility Lee couldn't see the end of the runway. Bad choice! Jockeying his throttles, Lee tried to slow his approach without stalling, but a decision had to be made. Abort!

He rammed in full power and pulled up his gear. His P-38 cleared Bubba's by fifty feet. He reached for his throat mike.

"Red Three going around." he called. "Red Two is dead on the runway."

Lee climbed to five hundred feet and began his first left turn for the go-around. As he paralleled the strip on his downwind leg he would have to count the P-38s coming from the opposite direction. A long, downwind leg would be necessary to avoid cutting in on the last of the approaching planes. He saw Bubba's ship turn off the runway onto the taxiway.

"I'm Three," Lee said aloud. "There went Four, Five, Six, Seven, Eight. Here comes Nine…Ten…"

But he couldn't find Eleven and Twelve. He was far past the strip and should be turning base leg, but where were Eleven and Twelve? Just as he reached for his mike switch the answer came. There were no Eleven and Twelve. With Robert and Cal gone, Gopher Squadron presently numbered only ten ships.

Lee knew he had to make this good. All the others were now following him. The pounding of his heart now rivaled the pounding in his head. He turned base leg and almost immediately turned again on final. The heavy rain turned his view through his windscreen into a blurry, undefined scenario. Then, ahead and slightly to his left appeared the runway. He made the necessary adjustments, dropped his landing gear and full flaps, and picked a spot farther up the runway from Bubba's choice. He had to avoid whatever Bubba had tangled with.

"Lead plane, Gopher Squadron, go around again," crackled the static-filled radio. "We've got damaged matting to repair."

"Roger. Gophers, go around again," Lee responded.

By the time the "all-clear" came after his fourth pass, he was feeling even more tired and tense, but he had the familiarity gained through the previous passes. He dropped his gear and flaps, then picked his spot. He cut the throttles, flared, and felt his mains settle into the juicy mud. But he held his nose high until it had to come down for lack of speed. The whooshing noise from the water-covered matting suddenly changed to familiar vibrations and Lee knew he had outrun the flooded portion of the matting. He applied his brakes gently and felt the huge craft begin to slow. He hoped Sandy had maintained a large enough interval, imagining for a moment the terrible sound of Sandy's props tearing into his tail section.

With Mo and Bubba far out of the picture, another FOLLOW ME jeep had pulled in to pick up Lee, and he followed it until he was finally guided into his parking slot on the line. He swirled the big ship around in the mud and halted. The nose bounced up and down on the nose gear shock absorber for a couple of seconds.

Breathing a sigh of relief, he cut the engines and simply sat there, grateful for two things. One, he was safely down, and two, he hadn't put out the radio call for Numbers Eleven and Twelve. Any aspirations for leadership would have splashed into the mud with that call. Finally, he proceeded with his post-flight check. Then he simply sat there listening to the rain pattering steadily on the Plexiglass canopy while the remaining Gophers taxied up. Minutes later he saw a canvas-covered truck drive slowly up the line, stopping at each Lightning to pick up its pilot.

When the Gophers had gathered under the thatched roof of the Ops shack, Mo Brennan called them to order. Although he was as thoroughly soaked as the rest, he smiled as he surveyed the exhausted pilots. Lee decided that Mo Brennan had nerves of steel or he was one hell of an actor.

"Okay, Gophers," Mo began. "Good news for you. Because of inclement weather we've been assured that the Japs have canceled all air raids scheduled for this base today."

"Wow!" came a voice from the back.

"Oh, no, I hear one up there right now," said another.

Mo's smile broadened. "Considering the elements, you did a hell of a job getting in here! We've sent the Goose and the Gooney over to Finschafen to wait it out. We wouldn't want to lose our crew chiefs and our toothbrushes." He grinned that Mo Brennan grin and took a drag on his cigarette. "I'll have Sergeant Worley check the ships thoroughly in the morning. We know that Bubba has a sprained ankle on his. A piece of matting came loose and bent his right main gear. Anything else you want to call their attention to, list it here on this clipboard.

"Now," Mo continued, "you have no personal gear, and it's really too wet to check out bedding and stuff from Supply, so Sergeant—what's your name again, Sergeant?"

"Frank, sir, Sergeant Frank."

"Sergeant Frank will lead us over to the mess tent for early chow. Then we'll just kill a little time to let this weather blow over so the other two ships can get in."

Lee picked up the sound of distant engines far to the south. As the radials grew closer and louder, he decided it was a B-24, likely on three engines. All conversation stopped and all heads turned to the south, silently tracking the approach of the disabled bomber. The engines suddenly accelerated to a loud roar. Then came a loud *Thump! Thump!* and the engines stopped. Then followed a sound Lee had never before heard, a grinding, metallic sound that seemed to be wrapped in a giant, ongoing ocean wave. The weird combination gradually slowed and faded away.

Lee and the other pilots knew what had happened. The B-24 had crashed on or near the airstrip, bouncing twice and then sliding for some distance before it stop—*Whumppp!*

"Oh, no-o-o," someone groaned.

Lee felt his stomach knot up at the sound of the exploding aircraft. He could only hope that the crew got out. Unfortunately the interval of time between the end of the slide and the explosion seemed too short, much too short for any escape.

After a full minute of silence, Mo said, "Okay, Gophers, there's nothing we can do to help those guys. The well just went dry for them. Let's go eat."

"Eat?" Someone asked.

Chapter 23

Word quickly filtered up through the rain that the crash of the crippled B-24 had killed all ten crewmen. As the storm began to relent, bombers and transport planes came rushing home to Nadzab from various directions. But Lee found himself tensing up. The sound of each approaching aircraft captured his attention, and he involuntarily tracked its sound to the conclusion of its landing as though to guide it safely past the point of disaster.

The numbers bounced about in Lee's head. One bomber down—ten men dead. One Lightning down—one man dead. The comparison, macabre as it was, brought Lee at least a slight relief. While he shared some responsibility for every man in the squadron, only two men would have died had he piled into Bubba that afternoon.

By 1800 hours the storm had drifted off and the tropical sun had rushed in to burn off the storm's residue. The humidity had been high at Dobo that morning, but the post-storm atmosphere at Nadzab was beyond humid—it was steamy. Lee felt fortunate that he had acquired two pairs of engineer boots. He had cut the tops down to about eight inches to speed up drying time. But until his B-4 bag arrived with his dry spares, he would have to squish around in the soggy ones. He needed to add a pair of tie-on boots that he might keep dry for flying.

The Golden Goose and the Gooneybird came in together at 1815 hours. At Mo's direction, Lee had lined up two trucks. One hauled the pilots' personal gear to their tents, while the other delivered the crew chiefs and their gear to the tent section for enlisted men.

In contrast to Dobodura, the base at Nadzab had been built on a huge expanse of open, flatland nestled between two mountain ranges and just above the convergence of two rivers, the Erap and the Markham. The gentle Markham traveled many miles down its valley from the northwest and curled around the base on the west and south sides. Between storms, the Markham shrank to only a trickling stream. But at the southeast corner of the base it was joined by the fierce, muddy Erap River, which originated in the high Finnisterre Mountains just east of the base. The combined flow then headed south down the forty miles to the Huon Gulf at Lae.

Nadzab and the flat valley that surrounded it had been swiftly and easily captured in the first large-scale paratrooper assault of the Pacific campaign in September of 1943. Except for the native village, there had been little there but a huge blanket of tall kunai grass. Since the enemy had seen no reason to view Nadzab as a target, they were caught totally unprepared to defend it.

The Army Engineers had gone to work immediately to convert the land into a huge airbase with five airstrips. While the new base had to have been an attractive target to the Japanese air forces, it had the advantage of its location behind a screen of advanced Allied bases. Enemy aircraft had to fly over or near several American bases to get at Nadzab, so their visits, except for Charlie, had been infrequent. It had been months since the last heavy air attack.

The village of Nadzab lay in the Y formed by the confluence of the two rivers and downstream from the American base. Farther to the east, the Royal Australian Air Force's Newton Airstrip, which was actually two 6000-foot strips, had been built in only twenty-seven days, a phenomenal engineering achievement.

Nadzab consisted of three parallel airstrips laid out east to west, with Number One in the center, flanked by Number Three on the north, and Number Two on the south. Between Number Two and the Markham River lay an orderly community of fifty-six pyramid tents serviced by a well-planned network of roads and lanes. East of the tents sat the Operations, Intelligence, and Orderly shacks for the three squadrons of the 483rd Fighter Group. The mess halls for enlisted men and officers, wooden structures with corrugated steel roofs, had been constructed to the west of the tent community. Two large hospital tents stood on the north side of the base, along with another tent city and appropriate command buildings.

The truck in which Lee rode wound its way through the village of tents, turned down a short lane, and stopped. Lee noted that the Mo Brennan magic apparently had worked again. The six large, new tents, three on each side of the wide lane, were assigned to the pilots of the three squadrons of the 483rd Fighter Group. The tents had solid, well-constructed though rough mahogany floors built about two feet above ground level, and their canvas looked fresh out of the box. The Gophers felt as if they were moving into their own luxurious, new apartments, and the move up in neighborhoods gave an immediate lift to their spirits.

Mo had, at Lee's suggestion, issued the order that the nine Gophers draw straws for their tent assignments. Until their two replacements arrived, that meant five men in one tent and four in the other. Mo wanted the two replacements to fill the additional two beds in the four-man aggregation so the two newcomers would have each other for support. Lee conducted the drawing, confident that he would be free at last. The odds said he couldn't get stuck with Black Bart again. Reluctantly, he jotted down the results to take back to Mo, anticipating some flak from his superior.

TENT ONE	TENT TWO
Gus	Sandy Sadler
Greenie	Bubba Nash
Burner Hedman	Bart Barton
Chub Forbes	Lee Marks
Smokey Stover	--------
--------	--------

Lee could only laugh sardonically as he stuffed the slip into his shirt pocket. Not only had he drawn Black Bart but he would also have Bubba in the mix yet again. In fact, with Sandy also in the tent, the mismatched foursome from Dobodura had somehow remained intact. He had been tempted to use the Mo Brennan approach to the problem, simply assign the men and then get Mo to approve it. But at the last minute, he had decided to apply short straw democracy. Never again, he vowed. Anyway, he reasoned, it might be interesting to see how the new Bubba related to the old Bart.

With his gear stowed in the tent, Lee walked the short distance to Ops, to the east of the tents. Mo and Colonel Sledge Hammer were huddled in one corner when Lee approached.

"Hey, Killer!" Mo greeted. "How did the democratic process work out?"

"Let me guess," said Colonel Hammer. "It backfired on you."

Lee could only grin and nod. "I should have been more devious."

"I told you that," said Mo, "but you had to try it your way. Are the men getting settled in? Like your new houses?"

"Great. My refrigerator doesn't hold its temperature very well, though."

"I'll get somebody right on it," Colonel Hammer said, straight-faced.

"It's nice to have dry boots for a change," Lee offered. "When will the crates be in, some time tomorrow?"

"Tomorrow afternoon at the earliest," Mo said. "We've been trying to come up with a good place to park them. There doesn't seem to be much privacy anywhere on this base. It's like trying to hide something in the town square."

"You'd think that somewhere around here there ought to be a huge storage area to accommodate all the different groups that are here," said the colonel. "It'd seem to me that the best place would be right in among them. That way, there would be people coming and going all the time, carrying things in, carrying things out. Of course, there's something to be said for a number of smaller storage areas, too. At least one bomb couldn't take them all out." He paused. "Anyway, it's your problem, not mine. Lee, take the jeep and go look around. And while you're at it, you two had better check on your flight line. See that you could get airborne if you had to."

"Good idea," said Mo. "Come on, Lee. Let's take a tour. You drive."

They piled into the headquarters jeep. Lee jerked it violently when he engaged the clutch.

Mo seemed unfazed. He sat lazily sprawled in the right-hand seat, half in and half out of the vehicle, his cigarette hand dangling over the side.

"Sorry," Lee said with a laugh. "If I forget to retract the gear, let me know."

"Since you're flying so low, just be careful how you hit those puddles," Mo countered.

"Oops!" said Lee, slamming on the brakes. "I wonder if I should have turned there."

"Here, let's take a look at this," Mo said.

He reached into a shirt pocket, extracted a piece of paper, unfolded it, and held it up before Lee. Someone had very hastily sketched a map of the base. One glance told Lee he had seen but a portion of the sprawling base. Coming in during the storm, he'd concentrated on only one landing strip and had seen nothing of the rest of the huge complex.

Nadzab was unique in that the base was built completely by the U.S. Army Engineers, whereas most Allied bases in New Guinea were captured from the Japanese and then expanded to suit the needs of the Allies. The runways, tents, thatched-roof pole structures, and steel-roofed buildings of the base were carefully laid out within the network of roads and lanes. Trenches and ditches had been dug to improve the drainage while providing air raid protection.

Lee and Mo explored the roads surrounding Strip Number Two. They had completely circled the strip when Mo pointed to a natural clearing just south of the row of 483rd tents. "I think that's what we're looking for, Lee," he said. "Buzz over there. Let's take a look."

Lee knew immediately they had found the spot for the storage crates, a small and isolated spot south of everything else, truly out in the suburbs, and just large enough for the storage crates. He jerked to a stop and they sat for a moment studying the layout.

"Not in a general storage area like the colonel wanted, but I think it'll work out nicely. It's really more like we had in Dobo, don't you think?" Mo asked.

"Did the Dobo layout cause you any problems?"

"No. We just had to watch carefully and be a little more discreet, that's all," Mo said. He got out and walked the area. "This is the spot, all right, and it's right behind your tents. Great to keep an eye on it." Then he rejoined Lee in the jeep.

"Do you have the inventory list with you?" Lee asked.

"Right here in my pocket," Mo replied. "Why?"

"Well…I have an idea. Thought I'd run it by you," Lee said. "How many Jap swords do we have?"

"Ahhh," Mo counted, "Twelve. Got twelve of them."

"And how many daggers?"

"Looks like ten. Why?"

"Anything else that you have eight or more?"

"Well—yes. We've got nine field glasses—seven flags." Mo turned and looked directly at Lee. "What the hell are you cooking up?"

"Try this on," began Lee, "each Gopher who's made Ace gets field glasses as a sort of in-house trophy. When he gets to ten—double ace—he gets a dagger. And when he gets to fifteen, he gets a sword. Then, if he reaches twenty…he gets your tent."

"Damned good idea, Lee! I'll just have to watch, and when a guy gets to nineteen he's grounded. You know, I think you're beginning to catch on. That's good. Corporate perks—that's good."

"Thanks. But there's still one problem I've got to solve to make it work," said Lee. "If these guys leave those trophies with their gear in the tents, the stuff will disappear for sure. Yet, we can't give them access to the corporate crate. Got an answer?"

"No problem, Lee. We'll just have to, uhh, *acquire* another crate to use as the squadron vault. If they want, they can tag their stuff and we'll lock it up for them. I'll have Sergeant Jernigan check the incoming shipments and get us a crate as soon as one empties."

When Lee and Mo reported back to Colonel Hammer, Mo relayed Lee's idea for corporate perks. Later, as Lee was leaving, Mo pulled him aside.

"Sorry, Lee, I should have seen that coming," Mo said.

"Yeah," Lee said with a laugh, "*you* should have known better. I'm too green to handle that stuff right, but you aren't."

"Oh, well," consoled Mo, "Sledge is right. If we're going to give Fighter Group trophies to aces in the 125th, we really can't exclude the aces of the 126th and 127th. But it's going to put a hell of a stress on our inventory. We're going to have to do some serious trading. You know, it's possible these natives around Nadzab are all traded out. It could be they've already recovered every Jap souvenir within fifty miles."

"Now, that's something I might have said," countered Lee. "But my CO, who's the master trader would say, 'Don't worry. There have to still be some Japs around. And these natives know exactly where they are. And those Japs don't have a chance. They'll disappear one by one."

"Damn, but you're catching on fast!"

A quick drive past the Gopher Lightnings showed everything as orderly as could be expected. Only the crew chiefs tended the aircraft with the small sets of emergency tools they had brought along. Clearly, it was only tinker time. But Sergeant Worley assured Mo and Lee that all ships were fueled, armed, and ready for quick take-off if necessary.

Mo dropped Lee at an intersection and then scooted off headed toward his own tent. As Lee walked down the short lane on which he now lived, he picked up voices, familiar and angry voices.

"Look, damn it!" bellowed Black Bart. "I really don't give a shit if you like it or not."

"I'm not afraid of you," shouted Bubba. "Those days are over. You got it? Over!"

Lee eased up behind the neighboring tent.

"Shssh!" hissed a voice close beside Lee from inside the tent.

Lee turned and through the mosquito netting he saw Smokey sprawled on his cot, a finger to his lips, a twinkle in his eyes. Then Lee realized that all five occupants of the tent were amused spectators to the brewing battle next door.

"Okay, Little Boy," said Bart. "If you're done now, why don't you just pick up your marbles and go home?"

"Why you—"

Bubba came up off his cot like a rocket. He took a mighty swing at Bart. Bart simply ducked the blow and retaliated with a right fist to Bubba's jaw. The gangly lieutenant with the new found courage went sprawling over an empty cot. He slid off the cot and thumped to the floor where he sat, rubbing his jaw and staring angrily at Black Bart.

Lee felt the heat rising within. Certainly, Bubba had asked for it. But Lee knew that if he didn't do something about the perpetual feud, he and Sandy were in for a miserable home life.

"I—I guess it's time," Lee said to nobody in particular.

"Guess it is," replied Smokey. "Do a good job so we can get some sleep around here."

Lee walked into the tent and headed for Bubba.

"Lee! Did you see what he did?" Bubba asked.

"Shut up!" Lee said, pointing a finger right at Bubba's nose.

"But he—"

"I said, 'Shut up!'"

Lee turned to Black Bart. The incessant troublemaker looked from Bubba to Lee with a pleased grin on his face. Lee recognized the adrenalin shot that came with victory.

"Bart," Lee said quietly, "we've all had enough of your bitching and your agitating, so I'm telling you this—if you want to stay in this tent there'll be no more bitching. There'll be no more agitating. And there'll be no more hands on Bubba or anyone else. Got it?"

"Says you," spouted Bart. "Who the hell do you think you are? Just 'cause you're Brennan's fair-haired boy doesn't mean shit to me. Until you outrank me, you don't give me any orders."

"I'm giving you one now," said Lee, "and it's rather simple. Shut up—permanently!"

Lee caught the telltale sign, a clenched fist, and was ready. When the roundhouse right came, he deflected it with his left arm and followed with a hard right to Black Bart's belly. Spit sprayed as Bart doubled over. Before he could even finish the motion, Lee followed with a crunching left to the side of Bart's face sending him limply to the wooden floor. After a few seconds, Bart rolled over and looked up at Lee. The adrenalin was gone. The arrogance was gone. All that remained was a glazed look that ranked somewhere between surprise and fear.

Lee snatched up Bart's B-4 bag and stepped to the door of the tent.

"Okay, Bart, it's in or out. Quick! In or out!"

Bart said nothing, but he slowly nodded his concession.

A loud chorus of cheers erupted from the surrounding tents.

"Well done!"

"Glad *that's* settled!"

"Remind me not to get *you* mad," called the husky voice of Burner Hedman.

Lee hardly heard the supportive comments. As he rubbed his left hand, his mind bobbled between two scenes. In one, he saw the tough leader of a south Chicago Polish neighborhood gang telling him, "Allus go fer de gut wit' yer *on* hand and go fer de head wit' yer *off* hand. Dat way, you break anything, it'll be yer *off* hand. In the other he saw himself facing Mo, Colonel Hammer, and serious trouble.

Chapter 24

"Lee, I think you've gone and done it now," said Sandy. "He said you should report to him at Ops immediately or sooner!"

"Who? Major Brennan?" Lee asked as he pulled his trousers up.

"You should be so lucky. It was Colonel Hammer," Sandy replied. "I think you're about to find out why he's called Sledge Hammer."

Lee hurriedly pulled his boots on, grabbed for his hat, and bolted from the tent. The eastern sky offered its light gray prelude to sunrise as he hustled along the lane. There were no clouds in the sky, but Lee felt he was headed into a typhoon. As he approached the Ops shack, he tried to organize his responses to the questions he knew were coming, but his mind simply wouldn't focus. When he turned to enter the shack, he heard a voice from behind him.

"Lieutenant Marks! Over here!"

Lee wheeled about and saw Major Brennan and Colonel Hammer standing some distance away in the middle of the road. As he strode toward them, it struck him as odd that they would pick such a strange place to have a meeting. It also struck him that Colonel Hammer's steely eyes may have just come out of the forge.

"Marks," the colonel said bruskly, "are you right-handed?"

"Yes—sir," Lee replied.

"Hold out your right hand."

Unsure of where the confrontation was headed, Lee looked at Mo for some sign. But Mo simply stared past Lee into space. Lee held out his right hand, palm up. Colonel Hammer reached out and turned it over palm down. He examined the knuckles and the back of Lee's hand thoroughly. During the process, Lee slid his tender, bruised left hand slightly behind him.

"Just as I thought," he said gruffly. "Not a mark on it." He looked up at Lee. "Marks, you've been accused of striking a fellow officer. Would you do such a thing?"

"No, sir," Lee said, "except in self defense."

"You hear that, Major Brennan?" Colonel Hammer said. "He *would* do it in self defense!"

"Well, that clarifies everything," Mo said. "Either he didn't do it, or he did it in self defense. Personally, since his hand shows no marks or damage, I'm inclined to believe we were given a false accusation."

Lee tried to sort through his confusion. Then he saw Mo's smiling eyes. Even the glint in Colonel Hammer's eyes had softened. Lee grinned sheepishly.

"Get that goddamned grin off your face, Lieutenant!" the colonel barked. "This is no laughing matter. Now I may have to investigate the incident, and there's nothing funny about that. I've got lots better things to do with my time." Then, lowering his voice, he said to Lee, "You understand what just happened here?"

"Yes, sir."

"Good. You had chow yet?"

"No, Sir."

"Then you'd better get over there. You can't work on an empty stomach."

"Check in with me when you've eaten," Mo said as he turned to walk off with Colonel Hammer.

Lee knew he'd just been granted a reprieve—the *system* at work. But in this case, though the process was corrupt, the outcome served justice. He wondered if he had seen the end of the matter.

He had just attacked his green eggs when Bubba slid in beside him.

"Lee, I got to thank you for what you did last night," Bubba said. "Damn, I wish I could handle myself the way you did!"

Lee chewed, then swallowed and turned to Bubba.

"I haven't the faintest idea what you're talking about," Lee said.

"Last night—when you hit—"

"I think you must be mistaking me for someone else," Lee cut in.

"How could I mistake you for someone—o-h-h-h-h."

Bubba looked at Lee, smiled broadly, nodded his head, and then dug into his breakfast.

"Now," said Lee, "that we agree that I didn't do what you thought you saw me do, I have some excellent advice for you, Bubba. Don't, I repeat, *don't* start fights you can't win. Even more important, don't, I repeat, *don't* start *any* fights until you've had some lessons and a lot of practice at handling yourself. You are no Joe Louis. Do—you—understand?"

"Now that I've seen you do it, I'll bet I can take him—"

"Bubba!" Lee slammed his fork to the table. "What's with you? Just because you finally found some courage you think you can lick the world?"

"Well, not the world...."

"Bubba, courage is important," Lee said, "but it takes more than courage to fight. It takes strength and skill, and you, my friend, score a big, fat zero in both departments. Now, I'm glad for what your experience did for you the other day, but unless you wrap all that newfound courage in some common sense, it's going to get you killed. The kind of courage you're carrying around is really nothing but stupidity." He paused and looked into Bubba's eyes. "Am I getting through to you? Are you listening? Or are you going to have to get killed before you can understand?"

Bubba's eyes seemed to reflect confusion blended with disappointment.

Lee abandoned his project at that point, washed up his mess kit, and headed north to the flight line. There had been some talk about getting the Gopher P-38s into revetments for their protection. He was anxious to see if more had come of the idea. In his ride about the base with Mo he hadn't noticed any unoccupied revetments.

As he puttered about his ship, he kept an eye on the road, watching for the trucks that had come up on the LST. With them would come the other two-thirds of the ground crew personnel, the scaffolding, heavy tools, tractors, and—the crates.

A curious group of people came walking slowly up the road. He had heard of the phenomenon at Dobo, and now, here it was right before him. Four very dark brown native women carried baskets of laundry. Each wore only a white cloth wrapped around her lower abdomen, and each had fully exposed breasts that bounced nicely as she walked. One of the young women was in the advanced stages of pregnancy, but she cheerily walked along carrying her basket in front of her. It appeared to Lee that she was carrying her immense belly in the laundry basket. The women chattered and laughed as they walked. Lee watched as they headed down the lane toward the mess tent.

Curious, Lee caught a passing sergeant and asked about the procession.

"Oh, they come up every day or two, pick up laundry for some of the guys," said the sergeant. "If you want them to wash for you, they're always looking for more customers."

"What's the deal?"

"They wash in the river. They're really kind of hard on the clothes—beat the shit out them on the rocks. You can pay them with most anything, but it's best to make the deal in advance. Some of the things they really like are old clothes, spools of thread, matches, and cartons of cigs for their men. They're really pretty nice people," said the sergeant. "Only speak a few words of English. A couple of the men learned pretty good English from the missionaries. They're the straw bosses for two of the work crews. One crew works on roads for the engineers and the other does odd jobs, loading and unloading stuff mostly. Some of the women work at the hospitals."

"And they're all friendly?" asked Lee.

"Oh, they don't take scalps or collect heads, if that's what you mean. Most of those bad guys live high up in the central mountains. The ones from the village are very friendly. Many of them work on the base. We do get some visitors from out in the jungle. They're not quite so predictable, but most of them are okay, too. They come in to trade souvenirs like woven bags, tooth-and-shell necklaces, and war clubs. Sometimes they have some Jap stuff, you know, swords, flags, helmets, stuff like that."

Lee listened carefully. He was learning valuable things for the corporate operations. It sounded like the out-of-towners were the natives he needed most to reach.

"And what do they all treasure the most?" Lee asked, suspecting he already knew the answer.

"G.I. clothes, matches, tools, things they can use for fishing, like hand grenades."

"Hand grenades?" Lee asked.

"Yeah. Our guys taught 'em that one. Drop the grenade into the water and *Pooom!* Then go out and scoop up all the dead or stunned fish. These guys were pretty smart. The grenade fishing didn't work too well in the river because it flowed by too fast. So downstream a couple of miles, they dug two canals into low-lying areas, you know, kind of created their own backwater ponds. Every few days they drop a couple of grenades in."

"And we don't get nervous—these natives running around among us with hand grenades?" Lee asked.

"Nah," the sergeant said with a wide grin on his face. "They like us, almost *need* us. Now that we've run the Japs off, this war's the best thing they could ask for. Hell, in four months we've advanced their world more than they had in the last 4,000 years."

The comment reminded Lee of something Bob had said as they parted in Dobodura.

"But I wouldn't mess with their women," the sergeant went on. "Some of the tribes are pretty loose about sharing, but some of them draw a hard and fast line there. Can never be too sure which ones. By the way, did you hear about the nurses?"

"Nurses?" Lee asked.

"Yeah. We finally got some real live nurses. They're over at the main hospital. Anyway, they decided one day that it really wasn't too cool to have their native helpers shaking their bare boobs in the patients' faces. They figured those poor guys have enough frustration without that. So each of the nurses went through her B-4 bag, and that night they sent each of the helpers home with a bra. You know, brassiere?" he said, motioning across his chest. Then he stopped and laughed. "And the next morning their helpers came to work at the hospital—wearing the bras round their waists and using them for pockets! Hey, Lieutenant, I gotta go!" The sergeant took off at a fast pace toward the enlisted men's camp.

The trucks arrived that afternoon at 1430 hours. Mashy looked surprisingly good.

"You look pretty bright for a seasick land bird," Lee said.

"You know what, Lieutenant? I was so busy raking in the money, I forgot to get sick. In fact, I've found a cure for sea sickness—called poker. Should have been there. Hell of a cruise!"

Lee left the ground crew to unload and set up the flight line equipment. He jumped into one of the two trucks carrying the crates and pointed the way to the secluded spot he and Mo had discovered. He had already arranged for an engineer to be there with a bulldozer for unloading. In no time the crates were off the trucks and lined up so that the doors faced away from the base toward a large clump of trees and the Markham River.

When the work crew was gone, Lee checked the corporate crate. Everything made it. No breakage. But there, lying on a case of Scotch was something new, something he'd not seen before, a sign that said, KILROY WAS HERE. As he restacked the booze and sorted the trophies into groups he rechecked the inventory. Nothing missing. He locked up and dragged a huge tarp over the crate. He felt enthused about his award system. He couldn't wait to inaugurate it. It had to go over big. How could anyone object to free war trophies they hadn't expected?

After evening chow, Lee huddled in Ops with Mo and Colonel Hammer. Lee tossed his slip bearing the names and numbers of Ace Award winners among the Gophers onto the table. Captains Robesky and Bryant had previously submitted those from the 126th and 127th Squadrons.

"Damn it, Mo," said the colonel. "Look at this—just look at the differences! Your guys have four aces, three doubles, and a triple. Hollings Bryant and the 126th have three aces and one double. Dick Robesky's 127th has four aces and one double. Hell, you guys have more aces than the other two squadrons combined." He pursed his lips and shook his head slowly. "Do you two give lessons?"

Lee and Mo merely looked at each other and smiled.

"Speaking of lessons…." The colonel lit a cigarette and took a swig of his coffee. "Lee, you're about to be approached by Barton."

"Ohhh, not again!" Lee groaned.

"It's not like that. He's going to apologize and ask for your help—exactly that—lessons."

"He's *what?*"

"That's right, an apology and a plea for help. Can you handle that?"

"Well, sure I can," Lee said. "But I'll have to see it to believe it."

"Oh, you're going to see it all right. And if he doesn't have his tail all the way between his legs, I want to know about it immediately," Colonel Hammer said. "You follow?"

"I follow."

"And if he's anything less than cooperative, you just remind him that he's to cooperate or finish the war unloading trucks and digging latrines. Those are the terms I've laid on him."

"I'll do everything I can, Colonel. But Black Bart *change?*" Lee rolled his eyes.

"Well," said Mo, "we've set it up for you, but I have to agree it's a hell of a challenge."

Lee made it a busy day. He worked with his ground crew on The Marksman. He took on some administrative chores for Mo. That evening, as he headed for the tent to turn in, he stepped into the mess for a quick cup of coffee. The cavernous building was nearly empty. He picked a solitary spot and sat down. After recounting the activities of the day, he spent several minutes thinking ahead to the next day. Mo had said they were scheduled for another escort mission to Kavieng.

When Lee recalled their previous mission to Kavieng, Robert and Cal popped into his consciousness. He wondered how they were doing. Then it struck him that they might not even be alive. The Japs frequently executed captured pilots once they determined they would get no further information from them. Ugly thoughts of torture ran through his mind. Perhaps his friends would be better off dead. He tried to convince himself that they *were* better off dead. And that prospect seemed most likely, given the Japanese attitude toward captured enemies and the fact that many of the isolated Japanese troops were already on starvation diets.

"No, Dick, it's not the *idea* that I'm against," said a hushed voice from the table behind Lee. "In fact, it's really a pretty good idea. Might help a little with morale."

Lee peeked over his shoulder. Apparently, while he had been deep in thought, the commanding officers of the other two squadrons within the 483rd Fighter Group had seated themselves a couple of tables over with their backs to him. He remembered Captain Dick Robesky of the 127th Bobcat Squadron, the officer he had met on the flight from Townsville. The other captain he knew to be Hollings Bryant, CO of the 126th Pony Squadron. Bryant was a skinny, little man who carried himself like an accountant.

It was Captain Bryant who was speaking. "It's the *way* he does things like a back alley hoodlum that bothers me," said Captain Bryant. "Well, that and the fact that he and Sledge are thick as thieves."

Robesky laughed softly. "Hollings, they *are* thieves. Does that bother you? Have they done anything to directly hurt you or your men?"

"Well, yes," answered Bryant. "He makes my guys look bad. I've got a whole bunch of experienced pilots who've been around for some time. They've paid their dues and they're giving all they've got. But all this emphasis on Jap planes shot down. Hell, Dick, you know it as well as I do. Sledge gives him the assignments that get Zeros and Betties, while you and I are down doing ground attack on shipping, damned dangerous work by the way."

Lee felt the creepie crawlies under his shirt. He wished he could simply evaporate. Sooner or later Captain Robesky would turn around and realize that Lee was hearing their conversation. Carefully he slid off the bench and slipped out through the nearest exit.

Chapter 25

"Gus says that when I call a squadron meeting it's always for something bad," Mo said to open the morning meeting of Gopher Squadron.

Lee doubted that Gus had ever said such a thing. He looked over at his friend. Gus sat bent over on a box, staring at the ground, and ever so slightly shaking his head.

"Well, this meeting is not about bad news," Mo went on. "Sledge and I were chatting the other day, trying to think of things we haven't done for you guys. In walks Lee with an idea—and we think it's a great idea." He paused and smiled in Lee's direction. "You may already know that some of us get pretty heavily involved in the trading circuit, partly for something to do and partly because it's about the only way out here to get the things we need. So, Lee's idea is to use some of those things we come upon for a reward system that he devised. I call it 'corporate perks.'" Mo went on to explain the awards for ace, double-ace, and triple-ace.

Lee watched the pilots for their reactions. While nobody jumped up and down with excitement, they did seem enthusiastic about the system. Of course, with six of the present ten squadron members eligible for awards, Lee wouldn't have expected a negative response. He stepped up to help Mo with the presentations.

"And the eight who have qualified as ace are now inducted into the Order of the Glasses," Mo said. "To them we offer the just rewards." Lee distributed Japanese field glasses to Gus, Greenie, Burner, Sandy, Robert, Smokey, Mo, and himself.

The presentation triggered a round of cheers, compliments, and applause that validated Lee's idea. He was glad he had followed through on it.

"To the double-aces who are now members of the Order of the Dagger...." Lee presented daggers to Gus, Greenie, Mo, and himself. The response seemed even louder to Lee. Then he picked up the sword from the table behind him and stepped forward.

"There aren't many in the whole Army Air Force," Lee said to the group, "who would qualify for our Order of the Sword, but our CO is one of them." He turned, handed the officers' sword with its ornate scabbard to Mo, and then added a sweeping bow gesture as the pilots applauded loudly.

"Thanks, Lee," Mo said with a warm smile. He admired the sword for a moment, then placed it back on the table and turned to the group. "I think this is a good moment, not because I got three prizes, but because we've started something good." His eyes swept over the group. "And it is my wish, my hope, my goal to see every man in this squadron looking at me through Jap field glasses. And we're going to do everything we can to make that happen. But when you've all earned daggers, I'll have to say, 'Be careful with those things, they're sharp!'"

The group laughed. Then Lee explained that within a day or two they hoped to have a relatively secure place to keep their treasures if they preferred not to chance storing them with their personal things in the tents.

"Okay," said Mo, "it's back to work. We're on for escort to Kavieng at 1100 hours. I got us assigned to high escort over the B-25s. It could be a milk run, but over Kavieng, it's more likely to be a wild one. We'll be the second attack group today, so there'll be no element of surprise. And there'll be another group after us. The brass is really socking it to Kavieng for a few days to soften them up. I won't go into any more detail than that. You don't want to know."

No, Lee thought, it's better for captive pilots to know nothing of the Allies' planning.

"If we get the B-25s through without too much trouble, and if Duckbutt, the radar picket destroyer, gives them the "all clear" for the trip home, we'll go down and try to put some frosting on the cake. If we do, look for: one—gun installations, two—aircraft, and three—other fixtures, in that order. We want to do lots of damage, but most important we want to make it easier and safer for the third group to go in. Most of you are armed with armor piercing, no tracers. But I'm having Smokey and Bart stay with tracers for now. There's a chance of some weather on the way home. Get some coffee and do what you have to do. I'll see you on the flight line at 1015 hours. Remember, keep your head on a swivel."

He turned to leave, then stopped. "Oh, one other thing. This will be your first flight out of Nadzab. Since you didn't get to see it when we flew in here, make it a point to study the layout after take-off. Since we've got to get altitude to clear the Finnestere Mountains anyway, we'll rendezvous at 10,000 angels just east of the base. That'll give you some climbing circles to look things over. If we should come home in another storm, you'll be glad you did."

An hour later, the Gopher pilots began collecting around a makeshift table at the near end of the squadron flight line. It was too early to begin flight preparations, but there was insufficient time to become involved in anything else.

"They say that when you're getting close to the battle fatigue line, you begin to feel like the cockpit's closing in on you," Burner Hedman was saying as Lee joined the group. "I got a chance to crawl into the cockpit of a captured ME-109 once. Now that's a goddamned small cockpit, I'll tell you. I was so crowded I had to climb out on the wing to find room to think."

"What I want to know," replied Sandy, "for the first time in your life you began to think. Why'd you quit?"

"Okay, wise guy," Burner retorted, "I just hope you have enough sense to look for a place to land when the rubber bands break and your propellers stop turning."

"At least I don't have to get so close to a Betty that I can smell the tail gunner's bad breath before I remember to shoot."

Lee enjoyed their verbal jousting. Done in a friendly tone, their barbs had none of the poison of a Black Bart comment. Most of the squadron mates engaged in such kidding, but they usually sat back as spectators when the sharp minds and tongues of Sandy Sadler and Burner Hedman began another friendly duel. The crisp dialogue had begun to slow when a third voice abruptly changed the tone.

"I wonder what's happened to Robert and Cal," said Smokey Stover.

"Not a good time to think about them," mumbled Chub Forbes.

"I disagree," said Smokey. "I think they deserve our thoughts, *especially* right before a mission. And if we think about what happened, or might have happened to them, we just might be a little sharper."

"Okay!" called Mo Brennan as he strode past. "Time to mount up and head 'em out. Remember—"

"Head on a swivel," the group chorused in unison.

The launch into this Kavieng mission contrasted with the previous sortie out of Dobodura. With the high, rugged Finnestere Mountains just east of the Nadzab base, eastbound flights were forced to climb rapidly in a spiral pattern to gain sufficient altitude to clear the mountains. Mo had been right. The circular climb gave the Gophers time to study the layout of the base beneath them.

Lee had been concerned about possible overlaps of traffic around the U.S. base and the Newton Strips of the Aussies. But from the air he could clearly see that the Aussie strips were considerably east of the U.S. traffic pattern. There should be no dangers there as long as every pilot could see well enough to stay in his own traffic pattern.

The Gophers formed up at 10,000 angels and headed east over the mountains. The crisp, angular valleys and shadows of the rugged range sent a clear message; this was not a place to go down. Even if one parachuted down safely, finding his way down the mountains would be a difficult and treacherous trek. In bad weather, Lee decided, it would be wise to follow the coastline around the Huon Gulf to Lae and then head up the Markham River as they had done in their first flight into Nadzab.

Not only did the ominous mountains reach up to claim the unwary, but they also hid thousands of very unhappy Japanese soldiers who had been forced to evacuate the coastal bases and head for the hills. Lee's mind drifted for a moment to the predicament into which those enemy soldiers had escaped. If I were one of their officers, he thought, I'd try to pull together a large enough group to slip down out of the mountains and retake Nadzab. After all, we're air force pilots, support personnel, and engineers, not infantry and artillery.

Halfway across the Bismarck Sea, the Lightnings overtook the two squadrons of solid-nose B-25s they were to escort. The Gophers throttled back to keep their protective umbrella high above the medium bombers. While one couldn't look directly at the sun, now high in the southeast, for very long, frequent flitting examinations were necessary. Lee felt better when Mo led them on up to 22,000 feet. The higher the squadron flew, the less vulnerable they were to attack from above.

"Mo here. String 'em out now, but don't drop your bottles."

Lee dropped back to allow Bubba to slide in between Mo and himself. Up ahead, he saw numerous clouds of gray and black smoke climbing skyward, obvious results of the first wave of American bombers. Far to his right he saw another cluster of battle clouds over Rabaul. Apparently attacks had once again been coordinated to keep the Japanese forces at Rabaul busy defending themselves. Twice now the plan seemed to have worked.

The Mitchell bombers shrank in size as they went down close to ocean level for their attack. Lee expected Mo to split the squadron and send one or two flights down closer to the action for quicker response should Japanese fighters show up. Then he noticed a second squadron of P-38s, Captain Robesky's Bobcat Squadron, down around 10,000 feet.

Lee had just finished another three-sixty scan when he saw the birth of a battle unfold far below. A large group of Jap fighters were headed west from Kavieng, obviously to meet the American bombers and thin their ranks before the anti-aircraft batteries took over. But the Bobcat Squadron had split by flights and were heading into the Japs from different directions. Lee found it fascinating. It was as though he had a seat on the fifty-yard line for the—

"All right, Gophers," came Mo's voice. "You keep your eyes on the attic. *I'll watch the game.*"

As they circled high above Kavieng Bay, Lee stole occasional glances at the battle below. It seemed to be going like it should. The Lightnings were all tangled up with the Zeros and the B-25s with their eight forward-firing machine guns were down among the ships, skip-bombing and strafing. New clouds of smoke added to the scene. Some were dark black mushrooms that suggested that fuel tanks had been hit. Several arcs and spirals of smoke traced the fatal fall of fighter planes, but at his altitude Lee couldn't identify them.

He became uncomfortable with his role. For the first time, the battle raged below while he circled high above, looking for a fight and finding none. It shouldn't be going like this. He increased his vigilance. It shouldn't be so easy. He tried various tricks for looking into the sun, but he found no Jap planes there. Certainly within minutes Mo would start them downward to begin their strafing attacks. Gun emplacements were to be the primary targets and they were hard to recognize at high speeds until the twinkling tracers began coming upward.

With their attack finally concluded, the bombers swept out of the harbor at wave-top altitude, then began to climb and form up for the trip home. Mo extended the Gophers' oval-shaped flight pattern eastward. Lee expected an order to start downward for strafing attacks, but none came. Instead, an unfamiliar voice came over the mission channel.

"Yeahhh, Thirty-eights, we pasted them pretty good. Our last flight caught no ground fire. I think you can probably save your ammo and take us home."

"Roger, Big Brothers," Mo replied. "Home, it is."

Mo's immediate acquiescence surprised Lee.

"Kavieng group, this is Duckbutt. We show you clear to home. No bogies."

"Roger, Duckbutt," replied the bomber leader. "We have three down and four with clipped wings. Keep an eye on us, please."

"Roger Wilco."

"Uhh, Duckbutt," came Captain Robesky's voice. "Bobcat Squadron at 10,000 angels. We have two down and two wounded birds also."

"Roger, Bobcat. We'll watch. Be advised, you're headed for weather."

As Gopher Squadron made their turn to head for New Guinea, Lee saw a massive cloud line to the west. It was hard to judge the distance, but he guessed the line was near the coast. It extended fifty to a hundred miles to the north and as far as the eye could see to the south. It did not look inviting. The billowing tops of the cumulus headers rose to perhaps 30,000 feet, and in the light of the southeast sun the clouds reflected tones of bright silver-white with gold tints here and there. But the bases of those clouds were solid, dark gray, and really nasty.

Lee could almost feel the other pilots tensing up with him. That ugly mass had socked in all of the bases in the area of the Huon Peninsula. The only options left to them might be Cape Gloucester, the small base at the western tip of the island of New Britain, or Arawe on the southwest shore of the large island. But by the time they reached the cape, the storm may have captured those bases as well.

"Big Brothers, Gopher Leader here," called Mo. "That shit is ugly. What's your fuel situation?"

"Uhh, Gopher Leader, we don't have enough to play those games, especially with some tired birds. It'll be tight getting us in at the first two strips, but we'll have to do it."

"Roger, Big Brother. Roby, maybe your Bobcats should do the same?"

"Roger, Mo," said Captain Robesky. "We've got too many problems to head into that mess."

"It looks like it's shorter on the north end," replied Mo. "We'll head for Saidor and see if we can sneak around behind it and get down the valley. Gophers, tighten it up. If we get into the soup, I'll call my turns. Be steady, smooth, and don't panic. Breaking right to two-seven-zero. Let's go down."

As the squadron angled for Saidor and lower altitude, Lee knew they were in for a frisky ride. If lucky, the ceiling, the bottom of the storm, would be high enough that they could safely fly beneath it. If so, they would find Saidor, angle southwest and pick their way through a lower mountain range to the Markham River valley. Then they would follow the valley home to Nadzab. It sounded so simple.

He tried to gauge the north end of the storm. Storm cells didn't usually end abruptly and suddenly turn into blue sky. Rather, they broke up into smaller and smaller units, farther and farther apart. If the storm broke up somewhere near Saidor, they might manage to pick their way through. But if the monster held solid all the way to the Japanese stronghold at Madang, they would be forced to set down at Saidor or find a way through. Lee preferred the Saidor option. In New Guinea, mountains had a way of popping out of storm clouds and spelling D-E-A-D.

By the time the Gophers had descended to 10,000 feet, they had nearly reached the immense dark gray wall that towered thousands of feet above them. The frequent bolts of lightning buried in the maelstrom flashed their deadly light through the ominous thunderheads and served as a final warning to the P-38 pilots. Suddenly, Lee's 17,000-pound unit of high tech aircraft seemed about as large and powerful as a chicken feather. The war meant nothing. The Army chain of command meant nothing. Only survival mattered. He knew he would have to discipline himself to consider his squadron mates. He hoped they would do the same.

"It shows signs of breaking a little," came Mo's voice. But the increased static told Lee that their radio communication was close to breaking up also. "There's a hole in the crap ahead on the left. We'll give it a try. If we can get through at ten angels, we don't have to worry about the mountains. Tighten up now, Gophers. Make sure you're on a full tank. We'll ease off on the airspeed to two-ten. Coming left to two-two-zero, now."

Lee focused on Bubba as he banked left and followed into the open space in the clouds. The opening was about half a mile wide. Would it get bigger or smaller?

No sooner had all of the Gophers committed to the small canyon in the clouds than the answer became clear. Neither. They had flown into what amounted to a box canyon that ended abruptly after a mile of two.

"Gophers, down to ninety-five angels," came Mo's voice.

Lee tightened some more as he followed Bubba down. The charts indicated that the mountains west of Saidor topped off at 8,000 feet. Two things about that bothered Lee. Were the Gophers in fact *west* of Saidor? And who measured the mountains?

Mo had made a sound choice, though. At 9,700 feet they broke through the ceiling. Back of them and to their right lay the base at Saidor, while ahead and below were the dreaded mountain tops. It looked like they could make the Markham River valley. Certainly, they could swing around and land at Saidor. Lee knew Mo's decision even before the radio crackled.

"Gophers, we—home," came the broken message.

Twenty minutes later, Mo led them down and into a ninety-degree turn to their left. They had reached the Markham. Another ten minutes found them opening their spacing to enter the pattern for Strip Number Two.

As Lee's nose wheel eased slowly down to the runway surface, he realized how damp and clammy his body felt. The long flight home had provided as much tension as any of the previous battles, though they hadn't come within miles of an enemy aircraft. The well-known warning that the unpredictable New Guinea weather accounted for as many losses as did the Japanese had just been reaffirmed.

Later, as Lee walked with Mo toward the Intel section, he questioned Mo's decision not to go down for a strafing attack on Kavieng.

"Is your question a criticism, or is it an attempt to learn?" Mo responded.

"Oh, to learn. I know you had good reasons. You always do."

"I'll go humble on you, Lee," Mo said with a glint in his eye. "I *usually* have good reasons. This time, I had two. One—I thought it would be good for our guys to ride a milk run for a change. And two—another twenty or thirty minutes over the target would have made that trip home a lot tougher than it was."

"But what about our orders?"

"Orders?" Mo tossed his cigarette and stepped on it. "Orders from above—we bend. Orders from me—we follow. Don't ever forget that.

Chapter 26

"Congratulations, Killer!" said Mo. "Let me correct that. Congratulations, First Lieutenant Marks." He plunked his tray onto the rough table and sat down across from Lee.

"It came through?" asked Lee. "Already?"

"Sledge went after it pretty aggressively." Mo hesitated, then smiled and said, "I guess I'm supposed to do it like they do in the movies, give you my old bar and demand that you uphold the tradition it represents. Truth is, I tossed mine into the jungle when I made captain."

"Hey, no problem," Lee said. The smile that captured his face was not to be denied. "You know, I hadn't thought of this promotion as that big a deal. But now that it's here so soon, I can't stop smiling."

"Smile, Killer, you earned it. I wanted to run you right up to captain, but Sledge said he didn't want to push his luck. We'll get you there as soon as we can, though. We've got two new kids due in today, both rookies. They'll be in White and Blue Flights, but I'm counting on you to do what you can to help them fit in and learn."

"Of course," said Lee. "What do we know about them?"

"Haven't looked over their files yet. Sledge is giving us two ships from Headquarters Squadron—to help out—he says. That's what he says. Actually, we found out there are new Model Ls heading this way, and if Headquarters Squadron is short on planes, Sledge will get first crack at them." Mo smiled. "Sound a little like someone you know?"

Lee grinned, then said, "Mo, there's something I have to ask you. You'll probably say it's none of my business, but I have to ask anyway."

"We've got no more problems, Killer. Shoot."

"Well," Lee began, "I consider myself a pretty good judge of character. I happen to think Gus is a good guy, a good pilot, and a good leader. Why have you got it in for him?"

Lee hoped he wasn't too obvious in holding his breath. He had probably just stepped over the line in this new relationship, but he hadn't found a better way to deal with the matter.

Mo slid his hat back a notch, dipped his chin, and stared up coldly at Lee for a moment.

"You're right. It's none of your business," he pronounced. "And why, might I ask, do you think it is?"

"I could say that's none of your business," Lee returned, "but I won't play that game. I asked for three reasons. One, I don't have to be a Lockheed engineer to see that you're giving Gus the short end. Two, we're trying to make this squadron a tight, cohesive organization, a leadership unit. That'll never happen if the leader carries a grudge against a good man who's respected by all the others. Eventually it'll divide the squadron, Mo. And three, it's looking like I could be the knife blade that cuts the pie. I don't want to do that, Mo."

Keeping his stare locked onto Lee, Mo leaned back, took a long drag on his cigarette, and exhaled. Then he leaned forward with both elbows on the table and glanced quickly from side to side. When the response came, his voice was low and soft, but it bristled like a porcupine.

"Yes, you are out of line, Marks. How I handle the men under my command is none of your business."

"It is if you want me to ride shotgun for you." Lee felt the heat rising. "Mo, I'm really happy to get this promotion. I want promotions as much as anybody. But you implied that Gus and Greenie would get theirs along with me. There will be guys in the squadron who are wondering why they didn't, and they'll be glaring at me while they wonder. The squadron roster must have room for at least two captains, so whether nor not you meant to, you've already dragged this old knife blade through the pie and left a deep cut." Lee took a drink of tepid coffee. "I think I can manage to smooth over this cut, but I doubt I can pull it off twice."

"Meaning?" Mo turned on his hint of a grin that served as a question mark.

"Meaning I told Gus and Greenie that I'll never accept captain unless they get it, too."

"You did that?" Mo asked. "I certainly overestimated your political skills."

"No," said Lee, "I think you underestimated my ethics."

Suddenly the protective fog of emotions evaporated, and Lee found himself sitting there totally naked facing his superior. He swallowed the lump in his throat, but he forced himself to hold eye contact with Mo.

"You know, Marks, you're really out of—"

"Just one more thing," Lee cut in, "before you throw me back to Tail End Charlie behind Black Bart. I just put water on a brush fire for you, a fire that was growing really fast. I'd call that an excellent political move, wouldn't you?" From somewhere Lee found a grin, and when he realized it he forced the grin to expand.

Mo seemed to study Lee for some time. Then abruptly he, too, broke into a wide smile.

"Touché, Killer," he said. "I'll give you that one. Good move. But," he continued with a sober stare, "don't push your luck. I'll take your help and take it with appreciation. But challenges? Uh-uh. Remember, I can always toss this fish back where I found him."

"This wasn't a challenge, Mo," Lee said. "I was just—helping."

"And you did," Mo responded with surprising warmth. "You realize that if I get captain's bars for Gus and Greenie, the high brass might turn you down when it's your time?"

"But what if you've got a great squadron of eleven pilots who are accomplishing wonders under your command—because they really believe in you? And if you get light colonel? That would leave room for Gus or Greenie to make major and open up a captain's slot, wouldn't it?"

"Goddamn, Killer," Mo said under his breath. "And I said you lacked political skills?" He shook his head slowly for a moment. "Okay, let's try it your way."

Lee's tension eased suddenly. He hadn't expected such a favorable conclusion. His respect for Mo Brandon swelled like a balloon within him. Mo could have exploded and shot him right out of the water. He didn't. He listened with an open mind and accepted an opinion contrary to his own. But Lee's original question still lay unanswered.

"Just one thing, Mo," Lee said. "The Gus thing?"

"Just leave it alone," Mo snapped. "Just drop it." He got up from the table, grabbed his utensils, and left. Lee knew he'd have to find the answer some other way.

Sometime later, Lee made it to the flight line. The rain had stopped, but heavy storms throughout the area had scrubbed their ground attack mission to Madang. He found Bubba up on a ladder studying the strange piece of nose art on his new ship. Each side of Bubba's P-38 bore a Japanese submarine—nothing more, just the submarine.

"I—uh—kind of like your paint job," said Lee. "It's—unique. Is there some special message there?"

"Okay, Lee, have your damned fun," Bubba called down to him. "I know. You told me there wouldn't be enough time for Corporal Jones to finish his painting before we had to leave."

"It really is unique, Bubba. When the Jap pilots cozy up to you, trying like hell to figure out why you have one of their subs on your ship, you just blow them out of the blue, right? You know, it just might work."

"Okay! Okay! When you get done rubbing it in, tell me what the hell I can do with this. I don't have Corporal Jones here, so I'll probably have to finish it myself."

"Are you any good at lettering?" Lee asked.

"Fairly good. No good at painting objects though."

"No need to paint objects. Below the sub you just paint, "BUBBA'S SUBBA. I'll bet there won't be another ship in the whole Fifth Air Force with nose art anything like it."

"God—damn! You're right! What a great idea!" Bubba's exuberance nearly launched him from his precarious perch. He caught his balance and steadied the ladder.

"Okay, now tell me, what was it supposed to be?" Lee asked.

"Oh, the corporal was going to paint a P-38 with arms, hands, and claws instead of landing gears. It would be holding the Jap sub in its claws."

"Too bad," said Lee. "The kid's ideas are as good as his painting, aren't they?"

"Hope he's not too mad. We left so quickly he didn't get paid his whiskey. The major will pay for it again, won't he?"

"Uh-uh. Afraid the second one's on you. You should get a couple of fifths ready and send them with the Golden Goose next time she heads for Dobo. But you'd better get busy with your painting before those clouds dump again."

As Lee headed on down the flight line, the sun burst suddenly through an opening in the storm clouds, adding to his rising spirit. Things were looking up for him, Gopher Squadron, and the Allied campaign in general.

On March third, Allied forces had captured the Japanese base at Momote on Los Negros in the Admiralties. With the March seventh capture of Seeadler Harbor on Manus Island, the Americans had essentially gained control of the Admiralties. While the clean-up fighting in the island group would go on for days or weeks, the outcome was no longer in doubt.

The Gophers had flown several missions against Kavieng in mid-March, but with Japanese air defenses all but knocked out, the assignments had changed from escort duty to low-level ground and harbor attacks. The strafing runs brought mixed feelings. When Lee could clearly see his targets, sometimes clusters of Japanese troops, his five devastating weapons could take out as many as fifty of them in one pass, fifty who would not be available to shoot at the invading U.S. forces. His contribution to the effort was almost measurable, and he liked that. But during some strafing runs he had perhaps a hundred enemy soldiers firing small weapons at him. Despite a couple of panels of armor cockpit protection, he was flying an aluminum aircraft that was vulnerable to bullets. Captain Hollings Bryant was right. Aerial combat was safer.

On March 21st, Kavieng fell and the noose around Rabaul had been knotted. The Americans had previously captured Guadalcanal and Bougainville and thus controlled the Solomon Islands just southeast of Rabaul. The powerful Japanese installation could now be denied most of the supplies it needed to remain operational. The obvious plan for the Allies called for a period of relentless blockade followed by invasion. But Mo had picked up word that General MacArthur had decided against wasting time and American lives on an invasion of Rabaul. He had Rabaul in a bottle. By using Navy and Marine air power based in the Solomons to peck away at the only weapons the enemy had left, their aircraft, he could in effect cork the bottle.

Before losing the Admiralties and Kavieng to the Americans, the Japanese evacuated their functional aircraft to their stronghold at Wewak. With their Navy air arm in dire straits, they turned over command of their New Guinea air war to the Fourth Air Army.

No sooner had Momote, Seeadler Harbor, and Kavieng been secured than the U.S. Fifth Air Force turned its full strength against the string of Japanese bases along the north coast of New Guinea. Beginning with Madang and extending westward to Hansa Bay and Wewak, bomber and fighter commands hammered away at Japanese shipping and airbases.

The Lockheed Lightning was indeed proving its versatility. Since all three targets were within 225 miles of Nadzab, the Gophers occasionally found their one hundred-sixty-five-gallon belly tanks replaced by 500-pound bombs. On successive days, the Gophers found themselves filling the role of escort fighters, bombers, and ground attack planes. Their superior speed, range, and payload capabilities made them excellent bombers. Their speed made them difficult targets for the enemy anti-aircraft gunners. And once their mid-level bomb attack had been completed, the Lightnings could go down on the deck and use their machine guns and cannon to rip through the enemy troops and installations.

Like the other pilots, Lee had adjusted to the flight characteristics of his heavy-laden Lightning when carrying two five-hundred-pound bombs. And like the others, he felt a rush of relief each time the last bomb cleared its shackles and fell away. Attempting to land back at Nadzab with a dangling 500-pound bomb that had only partially released seriously threatened a fighter pilot's life expectancy. He shuddered when he learned that some Lightnings were being modified to carry four 500-pound bombs or two 1,000-pound bombs, loads that approached the capabilities of the medium bombers.

Upon returning from a low-level attack at Madang, Lee found a crowd of pilots and ground crewmen gathered around Burner Hedstrom's ship. The exuberant gathering was examining a sizeable dent in the leading edge of Burner's horizontal stabilizer, the small wing-like slab that connected the two booms together at the tail.

"What did you hit, Burner, an 80-millimeter gun barrel?" Sandy asked.

"Naw, I gotta admit it was nothing that glamorous, Sandy. I was right tight on the deck, and when I pulled up I caught the radio antenna tower. Now *that's* getting right close to your work!"

"Man, going in that tight, you must have knocked their radios out." Sandy said.

"Don't really know," Burner replied, "but I got two laundry tubs, a clothes line, two shirts, and some of those funny undershorts the Japs wear."

It was on a March 27 escort mission to Dagua, one of the three Japanese airdromes at Wewak, that the Gophers ran up against a formidable challenge by the Japanese Fourth Air Army. Two previous strikes that day had blown away any element of surprise. As the two dozen B-24 heavies lined up for their bombing run at 12,000 feet, a mass of perhaps forty Oscars and A6M5 Zeros came out of the sun from 20,000 feet. While the Oscars continued on down toward the bombers, the Zeros clearly had targeted the Gopher Lightnings.

"Quick switch and drop 'em!" Mo called. "Up and right for a head-on."

While climbing into a swarm of Zeros was generally considered a bad practice, the Gophers had little choice. Some had not even completed the turn when the Jap tracers began tracking into the squadron, and the Lightning pilots found themselves in a role reversal. This time, they were the hunted. Lee hoped that Captain Bryant's Pony Squadron was in a position to take on the Oscars because the Gophers would be lucky to defend themselves against the Zeros.

Lee and Sandy cut the climbing turn sharply and matched up immediately with two diving attackers. Lee fired a moment before his adversary opened up, and the battle proved to be a replay of the fastest gun contest. No sooner had the enemy's first tracers come at Lee than the Zero pulled up, flipped over and exploded. A glance to the right found Sandy's target flashing past on only one wing. But even without a look at his airspeed indicator, Lee knew he and his wingman were perched at a dangerous angle with their airspeed dropping rapidly. There were still a few Zeros diving from above, but they seemed to be focused on other Lightnings.

Lee had lost all track of the other Gophers, and with the terrible blind spot beneath his P-38 a turn either way could lead to a mid-air collision. He pushed the control yoke ahead full, trusting that Sandy would alertly follow. Once past the potential stall and heading downward in a shallow dive to regain their lost airspeed, Lee's head swiveled up, down, and around as fast as he could move it. For now they seemed to be clear from above.

"Sandy, let's take a look around," Lee called.

"Roger."

A steeply banked left turn gave Lee a look at the events beneath them. Everywhere he looked he saw an entanglement of the distinctive Lightnings and the smaller Zeros. Several trails of smoke led to the sea beneath. The Jap fighters who were not currently engaged were climbing to regain altitude from several thousand feet below the two Gophers. Their strategy mirrored that usually followed by the Lightnings, dive through the enemy, then climb up for another pass. Lee led Sandy toward the best position from which to dive on the climbing Zeros. They had nearly reached the vantage point when a Lightning about two thousand feet below caught Lee's attention. The P-38 was a loner and streamed smoke from the right engine. Worse, about 600 yards behind him followed three Zeros moving in for the kill.

"Somebody needs help, Sandy. Below—right," called Lee.

"Looks like two of ours already to the rescue," Sandy responded.

A second look confirmed it. Two other Gophers were apparently angling toward the three Jap fighters.

"Okay, Sandy, let's take those coming up the elevator."

The attack on the climbing Zeros would call for deflection shots, but this time the Zeros had given away airspeed in their haste to regain altitude, and that would ease the difficulty of the shot. Lee picked the leader of the group of four Zeros and fired two short bursts. He thought he had hit it, but apparently not. As the plane with its red insignia spots grew larger and larger, he squeezed the button behind the control yoke a third time. The agile fighter seemed to stop momentarily and then drop into a steep dive with heavy smoke trailing behind. The pilot of Sandy's target either took some body hits or decided the game wasn't for him. He did a sharp one-eighty and began a shallow dive in the opposite direction. The remaining two Zeros apparently liked his judgment, for they followed in the tight turn and disappeared below and behind the two Lightnings.

Lee and Sandy leveled off and checked to be sure the three escaping Zeros really had thrown in the towel. Looking over the battle scene, they found the heavies at the end of their run and turning for home. Except for one or two distant skirmishes between Lightnings and Jap fighters, it seemed the battle was over. But with Japanese bases at Alexschafen, Hansa Bay, and Madang along the course for home, the two escorting squadrons would stay with the bombers.

When the Gophers formed up on Mo at 15,000 feet, Red Flight seemed intact. One of the three planes of the shorthanded White Flight trailed a thin stream of coolant. But only two of the three-plane Blue Flight joined the formation, and they were without their flight leader, Gus. Lee knew then that the smoking Lightning under attack by three Zeros had to be Gus. The two Lightnings closing in on Gus's attackers must have gotten there too late.

"Anyone see what happened to Gus?" Lee called.

"He ducked underneath me where I couldn't see him," responded Smokey Stover. "When I came around to look for him I got a Zero on my tail. Never saw him again. I didn't see any chutes. Did anybody else see one?"

"Okay, Gophers," called Mo, "let's pay attention to things. We've still got to get our big brothers home."

Lee concentrated doubly hard on his flying to try to divert his mind. It worked for brief periods but then Gus would be right back with him. If there was one man in the squadron who deserved more than the others to get safely back to the States, it had to be First Lieutenant Edward Gustafson. His blend of flying skills, fighting spirit, leadership, compassion, and patience through the unfair treatment given him by Mo set him apart from the others. Lee replayed the encouragement and advice Gus had given him while he was dealing with his own set of Mo Brennan manipulations. Without the support given by Gus, Lee knew he would have made critical mistakes and ended up on Mo's list for good.

Far ahead and to Lee's right, an enormous bank of silver-white cumulus clouds formed a sunlit crown that engulfed the high peak of Mount Wilhelm. As Lee wiped away tears and studied the phenomenon, he was sure he saw Gus's face in the fluffy setting. It seemed to be Gus at his best, at peace with things, and telling Lee that it was meant to be—it was okay. Lee shook it off and looked away. A part of his mind told him he was seeing only what he wanted to see.

But when he looked back, Gus was still there—only he was smiling.

"Yes!" Lee said aloud. "Yes! We've lost you, Gus, but I think you're telling me you're okay. You're better off than the rest of us. Right?" As Lee watched, the smiling face of his friend faded into the silvery mass.

"Marks! Is there a reason you're breaking formation?" crackled Mo's voice over the mission channel. "How about coming back down here with the rest of us?"

"Roger."

Back at Nadzab, the Gopher pilots huddled at the end of the flight line around the makeshift table. Nobody had much to say, but a gigantic magnet seemed to hold the men to the cluster. It was Smokey Stover who finally broke the silence.

"God, I'm sorry, Gus," he said as he looked at the ground with tears streaming down his face. "You cut under me—and I just lost you. I'm sorry, man. I should have been there."

Lee put his hand on Smokey's shoulder.

"It's okay, Smokey," said Lee. "It's okay. I think he knows you did everything you could." Lee turned to the northwest, toward Mt. Wilhelm. "I think he's up there telling us we have to go on, that he's better off than the rest of us."

"Do you really think so? What makes you think that?" Smokey managed.

"I—I can't explain it," Lee replied, "but I really believe it."

Slowly, reluctantly, the group broke up and headed for Ops. *This is good*, Lee thought as he sluffed along the path. *This is good that these guys feel that much for one man. Now we have to help one another get past it. The guy went down doing what we're all here to do. We can't just stop.*

"Lee? Lee? Can we talk? Just for a minute?"

Lee felt a tug at his elbow and turned to find Bubba. He pulled off to one side of the path and stopped.

"Lee, I can't talk to anyone else about this, but I'm really torn up," Bubba.

"Bubba, I think we all are."

"Damn, I'm talking about more than losing Gus. I'm talking about how it happened."

Then Lee saw in his protégé's face a fear that was new. It bore no resemblance to the kid who couldn't deal with wormy Army food, and it seemed totally incongruous with the arrogant bravado of the flyer who had faced down a Japanese submarine.

"Okay, talk to me, Bubba. What's got you?"

"Lee, I think we could have saved Gus. He didn't have to go down."

"What do you mean, Bubba?" Lee asked.

"Mo and I were moving in on the three Zeros that had Gus cornered. At least I *thought* that was what we were doing. We'd have had them, too. We could have nailed at least two of them, maybe all three."

"I saw you, thought sure that's what you were doing. And you didn't?"

"No." Bubba hesitated, looked around, then continued in a lowered voice. "Mo suddenly broke off after two others. I didn't know what to do, but I'm his wingman so I followed him. We got both of them. But Gus?"

Lee's imagination roared off at full throttle . Would Mo really?... No, nobody would do that, not even Black Bart. But still....

"Lee, what do I do?" asked the shaken Bubba. "What do I say in debriefing?"

"Bubba, there has to be an explanation. I don't think I'd mention it to anyone."

Chapter 27

Lea had just finished rinsing his mess kit after breakfast when he felt Mo's tap on his shoulder.

"Get a refill on the coffee and meet me over in the corner," said Mo.

When Lee straightened and turned around, Mo had disappeared, leaving Lee wondering what ever happened to the words, "Good morning." But he finished his chores and with coffee in hand joined Mo in a secluded corner of the mess hall. One glance told Lee that Mo had a burr under his saddle.

"Where the hell does your wingman get off telling Intel that I was in a position to get those Nips off Gus's tail? What kind of bullshit is *this?*" There was not a trace of the fixed, meaningless Brennan smile.

"I purposely did *not* mention that in my debriefing," Lee said, "but it looked to us like you and Bubba were headed for the three Zeros chasing Gus. And since you were the closest to them, we went after four others that were trying to get altitude on us."

"No you don't, Marks. Don't try to hang that on me." Mo leaned forward and pointed a finger at Lee. "You and Sadler had the altitude and angle, so we broke off and nailed two others. If anybody left Gus dangling out there it was you and Sadler. That's bad enough, but when you try to pass the buck to me you're asking for a shit pot full of trouble. Now, all you have to do is convince me that's *not* what's happening here."

Lee felt a tornado rise up within him. Mo's anger had caught him off guard, but the implication that he and Sandy were responsible for the loss of Gus was enough to light the fuse. He turned away for a few seconds and struggled to gather his patience. It helped a little.

"Mo," he said, "nobody's trying to hang that on you. You made a judgment call based on what you perceived to be the facts. I did the same. To tell you the truth, I think we both screwed up. You assumed, and I assumed, but we didn't communicate—simple as that. Now I'm going to have to live with that, and so are you, so we'd better get started."

Mo looked away. He carelessly tossed his cigarette at the cut-off fruit juice can that served as an ashtray and stabbed two fingers into his shirt pocket for another cigarette. His hand trembled slightly as he lit the new one.

"Ah, shit," he said, grabbing his coffee cup. "Let's get out of here."

They had stashed their utensils and were half way to the flight line when Mo spoke.

"You know, you're right. We both messed up—should have used the radio. You know, you're right too often lately. You'd better be wrong one of these days or I'm going to have to replace you." He strode on down the path, his eyes fixed straight ahead.

"I'll take care of that—tomorrow," Lee replied.

The sarcastic humor did nothing to salve the pain that Lee felt, but it did begin to swing the door shut on the painful subject.

"Am I right, we've got nothing scheduled today?" Lee asked.

"That's right. But I want you to find the two new guys, take them up where you can find the least traffic, and put them through the mill." Mo stopped suddenly and turned to Lee. "Hey, while you're at it, take Barton with you. Maybe if he feels threatened by the two new rookies, he'll pay attention."

"That's a good theory, Mo. I doubt it'll work, but I'll try it."

Lee searched out the two new pilots. Their raw enthusiasm brought a smile to his face. Only months before, Lee Marks had been in that role.

Second Lieutenant Tony Margo had the looks, voice, and personality of a movie hero. He swaggered slightly when he walked, and his demeanor reeked of confidence. He could have been the fighter pilot on a recruiting poster. Ironically, his compadre, James Stewart, bore the name of the famous movie star who had also become an Army Air Force pilot. Any similarities ended there, and while Stewart wore the wings of a pilot, he looked like a dime store clerk. The short, stocky blond with blue eyes and thinning hair came across as shy and unsure of himself.

It looked like the Gophers had inherited two more extremies, as Lee liked to call them. Why couldn't Fighter Command have found them some middle-of-the-roaders who could readily blend in with their squadron mates? He was anxious to see the pair fly and find out what they really had there. He was about to brief them for the morning flight when Black Bart sidled up.

"The major sent word that I was to find you here and go flying with you," Bart said dryly.

"Yeah," said Lee. He introduced Bart to the two new pilots. Then, on an impulse, he said, "I want you to help me with these guys, help get them adjusted to our ways, check out their moves, and teach them a few of ours."

"You—" Bart cocked his head to one side and looked at Lee out of the corners of his eyes. "You—" He blinked and faced Lee.

"Are you free to go now?" Lee asked.

"Uh, sure. Got nothing better to do," Bart said.

"Okay. Here's what we'll do," Lee said to the three pilots. "We'll take off in pairs. Call signs, I'm Lee, he's Bart." He looked inquiringly at the newcomers.

"I'm Tony," said Margo.

"I guess I kind of got stuck with Stew," said Stewart.

"You want to change it? Now's the time," Lee offered.

"No, I guess I'll go on being Stew."

"He kind of looks like stew, don't you think?" Tony Margo said.

"Okay," said Lee, "here's the drill. I'll take Stew. Bart, you take Tony. We'll take off in pairs and head for the Huon Gulf southeast from Lae to get out of the traffic. I'll call the moves, Channel Three, as we go. We'll do some formation flying, changes in formations, changes in positions, and then we'll get into some combat moves. Keep track of each other and keep your heads moving at all times. Be sure to check the sun often. We *are* in a war zone."

Lee led the way taxiing to Strip Number Two, and thirty minutes later the unusual combination began their drills at 20,000 feet out over the Huon Gulf. The session proved to be productive, and Lee found his own instinctive teaching techniques surprisingly effective. At times he had the others follow him through moves, followed by maneuvers in which he had Bart take the lead. Lee then dropped back into the Number Four slot so he could watch the others. After running the list of maneuvers at high altitude, Lee took them down to 7,000 feet and repeated some of the moves to experience the differences in changing to the low altitude flight characteristics of the J-model Lightnings. Finally, he wrapped up the session with practice using the Fowler flaps to sharpen up low-speed turns and the dive flaps to pull high-speed turns.

Confident that all three pilots could handle the turns without losing control, he led them home. He felt reasonably satisfied with Tony Margo's heavy-handed performance and surprisingly impressed with Stew's flying. Once again, looks had deceived. The shy, pudgy flyer had quick reflexes and a smooth touch with the controls, unlike those who handled the Lightning like it was a bulldozer.

While previously he had seldom been in a position to observe Black Bart's flying, Lee felt that morning that his antagonist had indeed really flown his aircraft. Perhaps Lee should stop thinking of Bart as a truck driver. But Bart's gunnery was still suspect. Lee wondered if he would now be ready to listen to suggestions. If so, Lee might be able to help him improve his shooting, particularly his patience and concentration, without ever leaving the ground. But most of all, Lee hoped that his respectful treatment of Bart had cracked that hard shell of resentment. After buttoning up his Marksman, Lee caught up with Bart as he walked up the line.

"Well," opened Lee, "what did you think of your man's flying? Is he any good?"

"Save your condescending bullshit, Marks," Black Bart said. He turned and glared at Lee as they walked side-by-side. "You don't give a shit what I think of the new man. You can stick the game playing right up your ass—sideways."

Bart's reaction disappointed Lee, but it did not surprise him. Nothing had changed.

"Okay, Barton. I've tried to mend our fence. Have it your way."

Chapter 28

▼

"Habba-habba. Habba-habba."

Lee pulled on his low-cut engineer boots and looked to the door of the tent. There stood a tall, slender black man, perhaps even a shade darker than Bob and Bill. His huge puffball of fuzzie hair showed streaks of gray, and in his nose was fixed a four-inch bone. But the shiny face that surrounded the bone came across as one big smile. The wrinkles in his forehead seemed to smile. His eyes smiled. And his thick lips, stained red from the juice of the addictive betel nuts, parted in a toothy smile. A wide band of layered parachute silk was wrapped around his hips.

"Habba-habba. Habba-habba," he repeated, pointing first at Lee and then himself.

"Habba-habba," said Lee. He *thought* the greeting translated as, "You friend. All is okay." He hoped so. If not, it was a little like signing a blank check. When he motioned for the man to enter the tent, the visitor's face sobered. He flinched and stepped back, then waved for Lee to step outside. Lee smiled, acknowledged the unspoken protocol, and joined the man on the rickety porch.

"Alvin," the man said, pointing to himself. "Alvin." Then he pointed at Lee.

"Lee—Lee," Lee replied, pointing to himself.

"Lee-Lee." His grin broadened and he repeated, "Lee-Lee."

"No." Lee again pointed to himself. "Just *Lee*."

Alvin's face contorted. One eyebrow raised.

"Just Lee?" he said. His smile returned. "*Just* Lee!"

Lee had finally identified his problem. With deliberate caution, he drilled with Alvin until the confusion had lifted and he had once again become "Lee."

"Trade?" asked Alvin. "Trade?" He pointed to a sizeable bundle he carried that was wrapped in parachute silk.

"Trade," Lee replied. Unlike his first experience with Bob and Bill, Lee had prepared for this visit. He stepped into the tent and gathered up his goods. He had accumulated several well-worn shirts and trousers, three cartons of Lucky Strikes, the silk and shrouds of one damaged parachute, half a dozen empty fruit juice cans, and a pouch of buttons and beads.

Alvin lit up like an ebony candle when he saw the potential. And when he unwrapped his offerings Lee brightened as well. Alvin had brought the customary and most desirable combat gear from perhaps three Jap officers and two enlisted men: swords, daggers, field glasses, pistols, rifles, canteens, and flags. Lee wondered if it was time for Alvin to bring out the human ears.

In a short burst of pseudo negotiations, the pair soon arrived at an even trade, one collection for the other, and both entrepreneurs bowed and smiled, pleased with their prizes.

"You—village?" Lee asked, pointing off toward the east. Several repetitions finally elicited a negative headshake and a gesture toward the mountains.

"Good!" Lee said with a broad smile. "Good!" He extended his hand and was somewhat surprised when Alvin quickly grasped it and shook it enthusiastically. With an unfaltering smile, Alvin bundled up his acquisitions, gave a last wave to Lee, and headed for the river on the west side of the base. Lee watched his visitor slosh across the shallow river and disappear in the tall kunai grass.

Lee made a list of the items and carefully wrapped his accumulation in a blanket. Then he bound the long bundle with a parachute shroud and slung it across his back. The two rifles made the load surprisingly heavy as he headed out back to the storage crate near the river, but he felt warmed by the experience. Like his old trading partner, Bob, Alvin was indeed a friendly man. Lee chuckled at the "Lee-Lee" problem. Yet, despite the language barrier, his contact with Alvin had been a pleasure.

At Dobodura Lee had heard many tales of the dedicated support given by the natives. They worked at unloading ships, carrying supplies, and building roads, and from the first battles against the Japanese troops, the natives had proven to be strong and extremely kind litter bearers, often going to great lengths to make wounded soldiers more comfortable. Most of the natives had been badly mistreated by the Japanese soldiers, and theirs was a culture that didn't forget. Lee shuddered at the probable fate of the Japs whose belongings he now carried.

A smile crossed his face, however, when he reasoned that his trading with the natives actually contributed to the war effort. By providing the natives with useful items, the G.I. traders were in effect putting out a bounty for enemy troops. Where and how the enemies were eliminated was really not important. Then Lee remembered the pair of ears Bob had offered and his warm moment of satisfaction succumbed to a sudden chill.

Lee stowed the goods and made his way to Mo's tent where he found his leader outside propping wet boots upside down in the sun on long sticks driven into the ground.

"Hey, Killer, good timing. Come on in. We've got the apartment to ourselves."

Lee followed Mo up and into the tent. He sat down gingerly on the bunk across from Mo's while Mo unlocked a small crate and pulled out a bottle of Jack Daniels.

"What they don't know won't hurt them," he said, gesturing to the empty bunks. He poured a generous portion into a tin cup and handed it to Lee.

"Ooh, easy now," Lee said, pouring half of his whiskey back into Mo's cup. "It's still pretty early in the afternoon for me."

"Good sense," said Mo. "You know how it affects you. I know how it doesn't affect me. Have you seen the board for tomorrow?" He took a large swallow from his cup. His face contorted and he shook his head violently. "Aaahh…."

"No, but from the look on your face I'd guess we've got a doozy coming up."

"Hollandia."

"Hollandia?" Lee repeated, incredulously. "That's huge! But it's over 450 miles from here. Why not Madang, or Hansa Bay, or Wewak?"

"Well, in a way we *are* hitting those three," Mo said. "My take on it is, we're getting ready to invade Madang, probably in the final stages of prep. But we can't just ignore all that airpower the Nips have up at Hollandia. So, we've got to take steps to neutralize them, shoot up as many as we can and at least leave them with a lot of repairs to be made."

"Oof," muttered Lee. "But I guess the brass know best."

"Hell no, they don't know best!" countered Mo. "But they do have the rank, and they do make the calls. Trust me, though. One of these days we're going to have a real fiasco. Some of their stupid decision-making is going to leave you and me in a shit pot full of trouble. We're long overdue."

"But by-passing Madang, Hansa Bay, and Wewak to go after Hollandia?" Lee said. "That doesn't make sense."

"Oh, we're not by-passing them. They're going to get hit hard at the same time. But the P-39s, P-40s, and the Aussie stuff can get to them. We're the only ones with the range to take the bombers to Hollandia."

"Okay, that does make more sense, I think."

"Now, let's reorganize the Gophers. You saw the new guys fly. What do you think?"

"I think," Lee began, "before we place the new guys, we ought to take a look at Blue Flight and see what we can do to beef it up. Without Gus, all we have there is Chub Forbes with five kills. Black Bart's a zero and that probably won't change."

"Great minds work alike," Mo said. "We'll come back to Barton in a minute, but I agree with you on Blue Flight. How would you do it?"

"Much as I *don't* like it," Lee began, "the first thing I'd do is move Sandy or me back to Blue Leader. Then I'd rethink things from there."

"Damn! You're leadership stuff, you know that? That's exactly where I'm coming from. Now, since we're still a man short, I want to keep Sandy in Red for now. When we've got our replacement to fill out the squadron, we can take another look at it. So…if Sandy stays with me, what would you do next?"

"You really want to know?" Lee asked.

"Absolutely. You're taking on the biggest chore in the squadron, trying to make something out of Blue Flight. You should have some say in this."

"Well, okay, here's what I'd do. I'd leave Red Flight a three-man unit for now—still plenty strong with you, Bubba, and Sandy. I'd put Tony Margo, the weaker of the two new guys in White Number Four spot, and set up Blue Flight so Stewart is my wingman and Chub Forbes is Number Three…and stuck with Black Bart as his wingman. Believe me, I've nothing against Chub. I really like him. But with this lineup, everybody in the squadron has a proven wingman, except for Smokey Stover, Chub Forbes, and me. Chub deserves better than this, but I don't see a better way. Do you?"

"Nope," Mo said with a wide grin. "You've done almost what I would do, except for one question—Barton. How did your training flight go this morning?"

Lee carefully summarized the morning session. He purposely did not cap it with Bart's exact words, but he did paint an accurate picture of the ugly state of things.

"I think," Mo began slowly, "it might be time to ground him."

"You can do that?" Lee took another sip of the strong whiskey.

"I have to be able to justify it, but I can do that. The fact is, besides having a rotten attitude and refusing to join the team, he can't hit a Jap plane. I could include him only on ground attack missions. He *can* hit the ground—but then it's a pretty big planet. So far, about the only thing we've accomplished with Barton flying is we've increased the risk of losing a P-38." Mo lit a cigarette, gestured crisply toward Lee and asked, "Where we going to fly him? Do you want him as your wingman? Does anybody?" Without waiting for an answer, Mo rolled on, "And now, with him so busy being mad at the world, putting him in the Number Four slot is like having the fox guarding the henhouse."

"Do you think a stern warning before grounding him would wake him up?"

"He's already had that warning, from Sledge himself. Tell you what. If Sledge agrees with me, I'm going to leave Barton behind tomorrow. It's a big, big operation, and one less, or should I say "harm-less," fighter shouldn't make much difference. If he doesn't pick up the phone on *this* call, we'll look into a transfer. That means you and I will have three-plane elements tomorrow, but I'd have to say pretty good three-plane elements."

"Sounds good," Lee said. "Big mission—how big is *big?*" He looked at the remaining whiskey in his cup. While certainly not a teetotaler, Lee had yet to develop a taste for straight, warm whisky. He sipped a little and decided to drag it out as long as possible. He was sure, even without asking, that Mo had no water for a mix.

"We're not supposed to know this yet, but I think we're looking at something like fifty-plus heavies and the whole 483rd Fighter Group for cover."

"Wow, that *is* big for a New Guinea mission. Sounds more like Eighth Air Force over Germany."

"Have you thought any more about our plan?" Mo asked

"Yeah," Lee said, "I have. And it makes good sense. As long as we don't hurt anybody else, why *not* make ourselves look good?" Lee thought he detected a tiny physical reaction with the words, "don't hurt anybody else," but he sloughed the thought away.

"It's been slowing down through late February and early March," Mo said. "The Japs have been saving their aircraft and concentrating them along the coast west of us to beat us up on our way to the Philippines. But the last mission did help our score. Adding those seven kills, the Gophers are now up to seventy-one, plus the 28 that Gus, Greenie, and I had before the squadron was formed. We're still behind the 475th Fighter Group, but we're gaining on them."

"Problem is," Lee offered, "we're losing too many. Of our original twelve pilots, we've lost four. That's thirty-three percent." Lee looked at Mo. "You know, we haven't been up to our full strength since our first mission. We're *still* short one."

"Sledge and I have to share the blame for that. When the 483rd was organized, we should have tried to get the brass to set up the squadron in four flights instead of three. Then, even with losses, we'd still be flying three full flights or more. But—we thought we'd have tighter units with three flights. Didn't anticipate this many losses. Simple as that."

"On the bright side," said Lee, "we've lost four against their seventy-one. That's huge."

"But you said it," said Mo. "We've lost a third of our pilots—in only two months. Any thoughts on stopping the bleeding?"

"I guess...." Lee stopped and swallowed the last of the Jack Daniels. "I guess I'd look at the possibility of adding a flight to the squadron. Then, maybe we should take a careful look at how we lost the guys. Maybe there were mistakes made that we can correct."

"Yeah. That's good." Mo looked at the floor. "Of course, we already know how we lost Gus." He hesitated, then stood up quickly, gathered the two tin cups together, and locked up the bar crate. "I don't want to walk that road anymore today. Let's get over to the flight line and light a fire under the ground crews to make sure every ship is ready for the long haul tomorrow. And on the way, I've got to change tomorrow's Assignment Board. Got to ground Barton and revise the flight assignments.

Chapter 29

"Jeez," said Bubba as he reached for his coffee, "I hope we can just fight the damned Japs today. I'm getting tired of duking it out with the God of Tropical Storms."

"Yeah, we've had so goddamned much rain this month that even the jeeps are growing webbed feet," offered Burner Hedman.

"You know," added Sandy, "that it's time to dry out your boots when the creepie crawlies in them start squealing for life jackets."

"Cheer up, guys," said Lee. "We're almost out of the rainy season."

"Sure, sure," countered Burner. "That's what Noah said just before the storm."

Lee laughed, then studied his mates who had gathered around the makeshift table on the flight line after morning chow. The group featured the new Bubba, Sandy's freckled humor, Burner's mixture of contrived boasting and half-hearted bitching, and Black Bart, who was seated some distance away, moping in his cloud of isolation.

"It's going to be kind of strange today," said Sandy. "This is the first time the whole 483rd is scheduled together on the same mission."

"Won't be the whole fighter group," observed Bubba. "We're still short one, the 126th is short two, and three guys in the 127th are down with malaria."

"Whew!" said Burner. "You know how lucky we've been? No real problems so far with either dysentery or malaria. Better overdose on Atabrine, everybody. Don't back off until you're so yellow that the Zero pilots stop shooting and start bowing."

"Missing the point," grumbled Black Bart from his seat outside of the group. "The people in our squadron get killed before they have time to get sick."

"Bart," said Burner Hedman, his eyes flashing the power that was Burner Hedman, "You're already sick, so goddamned sick they jerked you from this mission today. Why don't you go bury your head in the latrine."

Bart returned the glare but said nothing. He simply stood and quietly skulked off toward the tent city.

"Do you think he's getting the message?" Sandy asked.

"I don't think he'll *ever* get the message," said Burner. "There's a short circuit there," he added, tapping the side of his head.

"I still have hope," Lee said, "but not much, I guess."

Lee withdrew to his Marksman a few yards from the gathering, and the group returned to their tension-busting banter. Mashy had finished loading the ammunition. He gave the inner workings one last, thorough check before buttoning up the nose compartment.

"I guess I'm outa line, Lieutenant," said Mashy, "but I gotta tell you, that Lieutenant Barton is a gen-u-wine nutcase."

"No comment," Lee said.

"Yeah, I wouldn't expect you to answer that. You're not like him. You're a real processional." Mashy double-checked the fasteners, then started down from his scaffold. "He reminds me of a baseball star I knew. Every time he made a play or hit a home run, the people clapped like hell and gave him a standing obation. His head got bigger and bigger until he got so obnoxitratious even his friends couldn't stand him."

"Did he ever figure it out?" Lee asked.

"Never did. I heard he still thought he was God when a German Stuka dropped a bomb on him in North Africa. She's all set, Lieutenant. You won't have any problems. I'll bet on it."

"Great, Mashy. Thanks for being so careful. My momma thanks you, too." Lee returned to the group of pilots.

"Even though my guns were jammed," Burner was saying, "I got another kill. I got behind this Zero, and when he saw me he cut such a sharp left turn his prop tore a chunk out of his tail."

An hour later the Gophers had been briefed and were climbing out on a heading of three-one-five degrees toward the Japanese stronghold at Hollandia. Just past the small U.S. auxiliary base at Gusap, Lee sighted the B-24s they were to escort. A lump of pride grew in his throat as they overtook the incredible mass of four-engine bombers. The clusters of fat-bodied, double-tailed Liberators spread over several square miles. Lee had heard numbers like fifty and sixty, but to actually *see* such a group of flying destruction was something else. He imagined that the mission was indeed similar to the Eighth Air Force missions over Germany, and he wondered how anything could survive the tons of high explosives they carried.

The 483rd Fighter Group took to their escort positions at varying altitudes above the bombers. They throttled back, leaned their mixtures, and settled in for what was to be their longest mission so far. As they passed some thirty miles west of the Jap base at Madang, Lee sharpened his vigilance. From here on in they were in enemy territory. They would be skirting to the west of Jap bases at Madang, Hansa Bay, Wewak, and Aitape on their way to Hollandia. And while the Japanese radar was still much less effective than the U.S. technology, Lee doubted that a formation of nearly a hundred large aircraft could pass four Japanese bases undetected.

An hour later the formation altered course slightly to swing farther to the west around Aitape. As they returned to their original course to Hollandia, Lee spotted columns of smoke ahead. Various shades of gray to black told him the early strike mission had come off as scheduled. A large group of B-25 mediums was to have gone in low dropping deadly parafrags called Daisey Cutters, actually small bomblets loaded with shrapnel. The parafrags were suspended from tiny parachutes to give the bombers time to clear before exploding near ground level. If effective, the attack would tear up fighter planes and anti-aircraft installations, thus reducing the risks for the main attack force, without destroying runways the Allies would need.

The bombers split into three groups, each headed for an airdrome now clearly marked by its smoke. Lee's group continued straight on toward huge Lake Sentani and the Sentani Airdrome. The other two groups split for Hollandia and Cyclops. But before the runways had become visible, a dozen Oscars could be seen climbing rapidly a couple of miles to the east.

"Bogeys at four o'clock coming up to meet us," crackled Mo's voice. "Switch and drop. String 'em out. Notice the ragged formation. I think they've been hurt—they're scrambling and disorganized. Lee, go down after them. Greenie, follow. Red, stay up here."

"Roger," replied Lee and Greenie in succession.

With a warning waggle of his wings, Lee banked to the right and started down. The Gophers would have the advantage of both altitude and speed. It looked like his flight could hit the Oscars before they reached the bombers at 12,000 feet. The Jap fighters seemed not to have spotted the diving Lightnings for they continued their climb, obviously intending to come around and hit the bombers from above and behind.

Lee saw a rare opportunity to catch the Oscars like sitting ducks and he allowed his airspeed to push 400 mph. He lined up on the lead enemy fighter on the left, allowing his flight mates clear shots to those on the right. He lined up his target, then nosed up slightly to lead him. It seemed all too eas—

Suddenly, the Japanese fighters broke their hastily contrived formation, darting in all directions like shrapnel from an exploding bomb. Lee's target scampered left and out of his line of sight. He gave up on that one and looked for a secondary target. He saw Oscars all over the place, but none in front of Lee Marks and the Blue Flight.

"Okay, Blue, coming up around to the left. Keep your eyes open," Lee called.

He cut the turn short and increased his angle to get his group back on top as quickly as possible. By the time he had completed the climbing three-sixty, the situation had deteriorated into chaos, an old-fashioned dogfight in which a mid-air collision was almost as likely as taking hits from an enemy fighter. The only plus Lee could find was that the dozen Jap Oscars were so entangled with the seven Lightnings they could not shake free to attack the Liberators.

"Lee! Stew!" came a frantic call from Chub Forbes, "Give me some help! Two on my tail and I can't shake 'em!"

Lee twisted to look over his right shoulder.

"Take 'em down and right, Chub! Stew, stick with me."

Lee took his Marksman into a sharp turn to the left to come around behind the Oscars. He and Stew had completed three-fourths of the turn when three Lightnings flashed past his nose from right to left. He caught the number on the third ship: 168. It was Sandy. The first two must have been Mo and Bubba. As he completed his turn he saw them blow the two Oscars off Chub's tail.

"Thanks, Mo," Lee called. "Good shooting."

Collecting Chub, Lee searched for targets. The Gophers were flying by the book, and it seemed to be working. No sooner would a few Lightnings dive through the Jap fighters and take out one or two than they would be followed by another pair of diving P-38s. The nimble Jap Oscars seemed to be confused. As soon as they locked onto a Lightning, two more appeared out of nowhere.

But they had no monopoly on confusion. Everywhere Lee took his two flight mates in search of targets, they were too late. They turned, twisted, climbed, and dived, but they never got a good shot at anything. Finally, Lee took his two followers and climbed for altitude above the bombers for a final check on their welfare. The big brothers flew on steadily, unmolested. But as the bombers approached the airdrome, the flak intensified and Lee took Blue Flight off to watch over the bombers from a distance.

When the bombers had outrun the flak, Mo called the Gophers to reassemble above the Liberators. The few remaining Oscars had turned toward the sea and safety. Except for the refueling stop at Gusap, Lee found the return flight as long and boring as he had feared.

Following Tony Margo on final approach to Nadzab, Lee settled The Marksman in as smoothly as ever. As the rumble of his tires on the steel matting subsided, he turned off the runway to his right. Then, he followed with a sharp right turn toward the Gopher flight line. He twisted his head to watch Stew, his new wingman, complete his landing.

Stew looked good. He had yet to slow enough to ease his nose wheel down to the matting when one of the dreaded demons of New Guinea airfields rose up to smite him. A protrusion in the perforated steel matting punctured his left main tire. The flat tire spewed shreds of rubber as it pulled the heavy Lightning hard to its left toward the parallel taxiway for Strip Number One.

Lee found himself standing on his own brakes in a futile effort to help his wingman. But stopping a 17,000-pound aircraft veering out-of-control at eighty miles per hour called for something beyond Lee, something not published in the P-38 flight manual. He felt his scalp tingle as he watched Number 167 skid farther and farther to its left on a path that meant certain collision with a taxiing B-25.

Only a hundred yards of bare ground separated the two planes when the landing gear of the Lightning suddenly retracted. The stricken bird settled smoothly to its belly. A vivid trail of sparks gave way to clouds of dust when Stew slid off the steel matting onto soft earth. Bursts of exhaust smoke behind the B-25 said its pilot had accelerated to avert the collision, but Lee's angle of vision told him the effort was in vain.

In the first fifty yards of its slide, Stew's speed hardly diminished, but once the friction took effect, the Lightning slowed rapidly, finally coming to rest about fifteen yards short of the helpless Mitchell bomber.

"Yeah!" Lee shouted. "Way to dump it, Stew!"

The grateful pilot of the B-25 reached out through his side window and tossed his hat into the air. His prop wash caught the disc-like object and hurled it back down the taxi strip.

By the time the dust had settled, Lee had parked his ship and shut it down. Skipping his post-flight checklist, he bolted from the cockpit, jumped down from the trailing edge of the wing and headed for Stew's Lightning. A crowd had gathered around the rookie pilot. Stew simply stood there, looking at the rumpled underside of his first assigned aircraft and shaking his head. He seemed relieved when he saw Lee approach.

"Do you think they'll ever give me another one?" he asked Lee.

"After the great move you just made, they owe you two," Lee replied. "I'm not sure I'd have thought to retract the gear."

"One thing about it," the cautious little pilot said. "It's sure easier to get down when you don't have to climb that rickety ladder."

"Uh, there's another thing about it," said Lee, nodding at the damaged P-38 with its propeller tips neatly folded back. That's Colonel Hammer's aircraft. He loaned us two ships from Headquarters Squadron, and that's one of them."

Chapter 30

Lee tried to read Mo's face as the he joined him on the walk up the flight line toward Ops. Within seconds he knew the effort had been wasted.

"Christ, Marks, didn't you warn Stewart about the matting?"

"No. Did you?"

Mo smiled his noncommittal smile, grunted, and trudged on. "You know, I had to coax Sledge to lend us his ship. Now Sergeant Worley thinks we might have to total it out. You want the privilege of telling Sledge?"

"Not really," said Lee, "I imagine the hammer will fall. But it wasn't Stew's fault. That could have been you or me—or the colonel himself. When a tire blows, it blows. And how many of us would have thought that quickly and had the guts to jerk the gear? He probably saved six lives and a B-25. Oh, oh, speak of the devil."

"Tell me I heard it wrong, Mo," said Colonel Hammer. His iron-clad voice resonated no more than was customary and his steely eyes showed only the usual glint. Still, Lee held his breath, waiting for the explosion.

"Sounds to me like the kid did a hell of a job," said the colonel. "That could have been a bad one, good for six letters home. Which one of you taught him that trick? You, Marks?"

"Uh, no, Colonel. Must have been Mo."

"Well, I don't overly labor the point with our rookies," said Mo. "But they all need to be briefed on that move since we do lose tires to the Marston matting."

"Good job, Mo. Hate to lose my ship, though." Sledge turned directly to Mo. "Maybe this is the time to use that ace you say you have up your sleeve, use it to get me a new ship. What do you think?"

"Maybe, Sledge," said Mo, "but I had hoped I could wait a little longer and then go for a larger order for new aircraft. Moresby and Townsville are getting more and more of the new Model Ls in from the States. I was hoping we could hold off until we could replace all of our J-models with the new L."

"Good point, Mo, but I need a ship." Sledge Hammer looked about as though studying the foot traffic on the dusty paths that formed a matrix at the center of the 483rd headquarters area. "I'll do some sniffing around, see what kind of a read I can get on the supply line into Moresby. Maybe I can work an angle to get a new ship and still keep your option open."

Lee took care of his debriefing with Lieutenant Nelson, then hung around over a cup of coffee with Mo in the Officers' Mess. At final count, the 125th Gopher Squadron had scored seven Oscars over Sentani Airdrome. And except for the wipe-out of Colonel Hammer's ship, the squadron suffered no losses or serious damage. Mo and Bubba had each added a kill. Lee felt certain his flight would have nailed those two Oscars had Mo's Red Flight not cut in on the action. And his own failure to get lined up on any other targets made the loss of those two scores a little harder to take.

With no scheduled activity for the rest of the day, Lee needed to get his mind on other things so he headed up the dusty path toward the tent. There would be pick-up volleyball and baseball games. He glanced down at the dust that had collected on his boots, then looked skyward. A cluster of low-drifting, dark gray cumulus clouds appeared ready to dump on them. He increased his pace and as he turned to hustle up the steps into their tent the first huge drops fell.

"Only in New Guinea," he mumbled, "dust one minute and rain the next."

"Hey, Lee! Strap yourself in," Bubba said, motioning to a chair at the crude center table. Alone in the tent, he sat at the wobbly table, a bottle of Scotch before him and a metal cup of the whiskey in one hand. "Lee, I got another one today. That's five. Lee Marks, meet Bubba Nash—Ace!" He gave a sloppy salute, then carelessly tossed a large swallow down, gulped and choked for a moment, coming up out of it with watery eyes.

Though startled again by his young protege's extraordinary transition from mollycoddled misfit to maladroit macho man, Lee brushed his fatherly concerns aside and sat down to join in the celebration. While Bubba didn't need Scotch, he did need to have his successes celebrated.

"That's five, Lee, *five!* That's more than four of the other Gophers, more than nineteen of the other thirty-five pilots in the 483rd Fighter Group! Boy, I can't wait for ol' Bart to get here."

"Uh-uh," Lee said. He reached out and grabbed the bottle, capped it, and set it on the floor beside him. "Two things wrong here, Bubba. You've got some things to learn about self-control as relating to booze and to fighting. You've got to learn that unless you watch it, the booze leads to fighting. Drunk or sober, *you* are no fighter. But then we've already covered that."

"Yeah, yeah, we've covered that. I know I'm not a fighter, not yet. I know that."

"But you're looking forward to lording it over Black Bart. You should know by now—"

"I do, I do. I wasn't going to lord it into a fight, just going to let him know that I'm a much better pilot than he is."

"You even start in that direction, my friend, and I'll have you chewing on a knuckle sandwich." Lee grabbed the bottle, stood up, and said, "C'mon, Ace Bubba. The rain has stopped, and I know a good place where we can go have a couple of snorts and a quiet, little celebration—without Bart." As Lee headed for the path that led to the clump of palm trees on the knoll overlooking the river Bubba caught up.

"Did you know, Lee, that good Scotch is hard to come by out here? Gin is everywhere, but to get good whiskey, you have to know how to go about it. Why I heard of a 475th pilot whose wife sends him whiskey in mouthwash bottles. Pretty neat, huh?"

They settled onto the log provided by a toppled palm tree at the familiar spot where Mo had taken Lee just days before. Lee hoped Mo wouldn't mind the two of them using his special place.

Lee poured each a fresh cup of Scotch. He wedged the bottle down between his feet. At the right moment he intended to accidentally kick the bottle over. "Okay," he toasted, "here's to Bubba Nash, the Gopher Squadron's newest ace and incredible secret weapon."

"Thank you, Lee," Bubba responded. "That sounded nice. I'm not used to people saying nice things about me, you know. It's always seemed that on an intellectual level people were afraid to meet me, and on a physical level they were too anxious to beat me. I guess that's how I got in the habit of crawling into the woodwork and only sticking my head out to say something once in a while so they wouldn't completely forget I was there."

"That must have been tough, Bubba. Did you manage to have any kind of a social life through high school and your two years of college?" Lee considered asking about girl friends but let the thought pass. He didn't want to embarrass

Bubba. It took a better imagination than Lee's to picture skinny Bubba, with his red face and round ears, with a girl friend.

"Oh, sure. I usually hung out with a couple of bookworm friends. I really didn't have too many choices. And then there was Janelle."

"Janelle?"

"Oh sure, my girl friend, Janelle. We went steady together through the last two years of high school and nearly two years of college."

Lee was stunned. "*You* had a girl friend?"

"We even did it—*seven* times," Bubba added.

"You did? Seven times? Approximately seven, or exactly seven?"

"Exactly seven—two years at Christmas, two years on her birthday, two years on my birthday, and once on Valentine's Day."

"What did you do on all your other dates, sit and look at the calendar?" Lee wished he could take it back, but Bubba seemed not to have heard the remark.

"She sent me a Dear John letter, you know," Bubba said, motioning to Lee for a refill.

"She did? When?"

"I got it just the other day, right after my tussle with the Jap sub."

"Bubba, you should have said something to me. That must have been very upsetting." Lee grappled with guilt. Here was poor Bubba, dealing with a Dear John, and he had lacked the sensitivity to pick up on it. He vowed silently to himself that he would—

"It was a real relief," Bubba went on. "See, after the first time Janelle considered us engaged. And each time we did it, we got more engaged. Then, after the seventh time she said there'd be no eighth time until we were married. She said, 'Seven times is for good luck. Eight times is just to fuck.' Really, I'm quite intelligent, Lee, but I never figured *that* one out."

"I suspect neither of us ever will, Bubba. Just count your blessings." Lee checked his watch. "Hey, Bubba, we'd better head for chow or we'll miss it. Long time till breakfast."

"If you wouldn't mind too much, Lee, I'd like to just sit here and talk till the Scotch is gone. Would you do that for me, Lee? It's kind of a special day for me. Pretend it's my birthday."

Lee did a quick self-assessment. On an empty stomach he had quickly developed a warm glow; the Scotch had begun to taste good; and Bubba needed the attention and support. Lee outvoted his reluctance, ditched the thought of spilling the booze, and the party went on. They talked more about personal things, about post-war aspirations, and then about their chances of surviving the war to follow through on those aspirations.

Darkness settled in. The lazy rain had begun again, but it kept the mosquitoes down. And sitting there soaking wet in the cool breeze on the hilltop logs really felt quite good. By 1900 hours the conversation had slowed and there were periods during which the two pilots simply sat there quietly in the rain staring out over the darkened base. It was strange, no lights yet.

Suddenly, as though scripted, the rain stopped; the stars reappeared; and the reverie of the little party was broken by a thundering *Pom! Pom! Pom!* The 90-millimeter anti-aircraft guns on the north perimeter had sounded the air raid alert.

"Too early for Charlie," Lee said. "Listen. I hear several of them. I think they're *serious*. We've got the ditch right here, but this time I'm not diving into that mud until I have to."

"M-m-me neither."

Lee and Bubba listened as the drone of the Jap bombers came their way.

"They're coming from the northwest, probably from Wewak or Madang. Not likely to be from Rabaul," Lee said. "Sounds like they're up about 10,000 feet."

The anti-aircraft batteries surrounding the base opened up. The non-stop *Pom! Pom! Pom! Pom!* of the nearest battery was matched by those of five other batteries and soon echoed by the aerial *Crack! Crack! Crack! Crack!* of their shells exploding high in the air. The unrelenting cacophony thumped Lee's ear drums and sent shivers up his spine. When the falling Japanese bombs began to add their *Whomp! Whomp! Whomp!* to the mix, Lee met with true terror for the first time, the terror felt in Nanking, London, and Manilla. This was a war that was new to the young pilots. In *this* war they were the helpless ones. This was *real* war.

"Bubba! Looks like most of the bombs are missing the flight line and the main parts of the base—but they're walking right toward us!" Lee shouted. "Bail out!"

The two young aviators ran a few steps and slid feet first into the five-foot drainage ditch that doubled as an air raid shelter. The fresh mud cushioned Lee's slide, and as he hugged the side of the trench he felt the slime oozing over the tops of his cut-off engineers' boots.

"Lee, did you bring the Scotch?"

"Forget it!"

"Those Nips aren't going to spoil *my* party," said Bubba. Lee glanced over his shoulder in time to see his friend claw his way up and out of the trench. The awkward towhead had made it a couple of steps toward the bottle when a bomb exploded in a nearby clump of trees with a mighty *Whomp!*. The concussion tossed Bubba backward like a leaf in the wind. His body did a mid-air flip and he landed face first in the muck of the trench.

"You okay, Bubba?" Lee shouted as he sloshed over to his cohort. "You okay?"

Bubba's contortions as he righted himself resembled those of a gigantic earthworm squirming in the soft muck. As he recovered his balance he scrawled up to the lip of the trench and shook both fists at the sky.

"You dirty bastards!" Bubba shouted. "You sons of bitches! I'm going to get you! You hear me? I'm going to get you! You hear me?"

Lee was taken aback by the latest remonstration coming from his enigmatic friend. And at that precise moment, the bombs stopped exploding. The firing of the anti-aircraft guns began to taper off. Lee found himself back in his world and watching what had to be the choice comedy of Bubba Nash's Army Air Force career.

Bubba's head and face were thickly plastered with mud. In the darkness, only two eyes and two round ears showed through the mask. There stood a monster from beneath the earth, shaking his fists and shouting epithets at the long-gone Jap bombers.

Lee broke up. He roared, a volcanic eruption of shrieking, gagging, choking, and laughing that had been repressed for all too many months. A part of him said, "Don't laugh at Bubba. Don't hurt him." But the sight of the gangly, mud-covered spook threatening the entire Japanese Air Army won out. His laughter rolled on, uncontrolled until he realized that the mud-covered spook was standing before him, quietly looking directly at him. It was enough to stem the tide of humor.

"You know something, Marks?" Bubba said. "You really look like hell." Then he, too, began to laugh. It was no longer the nasal, boyish snicker of the meek Bubba Nash, but more a deep, hearty belly laugh resonating with newfound maturity.

"I'll bet I do," sputtered Lee, "but God, it feels so good." He scrambled up and out of the ditch, then turned and gave Bubba a hand. "You okay?"

"I think so, but you know? I do have a real owy somewhere under all this mud. It's on the side of my head. Lee? I think I got whacked by a chunk of shrapnel." He ran his fingers through his once blond hair. "I can't tell, Lee. It stings, but with all the mud I can't tell if I'm bleeding."

"Come on, Bubba. Let's get you back to camp. Can you walk it okay?"

"Yeah. I think so."

The twosome struggled down the darkened path toward whatever was left of their civilization. About the time they reached the showers, the lights came back on. Without a word, Lee turned his friend fully dressed into one of the crude shower stalls, centered him, and pulled the rope. After a minute, he pushed Bubba aside and took a turn under the cool water. Then he towed Bubba over to the nearest light bulb for an examination.

"You know what?" Lee said. "I don't see any wound, any blood coming out."

Bubba ran another finger test. "Hey, I think you're right. It really smarts, but it isn't bleeding."

"Maybe you got hit by the flat side of something flying through the air," Lee speculated.

"Maybe so," Bubba said. "That's good enough for me. Hey, I know what. Let's go down to the flight line and see how Bubba's Subba and The Marksman came through it all."

"Good thinking, Bubba."

"And if they're all right, let's just finish our party." From behind him he whipped out the half-full bottle of Scotch and held it up.

"Whoa! Where'd you get *that?*"

"I always said those Japs can't hit anything," replied Bubba triumphantly. "Come on."

Some time later a strange convoy wheeled up to the rear of the mess. One very wet and very drunk lieutenant pushed and struggled with a bomb dolly over which was draped, face-down, the body of a second officer.

"A-y-y-y, Sarshen! A-y-y-y, Sarshen!"

"Yeah, what da ya want?" came Sergeant Warren's voice from within the kitchen.

"A-y-y-y, Sarshen! You got any coffee fer my frien'? I think he's…a liddle drunk."

The face of the sergeant appeared at the kitchen entrance. He quickly surveyed the situation and said, "Oh, Lieutenant Nash? Who's that you got there?"

"He'sh my frien'. He'sh allus lookin' after me. Good frien'…"

Chapter 31

It had to be an omen of good things to come. Lee could see it no other way. First Bubba gets whacked on the side of the head by shrapnel and comes away without a scratch. Then he himself gets whacked by a bottle of Scotch, gets falling down drunk, something he'd never done in his life, and wakes up—without a hangover. He was hungry, terribly hungry, but no hangover. It was a good thing, because Bubba had seized the opportunity to launch an early morning roast at Lee's expense. Lee shouldn't have minded. After all, Bubba had only recently found something he could crow about. And now he had added Lee to his list somewhere beneath the Jap submarine. Lee smiled. One couldn't get much lower than a submarine.

They passed a busy group of enlisted men and fuzzy-haired natives who were repairing shrapnel holes in tents that had suffered in the air raid. After each tent was lowered, a couple of the natives sewed patches over the holes and then treated each with a water proofing paste. Scuttlebutt had it that about a dozen enlisted men suffered shrapnel wounds during the air raid.

"It's good, Lee," Bubba quipped as they passed, "it's good you got a little last night."

"Got a little?"

"Yeah. The word is out that you were seen riding a dolly last night."

Lee smiled. But as they approached the mess tent, he felt sufficiently punished.

"Bubba," he said calmly, turning to look his compatriot in the eye, "that's enough now. Understand? Enough. No more."

Bubba stifled a laugh as Lee's message sank in. "But I was just—"

Lee simply slashed across his own throat with an index finger while staring Bubba Nash into silence. Deep down, though, he was glad to have served as the object of Bubba's jokes. The poor kid hadn't won many in his lifetime. But Lee was also aware that Bubba's role reversal could get out of hand. He hoped the gentle young man hadn't lost his good qualities to that Japanese submarine far out in the Bismarck Sea. If his personality swap gets wildly out of control, could he become another Black Bart?

The breakfast of rubbery pancakes suited Lee, matched his ravenous appetite better than the typical green eggs and wormy toast might have. There were those who searched through the pancakes for grubs. Since the cooked creatures were harder to find in pancakes, Lee and the majority preferred to close their eyes to the problem and use lots of the imitation maple syrup.

Hollandia's Sentani Airdrome was up once again as the target for the day. Gopher Squadron was to rendezvous with a squadron of A-20 twin-engine, light attack bombers near Gusap. The Lightnings would lead the low level attack and concentrate their strafing on anti-aircraft installations and aircraft on the ground. The fast A-20s would follow with a blanket of parafrags. The heavy bombers, escorted by the 475th Fighter Group, were attacking shipping in the harbors. Command was preserving the infrastructure of airdromes like Sentani by using the heavy bombers elsewhere. The neutralizing of the Japanese Air Army was on schedule.

By 0730 hours Gopher Squadron had reached 16,000 feet as they followed the Markham River Valley to the northwest through the mountains. The air seemed cooler than usual for the altitude, and Lee was glad he'd thrown on his jacket and warmer boots at the last minute. Gusap, the small emergency field along the Markham could hardly be seen through the developing layer of clouds. When they cleared the mountains and reached the Ramu River, they altered their course to a near-westerly heading of two-nine-four degrees.

The course would parallel the rugged Bismarck Mountains, one section of the enormous mountain range that ran east to west through the center of New Guinea for the island's entire length of 1200 miles. The prevailing logic said that such a course on the way to the numerous enemy bases along the north coast of New Guinea would keep the Fifth Air Force aircraft from enemy eyes and ears and therefore reduce the Japs' alert reaction time.

To Lee it was a comforting thought—if it worked. But with the thousands of Japanese infantry who had been forced to retreat to the jungles, Lee doubted that the Fifth Air Force could so much as visit the latrine without the Japanese Army knowing it and spreading the news up the line. As he peered down to the green mass far below through an occasional break in the thickening layer of clouds, he shivered lightly at the prospect of ever going down in this region. If a downed pilot didn't run into Japanese soldiers scattered through the jungles he stood a good chance of meeting up with area headhunters and cannibals. He smiled to himself as he recalled Burner Hedman's comment on the subject. "Hell," the burly lumberjack had said, "I don't really care if they eat me or what they do with me as long as I'm dead before they throw me in the pot." Lee's radio crackled.

"Uhhh, Gophers," droned Mo's voice. "This is getting too thick. We'll be on instruments soon—never make our rendezvous. Let's go down and see what's in the basement. Tighten it up now."

The descent reminded Lee of that first flight from Port Moresby to Dobodura. It seemed like years ago, but he remembered the tension of dropping half-blind through the violent clouds, wondering all the time when he was to smack into a mountainside. But as before, Mo seemed to have made travel reservations for them. He banked this way and that, from one opening to another, dropping off about 700 feet per minute.

They had no sooner broken out of the clouds into a steady rain at 1,100 feet when Mo gave the order to abort the mission.

"Gardenia advises we take the same road home," he said. "Coming around left—now."

Lee's disappointment got washed aside by relief. They had flown two hours, which meant two more to get home with nothing accomplished. But the sudden decision had reduced the powerful enemy forces they faced from two to one. With the Japs out of the day's picture, the Gophers only had to contend with Mother Nature…the same old mother who had taken so many Fifth Air Force pilots.

After what seemed like far too long, they crossed the Ramu River once again and made their turn to the right in order to negotiate the mountain pass that would take them into the Markham River Valley.

"Okay, you rodents," said Mo. "Back up to 10,000 angels. Tighten it up. No panic now."

Though there were times when Lee lost sight of White Flight ahead of him, he held to his course and trusted his instruments. His wing mates, Chub Forbes and Stew, remained glued to his wingtips. The fact that Blue Flight was, in fact, a group of only three ships gave Lee some relief. Bart was still grounded, and his P-38 had been assigned for the day to Stew. Lee knew as they crossed over and began their final descent that the worst was over. When they overflew Nadzab and found moderate visibility at 1,000 feet, the Gophers knew they were home.

They got the word upon reporting in that the heavies who had flown to attack the harbors had met no enemy fighters because the area was socked in. They could see nothing. So they headed down the coast on the way home, and as they reached the other heavy concentration of bases at Wewak the weather opened up for them. They and their escorts dropped everything they had, including the fighters' empty wing tanks.

The next day was April Fools' Day and Lee wondered, as the P-38s of the 483rd Fighter Group escorted the squadron of A-20s once again to Sentani Airdrome at Hollandia, just who the fools would be. Located just north of the large Sentani Lake were three enemy airdromes, Hollandia, Sentani, and Cyclops. A fourth drome, Tami, was located to the east of Humboldt Bay, nearer the ocean. According to the plan, the Gophers, followed by the A-20s, would come in low and fast from the west hoping to catch the Sentani defenses by surprise. The remaining two squadrons of P-38s would fly cover, ready to come down and protect the low-flying attackers. Other units would mount similar attacks on Hollandia and Cyclops dromes.

Col. Sledge Hammer had made a point of assigning the Pony and Bobcat Squadrons the cover duty so that, if airborne enemy fighters were to be encountered, the two squadrons would draw the combat.

"I've got to do this now and then," Sledge had told Mo and Lee privately, "for the sake of morale. Some are starting to complain that I've favored you Gophers a bit, and I can't have that."

Gopher Squadron came in on the deck very hot, crossing the west bay of Sentani Lake just south of the village of Jakonde, then angling slightly to the southeast toward the enemy radio installation on the far shore of the lake. Element by element they raked the station with their fire as they passed. Mo then led them in a slow left bank northward toward the Hollandia drome. But the Gophers knew what the Japs did not. Seemingly committed to an attack on the Hollandia drome they suddenly executed a sharp bank to the right which lined them up perfectly for their strafing run at Sentani.

Lee thought he saw, as his Blue Flight lined up for an unobstructed pass at Sentani, who the April fools would be that day, for what he saw was hard to believe—was it some kind of trick? There were enemy aircraft parked in rows along the runway just waiting to be nailed, yet none in the air. He felt the excitement that the Japanese pilots must have felt when they found a similar scene at Hickam Field during their infamous Pearl Harbor attack. But the anti-aircraft emplacements had to be knocked out to make things safer for the A-20s that followed.

The Gophers jinked slightly from side to side to fire on one gun pit, then another. Twice Lee saw his four fifties and the 20-millimeter canon rip up heavy machine gun emplacements, tossing men and collapsing weapons indiscriminately. Once over the perimeter ring of anti-aircraft guns, Lee sighted in on a row of parked Oscars. With the damage Red and White Flights had already inflicted, he and his two wing mates had to search and adjust quickly to find targets amid the billowing columns of black smoke.

Lee flamed one Oscar and one twin-engine Betty bomber. Approaching the far end of the field, it was time once again to search out gun emplacements. He felt yet another surge of adrenalin when he saw the blinking twinkies of a machine gun, clearly marking its own location. One on one, the P-38 was more than a match for an enemy machine gun, unless the enemy got sighted in first. Lee squeezed his 20-millimeter button in short bursts and the Jap weapon went dark.

Mo led them around to the right, as though they were executing a wide, right-hand landing pattern, and they reduced air speed for their second pass. Lee saw only one blinking weapon and it was quickly silenced by White Flight just ahead of him. But the heavy, black smoke made it extremely difficult to find targets. He managed to fire into another parked Oscar and see it blow up. As he pulled up and over the orange fireball, Lee felt a pang of regret; it was too bad these ground kills wouldn't add any Jap flags to the side of his cockpit.

The Gophers and the A-20s formed up to head home, and Lee looked over the Hollandia area. The massive base was surrounded by huge orchards of coconut palms planted in precise rows, once the plantation domain of Lever Brothers. With two large harbors, four airfields, and the mass of accompanying support buildings, Lee could more easily understand command's focus upon destroying the enemy and his weapons while preserving as much as possible of the Hollandia bases. When the vastly superior American engineers finished, Hollandia would make an impressive Allied base, comparable even to Port Moresby. And with the Allied conquests in the New Guinea war pointing clearly and perhaps eagerly toward MacArthur's return to the Philippines, Hollandia would serve well as a primary staging base.

When all the Gophers were nestled in their spots on the flight line back at Nadzab, Mo called them together.

"Unless you have any critical damage, have your crew chief just refuel, re-arm, and put your aircraft to bed for the night," he directed. "After chow tonight," he continued, "the 483rd is having a little get-together in that space over behind Ops. Bring your mess kits," he said. Then to Lee he added, "When everybody's been debriefed, get your kill counts updated and get the appropriate perks out of the storage crate."

Later, as the officers and enlisted men of Gopher, Pony, and Bobcat Squadrons gathered together, a wave of celebratory enthusiasm mushroomed. The Pony and Bobcat squadrons were excited. Their replays of the day's mission buzzed on and on. Finally on this mission they had found themselves in perfect position to intercept a group of eleven Oscars and four Zeros who were bent on breaking up the low-level attack. When the encounter closed, two Oscars and one remaining Zero scooted out of the action to save themselves for another day. One P-38 in Bobcat Squadron was badly hit and presumed lost trying to make it to Gusap. But it appeared that Sledge's mission assignments had served well.

"Okay, quiet down and listen up!" called Col. Hammer. When the buzz of voices had faded to nothing he continued, "You all did a good job today. We've had a recon up there shooting film so we can get a clearer picture of what's left. But we do know that you Gophers and your A-20 buddies wiped out a hell of a lot of their aircraft on the ground. Intelligence is still trying to figure out why they had so many planes parked instead of flying. Could be lack of fuel; could be lack of pilots; could be lack of brains." Laughter rolled through the group. "And while you Gophers were breaking their airplanes, the 126th and 127th were doing a great job upstairs. They knocked down twelve Oscars and Zeros. As you probably know, we lost one. There's still a chance he'll make it back."

Sledge Hammer stood there for a moment, a smile on his face, surveying the group before him.

"Now," he went on, "while you fighter jocks are kicking ass at Hollandia, your ground crews are sweating it out. And the rest of our support group are working right on through. I don't think any of us who fly can forget for a moment who puts us up there. Without all of you support personnel, we'd be sitting here on our butts twiddling our joysticks."

The fighter group responded with a burst of laughter and applause.

"Now, while all of that was going on today, our corporate public relations committee—that's Sergeant Jernigan and Corporal Muney—hauled ass for Lae, where some big navy stuff has docked. They took with them a load of our, uh, *corporate acquisitions.* You know, when it comes to trading, our Sergeant Jernigan is the master of all. And what does all this mean? When we trade with the swabbies, it means—"

"Ice Cream!"

"Whooo-eee!"

"Yaaay-Navy!"

Lee was off to one side, rechecking his awards list and the prizes he had brought from the corporate crate when the cheers and whistles exploded. He stopped and looked over the group. Not since his college days had he seen such a large group that happy.

"Here, Lieutenant Marks," said Sergeant Jernigan, after he had his helpers begin dishing up the ice cream, "This is a list of the stuff I took out for trading stock. You can deduct it from your inventory, too."

"Fine," said Lee. "Do you really think you've got enough ice cream for *all* these guys?"

"May not have enough for seconds, but otherwise we're fine. Twenty gallons. Had to do some real jury-rigging, though, to try to keep it cold."

"For twenty gallons I can't imagine that we have any souvenirs left in the crate."

"Hardly made a dent, Lieutenant. It's all about putting the right things under the noses of the right people. But you know what those damned swabbies did?"

Lee looked at the sergeant quizzically.

"Every time we took a lid off an ice cream container there was a slip of paper inside that said, 'Kilroy was here!'"

The ice cream social rolled along nicely. Groups of GIs settled here and there, many clusters simply sitting cross-legged on the ground. At one point, Lee interrupted the festivities long enough to make the awards. At this second award ceremony nearly all of the prizes went to members of the 126th and 127th Squadrons, a fact that brought Lee a good feeling. But he had to admit to a stronger emotion when he called Bubba Nash, Ace, up to collect his Order of the Glasses award. Lee chuckled at the proud, jock-like swagger as Bubba walked up and back.

By the time Lee got to the ice cream they had already served some seconds. He was too late. But as he stood aside and dealt with his disappointment, he saw Mo walk to the front of the group. With a broad smile, Mo made the usual gestures and the group quieted.

"Gentlemen! In a war like this we seldom have the opportunity to grant recognition so well-deserved like Col. Hammer has tonight. But before we break up tonight, I'd like to bring up three more men for appropriate recognition.

Lee wondered where Mo was going. He'd heard nothing of other awards.

It's come to my attention, thanks to Sergeant Jernigan, that three of you have birthdays this week. So let's have you stand up and collect your due. Captain Robesky! Sergeant Harrison! and Corporal Masters! Stand up, please!"

With the customary, "Gee whiz, do I have to?" reluctance, the three finally made it to their feet and were serenaded individually by a rousing, up-tempo verse of *Happy Birthday*.

As the party broke up, Lee sidled over to Mo.

"That was really nice of you, Mo. A really nice touch."

"You know, Killer?" Mo said, his smile widening, "I think they bought it. Now that we've got the awards ceremony over with, why don't you pick up a jug of Scotch and meet me down at the river."

Booze was the last thing on Lee's wish list that evening, but he nodded agreement and set off for the corporate crate. He glanced about as he left the gathering to see that his departure went unnoticed. But as he rounded the corner of the first large crate he nearly bumped into an enlisted man standing with his back turned, taking a leak.

"Man, good idea," Lee said. He stood up beside the corporal, opened his trousers, and commenced draining his own reservoir, somewhat surprised at his success under the conditions. When the corporal had gone, Lee grabbed a bottle of Scotch, relocked the crate and headed for the clump of palm trees where he found Mo waiting with two cups.

"I—I think I'll pass on the Scotch tonight," Lee said. "I don't want to push my luck."

"Oh?" Mo looked at him quizzically. He raised his own tin cup in a perfunctory toast and then drank a long slug. An awkward silence set in.

"I'm still wondering, Mo. They've got us flying way over to the west to Hollandia. Yet, we're bypassing Wewak and Madang, both much closer. I'd think we'd be softening up Madang, the next big invasion target along the coast."

"What do you think is going on?" Mo asked.

"Not sure, but I *think* we must have other units pounding Madang and Wewak while we go up and beat up on Hollandia. The Japs would certainly expect support from Hollandia when MacArthur invades Madang. And we draw the long straws because of our P-38 range?"

"Pretty good logic, Killer. I hope the Japs see it that way."

"Meaning?"

"Need to know," was Mo's final punctuation on the subject.

After another blank of silence, Lee heard himself say, "I don't know about you, Mo, but for me this whole week has had the sparkle of a mud bath. First mission, I couldn't hit a barn with a snowball. Second mission, we have to abort and fight our way home through the weather. And today, nothing but high-risk ground action, no flags at all. I guess it's just one of those times when we have to search for personal satisfaction."

"Look at it this way. We really creamed a lot of parked aircraft, planes we'd have to face in combat some day. And we did some good PR work with the 126th and 127th that should shut down their damned bitching for awhile." Mo took another swallow of Scotch, then cast an expectant look at Lee. He held the pose but said nothing. The customary fixed smile left Lee stymied.

"Uhhh, did I miss something there?" Lee asked.

"Yes."

"Okay…what's wrong?"

"Well, for starters, I can't really figure out how you ever manage to hit a Jap airplane…with vision as bad as yours."

"Vision?" Lee stopped. He tried to guess what was forthcoming. Mo simply sat there, staring at Lee, and lightly fingering the silver leaf insignia on his collar.

"Not only is your vision bad, Killer, but you're also color blind. How'd you get this far?"

The final clue popped the mystery open. Silver leaf—Mo's promotion had come through! Major Mo Brennan had traded his gold leaf for the silver leaf of a lieutenant colonel! Lee sputtered and stammered his way through half-cooked congratulations until he finally slowed and realized that he was adding nothing to the event.

"It's not such a big deal," Mo said. "It's a stepping stone. In my role here I can't really do a whole lot more as a light colonel than I did as a major. I sure as hell don't need the money. But down the road you and I are checking out of here. Before we do, I want to make bird colonel and see you at least a captain, maybe major. Major would be better. Then we go make some real hay."

"You know, Mo, I still have some trouble buying into your perspective on the future. I can see how this great success can benefit you. If you can go home as a bird colonel with a kill record rivaling Dick Bong's, why they probably *will* put up a statue in your home town. But me? I'm still a nobody. I don't really even *have* a home town, at least not one I can go back to."

"Ready now?" Mo motioned toward Lee's tin cup. Lee thrust it forward and Mo poured it half full. "You can always *make* a new hometown. That's easy as a war hero."

"To Lieutenant Colonel Mo Brennan," Lee toasted. "And this is only the beginning."

As they lowered their cups again, Mo's smile faded. Lee had developed the habit of trying to read his mentor's facial expressions as indicators of what was to come next. There was the wide grin, the peak of Mo's exuberance. There was the warm, pleasant smile, and then the benign, noncommittal smile that simply said, "I am smiling." From there Mo's face went into what Lee thought of as negative figures. The flat, straight face said, "I'm unhappy with you," and the reddened, distorted face said, "I'm thoroughly pissed and you are dead meat!" What Lee saw registered somewhere between "I am smiling" and "I'm unhappy with you."

Mo fumbled in one trouser pocket, finally extracting a half-pint metal hip flask. His concentration became intense as he filled the flask from the bottle of Scotch. With the task completed, he rammed the flask back into his trouser pocket and turned to Lee.

"You just said something—this is only the beginning." Mo's face was serious, but his eyes showed no anger. "This…today…or tomorrow could also be the *end*. Have you thought of that?"

"Well, of course, but I never suspected that you had those thoughts."

"I seldom do. I focus on the positive. But here in this lousy New Guinea war it could happen anytime, maybe the next time out. Killer, I want you to promise me a favor."

"Sure, Mo. Anything." Lee's gut tightened at the last word.

"I want you to promise that if I go down for the count, you'll write two letters for me. Well, it's really one letter, done twice."

"Okay…."

"Here are the names and addresses." Mo handed Lee a three-by-five card. On it were his parents' names and their address and also one John Hedrick, Minneapolis Daily Journal, along with the street address of the Minneapolis newspaper.

"I, uh…."

"You see, if I go down, Sledge will write the obligatory letter to my parents. But there are a few things wrong with that. Sledge is a lousy writer with absolutely no imagination. His letter will almost fit on that card, and it'll say only the usual bullshit, you know, 'fine officer and leader, excellent pilot as evidenced by his record.'" Mo paused to slop more whiskey into his cup and take a long drink. "You, on the other hand, know me better. You know what I've really accomplished out here, and you know the image I want presented back there…dead or alive. You follow?"

"I—I've never thought of myself as a creative writer, Mo. But for you, yes, I can do that. Who's this John Hedrick guy?"

"He's a highly respected columnist for the Star. I know him. He's the kind of guy who'd love to get his teeth into something like my New Guinea heroics.

He'll get me that statue. You'll do this for me? Make me God's gift to the war effort?"

"Do the best I possibly can, Mo."

"Okay, got that taken care of. Now let's talk a little more about the future." The customary smile was back. "I've put Greenie in for captain, and Sledge is rushing it through. By July we want Lee Marks to be a captain. Now, that's *really* pushing things—two promotions in three months. But if you can pile up a few more kills, shoot 'em up on the ground, and stay on the good side of your commanding officers, it can be done. You were right, you know. We do have the space in the squadron for two captains."

"Uh, Mo, it's my understanding that Fifth Air Force Fighter Command policy says that our tour is one year. And I heard that any promotions to captain require a commitment to stay here an extra four months. I'm not too sure I want to buy into that deal."

"But what you haven't heard, Killer, is that almost nobody is being shipped states-side anyway until we've landed in the Philippines and have worked our way well up into Luzon. Sledge says that comes from the top, from MacArthur. So what the hell's the difference? You're going to be here for a year anyway. But keep that one under your hat. Let someone else break the good news."

Suddenly the last elements of energy drained from Lee's reservoir. He felt beyond tired, more like weak. Was it the prospect of nine to thirteen more months of combat and jungle life? Was it the Scotch? Or both? He couldn't imagine keeping up the pace he'd been on for another nine months or longer. He felt like a grizzled, burned-out veteran after only three months. The kind of fierce aerial combat that would yield twelve kills, each one of which could easily have been him; the low-level strafing raids through the curtains of anti-aircraft fire; the abominable weather in which nobody should be flying; the coping with the inner workings of Mo Brennan; and the shepherding of the bumbling Bubba Nash—it all combined to make a foul, rancid existence topped with the tantrums of Black Bart. Thirteen months of that? As he watched Mo slurp another drink, then stare back at him through glassy eyes, it all began to come together.

"Got it figured out, huh, Killer?" Mo said. "Beginning to see who the real enemy is?"

Chapter 32

▼

The three squadrons of the 483rd Fighter Group roared out of Nadzab into the first signs of a brilliant, clear dawn, climbing steeply to altitude as they headed northwest up the Markham River Valley. Their mission, a repeat of the March 30, low-level attack on Sentani Airdrome at Hollandia, once again flying cover for the squadron of A-20 attack bombers. Command seemed intent on neutralizing the remaining Japanese air power on the four Hollandia bases, and they reasoned that pilots returning to the scene of their previous attack would more easily spot aircraft and equipment that had been rebuilt or moved.

What misgivings about the mission and flying Lee had carried into the cockpit with him that morning of April 3 faded as they reached 10,000 feet, cleared the mountains, and soared into a most gorgeous sunrise. He was glad, however, that the Allies had captured Kavieng and that this mission took them northward to Hollandia rather than eastward directly into the rising sun. The brilliant ball would have been a blinding beast for all of two hours. But that glorious morning sun will also, he thought, be a great place for the enemy to hide. And what aircraft they had left at Hollandia would likely be doing just that. The early morning departure did mean that they might return before the customary afternoon build-up of weather. Sledge and Mo had reinstated Black Bart into the lineup at Tail-end Charlie in Blue Flight. It was to be a trial, and Lee had to accept the decision.

The Gophers leveled off at 16,000 feet for the long journey to Hollandia, while Pony and Bobcat squadrons climbed on up to 22,000 feet to provide high cover. Lee's mind drifted to the chat of the previous evening with Mo. He was still surprised at Mo's open admission of mortality. Lee would never have predicted that conversation. And somehow, the thought that at any time he might find himself flying these missions without Mo's leadership put him on edge. The time might quickly come when he himself might have to issue the orders in combat and, perhaps worse, make the hairy decisions for the whole squadron when trying to find the way home in impossible weather. The thought sent a chill through his P-38 cockpit.

Through a restless night and the morning's pre-flight routine, Lee had tried to keep his mind away from the matter of battle fatigue. Having to deal with just the thought of fatigue after only three months in combat embarrassed him. It was certainly a subject he would not discuss with the other pilots, at least not for some time to come. If he was, in fact, falling into a battle with the dreaded F-word, he reasoned he would have to learn to power up his concentration and somehow overcome the depressive tide. To lose focus in their battles with the Japanese and the New Guinea weather would bring a quick trip to the exit.

Fifty miles short of Hollandia the coastline came into view, and Mo started the Gophers down to join up with the A-20s for the low-level attack. Pony and Bobcat squadrons would remain upstairs. With the blinding sun favoring the enemy, Lee felt comforted knowing the Gophers had the umbrella of protection.

At 15,000 feet their radio silence was suddenly shattered.

"Gophers and A-20s!" called Captain Robesky from the high cover position, "Bad guys coming down—your five o'clock! They slipped out of the sun behind and below us. We can't catch 'em in time!"

Lee snapped his head around for a look over his right shoulder. There they were, fifteen Oscars about 5,000 feet above the Lightnings and coming down fast. He expected Mo to turn and climb into them for a head-on. He turned his focus to Mo and the two flights ahead of Blue Flight.

"Gophers!" called Mo. "Switch and drop! Follow me down." His tanks had no sooner dropped from his wings than he peeled over to the right and began a steep dive for airspeed. At 12,000 feet, Mo pulled up into a fast climbing turn to come around toward the Oscars for a broadside and slightly downward attack. As Lee made the turn he could finally get a visual picture of the scene. Deflection shots at the fast-diving Oscars would be difficult, but—

"All right, Gophers," came Mo's voice. "Let's break up this party. Lead 'em enough, now."

Intent on reaching the bombers below, their adversaries had chosen to ignore the Gophers. Lee suspected the Japanese pilots were new, inexperienced replacements, rookie fighter pilots who tended to follow orders to the letter, allowing no flexibility for adjustment to unpredictable events. Lee knew it would be a tough shot, but twelve Lightnings each unloading four fifties, would spread a devastating gauntlet of fire. A glance up and to his left told him that Bobcat Squadron was coming down rapidly, gaining on the Oscars, and should be able to catch those who survived the Gopher attack before they could reach the A-20s. The hunters had become the hunted, caught in a two-pronged pincer. And the A-20s, who had to get down on the deck for the attack anyway, had simply taken the cue for an early departure.

As the distance to the Oscars closed, Lee could see the alignment favoring the Gophers more with each second that passed. Unless the enemy planes swerved suddenly toward Mo's group and forced them into a defensive mode, the speed the Gophers had picked up in their dive would enable them to slide into a comfortable three-quarter rear attack.

Analysis ceased when the action began. In but a minute the Lightnings blasted through the Oscar formation, sending debris flying among the numerous fireballs. The prospect of collision with planes or parts raised the hackles on Lee's neck.

He quickly flamed his first target, then pulled upward to his left and nailed another. When Blue Flight broke out on the other side of the Japanese group, Lee had collected a kill and a probable. And the ease with which he had done it fueled his excitement. It seemed like a fantasy. A few days before, he had been unable to get Blue Flight into position for a single shot. Wherever they went, the enemy had vanished. Today, each time he placed his right thumb on the trigger button, an Oscar conveniently appeared in his gun sight.

Gopher Squadron reassembled in a long, diving turn back toward the remnants of the Japanese formation. But Bobcat Squadron had indeed caught up and eliminated any threat to the bombers. They sent five flaming hulks into the jungle below, and the two remaining enemy fighters broke away and headed for the coast, a trail of smoke behind each. A quick count said the Gophers had finished off nine Jap fighters in the single pass.

The rest of the mission proved to be anti-climactic. On their way past the radio station near the lake, Red Flight completed the demolition job. One by one, Red, White, and Blue Flights made their low passes over the airdrome. But viable targets for strafing seemed hard to find. Everywhere Lee looked he saw devastation. Skeletons of blackened, burned out enemy planes covered the airdrome. Lee wondered what the trailing A-20s could possibly choose as targets for their destructive parafrag bombs. As he led Blue Flight up and out of their pass, he looked back at the rows and rows of tiny, descending parachutes that were blanketing the field. Each chute carried a fragmentation bomb whose spreading shrapnel was extremely deadly to man as well as aircraft.

When the Gophers had finished their debriefing back at Nadzab, Lee discovered that his good fortune had followed him home. His probable had been verified by Stew and Chub. He had come out of the brief skirmish with two kills, running his total to fourteen, amost a triple ace. Stew had scored his first two victories. Chub Forbes added one, running his total to five. Bart had somehow missed everything again. But even without a Barton contribution, Blue Flight had accounted for five Oscars. He quickly scanned the remainder of the sheet. Mo had scored one running his total to twenty-two; Bubba added one for a total of six; and Sandy also got a kill, topping his total at seven. In contrast, White Flight put up a graphic example of what Greenie called, "The fickle finger of fate." Despite having three of the more experienced combat pilots in Gopher Squadron, White only counted one kill, and that was credited to the rookie, Tony Margo. Lee could certainly understand the fickle finger—sometimes there was just no explanation.

Photo Recon sent another P-38-F-5 to Hollandia that afternoon, and when developed the photos confirmed that the recent raids on Hollandia's four airdromes had destroyed nearly 350 Japanese planes, the vast majority destroyed on the ground. The news blended with Sledge's order to "take a break," and the pilots and enlisted men of the 483rd breathed a collective sigh of relief. While the ground crews seized the stand-down time to catch up on maintenance and repairs, they kept at least one leg in the party atmosphere.

For several days, brisk breezes blew through Nadzab, bending the vast acres of kunai grass surrounding the base and converting all mud to a thick dust that rolled across the installation, blinding men and blanketing facilities. But still the pilots worked as hard at recreation as they had at the air war. The makeshift baseball field hosted one game after another, and constant repairs to the worn-out basketball net were the only interruptions to the ongoing pick-up games. Any shaded area that was blessed with only moderate moving air to break the stranglehold of tropical heat might find itself the site of a poker game.

Lee wandered over to the flight line to check on the progress of the maintenance work on The Marksman. He approached a mixed group of pilots and ground pounders in time to hear his assistant mechanic, Mac McTern, reading to the others from a book his mother had sent him.

"And here," the skinny, bare-chested blond said, "it says that New Guinea has few deadly poisonous snakes, not a single tiger, leopard, elephant, or wild horse. And there are only a few monkeys and pigs."

"With these goddamned mosquitoes, why would any of them *want* to live here?" Burner Hedman countered. "Hell, those animals certainly got to be smarter than the damned Japs."

"Mac, congratulations on making corporal," Lee said.

"Thanks, Lieutenant," the mechanic replied with enthusiasm, "and Mashy made sergeant, too."

Lee searched out Mashy and repeated his congratulations.

"Thanks," Mashy said, taking a swipe at the sweat that slid down his hairy chest. "Them guys up in the headsquatters shack know real talons when they see it."

Big Ole looked down from his stance on the wing beside Lee's cockpit, shook his head slowly, smiled, and rolled his eyes. Lee found the big crew chief's rare smile uplifting. Good a man as Big Ole was, his smile would never become a boring event. "I finally got a new radio compass for you, Lieutenant," Ole said, "and I found parts for the portside Fowler flap. You should be in good shape again. Just don't ask where I got 'em."

Lee sidled over to another small group, sized up the situation, and turned to move on.

"I don't care if you agree with me or not," Black Bart was saying. "The Japs are setting us up. They're not out of gas and they're not short on pilots. That's what they want us to think. You just wait until the Madang invasion starts. Then you'll find out why these last raids were so easy."

Lee gave Bart's theory long odds at best. He turned away to escape before his own mouth slipped open. Stopping at the newly constructed Drink Shack he bought a Coke. Though water-cooled only to a luke warm temperature, it provided a treat never far from his mind. Back in Basic Training he had become addicted to Coke. He had even caught himself thinking about the tangy soda while dealing with a powerful crosswind on what turned out to be a terrible, scary landing. The trip across from the states had provided a mandatory weaning.

After a three-day hiatus, the Gophers drew alert duty, the first in a long time. But it also served as an extension to their lazy time. They sought out shade near the flight line that day waiting for the sudden call that would send them scrambling into the air. Their only suffering came on the hot, dusty winds. Through recent weeks it had seemed that the rains came only when the Gophers flew, and the clear skies came when they remained groundlings. Lee felt inclined to agree with Smokey Stover when the handsome, black-haired pilot wiped the sweat from his Hollywood mustache and begged for the call that would get them up to a cooler environment.

The ground crews were frequently to be found climbing about on the Lightnings, refastening the canvas shrouds wrapped around the engines to protect them from the insidious dust. When Lee rubbed his itching eyes, he wondered how much good the shrouds did.

His earlier logic relating to military strategy seemed to come to life on April 8th and 9th. The squadron escorted B-24s to Madang, the enemy base that most scuttlebutt predicted would be the next Allied invasion target. Flying high cover, the Gophers watched the Liberators pound the harbor and base with 500-pound bombs. If the Lightnings served any purpose on the two missions, it could only be one of simultaneously providing comfort to the bomber pilots while perhaps intimidating the enemy. The experience did suggest that finally Black Bart might know what he's talking about. The Japs seemed to be saving their remaining planes to defend the western half of New Guinea and deny the U.S. a solid stepping stone to the Philippines.

Upon their return from the second mission, a grinning Mashy thanked Lee for saving all his ammunition. "Lieutenant, you're downright magnishifant. That's two days in a row you've saved me from a reload job. But if this goes on too long, they'll have me washing dishes."

Lee spent a couple of hours one afternoon, taking inventory and reshuffling the corporate crate. His tally checked out on all items but the booze. He seemed to be missing three bottles of gin. One of the other key holders must have used them for barter and forgotten to subtract them. He smiled as he thought of the losses they might have suffered. He opened the new crate, the "bank vault" used for the pilots to house their personal trophies. Each item was appropriately tagged; the crate seemed in order.

When the Gopher Squadron took to the skies again it was April 12th, and their assignment was a familiar one. The nighttime take-off would place them over the Bismarck Sea at dawn where they would patrol the coast between Madang and Wewak, searching for enemy boats of any type or size that might be moving reinforcements or supplies to Madang.

It seemed that command had read the enemy's minds, or perhaps their code, for at first light the group found a plethora of barges and small ships that had apparently tried to stretch the darkness just a bit longer. Some of their targets were churning their way landward to hide for the day. Others were tied up in coves and river outlets, desperately trying to rig belated camouflage over their vessels. Seldom did the Gophers find one vessel without finding several others in the trees and brush near by.

Although there came considerable risk from enemy groundfire, Mo's strategy worked well. With each attack the first flight in searched for "twinkies" and concentrated on silencing them. The following flights poured their fifties and 20-millimeter cannon shots into the boats, sinking several and blowing others up in spectacular fireballs.

The Gophers split up to cover a wider territory. Blue Flight caught two small cargo ships breaking for open water. They rode low in the water, probably still loaded and simply running for deeper, safer waters. Lee reached to press this throat mike on.

"All right, Blue," Lee called. "Let's try that ten-gun salute we've talked about. Chub, you and Bart go in on the closest one and quiet them down. Stew and I will follow on the hull."

He and Stew did a tight circle at 1,000 feet while Chub and Bart made two passes, pouring heavy strafing fire at the gun installations on the main deck. As they cleared, Lee and his wing mate went down on the deck, side by side but seventy-five yards apart, and bore in on the hull beneath the bridge a third of the way back from the bow. Lee fired first to mark the spot. Soon Stew added his cannon and armor-piercing fifties, and together they concentrated their incredible fire power on a small target area at the water line.

One remaining portside machine gun fired at Lee, and though he heard his Lightning take a couple of hits, he forced his concentration to his target. Coming in fast, he wouldn't have time to gauge the damage they'd done, but he knew the rhythmic bursts of fire were letting water into the hold of the rusty-hulled vessel. His left side peripheral vision told him the converging path of the two Lightnings had narrowed the gap between them to something less than twenty-five yards. He hoped Stew would remain attentive but cool. The bitter cordite from the firing guns invaded Lee's space like never before. Much more firing and the heat would jam his guns. He let go with one final salvo and glanced over at Stew. His wing mate was looking at him, a wide grin in his face. Never before had Lee found himself so close to another aircraft in flight. He pulled up and to the left, while his wing mate broke right.

"Ought to do it again," Lee called, "but I don't think we've got enough ammo to make it worth the trip. Let's just look it over."

He led the flight in a gentle circle at a safe distance. As they began their second rotation, it became obvious that the small freighter was listing to port. Lee extended their vigil for one more circle before leading Blue Flight back to their rendezvous point with Red and White Flights. They wouldn't get to see their target sink, but she was tilted close to capsizing. Her war was over. The ten-gun salute had worked.

Lee found Mo listening in as he was debriefed by Lieutenant Nelson. As he left the tent Mo joined him. They stopped at the confluence of the numerous paths. Mo grinned his non-committal grin.

"That was a hell of a stunt, Killer, a damned good way to get killed."

Lee turned to face his mentor and wished immediately that he hadn't. Mo's face said nothing, but his eyes—Lee had seen Mo in the sauce enough times to recognize the hint of glaze. Mo wasn't drunk, but he certainly was loose, loose enough to be dangerous in a P-38.

"I wouldn't do that trick with just anybody," Lee said.

"You must have a lot of trust in your new man, that Stewart."

"I do. In fact, there are only three others in the squadron that I'd trust with the ten-gun salute."

"And?..."

"Well, Sandy...and Bubba...."

"And?..."

Lee grinned at Mo. "And you, of course...when you're sober."

Mo stiffened and moved up face-to-face with Lee. The smile disappeared. The glassy eyes fired thunderbolts at Lee.

"I could sack your ass for a comment like that," Mo said, his face not a foot from Lee's.

It wasn't whiskey, Lee thought. It was gin.

"But you won't," Lee said quietly. He wheeled to head for the tent, then stopped and turned. "Don't worry, Mo. Unless it gets bad, it stays with me. And I won't mention *that*," he added, motioning to the pocket that he knew held Mo's flask. "But you really should let us know when and how much to deduct from the corporate stocks."

Chapter 33

"Okay, okay, okay!" spouted Bubba. "I agree. They've sent us out into weather a few times when we shouldn't have been flying."

A pair of pilots seated nearby in the officers' mess stopped their conversation and looked over at the small group of Gophers.

"Well, that's magnanimous of you to concede that," countered Sandy Sadler. His yellow-toned atabrine skin clashed with his freckles, but the reddish tips of his ears betrayed the Irish heat that had begun surfacing in recent days.

"But I still say," continued Bubba, "that some of these guys who go down in bad weather should have relied more on their instruments. They didn't all need to get killed."

"That's the kind of talk you hear from a guy who's sitting on his ass in a nice dry tent," injected Burner Hedman.

"Look," battled Bubba, "you've got your radio homing. At least some of the time your radio can get through for a vector to help you get back. And you've got your artificial horizon, turn and bank, airspeed, altimeter, regular compass, and radio compass. No reason not to keep the ship steady and level. And most important, if you know where you are at all times in clear weather, you'll know where you are most of the time in bad weather."

"And what about the mountains?" Sandy asked.

"It isn't like you've never seen them before. You ought to know by now where they are." Bubba turned a smug smile toward Sandy. "You guys act like those mountains are moving around in the fog and clouds, tracking you like some goddamned predator. Hell, they're fastened to the ground. They won't hit you. You have to hit *them*."

Lee sat and listened. He smiled at Bubba's debating skills. The kid had come a long way. His break-out into confident manhood seemed to be holding up. In this discussion, he leaned toward reckless optimism on the subject, but there was certainly validity to his point-of-view. After all, Mo had drummed the point home from the beginning, "Know where you are at all times."

Greenie entered, poured himself a cup of coffee and took a seat off by himself. Lee grabbed his own cup and moved over to join the White Flight leader.

"Your promotion come through yet?" Lee asked.

"Nope."

"Well, it will. You can put that in the bank."

"Says who? You?"

"Says Mo." Lee took in the irritation on Greenie's face. At present, Lee thought, Greenie had more reasons to be unhappy with things than any of the squadron mates. He was overdue for both a well-deserved promotion to captain and an R and R trip to Australia. And Mo had been on his case in recent days. With all that, Greenie had just had one of those missions in which White Flight went nearly scoreless while Red and Blue cleaned up. Lee was still three months away from Australia and probably that far from the next promotion, but he knew well the other frustrations.

"Before he went down," Greenie said, "Gus told me what you said, that you wouldn't accept captain until I got it, too. Is that true?" His hazel eyes probed from behind the slender, chiseled face.

"Sure is," Lee said, "and I meant it."

"Why doesn't that make me feel just Jim Dandy?"

Lee shrugged his return question.

"You don't get it, do you?"

Lee shrugged again and simply waited.

"Okay, Marks, just put yourself in my shoes. You're going to be promoted, not because Napoleon will admit you deserve it, but because he can't give his little buddy a promotion until you have yours. Feel good?"

"Good point," Lee said. "Anything else bothering you?"

"Nope. That's it. You know, Marks, several of us have had a stint at being Mo Brennan's special, right-hand man. Corky, then me, then Gus, and now, you." Greenie swallowed the last of his coffee and got up to leave. "Your day's coming…sooner than you think…if you don't get killed first." He turned and was gone.

"Oof," Lee said under his breath. He felt like he'd just taken one to the mid-section. And the punch brought his thoughts back once more to Mo Brennan. He had only heard of Corky Bales who flew in Mo's old outfit. With but a few missions completed Corky died in a mid-air collision with a Zero. Greenie had echoed Gus' angle on the Mo Brennan exec syndrome. And yes, Lee had to accept the fact that his days in Mo's good graces might also be numbered. He had already been through the flip-flop a couple of times. But then again, he had stood up to Mo's pressures. And it seemed he had Colonel Hammer's respect.

Lee wondered if the guts he had shown in the last scene with Mo over the drinking had been real self-confidence or temporary fuzz inflated by his successful ten-gun salute. "A good way to get killed," Mo had said. "What if that freighter had been loaded with high explosives?"

In retrospect, Lee had to admit that Mo may have taken several slugs of gin *after* landing, that he had flown the mission cold sober. He hoped so. The situation reminded Lee of an old musician friend who had played in South Chicago dance bands for years. "I always thought a drink helped relax me, get me get past my inhibitions," the friend had once said, "especially on gigs that involved improvisation, a jazz man's bread and butter. But when the cats went beyond the first drink they were kidding themselves. It didn't improve their playing. It only damaged their listening. They began to hear great jazz that wasn't there. Kind of sad, really."

When Lee recognized the negative impact of several of the morning's conversations, he felt the lighted fuse within him, and its heat was working its way upward. He vowed to douse the fire before it got out of hand. Within minutes he had hustled across the base to the athletic field, stripped to the waist, and found himself aligned with two bomber pilots in a game of three-on-three basketball. His favorite escape left no room for self-indulgence. The game forced him to concentrate, to be alert and quick. And with the games concluded, he knew the physical drain would purge the emotional strain.

On the way to the shower, Lee found Colonel Hammer just leaving. He was all decked out in fresh khakis that showed no perspiration stains. But they left his beat up and sweaty officers' hat rather out-of-place. He carried his wad of soiled clothes under one arm.

"Hey, Marks, I'm glad I ran into you," the colonel said. "I need to make sure you understand something."

"Understand something?"

"You do know that there's a price to pay for that silver bar I just got you?"

"A price to pay?"

"That's right. With your experience and higher rank, you'll be expected to think more like a leader." He paused and looked Lee in the eye. "Out here, you never know. Your life can change in less than the second it takes for one of your leaders to check out. You have to be ready." He started on down the path, then stopped and turned back to Lee. "But then, I imagine you have all that already figured out."

The next morning found the 483rd on their way to the coast to attack Madang. Finally, something in the Allied strategy made sense to Lee. Madang sat only a hundred miles north of their base at Nadzab and since it was one of the most obvious targets for the next invasion, it had to be softened up. While the results of the attacks on Hollandia were nothing short of spectacular, those missions required a 930-mile round-trip. In the New Guinea air war and its hostile weather, a lot of things could go wrong in 930 miles, including discomfort that became pain.

During the stand-down of recent days, scuttlebutt had it that the upcoming missions of the 483rd P-38s would shift almost exclusively from aerial combat to ground and sea attack. The ground crews had installed additional hard points, the pylons beneath the wings used to carry extra fuel tanks or bombs. And rumors had also begun circulating that in a few months Fifth Air Force Fighter Command would be adding air-to-surface rockets beneath the P-38 wings.

This morning found Lee riding herd on two 500-pound bombs, and he readily admitted to some nervousness. In advanced training back in the States, only a few practice missions had been devoted to bombing. And most of those involved harmless dummy bombs. The two powder kegs that were hung beneath his wings were not dummies, and they were not harmless. Since the arming process was new to the ground crews, and the actual bombing was relatively new to most of the pilots in Gopher Squadron, Lee found justification for his nerves. His biggest fear was having a bomb hang up and not release. He had heard of a P-40 pilot returning to land at his base with a bomb dangling precariously beneath his fuselage. The pilot apparently chose to head his ship toward the jungle and bail out, a decision, it was said, that he lived to regret. But he lived, Lee thought.

His jitters washed away as the Gophers gave away altitude to go in over the airdrome. Perhaps Command had suffered from momentary compassion in assigning Gopher Squadron to make their first bombing run in formation, flat and level, at 5,000 feet. With no bomb sights or technical aids, the pilots were to release their bombs on Mo's order. Man, Lee thought, that puts all the pressure on Mo. Had he ever done a bombing mission before? The words of Sledge Hammer came back to Lee as he released his payload, "…think more like a leader. Out here, you never know."

The Marksman surged upward as the 1,000-pound duo dropped away. Lee wished he could circle once to see what his bombs hit. He strained to see down and behind his huge wings, but the booms on both sides blocked the view. Up ahead the Gopher formation wobbled this way and that as the pilots tilted their ships for a view.

"Settle down, back there," came Mo's voice. "Forget about the bombs and watch for Jap fighters instead. Breaking left—now."

Lee felt let down. No results. He imagined for a moment that in all his previous combat missions he had flown and shot blindfolded, had never seen the enemy planes blow up, burn, come apart, or crash. All of his fifteen kills had been classified as probables. He had fired his guns at so many ground targets but had never seen any hits. Indeed, like playing Bingo without a card. He felt some apprehension with the concept of dive bombing—or skip bombing—or dropping napalm at 500 feet. But this? On this day they were simply truck drivers.

When they cleared debriefing back at Nadzab, Lee found the other pilots grumbling about the frustration. It helped him to know that his compatriots shared his feelings. And he thought he sensed the bond among the pilots firming up.

The 483rd Fighter Group repeated the attack four days later, on April 14th. For the Gophers the mission was exactly that, a repetition—except that the journey home took them head-on into bad weather. It proved to be a costly mission for Pony Squadron. Shortly after take-off, Lieutenant Bradson, one of their pilots, had to abort the mission. Apparently dysentary had caught up with him, and in his haste to land, he went in too hot and slid off the end of the runway, crumpling his landing gears and thoroughly messing up his ship, inside and out.

The story sobered Lee. *War really is hell*, he thought as he considered Bradson's frustration and humiliation. And we fighter pilots have been spared a lot of it. Until we crash, or explode, or get riddled with bullets, we're on a thrill ride. I don't even see the enemy I kill. I just shoot down his airplane and paint a funny, little flag on my ship.

"Hey, Lee!" came a familiar, booming voice.

Turning to track the voice he found Burner Hedman catching up with him.

"Lee, I gotta ask for a favor," said the powerful lumberjack. He put a massive mitt on Lee's shoulder and said, "Will you do me this favor? And not tell anyone about it?"

"Well, sure. I guess so," Lee said. "What's this about?"

"Lee, I got this goddamned toothache, a really bad one. It's been killing me for two days now," Hedman backed away, straightened, and looked at Lee questioningly, "and I can't trust any of those other guys. Can I trust you?"

"Of course."

"You're sure?"

"Burner, what do you want?"

"Lee, I gotta go see Doc Parker, the dentist. And—I'm scared shitless of dentists."

Lee studied the powerful frame that outweighed him by fifty or more pounds and stood two or three inches taller. The strength that rippled in Burner's arms and hands was awesome. But the fear in his eyes betrayed the human within the massive frame.

"You need some moral support, Burner? Come on, let's go." Lee lowered his voice to a mumble, "And don't worry. I won't tell anyone."

Captain Doc Parker's waiting room was a wooden slab bench outside the tilted shack that served as the base dentist's office. The patient chair was nothing more than an old hand-pumped barber chair. As Captain Parker carefully guided Burner into the aged device, he cautioned him to settle in slowly and gently so as not to tip the chair over.

"If you sit down carefully and don't get too active, you'll be balanced and the chair won't tip over," he said, giving Lee a wink and a smile. "Now, let's see what the trouble is here."

Within two minutes he concluded his poking and probing and announced, again with the wink, his diagnosis. "You've got a bad—no, I should say *rotten* wisdom tooth. It's got to come out. But I have to tell you, sometimes we find other complications in removing wisdom teeth."

"C-c-complications?" Burner asked.

"Occasionally we find others, extra wisdom teeth down beneath the one we're taking out, but don't worry. We'll get it done. Now," Captain Parker went on, "I don't have one of those new x-ray machines to tell us ahead of time just what we're getting into. And I don't have any of that new novocaine to deaden the area. But I can give you some pills for pain afterwards. Okay," he said, cuffing Burner on the shoulder, "let's get it done. Lieutenant," he said to Lee, "would you stand right here and steady the chair," he winked again, "just in case this little guy—gets active?"

Lee braced himself firmly against the chair. He would rather have been somewhere else. Perhaps this was another of the elements of leadership that Sledge

Hammer had referred to. At least the experience had shown him yet another of the foibles of human kind, one he would never have expected.

Captain Parker was a slight man, perhaps five-foot-eight and 130 pounds. But he grabbed his plier-like weapon, pressed one knee into the chair back beside Burner's massive body, grabbed that tooth and wrenched several times from side to side. The crunching of bone separating from bone ran a shiver through Lee.

"Aaaagh! Uhhhhh-Aaaaaagh!" came the helpless animal's roar. His eyes resembled two giant moons with mean, threatening spots in their centers.

In less than a minute the diminutive dentist came out victorious and held the trophy up for Burner to see.

"There! Wasn't that bad at all, was it?"

Burner shook his head as though shaking off the bewilderment that was pasted upon his face. Then he broke into a wide grin. "Not bad t'all?" he asked. "Zzit! Notting to it!" In but seconds, the bravado of the old Burner Hedman had reemerged. Captain Parker offered him some packs to stuff the cavity with, along with some pain and antibiotic pills.

"Notting to it," Burner said as they headed down the dusty path toward their tents. "Wat you worr'd 'bout, Lee? Tole you it'd be a snap, dint I?" The wide grin and the thankful eyes gave Lee his reward.

"You don't really mind…if I tell people how it went, do you?" Lee laughed.

"Hell, no! Go tell the world!" Burner held up his tooth and slapped Lee on the back.

Bubba joined Lee as he took a place at one of the rough-hewn tables that evening at mess. Lee felt enthusiastic about the huge clump of canned Australian bully beef and cabbage on his plate. While some of the men ranked the meal as low as shit on a shingle, Lee chose to think of the fare as something exotic. But then he liked Spam® as well. There was little the cooks could do to spoil it, and that made Lee more comfortable.

He had decided that Corporal Dooley, the KP helper who was dishing out the meal, had to be a back room psychologist. Lee watched him. As each man reached Dooley's station and held out his plate, he looked down to the fare being served. When Dooley dipped his scooper into the vat, he watched the man's face. The size of the helping he served depended upon the look on the man's face. When Lee smiled on bully beef and Spam® days, he was appropriately rewarded. It was a good system, Lee thought. Why punish someone who had to choke the meal down?

Bubba had decisively won the battle with Army food, and he had come to agree with Lee on the bully beef. He attacked the meal aggressively, and for some time his jammed-full mouth ruled out any conversation. Lee smiled at the miraculous turn-around.

"Hey, Lee," Bubba said as they dipped their utensils in the rinse tanks, "let's hit the river and tip a few tonight. I got a hold of some Aussy gin that's smoother than the rest."

"Oh, no," Lee replied. "Do it to me once, shame on you. Do it to me twice, shame on me. We have a mission in the morning. I'm not going to suffer through that combination."

"Aw, come on," pleaded Bubba.

"No."

"Well, how about walking down to the flight line with me?" Bubba asked expectantly.

"Oh, okay, Bubba. You got something on your mind?"

"Well, since you asked, have you noticed how owly some of the guys are getting lately? Geez, you say anything at all and they climb all over you. Even Sandy, and he used to be one of the nicest guys in the whole Fifth Fighter Command. I don't get it."

Lee recalled his talk with Mo and his own subsequent thoughts about battle fatigue. But Bubba seemed more content than any time since Lee first met him. Lee hated to derail that.

"I don't know, Bubba. Are you sure you're not just imagining it? After all, the old Bubba used to irritate some of the guys pretty badly with his stu—uhh—rather naive comments. Maybe they've still got some of that stuck in the craw. Think so?"

"Doubt it. They've had the new Bubba around long enough now to be past that."

"Well, then, I don't know," said Lee. "I guess I can't help you on that one."

Bubba stopped, took Lee by the elbow. "Doubt that, too," he said. "You've always been able to help me with anything. You don't suppose it's—"

"It's what?" Lee asked.

"Well, I heard bits of a conversation between Sandy and Smokey Stover yesterday."

"And?"

"Well, it's the going subject right now. Lots of the guys are talking about it, but I just ignored it."

"Talking about what?"

"About battle fatigue. They say it's like a disease, like everybody who lives in the next block has it, and we're afraid it's coming to our block. Could that be what's bothering the guys?"

"I guess it could be, Bubba. But I see it like this. Our emotional stamina is a personal thing. No one can decide that we will *all* be burned out at thirty missions, or fifty missions, or a hundred missions. We're all different. I think these guys are talking each other *into* that trap."

"Hey, that's a good line!" Bubba said.

"That's not a line," Lee countered. "It's an opinion that just became fact."

"I figured I'd use your explanation," laughed Bubba. "But I like that last line, too."

Lee felt relieved that Bubba could treat the matter so casually. While he himself had been dancing around the subject, Bubba had been carrying it up front in his shirt pocket.

"If that's the problem, Lee, it's up to the rest of us to perk them up, to boost morale. We can't just let them slide down the slope. That's too dangerous. I know I'll do my part."

"You're that strong, Bubba?"

"Oh, hell yes! I've never felt better about myself and my life. Now that I've got the demons back in their cages, I'm actually having fun over here!"

"Okay then, Old Bud, let's see if we can perk things up a bit," said Lee, "but, Bubba, don't—*do not*—lecture them on the subject. That'll do more harm than good. Okay?"

Bubba smiled. "You're still a jump ahead of me, aren't you, Lee? Okay, I promise not to lecture. In fact, I promise I won't even use the words, 'battle fatigue.' How's that? You want to see some leadership? Just watch me."

Chapter 34

An explosion of orders burst through the ranks after morning chow on Saturday, April 15th, and by 0900 hours most of the personnel of the Fifth Air Force Fighter Command at Nadzab had gathered in the bright morning sun on a flat, vacant expanse bordering Strip Number Two. The group commanders busily guided squadron commanders and their charges to assigned patches of dusty Nadzab real estate.

Several of the Gophers fell into a laughing jag as they watched Captain Hollings Bryant, the skittish CO of the 126th Pony Squadron, try to cajole his men into some semblance of order. Half of them argued with one another over the matter of what he expected them to do; the other half seemed to be debating the issue of why they should be doing it. Whatever their position, the results would have been unacceptable even for raw recruits fresh off the bus at boot camp. For that matter, Lee mused, it would be fun to watch their boot camp drill instructors try to deal with the relaxed chaos that prevailed on this dusty lot. It would be like barking their orders at a herd of deaf and fearless donkeys.

At 0930 an olive drab gooney bird glided in for a perfect wheel landing and taxied toward the assembly. The command, "Fall in!" passed on down through the mass of khaki-clad airmen and their support personnel. After an inordinate amount of pushing, shoving, and adjusting, the strikingly unmilitary group established lines that were surprisingly straight.

"General Sossaman, Fifth Fighter Command," Mo said to Lee, whom he had positioned at his side, "and the light colonel must be his aide."

"Don't you think *you'd* make a good aide? You've got the rank now," said Lee with a smile.

"Tennn—Hut!" came a command over the improvised P.A. system. After brief introductory remarks by the base commander, Colonel Manders, whom Lee knew only by sight, the group was put at ease and the fastest award ceremony Lee could have imagined began. To begin the first phase, with the highest honors, Mo, Lee, and nine others were called to form a closed rank in front of the main body of men.

The general's aide took the microphone, and in a most boring tone of voice called the selected pilots one-by-one to step forward. He rambled quickly through a brief synopsis of the individual's actions in combat that called for the award and then announced the award. At that point General Sossaman received the appropriate medal from Sgt. Jernigan, pinned it on the winner's khaki shirt, shook hands, and finished with a crisp, short salute.

Lee felt a little surprised at the emotion that swelled through him when Mo stepped out to receive his awards. To add to his Air Medal previously won, he was given six silver Oak Leaf Clusters and one bronze. And to take him another step beyond his Distinguished Flying Cross, he was awarded the Silver Star. Of the five major medals available, Mo had been awarded three, leaving only the Distinguished Service cross and the Medal of Honor. Lee could only guess at the number of oak leaf clusters Mo had won for repetitions on his first two medals.

"First Lieutenant Lee Marks."

Lee stepped forward, his eyes straight ahead, and assumed the best attention posture he could remember. The voice over the P.A. system suddenly became an extraneous background noise. He was both excited and ill at ease standing before the large group and its commanding general. He glanced up at a silver cumulus cloud that was drifting slowly over the nearest mountain. As he studied it, a portion of the misty cloud solidified into a face—it was Gus! And by the time General Sossaman had finished pinning the Air Medal and the Distinguished Flying Cross on him and handing him what felt like a handful of Oak Leaf Clusters for multiple qualifications on the Air Medal, Lee's eyes had each dropped a tear.

"Congratulations, Lieutenant Marks," the general said as he shook Lee's hand. "You've established an incredible record. There are a lot of people watching you. How does that make you feel?"

"Embarrassed," was the only sound that came from his mouth.

"Embarrassed? Why is that?"

"Good friends up there," Lee said, looking skyward, "who should be getting these."

"You're right, Marks. You see that you stick around. They'd want you to do that." The general released Lee's hand, stepped back and gave him a crisp salute.

Lee missed the rest of the ceremony. His emotions tumbled right, left, up, and down. His mind rambled from the medals to clouds, to Gus, to flying, to several of his combat experiences, to Porter, Logan, and Callahan. At one point he felt such anger he wanted to rip the medals off and throw them at that cloud. He awoke to a bumpy landing when Mo grabbed his arm.

"Congratulations, Killer! Obviously, you've got the general's attention. Our plan is *definitely* working. Come on. Let's go have a snort to celebrate."

In minutes, Lee found himself at the river in the shade of the clump of palm trees, sipping whiskey from a tin cup. He didn't remember the walk across the base or any conversation on the way. But when he turned toward the chosen path, he somehow left Gus behind.

"I tell you, Killer—"

"Mo!" Lee interrupted. "I'd like you to stop calling me that. I am *not* a killer. I'm just a P-38 jockey who so far has been in the right place at the right time. That could change the next time I pull my wheels up. And if it does, I don't want to go out with the title, Killer. Okay?"

"Why—sure, Killer! I can stop calling you that." He broke into a wide grin. "Fine, Lee. If I do it again, just give me a swift kick. Anyway, things are working out well for us. We've both got Air Medals up the kazoo, the D.F.C, and now I've added the Star. By the time we get to the west end of New Guinea, we'll both have the Silver Star and the Distinguished Service Cross. We'll be scratching for the top dog, the Medal of Honor. Hey, Minneapolis! Get started on that statue! And while you're at it, get going on another one for my friend here." He took a long slug of whiskey and wiped his lips with one sleeve. "Only make his a couple of inches shorter."

"That General Sossaman," Lee said, "he seemed like a sharp guy, a real person."

"He is. He's been around—was in the 49th Fighter Group when they fought the Japs off at Darwin, Australia. Man, that was a scary time. And they did it with P-39s and P-40s. He's a pretty regular guy. If the truth were known, he'd probably prefer to be doing what we're doing."

"He said to me, 'You see that you stick around.' Think he was really concerned for *my* welfare, or was he thinking politically—the fame that an overachiever brings to those above him?" Lee took a drink from his cup and tried to smooth his grimace.

"Hey, no doubt, Lee. He was thinking of political gain, particularly for the Army Air Force. But from what I know of General Sossaman, his concern for you was genuine. He's the key, you know, to our final AAF stage."

"Meaning?"

"Meaning, when we've added another twenty-five to thirty per cent to our resumes, we'll have a chance of shipping home to do war bond tours. And we want that—pictures and articles in all the newspapers and magazines, parades, interviews over the radio—those are the clinchers that launch us into our very successful, joint civilian career. Sossaman is the guy who can get that done. His recommendations go right to General Wurtsmith. And it's to Sledge's advantage to push us upward. The better we look, the better he looks."

Lee sat silently for a moment processing Mo's words. There had always been a blank that needed filling in, an explanation of just how one begins to convert this combat success to postwar civilian success. The war bond tours could serve as the conversion catalyst, call it seed money. And now, for the first time, Mo seemed to be suggesting that their Southwest Pacific tours of duty might be measured in weeks to months, rather than months to years. Suddenly, Mo's selfish logic seemed to shed some of the selfishness. It could work, Lee thought, but only if none of their mates suffered as a result of their maneuvers.

"Some of our hotter pilots," Mo went on, "are just getting to the point where they will become valuable as war bond promoters, pilots like Dick Bong, and MacGuire, and Joe Foss. The difference is, we're going to sell this program as a *pair* of wingmen. When the press says Brennan they say Marks; when they say Marks they say Brennan. The military will love it because we represent the very battle style that's beating the Germans and Japanese, the two-man element. Now, I see it this way. For a while as we head west across New Guinea, we want you to continue as a flight leader. You'll get more kills that way. But when we're getting close to our combined day of reward, we'll move you back up to my wingman slot to solidify the team image. Make sense?"

"Makes sense, Mo. And what you've said today clears some things up for me. But I've got to insist on something." Lee looked Mo in the eye. "There's one thing, one rule that I've got to have your word on, one law that can't be broken. We cannot allow any of our squadron mates to be hurt in any way because of our maneuvering. Some of them are already pretty low, and a kick in the pants from one of us isn't what they need."

"Are you saying, you think morale's down?"

"Yeah, I guess I am," Lee said. "Bubba says the guys are really low. They've heard about the freeze on R and R and on the rotation home. He told them that the ones who came in with us are three months away from R and R and nine months short of rotation home anyway, and none of us have been here long enough to justify slopping around in battle fatigue."

"The kid said that?" Mo asked. "That little wimp said that?"

"Guess you haven't noticed, Mo. He's not the little wimp anymore. The new gutsy Bubba is for real. It wasn't just a whisp of bravada. It's for real. And before long, the guys are going to start listening to him. He's very bright, you know, maybe smarter than any of us. And since he's also fully alert to the discussions going around on battle fatigue, he's ready to assume a leadership posture there, too."

"No shit? And I suppose he's eating everything they put in front of him, too." Mo took a swallow, then looked over his cup at Lee with a "Gotcha there" look.

"Well, almost. He still has a little trouble with the clumps of fat that show up in the bully beef. He 'saves' those for the garbage can."

"Okay!" chortled Mo. "I guess my maneuvers to get him eating and fighting worked out better than I ever expected."

"Sure did," agreed Lee. "And better yet, we've got another leadership element to back us up."

"Any others we can count on?"

"Sandy's been solid all along, but he's a little iffy right now. Burner can be counted on, mainly because he's tough and he's just too stubborn to give in to anything or anybody. Stew is good. He's too new to convince anybody else of much yet, but his attitude is right up there. He'll be good leadership down the road."

"Great, Lee. You're doing what I pay you for. Keep it up. Find the ones that'll work with us and get them to help with the losers. You know, Lee, we've got a hell of a lot of action in front of us, and things are going to heat up as we get closer to the west end of New Guinea. The Japs know we need that area secured before we can even think about invading the Philippines. Right now we're running short of Jap planes to shoot at, but there will be more as we move west, and when we get to the Philippines it'll be Rabaul all over again. We can't go into that with our tails dragging. I need your help to keep them sharp. If we don't get ourselves up and strong before we head west, too many of our guys will go down. Lee, I can't let my squadron get all shot to hell."

Lee felt a reprise of the pride he had felt earlier as Mo had received his medals. Behind Colonel Mo Brennan's selfish side there seemed to be a noble streak, at least at times.

"Kill—uhh, Lee, I know it's down the road a couple of months, but I'd like you to commit to staying on. Take the captaincy when it comes and accept the four more months. If you and I accomplish what I think we will, we'll be back in the States selling war bonds long before we even *get* to those four months."

"I think I can accept your logic, Mo, but I hardly have to decide on that today."

"Of course not. But I need to know our thinking is in tune. By the way, our new replacement is due in this afternoon from Dobo. I think his name is Roland Greenberg, a second Louie. I understand he's had some experience and he'll be bringing an older Model H with him. I want you to check him out. If he's had any real experience, let's slot him into Red Flight as T.E.Charlie with Sadler for now."

The two officers sat quietly looking out over the shallow, meandering river for some time. The interlude struck Lee as unusual. Typically, Mo talked. And when he hesitated, Lee injected himself. Seldom had there been silence. Lee thought of a couple items he would like to bring up, but he sensed that Mo's wheels were turning. He waited.

"You know, Lee, there's another, even bigger reason to get our morale up off the floorboards," Mo said slowly. "I mentioned it a few weeks back. We're long, long overdue for a huge, disastrous high command fuck-up—I mean a royal, never-seen-anything-like-it fuck-up, like getting sent out on ground support for our GIs and finding out that the troops 150 feet under our vulnerable bellies are Japanese, or getting sent to where we get bounced by fighters that outnumber us ten or twenty to one, or getting sent into a trap with antiaircraft emplacements that are all set for altitude and range and are just waiting for us. It's going to happen some day, Lee, and when it does, we can't have ten pilots with us who have their heads on crooked, feeling sorry for themselves."

Chapter 35

From the jungle oozed a mixed message of fresh after-the-rain-shower smells and the ever-present stench of mildew. But as he made his way back to the tent following morning chow and the follow-up stop at the latrine, Lee chose to concentrate on the fresh smells and the fact that the morning shower had passed over and cleared space for the sunrise.

The Gophers were on the board for another long escort haul to Hollandia this Sunday morning, April 16th, and while nothing could make the nearly 1,000 miles attractive, it would help to have sunshine and clear skies. Five to six hours locked into one position in the hard pilot's seat of the P-38 made even young bodies beg for mercy. As Lee skipped up the steps into the tent to don his flight gear, he was met by Sandy Sadler.

"I've got something here you're not going to believe," Sandy said smugly. "For the first time since we came from the States, *you've got mail!* I picked it up at mail call yesterday, but you came in late last night and I forgot to give it to you." Sandy beamed as he handed it to Lee.

"Since it was postmarked about two months ago, I guess a few more hours didn't mess anything up too much. Okay, Lee?"

"Uh, sure, Sandy, sure, okay, thanks."

One glance at the penmanship made the return address a moot point. While he had hoped it would be from his mother, Marie would run a close second. But what if she only wanted to strike out at him for, as the teenager might see it, ruining her life? Could he handle that? Did he need that right now? He bent to stuff the unopened letter into his B4 bag, but somehow, his fingers wouldn't let go of it. His watch said he had ten minutes before he had to head for the pre-flight briefing. Plunking himself down on his bunk, he nervously ripped open the envelope.

> February 14, 1944
>
> Dear Lee,
>
> I'm sorry it's taken me so long to rite. I wasn't sure what to say. But finely my conshince got the best of me and I had to rite. Mom is still being stubbern. You know Mom, But don't worry none about her. She'll come out of it. She's beginning to talk sort of nice about you, so it shun't take to long now.
>
> I just wanted to tell you not to worry about the Pete Loring thing. Number One—you did the rite thing. I was all wrong, ALL WRONG. Number Two—I heard Mom telling Mrs. Packowsky about how you defendet me, an Mom was all proud about it to.
>
> And Number Three, maybe best of all—I heard from Lutenant Gardner that when Pete's dad went in to sign the charges or whatever it is they do, the police chief talked him out of it. The chief told him that Pete had been begging for that for a long time and if Mr. Loring wanted to be the most unpoplar man in the presinkt, all he had to do was file charges against a war hero who was off in the Pacific defenting his spoiled roten son!
>
> I guess that did it. So you don't have to worry no more.
>
> I have to admit, it made me feel good to be seen crusin with Pete in his convertable. I was a real somebody. But like Mom sayd, there's a price to pay. I won't do that no more.
>
> Are you all right? Have you been wunded or anything? Do you get enough to eat?
>
> Can we send you stuff that you need? I spose it probly takes a week for male to get there, but thats all right. I'll be sending more male now, and maybe Mom can help to.
>
> I love you, big brother. And thanks for always being there when I need you. I hope you got this rite away.
>
> Your sister,
> Marie

With the fourth reading the tears had slowed. Lee carefully folded the letter back into the envelope and stowed it in his bag.

The walk to the flight line took half as long as usual. Lee hadn't realized how heavy the home burden had become—until the burden bag was suddenly emptied. For the first time, he had reason to hope that Mom would come around. But with her well-fed, well-maintained hate for his father as the only benchmark, Lee hadn't seen much room for optimism. The four-month scenario had shown Lee that there were really only two people in his life. And now, at least one of them had rebuilt her faith in him. He smiled to himself. Having started at the bottom—empty—he found it easy to view the glass as half full.

Near the end of the briefing, Lee realized that he'd listened to some and only heard some, when he should have been listening to all. He flipped back to the present when a couple of the pilots vociferously challenged the weather report.

"I don't care what the meteorologists say," came a voice from the rear. "Anybody who's been here a month can take a look at those skies out there and know that we're in for it."

"You say we'll be back before the afternoon build-up," challenged Burner Hedman. "If I'm reading it right, that afternoon build-up is six hours ahead of schedule. It's now a *morning* build-up."

"We all hope you boys are wrong," countered Colonel Hammer. "We've been assured that, while you might possibly encounter a few isolated showers, none of it will threaten the mission. But right or wrong, photo recon shows the Japs furiously rebuilding and repairing at the Hollandia airdromes. We can't just ignore it. We tried to preserve the airdromes for our own eventual use, but the enemy has apparently decided we were preserving the bases for their continued use. We have to take them out in the next few days. The order for this mission came right from the top. Good luck, Gentlemen. Give 'em hell."

By 0700 hours, the 483rd Fighter Group reached the northern portion of the Markham River Valley, flying two levels of cover for a group of fifty B-24s. Pony and Bobcat Squadrons cruised 2,000 feet above the bombers at 15,000 feet, while the Gophers flew high cover at 21,000 feet. The large aggregation charged through intermittent rain squalls. But they would no sooner find dry skies than they were once more enveloped by bad weather. Colonel Hammer's words came back to Lee, "…a few isolated showers, but nothing that will threaten the mission." What Lee saw just off his port wing looked like something considerably more than a few isolated showers.

They broke out of the weather north of the heavy Japanese concentrations at Wewak, and as they drew closer to the Hollandia stronghold, the heads of the

Lightning pilots began swiveling. They searched back and over their shoulders; they searched the rear view mirrors mounted outside and above their windscreens; they searched to the sides and front. Several small, rag-tag groups of enemy fighters climbed furiously to meet the heavies, but Pony and Bobcat Squadrons dropped on them like hawks and dispatched them quickly. Reduced to but a fraction of their former fighting strength, and manning their fighters with new, poorly trained pilots, these remnants of the once-feared and respected Fourth Japanese Air Army needed the elements of altitude and surprise to even hope for victory. On this day, they had neither.

Gopher Squadron missed the action. Lee might have picked up two, perhaps three more flags. But it was good for Pony and Bobcat Squadrons to fatten up their record. And not having had to switch and drop his belly tanks for combat, Lee had only begun to tap his main tanks. As they formed up for the trip home and adopted a course heading of one-two-zero degrees, Lee settled in for a long, long ride. As they left Hollandia farther and farther behind them, the size and frequency of the rain squalls increased. And between the squalls Lee now found light muck, but no sunshine. Occasional gaps in the cloud cover beneath them allowed a glimpse of a hazy, ethereal jungle, clear enough only to tell Lee that that way was *down*. It was not to be a relaxing flight home.

After ninety minutes, Mo directed them to a course heading of one-three-five degrees. Lee glanced at his watch and concurred with Mo's judgment. It was time to jump the hump, to clear the barrier of mountains that blocked their way into the Markham River Valley. The gophers were already at 15,000 feet, more than enough to safely clear the hump, so altitude was not a question—unless they were off course. Could Colonel Mo Brennan lead them *off* course? If the responsibility fell to him, could Lieutenant Lee Marks keep them *on* course?

"Damn, I'm glad it's your call, Mo," Lee said to himself.

The Gophers barreled through two more squalls. As the second began to thin out, Lee expected conditions to revert automatically back to light, ethereal muck. But what confronted the Gophers, perhaps twenty miles ahead, was a gigantic wall of clouds, the biggest and most frightening he had ever seen. They grew like giant mushrooms from a black base a few hundred feet above the ground to deepening gray and finally to silver-white masses reaching to over 30,000 feet. There could be no doubt in any of the pilots' minds. A nearly impregnable wall separated them from home.

One-by-one, the Gophers responded to Mo's reduction in airspeed. It was good, Lee thought. It would save fuel and it would buy them some reaction time as things got stickier. Of course, it also brought them down closer to their stall speed.

"Uh, Gophers, listen up," came Mo's voice. "We seem to be faced with a problem. You're looking at one of those isolated showers you heard about. We'll probably lose radio contact any time now. Too much chance for mid-airs in this garbage, so go every man for himself at this point. Two choices: one, try to poke your way through it, and two, take a heading of zero-six-zero degrees and go for the ocean. Then go low and try to follow the surf line into Saidor. Just remember, there are eighty-five other birds out here. Be alert, trust your - - - - -ments, - - - good - - - -."

"That's leadership," Lee said aloud. "No panic, normal tone of voice, ho hum."

A few quick turns of the head told Lee that the other three members of Blue Flight had, at least for the time being, elected to follow his lead. They were strung out in a loose echelon, back and to his right, a staggered single-file. He'd have felt better if each pilot had gone on his own. But, he reasoned, he would concentrate on getting Lee Marks and The Marksman home to Nadzab. If he made it and they managed to stay with him, they would make it.

He headed for the lower left portion of the massive formation, the area that showed signs of some breaks in the cloud. Probing one opening after another, he found himself caught in one dead-end after another. As he escaped his fourth run up against a wall, he glanced back and found only Stew still with him. Good, for Stew would know when to break off and go his own way. He would follow Lee out of judgment, not fear. He tried the radio, but it yielded only static.

Lee's mouth became dry, his pulse quickened. His shoulders ached from leaning forward, pulling at the shoulder straps. It was crazy. He couldn't see any better by leaning forward twelve inches, yet he couldn't stop leaning. And each time he encountered rain, the urge to lean grew in proportion to the amount of rain pounding against the cockpit pod.

Suddenly, as though Zeus, god of the heavens, had intervened, Lee's chance jumped at him. Off his starboard wingtip he saw a sizeable cavern showing in the ugly, black clouds. Some distance behind the opening, the clouds picked up a purple tinge. He banked toward the opening and saw that farther back, the purple changed to red, and beyond the red was an area of dazzling gold. Sunlight?

Lee tried once more to reach Stew via the radio. Only static. He turned to look for Stew. He was gone! His wingmate had disappeared. Lee was all alone. He could only hope it was a deliberate action on Stew's part. A part of him felt relieved, for now there was but one pilot depending on his skills and his judgment. He checked his fuel gauges. Enough for perhaps 20 minutes at best, but definitely not enough to try for the coast and Saidor. Decision made. He would go for the small field at Gusap. His altimeter read 8,100 feet, quite enough if he had already crossed over the hump, but a sure invitation to a crash if he had not yet crossed over, for the mountain range topped out at 10,000 feet.

Reminding himself to depend on his instruments to maintain level flight, he eased into the eerie, multicolored tunnel. Immediately, some giant, unseen hand grabbed the 17,000-pound fighter plane and tossed it about like a toy, this way and that. Lee could never have imagined such a ride—one wing high—immediately the other wing high—nose down—nose up—flat drop downward that sent his stomach to his throat—flat surge upward that pushed his stomach to his toes. He fought for control as the powerful forces strained the P-38's airframe. In the middle of all that violence, one bizarre thought flitted through his mind: Big Ole will be upset when he sees the popped rivets. But for the first time, Lee faced the real question, would Lockheed's sturdy machine survive the games of Zeus?

By the time Lee's ship reached the purple zone, the red and gold zones had evaporated, replaced by ugly, swirling, gray clouds, the very kind he had sought to escape. There was no Gus smiling from these clouds. But maybe Gus would emerge from one of the billowing crowns to show Lee the way. A sudden explosion told Lee a powerful fire hose had been turned against the P-38. Lee had experienced rain showers, rain storms, even blasts of rain, but he had never heard the roar of rain over his engines. And not seconds behind the blast, a series of lightning bolts crisscrossed through the clouds around him.

Lee's eyes locked onto the principal instruments that were now his keys to life. There was nothing to be seen through the cockpit windows, at least nothing he wanted to see. The instruments were his only chance. By relying on the artificial horizon, the turn-and-bank indicator, airspeed, altimeter, and compass, he had a chance to buy additional flying time, and that time might buy his life back.

But this wasn't an instrument flying exercise. This was about maintaining straight and level flight in the middle of a monstrous cumulonimbus cloud, a force so powerful it could throw the sturdy P-38 into any position in an instant, or it could simply snap the wings off. Lee knew quickly that his was a lost cause. No matter how hard he concentrated on level flight, he couldn't counteract the forces against him.

His mind now accepted an alternative that had never been considered before—jump! While he wrestled with the control yoke with one hand, he did a quick inventory with the other hand: forty-five securely snapped into its holster; jungle kit; knife; chute harness secured. He was all set, he thought, but a reluctance to abandon a familiar, if fearful environment for the unknown caused him to hesitate. Just then a sporadic, jerking sensation racked the ship, bringing Lee's head up. The starboard engine sputtered, roared back to life, and then abruptly stopped. His mind immediately started through the emergency drills to restart the engine, drills that came close to demanding three hands. Out of the question. He feathered the prop, then worked the control yoke hard left to use the ailerons to try to keep the starboard wing up.

He cranked the side windows partially down, released his seat harness and then the upper canopy. It flew backward in the slipstream, ripped itself loose and was gone. Battered by ferocious winds carrying rain drops that felt like tiny knives at that speed, he released his grip on the yoke and wormed his way up to get his legs under him. And as the dead engine pulled that side down and rolled the stricken craft over, a horrendous blast of wind and water tore Lee from the cockpit and tossed him into the maelstrom. His breathless body tumbled like a rag doll in a washing machine. He found the D-ring and pulled the ripcord, then immediately feared he had pulled it too soon. He waited for a sign that he had been snagged by the ship. But the tumbling continued until suddenly a violent shock wrenched his body, sending a sharp pain upward from his groin.

A barely visible silken crown above him seemed to smile down at him. At the mercy of such powerful winds and the cutting raindrops that pelted his face, he knew that he'd better be watching for a good landing place. He was about to tilt his head downward for a glimpse beneath when his body splashed into water. As he struggled to right himself and get his head above water, his thoughts raced. He was in the ocean! Could he be in the ocean? He should be miles from it! He hadn't even inflated his Mae West! He had to get out of that damned parachute harness! Not much air left! Got to breathe!

While his hands fumbled frantically to release the straps and activate the inflatable life jacket, one foot struck something. Then the other foot touched it. Though it seemed to take hours, Lee rid himself of the cumbersome parachute, ballooned his life jacket, and got his head above water. As he relaxed his body, his feet touched the submerged object again. Shark? A paralyzing chill rippled through him. He cleared his eyes in the vain hope of spotting a boat, or even a reef, anything that could get him out of the water.

A growling, crackling thunderbolt drove itself to the surface nearby, and its explosive light gave Lee several seconds in which to explore. There—there in the driving rain, not ten yards away, was land. Not the beach, coral, or rock of the seashore, but a swampy, grass-covered bank. Cautiously, he lowered his feet once more. They touched and then sank slightly into what he knew now was mud.

Standing erect, Lee was shoulder-deep in what was apparently a river. With a shout of relief, he slogged his way through the sludge, climbed up on the bank, and rolled to his back. The rain stung his face, but it felt good, so good.

Lee chuckled at the first signs of the familiar, post-crisis trembles. The shaking spread through his arms and legs, and he snickered, giggled, and finally succumbed to uncontrolled laughter. He recounted the events of the last few minutes. He had flown like an idiot. He had broken nearly every rule on jump procedure. He jumped from only three or four hundred feet. And then, when he was certain he was about to drown in the Pacific with a shark after him, all he had to do was stand up. He tore at the turf with his hands and then extended his arms toward the rain clouds above his face.

"I'm alive!" he shouted, crumpling the grass and mud in his hands and allowing the mixture to sprinkle onto his face. "Lee Marks is alive! Zeus, you hear that? Alive!"

When the hysteria had finally spent itself, Lee became conscious of his surroundings. Cautiously, he worked himself to his feet and tested his limbs. There was a painful bruise above his right knee, probably from the windscreen frame as he went out. His groin was tender, undoubtedly from the parachute straps and the shock of the opening. His left shoulder sent a stabbing pain when he attempted to raise that arm above his head. He reasoned that he should be able to live with that until it healed.

Surveying the area, he saw a gigantic tree at the jungle's edge and made for it. The tree had enormous limbs and large, broad leaves. Lee slumped down against the thick trunk, partially sheltered from the relentless rain. There he checked his emergency rations, dried his Colt .45 and its holster the best he could, and rummaged for his compass.

He stood up to watch for debris floating in the river. If the river flowed to the west, it would eventually join the Markham, probably somewhere north of the small base at Gusap. Just then a sizeable tree limb floated past, and he had his answer.

"Westward we go, Marks," he announced.

Lee stepped out from behind the tree into a wall of rain. He quickly retreated, reasoning that even the natives wouldn't be out in such weather. But then, he thought, neither will the mosquitoes. He'd better get on with it. With the determination of a boy who wants to be home for dinner, he struck out to the west along the riverbank.

The going was relatively easy at first with only the tall kunai grass and water-filled ditches that fed into the river to contend with. But after a few confrontations with thick jungle that grew to the water's edge, he decided there had to be a better way. Greenie's preaching came back to him, "If you can find a river, stay with it. Rivers go places, and people live along rivers."

But hacking his way through the jungle could take days, even weeks.

Lee looked at the swiftly flowing river and decided it was his ticket out. Then he faced the question, "How?" Sighting a floating log that was jammed against the river bank, he decided to build a raft. Soon he had located a second log. His shoulder screamed at him as he struggled to drag it partially up on the river bank beside the first log. The raft would be more stable with a third log to keep him right-side-up, but further search of the area came up short. The craft would be a two-logger. He searched the banks downstream hoping to find his parachute snagged up along the way. With the strong shrouds, he'd have it made. But he found no chute.

The wind died down, and the rain fell off to a steady shower. His watch said it was 1430 hours. Remembering the darkness of the jungle at night, Lee hurried into the thicket to search for vines. By the time he had the logs bound together, he had developed a newfound respect for Huck Finn, Tarzan, and Jungle Jim. The vines that were pliable enough to be wound about the logs and secured with any kind of a knot would break under the slightest stress. The sturdier vines refused his knots. A compromise was eventually reached, and Lee's ship was ready for the launching.

With a final check of his equipment, he carefully bellied onto the two-log raft and began paddling with his hands toward midstream. His craft was unsteady, but he found a point of balance that he could maintain by being careful. He was elated with his ship-building, and as he coasted along with the current, he found himself singing lightly under his breath, "Cruis—ing down the riv—errr, on a Sun—day aft—ter—noon..."

The jungle along both banks grew thicker and thicker, and Lee was glad he had decided on the waterway. When he thought of the mosquitoes and other insects, the reptiles and other animals in the jungle, he shuddered and the song choked up in his throat.

Lee had floated a mile or two when he approached a sharp bend in the river. The current seemed to be moving him more swiftly, and his tension mounted. In his flights over the jungle he had seen several waterfalls of fifty to one hundred feet. He could see no white water ahead, but for some reason his unstable craft was gaining momentum. He began to paddle hard to his left, toward the nearest bank. The paddling motion sent severe stingers through his shoulder.

The bank was within ten feet when his log craft suddenly tilted downward. Water splashed in his face. He clung tightly to the logs, straining to see ahead, but the turbulent water blinded him. A jarring collision ripped the logs apart, rolling him off. The bottom dropped out. He felt weightless one second and heavy as a boulder the next as he crashed against the bottom of the river bed. Thrashing about, he fought to right himself and somehow managed to throw his good arm over the smaller of the logs. He embraced the object and held on.

As the current slowed and the water calmed, Lee looked back and marveled. He had indeed drifted over a fifteen-foot waterfall. And while the cushion-effect of the water at the bottom had spared him serious injury, riding two immense logs, both of which were much sturdier than he, down that chute was not the wisest choice.

He drifted along making good time, but he was tired and it was becoming more difficult to maintain his hold on the slippery log. His shoulder throbbed incessantly, so he turned his loyal log toward shore and kicked hard for propulsion. About fifty yards downstream, something foreign to the jungle caught his eye and he made for it. The shapeless white object defied identification until Lee's log bumped against the tree to which it was attached. Caught in the gnarled branches of the downed tree was the familiar white silk of his parachute. Equally as valuable, a variety of tree trunks and large limbs had collected against the downed tree.

Although his shoulder screamed at him with every movement, Lee set about building a second raft using the parachute shrouds to tie the logs together. His watch had stopped, but he knew he would soon run out of daylight. The thought of spending the night in the jungle gave him added incentive. Tying the remainder of his cannibalized parachute to his new, three-log raft, he took to the waterway once more. But this time, he piloted his craft in silence.

The increased stability of his new craft was such that he could occasionally rise to his knees for a clearer look downriver. The current was steady but swift, so little effort was required on his part. He found that he could steer the raft enough to keep it aligned with the river by dragging one foot and the matching hand in the water. The rain stopped, but the sky remained overcast.

Lee's best guess allowed for one, perhaps two hours of daylight, then total blackness. Should he use the remaining daylight to find a secure niche along the banks and get settled for the night? Or should he gamble and use the light to sail on in hopes of finding a native village?

There had to be natives somewhere along this river, but would they be friendly? It was generally accepted that most of the lowlands natives bitterly hated the Japanese and would go to great lengths to aid Americans. But there had been tales of natives who were hostile toward both sides.

He hoped he was well below the highlands that were home to tribes of cannibals.

Find a spot and get settled for the night? he asked himself again. What would he do to get settled, chop down trees and build a house? He could use the parachute to make a tent. No, no matter when he tied up to shore, this night would be spent right there on his raft—the safest place he could find.

The decision made, he headed on downstream. Just as he pulled out his compass for another check, the river began a series of bends. He guessed that, in a stretch of perhaps two miles, he had come up with a heading on each of the major four points of the compass. He cursed the geography of New Guinea. He cursed the damned war. And he cursed his rotten luck.

POP! A shot—it sounded like a thirty-caliber rifle shot. Lee flattened on his raft and fumbled with his shoulder holster, trying to remove the weapon. Would it even fire? Where did the shot come from? Could there be Japanese in this area? Certainly could. Perhaps he wasn't at all where he thought he was. He could try to paddle to one shore or the other, but which one? Maybe the Japs were shooting at something else. Maybe they hadn't spotted him. Maybe he could just hunker down on his raft and drift on past undiscovered. He worked the white clump of parachute silk beneath his body to hide it.

Scanning the shores he expected to see rifle muzzles pointed at him from behind every tree, every clump of brush. Then, ahead, right bank—something moved! He slowly shifted his aim toward the movement. No doubt about it! There was someone there!

"Hurry up, you guys! Get down here!" called a voice with a touch of Texas. "We've got another wet pigeon coming in," added the GI on the shore as he pumped another shot into the air.

Chapter 36

▼

Lee caught the rope thrown to him on the third attempt, and his bizarre watercraft was pulled to shore. He grabbed the wet wad of white silk, jumped ashore, then stopped for a moment, turned and tossed the chute back onto the raft. He tied the raft to a nearby palm stump.

"Save the raft—I may need it to get home to Nadzab," he said to the three enlisted men who had pulled him in. They looked at one another and shrugged.

"Sir, this is Gusap," said a corporal, "and I don't mean to hurry you, but there's a Gooney due in any minute. You just have time to get checked by the medic and maybe grab a bite to eat."

"Thanks, Corporal," Lee said, slogging along heavy-footed, his saturated boots squishing with each step. "Have any others made it in here?"

The corporal didn't answer, but as they stepped out past the next hut, he pointed to two dozen or more pilots and crewmen gathered near the airstrip. Several were laid out on stretchers. Lee felt his anger rising to a boil.

"Did they all come in from the jungle?" he asked.

"No, some of them piled up trying to fly in here."

"Damn!" Lee exclaimed. "Think of how many are still out there somewhere."

"I'd rather not, sir. The medic's over there. Good luck, sir."

As he headed for the medic's hut, Lee felt swamped by a cascade of feelings that took him back to the turbulence of the wild storm. His painful shoulder increased its torment. The bruises ached. His head throbbed. Then sudden nausea invaded, threatening to turn him inside out at any moment. The irrationality of the whole situation pecked at his brain, its paralyzing force washing away the last of the elation he had felt upon reaching Gusap. One whiff of the medicinal atmosphere, and Lee stooped over near the entrance. The gagging and choking produced little, but the acidic juices that went up his nose carried the jolt of smelling salts.

"Feeling tough, huh, Lieutenant?" sang the doctor.

Lee straightened and spun around to face the man. He dug deep within himself, searching for some control of his rage.

"Sorry," the doctor drawled as he motioned toward his examination table. In but two minutes Lee had received the official diagnosis for what he already knew. "Actually," the doctor said, "you're in pretty good shape. You're a lucky man. Better see if you can steal a bite to eat." The tone of his voice, his words, and the manner in which he turned his back on Lee did nothing to soothe Lee's inner turmoil. Somehow, Lee didn't feel lucky—thoroughly pissed—but not lucky.

Minutes later, with a muffin-like creature covered with something that resembled marmalade in each hand, Lee climbed the ladder into the crowded C-47 and worked his way over and around stretcher cases to an open spot half-way up the sloping walkway. He squatted cross-legged on the floor between the head of one stretcher patient and the feet of the next. Once settled, he closed his eyes and shut out the world while he devoured the two cakes. They tasted surprisingly good. A cup of coffee would have put the delightful snack over the top. He sat there, eyes closed, searching for the Lee Marks who had begun the mission that morning.

The port engine whined, coughed, and sputtered to life, followed shortly by the starboard engine. Then the two power plants swelled to a roar, sending familiar vibrations rippling through its occupants as the Gooneybird taxied over rough ground. Lee felt the aircraft swivel sharply to the left. The engines ran up to full power and soon the rumbling of the landing gears silenced as the ground fell away beneath them. Lee heard the gears thump up into their wells, and he sensed the flaps being returned to normal position. He felt thankful that the trip would take little more than a half-hour.

As the cloud of blue cigarette smoke began to spread, permeating every corner of the aircraft cabin, Lee's body began to relax. He sat there with his eyes closed. Sleep would be nice, he thought. To maintain his balance in the squat position, he placed one hand on the deck beside him, then the other hand. But his left hand didn't connect to the floor as his right hand had. Instead, it had found something warm and wet.

His eyes popped open to find his hand resting in a pool of blood that had trailed from the body of the man just ahead of him. Flinching, he jerked his hand up, looked at it, then searched around him for something to wipe the blood off. Two pilots who sat on the bench seat just above Lee stared down at him. Embarrassed, Lee wiped the blood off on his own trouser leg. When he looked up again, the glazed stare of the twosome had not changed. He shrugged and smiled at them; they only stared. The expanding pool of blood crept slowly toward Lee. It would soon be upon him, and he saw no avenue of escape. There simply was no room for movement. His attention fell to the man's badly mangled and only partially wrapped foot. Lee's eyes followed up a bandaged, bleeding, grotesquely-twisted leg to a mid-section that was tightly bound with thick layers of bandage. Blood seeped through the heavy binder, trickled down the man's side, and collected on the canvas beneath him. The young man's bruised and battered face showed two motionless eyes that stared through the fog of morphine to the cabin ceiling. His lips moved slightly, as though trying to talk.

As Lee wiped his blood-stained hand once more, he discovered two things. One, he couldn't get all the blood off. And two, he himself had indeed been lucky, so lucky. He glanced about the cabin and shivered as he saw arms in slings, legs in splints, bleeding bandages, and even open, unwrapped wounds. In an instant, the mutilated bodies and all-present blood washed the self-pity from Lee Marks, for this—*this* was the *real* war. Twice before, he thought he had found it—the frightening bombs, the loss of friends—but the blood soaking into his trouser leg offered a much more graphic definition. In view of the desecration surrounding him, his own experience had been little more than an inconvenience. But as his compassion warmed, the anger burned.

He tried to let the rhythm of the engine noise and the metallic complaints of the old, used, and abused aircraft envelope and insulate him from the horrors that surrounded him. But eyes open or eyes shut, the helpless feelings persisted. He felt a hand on his shoulder.

"See if you can slow the bleeding," came a voice from behind Lee. The man seated on the bench above and behind Lee pressed over him from behind, took Lee's hand, located a pressure point on the bleeding victim's leg, and pressed Lee's fingers firmly on the spot. "Let up a bit every couple of minutes."

"Do the best I can," said Lee.

The hand from behind patted him on the shoulder. "You got it."

Within minutes, Lee's anger faded to a warm glow within. He had slowed the bleeding noticeably. He was giving the poor guy a chance to make it. Perhaps someone would do the same for him some day. When it comes right down to it, he thought, this is what it's all about. He concentrated so hard on his task that he found himself startled when the Gooneybird flared out for touchdown at Nadzab.

Teams of medics immediately began removing the stretchers. Lee had to release his grip and tilt back against the helper behind him to make room for them to pass.

"Do you think he'll make it?" Lee asked the man.

"Naw. He's been gone for twenty minutes. But it sure as hell ain't your fault," said the man.

As Lee stumbled down the ladder into pounding rain at Nadzab, his heart was in his shoes. Tears streamed down his face. And anger seethed within. It was all so pointless, so unnecessary. Some man sporting stars had refused to reconsider a single order, and that stupid error had killed this poor guy and probably many others like him. No one person should have that kind of power. Mo was right when he said, "The whole system stinks, so you'd better figure it out and make it work for you. If you don't…it'll kill you."

He'd tell Mo he now agreed—a sudden chill ran through him. For the first time since the squadron split up in the storm he had thought of his squadron mates. He had been too wrapped up in himself? Maybe Mo didn't make it. But Mo always made it. What about the others? Bubba, Stew, Sandy, Burner, Greenie? He saw none of the faces he needed most.

Suddenly, from nowhere appeared Mo Brennan. "Any more Gophers on that bird?" he asked as he brushed on past Lee. Mo vaulted up the steel steps and disappeared into the cabin.

"Well, screw you," Lee muttered. "You can take your damned war and shove it." He turned and walked slowly toward the mess tent.

"I suppose I should check in to debrief," he said to himself. "Screw them, too! They're the idiots who put us through this stupid, meaningless mess. If they want me, they can find me."

"Did you say something to me?" asked the officer who was walking just ahead of Lee. "No." Lee noticed the man's rank, a colonel. "Yes…yes, I did." He bumped past the officer and entered the mess.

"You got anything fit to eat in this place?" he demanded of the sweaty sergeant who was stirring something in a large vat.

"Yes, *sir*!" the sergeant said, scowling, "some wonderful stew, just like mother used to make." He slopped a helping onto a tray and slid it across to Lee.

Lee eyed the concoction, returned the angry stare for a moment, then snatched up the tray. As bad as the stew looked, it tasted good, and he devoured it instantly. By the time he had refilled his coffee cup, he felt much better. He went out of his way to give the surly sergeant a smile and a thumbs up sign. Back at the table, he bummed a cigarette from a pilot from the 475th Fighter Group.

As he lit up and took his first drag, he imagined himself in a mirror. Now he was a smoker? An angry, surly, pissed-off son of a bitch who no longer cared about anything or anybody, including himself? That didn't sound like the Lee Marks he knew, but then maybe he had been wrong about himself, too. It seemed like the futility of war had suddenly penetrated his soul, too. Perhaps it took war to clear one's vision in the mirror.

He sat by himself, sipping his coffee and smoking, absorbing the somber atmosphere that had engulfed the entire mess. He watched the solemn procession of late diners come and go. There were angry voices to be heard everywhere. But then, there were usually a few angry voices to be heard. What pricked Lee's consciousness even more was the absence of laughter.

Lee recalled that Sunday back in December of 1941 when Japanese bombs had so shaken the nation that they were felt in the student union in Champagne, Illinois. Students had collected in small groups throughout the day and into the evening. Some vociferously decried the act of aggression, while others quietly gazed into space. Their feelings, Lee surmised, were probably a combination of generous concern for those whose lives had already been shattered and selfish fear for their own futures.

"This seat taken?" a voice beside Lee asked. He looked up to meet the weary eyes of Mo Brennan. There was no smile. Beads of water clung to his forehead, threatening to drop with the slightest movement. His khakis were soaked through, and his unbuttoned shirt exposed a damp mass of curly, brown hair. Even before Lee could respond, Mo plunked his cup on the table and took a seat. He stared at Lee, a stare aimed somewhere below the eyes, perhaps at the nose, or the mouth. His eyes remained fixed for several seconds.

Lee watched him, then nervously moved his own gaze around the mess and back again. Still no change. As he studied the strange figure before him, Lee felt his own anger subside. He couldn't even imagine what Mo must have gone through that day.

"You all right, Mo?"

"A stupid, goddamned waste," Mo muttered, "stupid, goddamned waste."

"How bad are we?"

Mo didn't answer, so Lee repeated the question.

"Huh? Oh...can't tell yet," Mo said. "Right now, the whole operation is missing thirty-one planes—maybe 140 pilots and crewmen—lost a batch of the B-24s. Nash collided with one at Saidor. He's gone. Son of a bitch, it's hot! I thought it might cool down after all this rain, but it sure hasn't." His eyes met Lee's for the first time. "You okay?"

Lee felt sympathy surging through himself. Here was his strong man, his mentor, his leader sitting there closer to defeat than he'd ever seen him. He found himself giving some leeway to the friend who had ignored him at the airstrip. Mo had to be carrying a heavy load.

"Yeah, I'm okay, Mo. How did you get home?"

"Just pure shitting luck. When we got boxed in I went down on the deck, broke out at about 400 feet, and found the river. Just followed it home. Too bad Nash didn't stay with me."

Suddenly, the message filtered through to Lee.

"Did you say Bubba bought it?" Lee sat there stunned. Bubba dead? The new Bubba who had finally found self-respect now dead?

"They told me that one of the gunners on the B-24 might make it," Mo said. "The rest all checked out—bad fire. Sadler, you, and your new guy, Stewart, all lost your ships but got back. We're still waiting for word on Stover. If he doesn't make it, we'll have to find two replacements and at least five new ships. Make that six. We owe one to Sledge for Stewart's wipe-out."

Lee pondered the logistics. How long would it take to find two new pilots and six replacement P-38s? Bubba dead? Not possible—not the *new* Bubba. And Smokey Stover gone? No, Smokey would have to make it back. He's just the old, reliable, average-type guy who does his job, not the kind of guy who gets killed.

Suddenly, dead-numbing fatigue washed through him. Without a word to Mo, he struggled to his feet, left the mess and half-staggered up the path to his tent. Sandy and Black Bart were already asleep. Lee stood for a moment over the bunk that had been Bubba's. Then he stripped off his soggy shirt, jerked his squishing boots and socks off, slid out of his wet trousers, flopped on the bunk, and closed the mosquito netting. Even as his defeated body went numb, his mind raced on through one final spurt of disordered thoughts.

His Marksman was gone. Bubba's parents will be devastated. Their only child burned to a crisp? Would Command replace the lost ships with Lightnings? Would Bubba somehow reappear? He himself had no plane. But maybe it wasn't Bubba. Maybe it was another P-38 who collided with the bomber on landing at Saidor. What if the top brass folded up Gopher Squadron and transferred the men into other units? The whirling dervish threw Lee's head into a flat, uncontrollable tail spin, the kind that could only end in a crash. Monstrous puffs of cumulonimbus clouds swirled around him as he spun out of control, their inner cores flashing from gray to purple, to red, to gold—and finally to black.

Chapter 37

▼

The two main landing gears thumped down and locked just as the olive drab C-47 emerged beneath a large thunderhead. The pilot throttled back and the craft flared out and touched the main wheels gently to the concrete at Seven-Mile Drome near Port Moresby. Lee knew the satisfaction the pilot drew from such a fine landing, particularly when all or most of the passengers were themselves pilots. It was a work of art to be shared.

Mo commandeered a jeep to take them to Fifth Air Force Headquarters. As they bumped on down the road, Mo reviewed his instructions to Lee.

"Now remember, you've got to keep cool. Be spit and polish. Do exactly like I've told you, say exactly the things I've told you to say and no more. Above all, act firm and positive. No sign of weakness. You do that and I'm betting you'll get us the ships."

"I think I've got it, Mo. But I still don't understand why you have *me* going in to see General Hayes to coax six new Model Ls out of him, while *you* are scraping up two replacement pilots. Shouldn't it be the other way around?"

"Well, maybe I'll explain it all later," Mo said. "For now I'll just say that if you do this thing right, you'll have a better chance of coming out a winner than even I would. Okay?"

Some time later, as Lee sat in General Hayes' outer office in the hotel building that served as headquarters, he rehearsed the curious instructions that he had committed to memory. "Above all," Mo had said, "keep to your lines. Don't add any more than you absolutely have to." Lee tried to swallow his nerves. No luck. He imagined himself stripping off a layer of nerves, like a thin layer of silk and stuffing it into a pocket. He had to find a way. This was *not* his kind of action.

Maybe he should just get up and walk out—tell Mo the general wasn't in, or perhaps—

"Lieutenant Marks," said the desk sergeant, "the general will see you now." He led Lee to the inner office and closed the door behind him.

Lee resisted the urge to scan the large, inner office and its furnishings. Instead he concentrated on the huge mahogany desk and the man seated behind it.

"Lieutenant Marks, sir," Lee said, snapping to attention with a crisp salute.

Brigadier General Hamilton Hayes was a slender but well-proportioned man in his late forties. He had an extremely handsome face beneath wavy black hair. Far down on his nose sat a tiny pair of reading glasses. The general seemed to exude warmth, yet the hazel eyes that looked over the small glasses were all business.

Lee stood there for what seemed like forever while General Hayes studied the papers in his hand. Lee suspected they were the forms that Mo and Sledge had filled out and sent with Lee.

Finally, General Hayes flipped the papers to the desktop and looked up.

"Well," he began, "considering the vast number of fighter squadrons we have in the Southwest Pacific Theater who are still flying obsolete P-39s and P-40s, this request seems not only out of order, but downright brazen. A couple of questions, Lieutenant Marks. Why didn't Colonel Brennan bring this requisition to me himself?"

The time had come. Lee must utter a canned response that still made no sense. But he gathered what false confidence he could find and launched Mo's plan.

"Sir," Lee said, "Colonel Brennan felt that since the three of us share a common bond—an understanding—this requisition submission is a mere formality. So, while I'm here, he's over searching for replacement pilots."

The general's face stiffened. His eyes blazed.

"And would you like to explain to me what this common bond is?"

"Sir, Colonel Brennan felt that the fourth member of our…common bond…would prefer that we expedite this matter quickly, and I believe he said 'quietly,' so that we can all look to the future rather than the past."

Lee couldn't be sure, but he thought he felt a puff of inner strength leak out from the handsome general. His eyes seemed less threatening; his shoulders sagged slightly.

"Well, yes," General Hayes said, "in view of your squadron's exemplary performance, the top priority almost has to float in your direction. But if I *should* decide to give you six new Model Ls, do we all understand that this will be the last special request granted by this office?"

Lee couldn't believe it. It had worked? That was the least convincing argument he had ever presented for anything of importance in his life, and he was about to win?

"Oh, yes, sir!" he replied. "Colonel Brennan said to tell you that he'd be sending all the copies of those other documents to you as soon as we get back to Nadzab with the six ships."

"That's—a given," the general said. He picked up another paper, studied it for a moment, then continued. "As—luck would have it—we just happen to have six unassigned, new P-38 Model L aircraft just ferried in from Townsville. If we stamp the forms high priority, you should be able to get out of here in the morning. We do need to clear out space at Seven-Mile as quickly as we can. Can you have the necessary pilots ready by morning?"

"Yes, sir!"

"Dismissed."

An hour later, over the best lunch Lee had ever met in an officers' mess, he relayed the story to Mo.

"Mo, this makes no sense at all, absolutely none," Lee said. "There wasn't a reason in hell that he should grant our request, and I'm out of there in five minutes with six new Lightnings—Model Ls at that."

"And at what point in the conversation did you feel you had scored?" Mo asked.

Lee thought for a moment. He looked at Mo quizzically and replied, "I think it was when I said that the fourth member of our…common bond…would prefer that we expedite this matter quickly and quietly so that we can all look to the future rather than the past. Mo, who's the fourth member?"

"Damn!" Mo exclaimed, slapping a hand on the table, "I knew that line would do it. Smooth as silk!"

"I think," Lee said, "that he thought I knew something that I don't. Mo, what is it that I knew that I don't? And who's the fourth member?"

Mo put his fork down, sipped his coffee, glanced to both sides, then leaned forward. "Just between us, now. Okay?"

"Uh, sure, okay."

"What you knew that you don't know," Mo began in a voice slightly louder than a whisper, "is that I have in my possession a photograph of the general caught in a compromising position."

"What, somebody's wife?" Lee asked.

"Uh-uh." Mo smiled, rolled his eyes once and said, "Somebody's husband."

When Lee recovered, the scripted conversation in the general's office rippled through his mind and began to make sense.

"So he's thinking that you've already shared his secret with me. How much farther might you take it? Is that it?"

"That's it." Mo's broad smile turned on. "Of course, I would never spread such gossip around, wouldn't consider it. And, of course, you wouldn't either."

"Man, you can damn well bet on *that!*"

"Okay, it's water *over* the damn. Now we've got to get ready for tomorrow. Got to get those ships out of here before we lose them to someone else. I've got two replacements lined up, believe it or not, Lieutenants Smith and Jones."

"Well, that makes four of us," Lee said. "I guess you and I each fly two ships home?"

"I'll have that covered as soon as I can get over to the radio shack and get a message to Sledge—do that right after coffee and a cigarette," said Mo. "He's waiting for the word. Harper can bring him, another pilot, Sergeant Worley, another crew chief, and an armorer down in the Golden Goose yet today. You got anything you need to do in the next couple of hours?"

"Well," began Lee, "I'd thought I might look up—no, I think I'll just hide somewhere."

"Hide?"

"Yeah, in case the general sends a hit squad out looking for me."

"While you're hiding, give some thought to who should get the three new ships after Sledge, you, and me." Mo stood and smiled his gotcha smile. "Bet you don't get this one right. See you over at the officers' quarters later." He slapped Lee on the back and left.

With an alteration by Colonel Hammer, Mo's plan came together, and the next day at 1300 hours six new Model L Lockheed Lightnings departed Seven-Mile Drome for Nadzab. The colonel had chosen not to entrust the precious new ships to new replacements when Gopher Squadron had several experienced pilots sitting there grounded at Nadzab for lack of aircraft.

Sledge had unknowingly accommodated Lee's choices for assignment of the new planes. Following the colonel's lead as they climbed out of Port Moresby were Mo, Lee, Greenie, Sandy Sadler, and Burner Hedman. The new pilots, Smith and Jones, would fly back aboard the Golden Goose with the ground pounders.

Colonel Hammer led the flight to the south over the water for a weapons test. Lee's four fifties and 20 mm cannon responded as they should, but he hoped they encountered no enemy planes on the way home. Strangers, hundreds of miles away, had sighted in their weapons. Lee would feel better when Sergeants Worley and Anderson had checked their work. A dogfight with the shifty Zeros was no place to find that your weapons shot east while your plane flew north.

The flight was uneventful, but nonetheless exciting. Lee found himself listening carefully to the rhythm of the more powerful Allison 1600-horsepower engines and scanning the instrumentation. While the engines were a substantial improvement over the Model J, the instruments were nearly identical. The most visible change was the exterior finish. The olive drab camouflage paint had given way to bright, polished aluminum. Scuttlebutt said the elimination of the camouflage paint scheme saved money and labor, and it reduced the Lightning's weight and friction, thereby increasing speed. And since the Fifth Air Force bases were becoming less vulnerable to Japanese attacks, camouflage was deemed unnecessary.

Lee loved the new ship from the first moment he boarded her. Somehow the bright silver finish had said, "speed" even before the engines were started. He felt the urge to break formation and wring her out, put her through her paces and see how she responded. But he managed to sit back, follow Colonel Hammer's lead, and enjoy a relaxing flight in the unusually clear New Guinea skies. After his disastrous flight on Black Sunday, he had found heaven. He gently rocked the Lightning from side to side, getting the feel of the new hydraulic aileron boost. A glance about the small formation found others doing the same. He drew additional comfort from the new, enlarged air scoops. While he himself had experienced few problems with overheating engines, the threat had hung constantly over the Gopher pilots.

Within a week, Gopher Squadron had become active once more. Old ships belonging to Mo, Greenie, and Burner Hedman were redistributed to Stew and the two new pilots, Smith and Jones. Nose art and numbers had been repainted. Lee had taken the two new pilots under his wing. While Smith and Jones seemed cooperative and listened carefully to his instructions, the pair left Lee with a question mark front and center. They both flew well—even demonstrated competency with the tense switch-over to single-engine flight—but neither showed the aggressiveness that was a characteristic of the early training classes. He passed along his reservations to Mo.

"I think they're too focused on staying alive," Mo said.

"I can't tell. It might be that they're just afraid they'll screw up," Lee replied.

A lengthy debate that would determine the make-up of each of the three flights followed. Lee could see immediately where the discussion would hit the wall. With the recent replacements, Gopher Squadron had taken on a new face, a face painted with the innocence of inexperience. They had the two rookies, Milton Smith and Oren Jones. Then, the next three pilots, Stew Stewart, Tony Margo, and Rolly Greenberg, each had one or two kills and at least a little experience. Of course, there was also Black Bart who, despite his experience, had no kills and had yet to demonstrate any reliability. That meant *six* weak links in the chain of twelve.

Lee's attempt to replace Black Bart with one of the new pilots was swept aside with a simple grunt from Mo. While Mo had intimated that Lee would have some influence in the realignment, it quickly became clear that the day was once again in the hands of Mo Brennan.

With his scribbling complete, Mo flipped the wrinkled paper across the table to Lee.

RED FLIGHT—30 total kills
Mo Brennan—Flight Leader—22
Sandy Sadler—Wingman—7
Rolly Greenberg—Element Leader—1
Milton Smith—Wingman—0

WHITE FLIGHT—21 total kills
Greenie—Flight Leader—12
Oren Jones—Wingman—0
Burner Headman—Element Leader—7
Tony Margo—Wingman—2

BLUE FLIGHT—22 total kills
Lee Marks—Flight Leader—15
Stew Stewart—Wingman—2
Chub Forbes—Element Leader—5
Black Bart Barton—Wingman—0

Despite finding himself stuck once again with Barton, Lee felt comfortable with his Blue Flight remaining untouched. At least he knew his pilots and what could or could not be expected of them. But Mo's placement of the two new pilots?

"It's okay, Mo," Lee began, "but you stuck Greenie with the new guy, Jones. Shouldn't Greenie at least get Tony Margo for his wingman?"

Mo's glare was short and his reply was quick.

"Simple. We match up the most experienced with the least experienced."

"Well, then, shouldn't you draw the other rookie, Smith, as your wingman and make Sandy the Element Leader with Greenberg as his—"

"You just don't get it, do you?" Mo cut in, his eyes burning into Lee. "I let you help out a little around here, but I still call the shots. End of subject." Mo got up, left the table, and trudged out of the mess.

Chapter 38

Five days after the Black Sunday disaster, a reconstituted Gopher Squadron headed up the Markham River Valley and over the mountains for a 250-mile flight to attack Wewak, the strong Jap base east of Hollandia on New Guinea's north coast. Nearly every perpetrator or conveyor of scuttlebutt agreed that Wewak would be the next Allied invasion target, and the event would take place within the week. Therefore it was logical that the Fifth Air Force would be pounding the base non-stop for the next few days.

As Lee looked down at the fifty or more B-25s loaded with parafrags, the recent events began to make more sense. They had flown several 900-mile missions to destroy the Jap air arm at Hollandia, apparently to reduce the enemy's capability to interfere with the imminent invasion of Wewak. But one event would never make sense to Lee—the Black Sunday mission, the ultimate screw-up by Command.

Lee felt strange as he scanned the other ships of Gopher Squadron. Half of the P-38s were bright silver, contrasting markedly with the older olive drab, and half of the ships were flown by replacement pilots, two of whom were fresh new yardbirds. And while his Marksman II had already demonstrated its superior power and agility, a hollow feeling in Lee's gut reminded him that much had changed. He had emerged from a fragile comfort zone into…he knew not what.

His new ship looked different, felt different, and even smelled different. The attitudes of the pilots seemed to bounce about like rubber balls. When one Gopher felt up and ready to go, the next seemed negative and often belligerent. Even the comradery of the original Gophers who remained had become unpredictable.

To Lee, and perhaps to others, the loss of Bubba penetrated the deepest. When Lee could, he squeezed the red-faced friend with his round ears and wispy, sun-bleached blond hair from his consciousness. But never for long. No matter how Lee tried to rationalize Bubba's death he ended up on the same page. It seemed so unfair. Just when the boy-man had finally surmounted the obstacles that had haunted him for most of his life, his victory was erased by a single piece of bad judgment. It wasn't the Japs who killed Bubba; it was his own commanding officers. Mo openly disagreed with Lee. Despite his own prediction that Command would soon screw up on a big one, Mo's stance had changed to one of denial. It was simply *the war*.

"Two groups of bad guys coming up! Two o'clock and ten o'clock. Switch, drop, and string it out," Lee's radio barked. "Gophers, we take the Oscars at ten. Roby, you do the others."

"Roger."

"Okay, Gophers, down we go."

Lee hadn't seen so many Japanese planes airborne for weeks. Captain Robesky's 127th Squadron banked right and started down toward a group of more than thirty Oscars. And the group coming up after the bombers from the left was perhaps even larger. Wewak must be important to them, very important, thought Lee as he tested his weapons.

He saw Red Flight bank farther to the left to take on a cluster of enemy planes. Greenie took his flight to the right, so Lee led his Blue Flight straight into the heart of the enemy formation. About half of the central group of Oscars turned up to meet Blue Flight, while the remainder headed for the bombers. But the split seemed to be random, totally disordered. Either the Japs had worked out a new playbook to confuse their enemies, or they were poorly trained and undisciplined. The answer came quickly as the lead Oscar that Lee was sighting in on suddenly pulled up and left into the path of one of his mates.

The orange to black fireball that erupted above and to the right of Blue Flight blew debris in all directions. Lee and Stew had the best positions to avoid the fallout. Lee glanced back to see Chub Forbes and Bart get through.

Strangely, that collision that marked the beginning of the battle for the Blues also seemed to signal the end of any confusion for them. It was as though the enemy had choreographed the battle to favor the four Lightnings. They shot their way through the formation, turned, climbed for altitude, then repeated the effort two more times. On each pass Lee's flight found Oscars exactly where they needed them for targets. During the second climbing turn, Lee recalled the earlier battle in which nothing he did could point his Lightning's nose to an enemy. In minutes, the Oscar formations were reduced by two-thirds and the remaining Jap pilots headed south to more peaceful skies.

Back at Nadzab, the debriefing revealed that the Gophers had scored an incredible 17 kills running their total to 89. Even more gratifying was the fact that every Gopher scored at least once—even Black Bart. And the two squadrons came home with no losses. The bombers lost four ships to AA. Lee was once again the high scorer with three, running his total to eighteen kills. His Blue Flight had shot down six Oscars. Mo added two more to his score for a total of twenty-four flags. He had made it into the top six group in the Pacific Theater.

And Aloysius Black Barton was ecstatic. As soon as one audience tired of his demonstration, using his hands as airplanes and explaining his intricate maneuvers, he turned his show on another. But with each performance Lee noted that Bart's exuberance became wrapped in slightly more professional tones.

Mo invited Lee to a "closed strategy session" on the knoll overlooking the Markham River. The ointment for the day was gin. Lee suspected that Mo had gained a head start on the gin, and when Mo's speech showed occasional slurs after only one drink, Lee knew. But Mo was exuberant, and with Lee's own emotions nearly matching Mo's, he wasn't about to engage in an argument on morals or ethics.

"Damn!" Mo said. "We really creamed them today. And with six replacement pilots, too. I doubt that Satan's Angels over in the 475th ever got seventeen in one mission."

"Most important," said Lee, "we got our adrenaluck back. We needed that."

"Adrenaluck?" Mo asked.

"Sure…our adrenaluck. Adrenalin and luck. It takes both and we've had neither lately. It'll be good for all of us, including you and me. Too bad we can't bottle *that*."

Mo flicked a glance in Lee's direction but said nothing.

The Fifth Air Force struck again at Wewak the following day. But instead of flying cover for the bombers, the Gophers preceded the low-level parafrag attack by A-20s with a strafing attack on gun positions. The mission proved to be a stark contrast to that of the previous day.

There were no Oscars to be found at such low level, and the heavy anti-aircraft machine gun emplacements numbered in the dozens.

Lee took a couple of light hits on the first pass. Then, on the second pass, he heard and felt a hard Thunk—Thunk! His starboard engine immediately began streaming coolant.

Lee felt the hairs prickle the back of his neck. It would be only a matter of minutes at best and he'd have to shut the engine down, and here he was, caught over an enemy stronghold with only 200 feet of altitude.

"Blue," he called, "I'm losing an engine. Help me get out of here. Then Chub and Bart can come back and finish the job."

"Roger," came Stew's response.

"Look out!" called Chub. "Three Oscars coming down on us from behind! Stay down on the deck, Lee, and we'll try to chase 'em off!"

Lee was anxious to gain altitude. Trying to convert to one engine at low altitude was not recommended. In fact, it was often a sure ticket out. But by remaining low, he could make it a little more difficult for his attackers. He watched the starboard engine's temperature gauge begin to climb. He checked over his shoulders and in the rear view mirror. His mates had all disappeared, as had two of the attackers. But one remaining Oscar was overtaking him as though he was sitting still. He felt several hits. He jinked sharply left and the attacker zoomed past.

As the Oscar began a sharp, climbing turn to the right, he suddenly lost his left wing. An olive drab P-38 flew over Lee and then the hapless enemy fighter as it went into a flat spin and did about three revolutions before crashing into the jungle.

"That takes care of him!" came a voice over the radio. "Go on up and I'll cover."

It sounded like…Black Bart's voice! Lee could wait no longer. He began climbing, watching for Oscars, checking his temperature gauge, and planning his conversion as he gained altitude. Flying in enemy territory with an obvious visible trail of coolant was like bleeding in shark infested waters. He had reached 4,000 feet when the gauge told him it was time. He cut both engines back, killed the starboard engine, feathered its prop, and cautiously eased power back into the port engine, carefully adjusting and trimming his control surfaces to compensate for the lost engine. If he could gain 500 feet a minute he'd have the altitude to clear the mountains. Methodically, he trimmed the ship to fly with as little effort on his part as possible. Lee relaxed a little and tried a quick search for positives.

If his port engine held up he should be able to clear the mountains at 9,000 feet. He was very familiar with these mountains and with clear skies could easily see the terrain. He had already bailed out successfully once, so if it came to that—

"Well, well," came Bart's voice. "Look what we have here! I sure hope that other engine doesn't quit on you. And I hope some Jap doesn't sneak past me and flame you. But you can count on me…old friend."

Lee tried to ignore Bart's subtle taunts. He wondered where Stew and Chub were. He hoped they'd not gotten themselves into serious trouble while trying to defend him. As he cleared the mountains he relaxed a little. It was downhill from there to Gusap, the small emergency field where he'd been pulled in on his raft. And if Barton was going to carry through on his earlier threat, he'd probably have made his move by now.

Lee knew there would be two things in his favor that would be working on Bart's mind. One, Lee's radio worked fine, and at the first sign of trouble from Bart, he could call it in. And two, having made two kills in as many days, some of Bart's hostility may have burned off.

As it turned out, Lee was right. The return flight went almost as well as it could on only one engine. When they reached Gusap, however, the field was obscured by thick, low-level smoke making any landing impossible. Lee feared the base had been attacked until he remembered that the natives were known to set strategic fires in the thick, tall kunai grass to aid in rounding up and killing wild pigs for food.

As he turned final at Nadzab, Lee felt grateful for his sound flying skills. The single-engine approach and landing was textbook. A snub-nosed tractor quickly hooked on and towed him home, followed by Black Bart.

"Thanks, Bart," Lee said as the two pilots came together after climbing down from their ships. Lee's gratitude was genuine, but he felt apprehensive. How would Bart react to this one?

To his surprise, Bart smiled broadly and reached to shake hands.

"You're welcome," he said. "It's possible you might have done the same thing for me. Right?"

"Absolutely," Lee said. "And Bart, congratulations on getting number two."

Shortly, the rest of the Gophers landed and taxied to their spots. Several had been hit by AA, but they all made it home, and with no injuries. Mo pulled Lee aside.

"How did that go?" he asked, nodding in Black Bart's direction.

"Some subtle threats, but I think he was just funning me. It went fine. And he saved my bacon when he tore that Oscar apart."

Mo broke into a big smile. "He got another one? Really? He hit another one?"

"Shssh."

"Oh—yeah. Well, maybe you've solved the problem, Killer."

Lee looked into Mo's eyes. The eyes might have been, as Lee thought of it, alcolized, but he couldn't be sure. And the smell of gin was less obvious than that of whiskey.

"No more 'Killer,'" Lee said, drawing a finger across his own throat in a slashing motion. He turned abruptly and walked away. It had become a matter of respect.

Days later on April 26th the Gopher Squadron once again flew high cover over B-24s to Wewak. With the pasting the Wewak installations were taking, Lee couldn't imagine much Japanese resistance against the forthcoming invasion. But then, the Allies had found before that the enemy had frequently found ways to go underground, endure incredible bombardment and yet rise up to fight on invasion day. The few Japanese fighters that rose to meet them were bottled up at lower altitudes by other escorts, and Gopher Squadron departed for home to close out a milk run on schedule with belly tanks intact and weapons unfired.

As Lee's flight was coasting in on their downwind leg at Nadzab, Lee looked to his left and could see Mo's ship on his final approach. But at a point well beyond normal flare-out and touch-down, Mo still had too much airspeed. It was doubtful that he could land and stop in time to avoid running off the end of the runway. It seemed obvious that he should abort the landing and go around. But that would be an open admission of inadequacy for everyone to see. Mo would have trouble with that.

"Go around, Mo! Go around!" Lee shouted to no one. Had the booze finally taken over? Mo was not one of the great pilots, but overshooting a landing? And with no mechanical problems? Under normal circumstances, an impossibility.

At the last second, Mo pulled up and turned left to re-enter the line-up behind Blue Flight on the downwind leg. Occupied with his own landing, Lee saw nothing of Mo's second attempt. The Gophers had all spun around in their respective parking spots when Mo Brandon came taxiing in. With his Marksman II shut down and ready to be buttoned up, Lee made for Mo's ship. Mo was out on one wing gesturing frantically to Sergeant Worley who stood there helpless in the onslaught. Lee heard nothing that was spoken until he drew close.

"Well, you find it!" shouted Mo. "You find the goddamned problem and fix it! Don't you tell *me* there's nothing wrong with the flaps!" Mo jumped angrily to the ground from the trailing edge of the wing.

"You all right, Mo?" Lee asked as he put a hand on Mo's shoulder.

Mo shook Lee's hand off. "Goddamned flaps!" he spouted. "I couldn't even get ten degrees flaps! These guys sit around playing poker, and I have to perform magic to get my goddamned plane back down!"

Lee eased around to face his mentor. No doubt about it. Lee could see the outline of Mo's flask in his front trouser pocket. It would probably go unnoticed by others, but Mo's eyes…and his demeanor?

"Mo," Lee said quietly, "you'd better slip over to mess and pour a couple of cups of coffee down before you go near the debriefing. No way you're going to slip past them today."

"Get off my toes, Marks! You don't tell me what to do. I think it's about time to throw you back where I found you." With that he turned and stomped off.

When Mo had disappeared, Lee approached Sergeant Worley. Together they tested the flaps through every possible configuration but actual flight. The flaps worked fine. As they talked, Lee watched the crew chief closely for any indication that he understood what was happening, but nothing showed.

"You're fine," Lee said, slapping Sergeant Worley on the shoulder. "Don't let it get to you. He's got a lot on his mind—under a lot of pressure."

Back at the tent Lee found two letters waiting for him. Both were from his mother. He hesitated before opening them. Then he reasoned, she wouldn't have bothered to write if the letters were bad. He tore into the two envelopes and quickly read the first, then the second. He'd have been hard put to describe the feelings the letters gave him. He knew it had been hard for his mom to write the letters. He had seen her take actions many times to demonstrate that she had been wrong, but to put it into words?

There was the time she'd become furious over the noise their next door neighbors were making one evening. She had stomped over, pounded on their door, and read them a first class riot act. The next day she learned the neighbors had received word their son, Melvin, had been killed in action. That same afternoon she carried over a full meal she had prepared: fried chicken, potatoes and gravy, vegetables, and dessert. Without a word, she delivered the meal and left. It was the best she could do.

While his mom had found few words of direct apology, the tone of the letters was a thoughtful blend of regret, love, and encouragement, and it lifted him to 10,000 feet in peaceful skies on a beautiful sunny morning. First Marie—and now Mom! He carefully tucked the letters away in his B-4, grabbed his mess kit, and took off at a brisk pace for evening mess. He had finished eating before he even noticed what he was eating. It didn't matter. He was about to leave the mess hall when a sudden surge in the conversation level swept slowly through the crowd.

When the rumble reached Lee's table he learned that the Allies had invaded Hollandia that day—not Wewak—but Hollandia! The air support had been provided by Navy planes from nearby aircraft carriers. And while mop-up operations were underway, the outcome was beyond doubt. In addition to Hollandia the invasion had led to the capture of the enemy base at Aitape, about ninety miles east of Hollandia on the north coast. The dual victories meant that the Allies, using their game of leapfrog, had skipped over and isolated three Japanese bases between Saidor and Aitape.

Lee was astounded, and judging from the conversations all around him, he was not alone.

The deceptive General MacArthur and his staff had done it again. They had not only fooled the Japs, they had fooled most of the Allied personnel. When everyone expected the Wewak invasion, he had simply skipped over Wewak and gone farther west to take Hollandia completely by surprise. The powerful base at Wewak, like Rabaul, would be isolated and left to die on the vine.

Lee was chatting with Captain Robesky when Colonel Hammer approached them.

"Where's Mo?" he asked.

"I—uh—don't know," said Lee. "He might be down on the flight line. He had some mechanical problems today."

"Lee, you find him. Tell him to shag his ass over to Ops, pronto. You, too, Roby. For that matter, Lee, you ought to be in on this. We just got orders. We move to Hollandia day after tomorrow."

Lee hustled off to find Mo. The reverie induced by the letters from his mother had been displaced by a sudden and stunning electric shock. Hollandia? Hollandia! And what condition would he find Mo in?

Chapter 39

"Yeah, yeah, I already got the word," Mo groused as he stomped out of his tent. He stopped nose to nose in front of Lee. "Okay, what are *you* looking at?"

"You," Lee said. He studied Mo's eyes, and he tried to smell the gin without being obvious. Nothing there, and Mo's eyes seemed as bright and clear as ever. Amazing. The only thing wrong—no smile. "Have you been through debriefing yet?" Lee asked. "Sledge has a meeting called for right now."

"You invited?"

"Uh huh."

"Okay, you go to the meeting. Tell him I was tied up down on the flight line, and I'll be right there. I'll buzz through Lt. Nelson as fast as I can."

"Already told him that," Lee said.

"Huh? Oh—thanks. See you in a few minutes."

Col. Hammer opened the meeting briskly, and from there things only got faster. Each of the three squadrons was represented by its CO, Exec, and Line Chief, while Col. Hammer was supported by his six-member Headquarters Squadron, Sgt. Jernigan, and another non-com.

Five minutes later, Mo slipped in beside Lee.

"Sgt. Jernigan is handing out copies of the checklists you followed on the move from Dobo," explained Col. Hammer. "We'll go through the group first to hear about the things that went snafu. Then we'll go from there."

* * * *

Hardly thirty-six hours had gone by when Gopher Squadron settled in at Hollandia on the Sentani runway of baked mud topped with steel matting. Ground troops and engineers were busy everywhere establishing new perimeter gun emplacements, pushing the skeletons of burned out Japanese aircraft off the field into huge piles, cleaning up debris, and repairing buildings. A separate crew of engineers had already regraded the airstrip and put down the Marston matting, anticipating the arrival of the heavy P-38s and B-25s. Although the Japanese planes were extremely light, Lee wondered how they ever got them up and down successfully when the airstrip was muddy.

The move went well. Some of the Gopher mechanics' equipment disappeared enroute, but under Mo's direction, other squadrons soon lost identical items. The weeks that followed proved to be busy for everyone in the 483rd.

Extraordinary progress had been made in the New Guinea campaign. The capture of Hollandia capped a gain of over 800 miles from the eastern tip of New Guinea where the Allies had begun. That meant they were about two-thirds of the way to the western tip, the end of any Japanese control on the island, and the stepping-off-point to the Philippines.

Morale among the members of the 483rd Fighter Group seemed to pick up, but Lee knew the morale would never again be as high as when it rode the enthusiastic wings of the original group of neophyte P-38 pilots. Pilots and ground support personnel performed well. But the attitudes behind the scenes became more typical GI. Sometimes Lee found the syndrome puzzling. The men would do a great job on something, then turn right back to bitching. And when they ran out of things to bitch about, they somehow found more. The comradery seemed to have become a mandatory and somewhat artificial thing, but it was still there.

"Why do you think it's happening?" Lee had asked Mo.

"Because the pilots know we're going to have more losses, and they've had it with losing *friends*. The ground pounders? They're just goddamned tired of the heat, rain, wind, dust…and boredom."

The Gopher pilots flew attack missions against Japanese bases farther west at Sarmi on the mainland and the islands of Wakde, Owi, Biak, and Noemfoor. Other assignments included duck hunting patrols to enforce the stranglehold on the by-passed Japanese bases. When off duty, personnel of all ranks pitched in to erect additional comforts as well as take advantage of drier weather to participate in sports. Cleared, level areas were abundant on the huge former Japanese base, so baseball games rolled on endlessly. When one group had to resume duties, another slipped in to replace them.

Surrounding the military bases on the flat coastal Hollandia plain were huge plantations of coconut palms that had been planted and nurtured by the Lever Brothers Corporation for many years before the Japanese occupation. Row upon row of tall palm trees, consistently spaced about ten feet apart, stood majestically over the earthlings, their symmetry inspiring one G.I. foible after another. One supply officer determined that the regular spacing of the trees was ideal for hanging hammocks and thereby reducing the number of tents needed. The first good rain put a damper on the concept. One group of bomber pilots marked out a softball diamond among the trees, reasoning that the well-spaced obstacles would make the game more interesting. Observers quickly labeled their game, "Palm Tree Pinball." It did generate humor, along with a few bruises.

Though he monitored the situation closely, Lee felt confident that Mo had separated his drinking from his flying. However, Mo's flying had become more aggressive, and his attitude reflected pure recklessness. He had picked up on Lee's concept of the ten gun salute, two Lightnings converging on a ship at angles that focused all of their joint firepower on one small area at the waterline. And he and Sandy had sent two small freighters to the bottom.

But Mo's techniques were beginning to test Sandy's will, as well as his skill.

"Damn it, Lee," Sandy said after one salute attack. "I kept pouring everything I had into that one spot, but I could feel us getting closer and closer and closer to each other. I wait and wait to hear Mo call, 'Break off.' Then I feel a bump! He's bumped my damned port wing—actually left a crease in the skin! Do I have to take chances like that? Beyond the call of duty? I think it's time for him to get a new wingman. Another game of chicken and this wingman will be shark bait."

Lee promised to talk to Mo about it, but he was careful not to promise an outcome. The matter of Mo's flying had, in fact, become Lee's current problem. In the past, Mo's heavy-handed flying had been tempered by a modicum of concentration and at least a touch of finesse. More and more it seemed like he was only interested in getting from Point A to Point B as quickly as possible.

But Lee's life had come together as well as could be expected in a combat zone. He had received another letter each from his mom and Marie. Coupled with that, the Gophers had not lost another pilot since reaching Hollandia. They had good tents on dry ground and they had picked through the captured Japanese goods to fashion furniture for the tents. Black Bart had come even close to rejoining the human race. And Mo's attitude toward Lee seemed less volatile.

Mo and Lee had taken to Jeeping over to the shores of nearby Sentani Lake where they would pass time sitting and drinking on a huge, shaded rock overlooking the lake. But Lee was becoming slightly more comfortable with Mo's drinking. Mo never suggested it until late in the day when it was a virtual certainty there would be no more flying. And while he occasionally got high enough to get his gear up, he never went out of control.

While the Gophers were not engaging in aerial combat as thick as they had faced in their early months together, they were once again encountering Japanese aircraft as they attacked the western bases. The enemies' inexperience showed, but occasionally a veteran squadron from the Japanese Air Army reminded them of the old adage about assumptions. By mid-June Mo had run his total kills to twenty-five and had moved into second place behind Dick Bong, but Lee had kept pace with him and stood at nineteen. It was never discussed, but both Lee and Mo knew that it was just a matter of time until Lee overtook Mo. Lee dreaded the day, but he saw no option. He couldn't let enemies escape simply to preserve relations with his commanding officer. Or could he?

"Hey, Lieutenant!"

Lee turned to find Mashy trotting up the dusty path to overtake him.

"Hey, Lieutenant, have I got good news for you!"

"I don't know, Mashy. The last time you had good news for me, you had set up that custom barbershop guaranteed to cut hair the way the customer wanted it. Your clipper pulled half of my hair out and wrecked the rest. It took me two months to grow back to normal."

"Oh, no, Lieutenant! This adventure is different," the bright-eyed armorer said. "You're gonna like what I've invented. I built a washing machine, you know, clothes washing machine? Everybody's tired of having the natives ruin their clothes pounding them on the damned rocks. Well, I got my hands on a little Jap cement mixer. I cleaned it all up and got the thing runnin' again. It makes a *perfect* washing machine."

"I—I don't know, Mashy. Your track record—"

"Here's the deal, Lieutenant! I'll do your clothes for a buck a week, and I'll do 'em *right!* Now how can you lose on that deal? You see, by doing a big business I can do the job really cheap—maybe 75 cents a week, and you get 'em done the way you like 'em. What do you say, Lieutenant? Sixty cents? You know, if I could get *your* enforcement, a lot of the others would give me a try."

"Hey, Lee!" It was Burner Hedman coming toward them. "Do you really let that guy load your weapons? I can't believe you're still alive. Boy, don't get dragged into his latest scheme. I tried him, and I'm all scratched to hell from my ankles to my shoulders—little particles of cement imbedded in my pants and shirt. I'll *never* get them out. On top of everything, it's Jap cement that's driving me crazy!"

Mashy simply threw up his hands and walked off mumbling, "Thankfullessness, that's what it is. Try to do something nice for 'em and they're not even thankfulless."

At dawn the next morning Gopher Squadron was airborne, headed for Biak, the strongest enemy base left along the north coast of New Guinea. Biak was actually a large island located in Geelvink Bay, a huge body of water that cut into New Guinea's north shore to the extent that it reached to within eighty miles of the south shore. Biak stretched to seventy-five miles in length and was perhaps ten miles wide at its widest point. A rib of mountains extended down the center from the eastern tip to the western tip. The shape and topography, if not the size of Biak, bore a strong resemblance to New Guinea itself.

Along the northern shore the Japanese had built Mokmer, their main air strip. It was heavily guarded by Zekes and Oscars, along with a seemingly endless line of anti-aircraft batteries that had been cut into the mountains overlooking the airstrip. The AA installations were well-protected in nooks, crannies, and caves and could actually shoot downward at aircraft making low level attacks on the air strip. Mixed among the AA were batteries of heavy artillery set to repel invasions from the sea.

Lee had visited Biak on two previous occasions, and it was not his favorite place. The Gophers' assignment on this mission was to bomb, then strafe the artillery and AA installations built into the north side of the mountains overlooking the base. Following their attack would come the A-20s for a parafrag run. It was anything but a safe assignment, for while the Lightning pilots were searching for targets hidden in the rocky mountain side, the enemy gunners had full view of their attackers. The Gopher pilots would have preferred a fair fight, but in the briefing Major Jackson had insisted that the heavies had "bombed the hell out of them for two days straight. There can't be too much left."

Mo's plan was to run the gauntlet in elements, each wingman to one side and slightly behind his element leader, varying the altitude from one element to the next to try to upset the Japs' range finding. The Gophers' 500-pound bombs had delayed action fuses set for ten seconds so the Lightnings could safely drop their loads from very low altitude. That one made Lee nervous. It was a well-known fact that bomb armorers had occasionally erred in setting the delays. Mo and Sandy went in low and fast. The following three elements followed at long intervals to allow the previously dropped bombs to explode before their arrival over the target.

Lee led Blue Flight in low to make it harder for the Jap gunners to draw a bead on them. He watched the eight pairs of bombs explode before him, then focused on an area that had not yet been hit. When he released his bombs, the Marksman jerked upward as though relieved to be free of its dangerous cargo. Lee hoped that their airspeed of over 350 would make them difficult targets to hit. Small arms fire plunked into his ship, but most of the AA was still firing too high.

Mo pulled far out over the lagoon and did a wide circle so as to bring them in from the opposite direction for their strafing run. This time they tightened up their formation so the enemy gunners would face a non-stop barrage of fire from the Lightnings. They pushed their airspeed almost to war emergency. At such low altitude and high speed, the rough mountainside became a blur. Lee squeezed off his 20-mm cannon and his four fifties in bursts, unsure of just how much he was hitting. He spaced his bursts to avoid overheating his weapons. Some heavier hits slammed into The Marksman, and as he screamed into a gentle climb at the west end of the island, he was already scanning his ship's exterior as well as its instruments. It was hard to believe that all those hits hadn't damaged something critical. All the controls seemed to work, and the gauges read normal. But up ahead Oren Jones trailed coolant.

"Burner, take Jonesy and head home," Mo's voice crackled.

"Roger."

"A big bunch of bad guys at nine o'clock high—headed for the A-20s. Looks like fifteen to eighteen of them. Let's try to draw them off. Close it up."

The Gophers gathered and began a fast climb for altitude. If they could reach the enemies' altitude in time they might come around behind them. At worst, they could turn directly into them for a side deflection shot and try to break them up. Lee felt he'd opt for the latter—too late to get behind them. He watched the sixteen Japanese planes closely. If they suddenly turned on the Gophers, offense and defense would swap sides quickly.

Then Lee noticed—

"Vals!" said Mo, "nothing but a bunch of old Vals. Don't know what they're doing up here, but they're sure not after our guys. Probably a training flight got caught in the war—ducks in a barrel. Best chance we'll ever have, but we're too short on ammo and fuel. We've got to go home." With that Mo banked right and set a course for Hollandia.

That evening, Mo and Lee sat sipping Scotch on their favorite rock. Lee had to concede that he was coming closer to liking the peculiar flavor, but it still tasted like licorice to him. The sinking sun had aligned itself across the lake with the remains of the radio station the Gophers had obliterated in their strafing attacks. In half-an-hour, dusk would set in, and with it would come hordes of mosquitoes. Mo suggested that the Japs had been breeding them in Sentani Lake as a secret weapon.

"You know," Mo said, "Hollandia right now is the driest place we've ever been. I wish somebody would tell the damned mosquitoes. I'm from Minnesota where they're the state bird, and *still* they irritate me!"

"Maybe the mosquitoes are the explanation," Lee said.

"Explanation for what?"

"For why you're flying so recklessly these days. I'm glad I'm back in Blue Flight so I don't have to do the things you do."

Mo grunted indignantly. "Well, as long as you're nice and safe back there, how I fly is really none of your business, is it?"

"You could say that. But, Mo, one of these days you're going to get Sandy, and maybe others, killed. That makes it my business, too."

"Well, Mr. Supervisor—all right, I concede the point," Mo said. He looked earnestly at Lee. "You think it's the booze, don't you?"

"What makes you say that?"

"Oh, you're always sniffing at me." Mo smiled. "You're not that slick, Marks."

Lee broke into a grin. "Not very subtle, huh?"

"What you need to understand is, the flying style is part of the plan. And you need to pick up on it."

"What? Now the plan is to get killed? You might still get your statue, but you sure won't win many elections. I don't think I'm ready for that."

"Hell, I'm not that reckless. But by flying looser and getting a little of the hot-dog reputation, we'll attract more media attention, and *that* fits the plan. You don't hear anyone talking about how cautious and careful Bong or McGuire are. And right now, I'm leading McGuire. Believe me, when the word of *that* gets around, the correspondents will be all over us."

Lee could see that nothing he could say would change Mo's mind. "Okay," he said, "then it's about time that I move up and be your wingman. Sandy can take over Blue Flight. Maybe he'll live long enough to finish his tour. If you get me killed, it's part of our plan. But Sandy isn't in the deal."

Mo offered Lee a refill, but Lee passed on it. Surprisingly, Mo then put the bottle aside and settled also for just the one drink.

"Okay," Mo responded, "you're my new wingman. But you know, you won't get as many kills there."

"Oh, but I will—I have to—because you're going to share the set-ups with me. That's part of the plan."

Mo stared at Lee for a moment. The broad smile returned to his face. "Well spoken. It shall be."

The next day found the Gopher Squadron grounded for repairs. Only a few ships had come away from Biak with serious mechanical or electrical problems, but nearly all of the Lightnings needed substantial scrutiny and patching.

Big Ole scowled when he looked at Lee and said, "I just hope when you get it and I get assigned to another pilot, that I get an ordinary pilot who's not crazy."

Lee was startled to hear the words from his soft-spoken crew chief. But the defiant look in Ole's eyes reminded Lee that The Marksman was Ole's ship. Lee was just the pilot.

Lee spent the morning over at the 475th Fighter Group. Now that his score placed him as a triple ace, the pilots of the red hot Satan's Angels, Clover, and Possum Squadrons had warmed up to him. He enjoyed getting in on their hangar flying and learning from their vast experience. But this particular trip had a special reason.

Charles Lindbergh had been with the 475th now for over a week, and Lee was among the many who were anxious to hear what the great aviator had to say. In addition to his famous trans-Atlantic flight, Lindbergh had probably flown more different aircraft than all of the pilots in the Fifth Fighter Command together.

He had spent time in pre-war Germany, studying the modernization of the Luftwaffe. Indeed, he had gotten into trouble and become labeled as a radical pacifist for certain naive remarks suggesting that Germany's build-up was strictly for defensive purposes and that U.S. aviation was in no condition to even consider taking on the Nazi machine. Despite being blackballed by President Roosevelt, Lindbergh had become perhaps the leading consultant to the American aviation industry. After doing some time on Guadalcanal with Marines and their F4U Corsairs he had maneuvered to become attached to Satan's Angels and had immediately found himself a place, though still a civilian, as a member of the flight that included top aces McGuire, Smith, and McDonald.

In addition to flying ground attack missions, Lindbergh had been experimenting with combining various engine settings involving leaner fuel mixture, increased manifold pressure, and a considerable reduction of cruise rpm to reduce fuel consumption. The pilots of the 475th were impressed with Lindbergh's knowledge and skills, but they were less than warm to his motive. By applying his suggestions, they would be able to extend the range of their Lightnings by as much as two hours. But most P-38 pilots felt that, while a five-hour mission was manageable but cruel, and a seven-hour mission was completely unfair, a nine-hour mission would be sheer torture.

Sitting on a parachute and emergency equipment, strapped into a hard bucket seat for nine hours? Lee doubted that Mo would buy into the plan, but he listened anyway, captivated by the slender adventurer's aviation wisdom. But when Mr. Lindbergh, as he was called, strayed into the philosophical realm, Lee found himself dealing with some consternation. It seemed to him that Lindbergh was the original "Mr. Nice Guy," and that he had a propensity for granting to the enemy the same respect that he himself was usually accorded.

Later, back at the 483rd, Lee reported in to Mo. When he passed on Lindbergh's recommendations for range extension, Mo cut him short.

"I didn't hear what you just said," Mo informed Lee, "and you didn't say what you just said. Understand? Above all, don't spread another word on this to anyone."

"Well, yeah, I get it. But the word will come down from on high—eventually."

"Eventually might be after you and I are gone. Leave it that way. If we're flying 2,000-mile missions, we won't have the fuel to engage enemy planes. You can see where that takes you and me."

Lee sacked out early that night. For some reason he felt more tired than usual, and there had been some scuttlebutt about a mission to Noemfoor the next day. It would be a long haul. He shuddered when he thought once more about the Lindberghian missions. Noemfoor was nearly 400 miles from Hollandia, typically a four-hour run, plus time over the target. Nine hours? He dearly loved flying, but nine hours? With the thought, he signed off and drifted away.

Bam! Bam! Bam! The three rifle shots brought Lee up and out of his bunk into bedlam. His tentmates scrambled about in the dark, colliding with one another. Outside, the stutter of 50-caliber machine guns joined the pandemonium, seemingly attracting more shots from rifles and Colt .45s, accompanied by chaotic shouting.

"What is it?" Lee searched for his colt.

"Japs! Japs out there!"

With his weapon in hand, Lee burst from the tent and sprawled face down in the dust, trying to get his bearings and form a picture of the situation. Several of the gun emplacements were firing into the thick, dark jungle about 200 yards away, and as men spilled from their tents the cacophony swelled with the familiar sounds of the handguns.

Fear bristled once more on the back of Lee's neck. But until he had a handle on the situation, he would stay where he was. Nonetheless, he cocked his Colt and made ready for whatever. He studied the dark wall of jungle. He saw very few muzzle flashes there—no, he saw *no* muzzle flashes there. The Japs must have retreated back into the jungle.

"Hold your fire! Hold your fire! Hold your fire!" The command echoed back and forth among the sand-bagged gun pits and the many pilots lying belly-down in the dust. As men on the front line began to get to their feet, Lee followed their example. If the Japs *hadn't* retreated and decided to resume firing, there were lots of Air Force bodies between the enemy and himself.

Slowly, he moved forward, ready to drop once more at the slightest sign of danger. As he approached the nearest gun pit, a frantic dialogue began to separate into distinct words.

"For Christ's sake, Murphy! Tell me it isn't true! Tell me it isn't true!"

"But Sarge, he was right there in my pit. Ain't no way I was goin' in there. It was him or me!"

"But look what you did. One Jap, and you got the whole damned base in an uproar! You didn't have to shoot him! Christ, Murphy, tell me it isn't true." pleaded the sergeant.

Dirty-faced pilots in dust-covered shorts and undershirts began gathering around the discussion. The murmur of the inquisitive increased to a soft, but steady drone. As Lee worked his way closer to the gun-pit, a couple of flashlights had begun probing the dark interior surrounded by sandbags.

"Aw, for Christ's sake, Murphy," hissed the sergeant. "It ain't no goddamned Jap. It's a fuckin' snake. Can't you tell the difference?" The drone of voices changed to laughter.

Lee edged up to the front line. Sure enough, there, writhing in the beams of the flashlights was a python, perhaps eight feet long and eight inches in diameter. The sergeant grabbed a bayonet from one of the guards, leaned in over the sandbag wall and decapitated the wounded creature. In minutes poor Murphy's story had made the rounds, and the embattled pilots and others made for their bunks.

Apparently Murphy had gone to a neighboring gun-pit to borrow some smokes. He chatted for a while with his fellow guard and then returned to his station. Lee could imagine how the hairs on Murphy's neck must have stood up when he walked in on the intruder.

Lee walked slowly back to the tents with one of Robesky's pilots who had been among the first P-38 pilots at Dobodura.

"Reminds me of a similar incident that happened right after I got to Dobo," the pilot said with a laugh. "Some mechanic went into the store room in the dark to get a tool. He heard some noises over in one corner behind an old metal filing cabinet. So what did he do? He tossed a grenade in there. You can imagine! The guns started going off! Everybody's shooting—nobody knows what they're shooting at. And just like this, after a hundred bucks worth of ammo is shot up, things slow down. And what did they find? He blew the file cabinet all to hell and made a shambles out of the storeroom. But he got the raider—an old rat looking for something to eat."

Back in his bunk, Lee had trouble getting back to sleep. The snake incident had brought home the fact that he was sleeping within 200 yards of the jungle to which the Japanese had retreated only days before. He wondered how far into the jungle the infantry had secured things. It was understood that the Japanese soldiers were most efficient fighters. They would survive on roots and roaches, if available, and go right on fighting. There had already been a couple of instances where single Jap soldiers had been found in camp after dark. No one knew exactly what their intent was. Lee imagined a stealthy invader slitting his throat as he slept.

It was thought by many that the enemy soldiers were simply looking for food. But it seemed the question of their intent had not been asked. At least, it certainly was not answered. The Japanese prowlers had been shot on sight.

Charles Lindbergh had that very day expounded on his theory that Americans had greatly reinforced Bushido, the Japanese fight-to-the-death philosophy. If the word was out that Americans took no prisoners and would slaughter them anyway, there was no point in letting oneself be captured.

Hours later, Lee found himself listening to every sound and studying every shadow.

Chapter 40

"Did you get any shots off last night, Lee?" Sandy asked.

"Uh, no. I didn't see anything to shoot at."

"I didn't see anything either, but I have to confess, I unloaded a few into the jungle."

One by one the Gophers gathered at their old table on the flight line. In an hour they were scheduled for a sea patrol between the new Allied base at Aitape and the Japanese at Wewak who were trapped by the Allied blockade.

"Boy, you sure don't want to go wandering around out there after dark," said Stew. "You'd look like Swiss cheese in five seconds. And in this climate, you'd be moldy in ten."

"Hell of a wake-up call, wasn't it," added Burner Hedman. "Scared the shit out of *me*."

"*That's* no surprise," barked Black Bart.

"Stuff it, Barton," retorted Burner. "You're not even *smart* enough to get scared."

"You know," said Tony Margo, "that snake wasn't really big enough to be dangerous."

"Well, he sure as hell wasn't going to crush anyone to death," said Sandy, "but they do bite, you know—pretty good set of jaws there."

"Hey, even worse," said Burner. "Some of the snakes I've curled up with had bad breath."

"Lee, what do you think of the new aileron boost on your Model L?" The abrupt change of subject came from the diminutive Chub Forbes, who was apprently uncomfortable with the subject.

"Great," said Lee, "but even with the aileron boost we can't think of trying to turn with a Zero." Lee thought for a moment, then added, "but we can turn a lot quicker than they *think* we can, and that might get us a few flags."

"Sure," said Black Bart, "those of us who were good enough to save our ships on Black Sunday have to stay with the old Model J. The hotshots who trashed their planes get rewarded with new ones. I'm good enough to save his ass," Bart said, waving toward Lee, "but I'm not good enough for a new ship?"

"You're not good enough to save his ass," said Sandy, "just lucky. That student pilot in the Oscar flew right into your line of fire. Except for a couple of incredible breaks you'd still be a virgin."

The sparring tapered off, and an hour later the Gophers were headed down the coast to look for supply boats trying to reach Wewak. Sandy's customary description of their sea patrols, "Lots of lookee—no findee," was inappropriate this day. Ten miles west of Wewak the Gophers discovered a small convoy ramming through open seas, obviously trying to run the blockade by sailing a straight line rather than slinking around in shallow coastal waters. A destroyer led the two small cargo ships and seven barges toward Wewak.

Mo put out a call for a nearby squadron of B-25s to join in. The bombs the mediums carried were armed with delayed action fuses, ideal for skip-bombing as were these targets.

"Red, we'll take out the tin can," came Mo's words. "The rest of you go for the barges. We've got help coming to handle the cargo ships."

Lee was incredulous. Their flight was taking on the heavily-armed destroyer? Leaving the cargo ships for later? He reached for his mike switch, then hesitated. Challenging Mo's command over the radio was a sure ticket to the loading docks. But this effort to show off would likely bring a quick ticket to something else. He followed Mo down to set up for a low run off the destroyer's starboard side. Greenberg and Smith would follow.

"Ten gun salute," called Mo. "Here we go. At the waterline just back of amidships…we'll try for the engine room."

The two Lightnings roared in pushing 330 mph at wave-top altitude. Immediately there were AA explosions above them accompanied by myriad lines of tracers arching toward them, searching them out. As they approached firing range, Lee concentrated on the target. But he couldn't forget that Mo Brennan was only fifty feet off his port wingtip.

They began pouring their combined two cannons and eight .50-caliber machine guns into the destroyer amidships. After feeling for the range with a couple of bursts, the Lightning pilots found their target. Lee knew he was smacking everything he had into the target area chosen by Mo. But the return fire from the ship began to track closer and closer to the two Lightnings.

A low AA shell burst to Mo's left. Mo swerved, and the next thing Lee knew he had a bright silver P-38 parked right in front of him. He could almost count the rivets. He jerked the yoke back and to the right. Mo disappeared in Lee's blind spot beneath. Lee waited for the crash. The certain disaster didn't come, but still Lee had no idea where Mo was. He continued his hard climb up and to his right. The longer he could avoid Mo, the better his chances became. Finally, Lee leveled off and searched for his leader. Had the event occurred in slow motion, Lee might have called Mo on the radio and asked where he was. But the sudden, violent move at their speed had left no time to even reach for the switch. Finally, Lee felt he had the opportunity to—

"Where you going, Killer? The fight's down *here*," Mo called.

"I—uhh—took a hit," Lee heard himself say. "My starboard engine sounds like it ate something it didn't like. I think I'd better head for home," Lee said.

"Roger. See if you can pick up someone to cover you."

See if I can pick up someone? The casual absurdity of Mo's advice matched that of Mo's attack. Lee felt glad he was headed home, and *that* bothered him. He'd never have believed he'd make up an excuse like that to escape a fight. But he'd said it. Now he *had* to head for Hollandia, and if he could get past the shakes that had invaded his body, he might manage a landing.

Back at Sentani strip, Big Ole had just pulled a large piece of AA shrapnel out of Lee's right side boom near the turbocharger, when Mo taxied in. Lee felt vindicated. While the shrapnel had not affected the starboard turbocharger, it was a large, ugly piece and could have shut that engine down. He turned to Big Ole, nodded toward the approaching Mo Brennan, put a finger to his lips, and then pointed at the turbocharger and motioned as though he was breaking something in his hands. Big Ole hesitated for a moment, then nodded that he had gotten the message.

Mo disembarked and strode quickly toward Lee.

"What the hell were you doing up there, Marks?" He spoke in subdued tones, almost a loud whisper, but the impact was heavy. "You're supposed to follow *me*, cover me, not take off on your own!"

"You cut right in front of me, almost wipe me out, and I'm supposed to *what?*" Lee shot back. He glanced about. Several of the Gopher pilots were facing away from them, but they had to be taking in the encounter. Lee wished he could cancel his reaction, but it was too late.

With a jerk of his head, Mo motioned Lee to follow him away from their audience.

Halfway up the path toward Ops, Mo stopped and turned to Lee once more. Mo's face was fixed in his combative smile, and his eyes burned into Lee threateningly.

"Now," Mo began, "are you saying that I almost caused a mid-air?"

Lee hesitated, trying to see into this jungle, trying to see the path this confrontation was taking.

"No other way to say it," he finally replied.

Mo drew a long breath and hesitated. Then his face relaxed as he exhaled.

"You know, from your perspective, I suppose it looked like that. But when that flak blew right beside me, I had no choice. I knew you'd be alert and pull up—and I knew where you were every instant. I was not about to fly into you."

"You're saying your maneuver was necessary and you were in complete control the whole time?"

"Absolutely."

Lee thought for a moment. Then the pathway into the jungle became clear.

"What you're really saying," began Lee, "is that you don't want that sudden turn to show up at debriefing. Right?"

Without blinking an eye, Mo replied, "Of course that's what I'm saying. What the hell did you *think* I was saying?"

"I—thought you were saying you didn't turn into me. What you're really saying is, Lee Marks took some hits and pulled up. You pulled up with him to cover him."

"Good," said Mo, "I thought for a minute we had a misunderstanding." He smiled. "Nobody got hurt, and it wouldn't help things to have a misunderstanding on record at Intel, now would it?"

By the next morning Lee had almost purged the experience from his mind. But he wondered how Rolly Greenberg and Milton Smith, the two new members of Red Flight who had been following close behind, had reported the incident. As Big Ole worked feverishly to remove shrapnel and patch the scars, Lee eased over to the new pilots and initiated a conversation on the previous day's events. To his surprise, neither pilot had seen anything unusual to report. They had been following in on the attack and awaiting their turn. The duo had been so focused on the destroyer that when Mo and Lee suddenly lurched up and away, they took it as their signal to bore on in and finish the job. And they were elated. They had added maximum fire to the spot and stopped the tin can dead in the water. The B-25s finished her off a few minutes later.

That evening after chow, Mo invited Lee to Jeep over to Lake Sentani again. Perched once more on their private rock overlooking the lake, Mo opened a new bottle of Scotch and poured their tin cups half full.

"Here's to tomorrow…and all the tomorrows after that," Mo toasted. He took a long slug and then added, "We've got a long one tomorrow—Manokwari. How does *that* make your tired butt feel? Over 400 miles each way and most of it through Jap territory."

"And that'll be a *short* trip if the brass hands down the Lindbergh tricks for long range flights," Lee commented. "It hurts my back, hips, and butt just to think of one-ways of over 800 miles."

"Anything else hurting?" Mo asked.

"Meaning?"

"Meaning, you got any problems with our little misunderstanding?"

"Only one. I'm still surprised that you made that move. It was so unlike you, Mo. I've always had complete confidence that you would do the right thing, carry through as planned, and set good examples for the—"

"Look, goddamn it." Mo cut in. "I don't need your questioning my every move. You're my wingman. That means, you back me up no matter what—now and in the future."

"I did, Mo, I did. I even followed up with Greenberg and Smith to make sure we didn't have a problem there."

"Oh, so now you're even talking about me to the men?"

"Not talking about you. Just getting them to talk to me so I'd know what they saw or what they *think* they saw. You know as well as I that the squadron morale is lower than it used to be. We've lost half of our original group. That does things to people, Mo. You said it yourself. And if the guys lose confidence in their leaders, the Gophers are in trouble."

"You saying you've lost confidence in me?"

"A little, yes." Lee searched for a way to keep the situation from becoming volatile.

"We don't deal in "littles" here, Killer. Either you're with me or you're against me," Mo pronounced, pointing a finger at Lee for emphasis. He drained his cup and refilled it. "You're forgetting something, Marks. I built this squadron—in just a few months. I led them to one of the best records in the South Pacific. Not you, not Greenie, not Gus, not anybody else. Mo Brennan did that, and Mo Brennan will continue to do that!"

The old cliche about discretion and valor ran through Lee's mind. He said nothing.

Mo gained momentum until he had whirled into a full-blown tirade, alternately listing Lee's mistakes and extolling his own tolerance of them. His eyes blazed with a fury that Lee hadn't seen before. Mo rattled on, listing every shortcoming that Lee had ever shown and then embellishing them freely. The facts and the fictional allegations were woven together so artistically that the barrage rocked Lee into submissive withdrawal. The accusations came across so well-ordered that it sounded as if Mo was reading from a list, a report, or a diary. For a moment, Lee felt he was hearing about someone else. Then, he consciously built armor around himself to shut out the hurricane. He felt like he was enclosed in a metal barrel. He could hear the rantings reverberating outside his cocoon, but the words made no sense.

Finally, Mo showed signs of tiring. His pace slowed. His volume dropped, and his violent dissertation ended with, "…I've always had tight control of my squadron and I'm not going to let that change, no matter what you say to anybody." He jerked his tin cup to his lips and carelessly slurped from it. Then he turned back to Lee and simply stared at him.

The end of the haranguing brought Lee to peek out of his barrel.

"You all done now?" he asked quietly.

Mo blinked.

"No, but *you're* close to it."

"Meaning?" A spark of familiar old anger suddenly ejected Lee from the barrel.

"Meaning, I'm stuck with you here, but I sure as hell don't have to carry you on my team back stateside."

"You never really *had* me on your team back stateside!" Lee snapped. "You just dangled it in front of me to keep your little boy Friday in line. You gave me the same recruitment speech you gave Gus, and Greenie, that other guy from your old squadron, and who knows how many more."

Lee knew he had stepped far over the line. It was too late to turn back so there was no reason to hold back. The glare in Mo's reddened eyes burned fiercely. Unready to turn the floor back to Mo, Lee drew a big breath and charged ahead.

"I can take your orders, Mo. I can put up with a lot of your manipulations—even your pie-in-the-sky promises. But the insulting treatment and the stupid, reckless flying that come out of that hip flask of yours—no more."

Lee looked away, lifted a shaky tin cup to his lips, and managed a swallow. The heat and the trembling that had captured his body took him back to an alley in Chicago. He had regretted his actions of that night, and now he fought the impulse once again. He drew a deep breath and turned back to Mo, ready for whatever violence or threats might come.

To his surprise, Mo Brennan seemed completely composed. He calmly took a drink, looked at Lee, pointed a finger at him, and said, "Tomorrow morning—you're going to wish today never happened. Let's go."

The little four-banger engine in the Jeep begged for mercy, screaming in its lower gears all the way back to the base. Neither man spoke. Lee held onto the seat frame with one hand and the windshield with the other as the bucking vehicle bounced one way and another. Inside he felt numb, and the only thought he could construct amid the terrible jouncing was, "Gus, I need to talk with you."

Chapter 41

Early, much too early on the morning of July 4th, Lee Marks lay in his bunk studying the darkness and listening to the early birds cranking up their chorus in the nearby jungle. He had slept fitfully—two nights in a row with little sleep. He couldn't stop replaying the dreadful showdown with Mo, and on top of that the long mission to Manokwari would begin at 0500 hours. Lee didn't want to go. In fact, he dreaded it. As he lay there, he even conjured up excuses to ground himself for the day. He had never done that. He could probably get away with it.

Something inside of him had caught hold, locked on, and told him not to fly on this day. After the close call of the previous mission and Mo's uncontrolled eruption, *this* Fourth of July could bring nothing good. An hour or so earlier he had finally managed to doze off when a face appeared to him. Gus—it was Gus! His friend simply looked down at him seriously and slowly shook his head. Even Gus was telling him not to go?

The pilots had discussed the issue of death warnings in hangar flying sessions. Tales abounded of deceased pilots who had shared premonitions that the upcoming mission would be their last. Lee had found the stories intriguing. But this story was *his,* and any intrigue was being washed aside by fear.

But to ditch out on a challenge? That snipped the very fiber that was Lee Marks. To cave in to Mo Brennan? He came out of his bunk like a mortar shot, and the pace continued as he performed his morning rituals, chowed down on rubbery pancakes, and headed down the dark path to the flight line. On the way, Sandy caught up with him.

"Lee, what the hell happened last night with Mo?"

"You know, I'm not really sure what happened. But I think I finally met the *real* Mo Brennan. And if I did—he's not a very nice guy."

"I think you're right about that," Sandy said. "Did you check the board this morning?"

"No, in my rush I guess I forgot."

"He's moved me back up to his wingman slot, slid Chub Forbes up to Blue Leader, and stuck you at the ass end again covering Black Bart."

Lee recalled the ominous warnings as he lay in his bunk. He took Sandy's arm and stopped him.

"That pretty well says it all, don't you think? Be careful today, Sandy. Be *very* careful."

The 483rd Fighter Group took off precisely at 0500 hours and climbed out on a course of two-seven-seven degrees. They would rendezvous at the northeast corner of Geelvink Bay with the 90th Bomb Group, The Jolly Rogers. From there they would escort the B-24 Liberators past the Japanese installations on the islands of Japen and Noemfoor. Noemfoor was the last sizeable Japanese base along their course to Manokwari. Scuttlebutt had it that Noemfoor would be the next target for Allied invasion. It would be nice to have another friendly island in the chain across Geelvink Bay. But the fact that they were escorting the Jolly Rogers, a rock-solid bomb group, was the only real bright spot Lee could find in the day's mission.

Bart had gleefully pointed up the change in assignments to anyone he thought might listen. But to a man, the Gophers turned their backs on him and went about their business. Their attitudes seemed to reflect Lee's own, at least to the extent that they approached the morning's mission with unspoken reluctance. Burner and Stew had each given him a slap on the back to let him know where they stood.

"You okay?" Greenie had asked, looking intently into Lee's eyes. "Finally got it, huh?"

As they picked up their bombers over Geelvink Bay, Lee seized the event to revitalize his fighter pilot instincts. Looking down at the huge formation of four-engine B-24s with their exhaust stacks spitting into the night he was reminded of where he was and why he was there. He resolved to sit on his emotions and fatigue and concentrate on a continual search for enemy fighters. It warmed him slightly when the sun rose behind the formation. Today the good guys would have the sun at their backs. Gopher Squadron eased over to cover the left flank of the bomber formation.

The armada passed over the long sliver of land that was Japen Island. It was occupied by Japanese soldiers, but it had no airbase large enough to pose a serious threat. Lee reminded himself, however, that only one Zero, Oscar, or Tony could present a very real threat.

Once past Noemfoor Island, Lee could begin to make out the peninsula and bay that marked the location of Manokwari. Things would be happening soon—

"Here they come up after the big boys," called Mo. "Switch, drop, and string 'em out."

Lee followed the Gopher Lightnings as they peeled off to the left. When he caught sight of the two dozen rapidly climbing Zeros who had yet to reach the altitude of the Liberators, he wondered if he was up to a full-scale skirmish. Maybe the best he could do was to try to keep Black Bart and himself alive. He watched Bart and kept his position behind and to Bart's right.

He could see a target for Bart, there seemed to be nothing ahead for himself.

Suddenly, Lee found himself toying with a strange notion, one that was bizarre, yet humorous. He dropped down to a position well below and only slightly behind Bart, and there coming straight for him was Bart's target, a Zero. He could see Bart's tracers firing long before they were in range. Lee waited. The Zero began firing. Lee sighted in and squeezed off two short bursts. The Zero, burst into flames, settled into a flat tailspin and began the long trip to Geelvink Bay. Halfway down it exploded. Lee dropped back once more and waited for Bart's next move.

After the Gophers' first pass through the enemy formation, the battle became a replay of so many previous missions. The Lightnings dived through in pairs, taking out a few enemy planes, then climbed back and around for another pass. Lee followed Bart faithfully, carefully watching his own mirror and over both shoulders for any Zeros trying to slip in behind them.

As Bart lined up each pass at a Zero, Lee sneaked into the position to help. And each time he found Bart firing too soon, simply wasting ammunition. Lee flamed a second Zero from beneath Black Bart's belly. It became apparent also that when Bart had a choice of two enemy planes, he inevitably chose the wrong one, passing up an easy kill for one that had every opportunity to evade him and did just that. Somehow, it did not surprise Lee. It was all about choices—a lot like life.

With the remnants of their detachment of Zeros retreating to the west, The Gophers reformed at 18,000 angels and watched the B-24s paste the Japanese installations at Manokwari on the north coast of New Guinea. The area became a huge blanket of gray and black puffs. It seemed impossible that any man or creature could survive such a devastating attack. Yet, somehow the enemy had survived many attacks like this one.

The massive formation of bombers and fighters had done their one-eighty turn and were headed for home, when Lee noticed traces of smoke sifting back through the Gopher formation.

He searched ahead for the source of the smoke. A trail of coolant appeared, tracking just to the left of the smoke, and both rapidly increased in intensity.

It was Mo. His starboard engine now showed flames licking out from the cowling, and his port engine was the source of the coolant. Clearly, Mo Brennan was in big, big trouble. At 18,000 feet, four hundred miles from home, in enemy territory, with both engines about to die, he had few choices.

"Okay, you rodents, listen up," came Mo's voice. "I'm going to have to park this thing somewhere. Greenie, you take 'em home."

"Roger," came Greenie's reply.

Mo's voice was as calm as with any transmission he had ever made. It was as though the Gophers were simply out on a training flight. Lee's anger toward his leader clashed with respect for Mo's self-control. He had always been strong when others were in trouble. But now *he* was in trouble, and his poise was just the sa—

"Marks, follow me down."

"You sure you—"

"That's an order, Marks."

"Roger. Uh, Mo, if you put her in a steep dive, you might be able to blow the fire out."

"That's why I wanted you with me, Marks. You think better than the rest." With that he shoved the nose down.

Lee followed. At 450 mph, the shuddering of compressibility began. Lee pulled his dive brake and suggested the same to Mo. He noticed that Mo held on longer before opening his brake. For a moment it seemed when they leveled off that Lee's idea had worked. But then, the flames showed again.

They were still at 10,000 feet, and though Japen Island sat directly below them, it was an extremely narrow sliver of land. Expecting to hit it by parachute from that altitude would be like mining fool's gold.

"This is getting a little hairy," said Mo. "Someone once told me these things carry a lot of gasoline in the wings. I'm not in the mood for a barbeque."

"Let's get down to a grand or two as fast as we can," Lee suggested. "That also gives them less time to plan a party for you."

"Goddamn! Why weren't you that smart yesterday?"

Lee choked off his reply just in time. At 4,000 feet, Lee could see vivid white caps on Geelvink Bay.

"Looks like a fairly brisk wind from the northeast," he said. "If you go for the north shore and drift past, you'll still be over land...and any Japs on the south shore likely won't see you coming."

Mo's ship was smoking badly. Lee thought the right wing tank should have exploded by now. Mo dropped to 2,000 feet, leveled off, and aimed his ship into the wind. When he was a quarter of a mile offshore, his Lightning rolled onto its back and Mo tumbled out. Rather than circle and help the enemy pinpoint Mo's location, Lee throttled back and set up a long, rectangular pattern at 3,000 feet. He watched Mo's chute open, then drift toward Japen Island. The stricken ship, still inverted, slipped its nose toward the water and went in with a moderate splash. At the eastern end of his pattern, Lee turned back. It was good. He was perhaps two miles east of Mo's chute, but he could see it clearly and should arrive on the spot shortly after Mo landed.

But the winds seemed determined to interfere with Mo's plan. While still a few hundred feet up, Mo had already drifted inland from the north shore. It looked like he would land near the middle of the thick jungle. That meant he'd have instant cover but it also meant lots of tall trees waiting to snag his chute and hang him up far above ground. As he headed toward Mo's drifting parachute, Lee dropped down to a hundred feet and skimmed above the tree tops. It would be harder for enemy troops to get a fix on his Lightning. He would cross Mo's path just after Mo settled into the trees. He would try to spot some nearby landmark.

With a sudden spurt, Mo drifted more quickly to Lee's left, missed the jungle, and splashed into the surf fifty yards off the south beach. Mo was quickly upright, unstrapping his chute and struggling to wade in toward the wide beach. But after negotiating the long stretch of shallow water he would still have 200 yards of beach to cross before reaching the jungle's edge. Lee waggled his wings as he flew past. He continued on to complete his pattern and did his one-eighty.

He finished his turn and searched again for Mo as he roared above the beach. What he saw slammed into his belly like an axe handle. There lay Mo on his back in the sand. Drawing closer, Lee could see Mo waving at him, waving and pointing on down the beach. About three dozen Jap soldiers had burst from the jungle and were racing toward Mo. Lee could make out flashes from their rifle barrels.

He took The Marksman right down on the beach, perhaps twenty feet above the sand, throttled back and began raking the beach ahead of him with his four fifties. He fish-tailed the ship slightly back and forth so as to spray every square yard with fire. Bodies lurched and dropped. Sand flew. Even at only 200 mph, the grizzly scene on the beach beneath sailed past in a blur. When he completed his turn at the other end, he found another group of soldiers breaking out of the jungle and racing toward Mo, obviously trying to trap him between the two groups.

Mo was up and running again and he was only yards from the jungle. Lee bore down on the second group. Once more bodies flailed and sand flew. He wished he could know how many of them he had hit. It would have a lot to do with Mo's chances of survival. As he left the group of sprawled soldiers behind he concentrated his fire once more on the survivors of his first attack. Perhaps a dozen Japs kneeled in the sand firing. But this time they were firing at Lee.

He could hear and feel bullets striking the Lightning. *Pung! Pung! Pung! Pung!* And the rapid, rhythmic hits told him there was at least one machine gun, probably a .30-caliber, down there. He thought he had wiped out the remaining soldiers of the first group, when something struck him in the left leg. It felt like someone had jabbed him fiercely with the end of a broomstick. He zoomed upward to 800 feet to make his turn for another pass. Halfway through his turn, the starboard engine abruptly quit. No coughing, no sputtering, just nothing. In the middle of a turn at low altitude? No place to follow the prescribed ritual for converting to single engine flight. He'd never pull it off!

To avoid flipping upside down, Lee quickly killed the remaining engine and found himself flying a 17,000-pound glider through the remainder of a turn at 500 feet altitude. Trying not to overreact and bank too sharply and thus dump the remainder of his meager altitude, he had just nursed the ship back to level when *Thud!* Lee's shoulder straps cut into his body. A brief silence as the Lightning bounced back into the air. Then another *Thud!* followed by a continuing *Whoooooosh!* as the ship slid through the sand like a boat on water. The Marksman turned slightly and angled toward the tree line. Lee hoped the ship would stop before he met the trees, but he had no sooner entertained the thought than *Bam! Crunnnnch!* This time the shoulder straps really punished him and his head snapped down and forward nearly to the control yoke.

His world had suddenly stopped. Only the pain told him he was alive.

Chapter 42

Lee's day had ended as it had begun. He had neither the reason nor the strength to move. If the pain in his left leg would go away, he would sleep. He was so tired, so tired.

Crack! Crack-Crack!

The three rifle shots burst through his plexiglass narrowly missing him. Two entered the cockpit behind his head and the third passed in front of him completely through the windows on both sides. But the intrusions jolted him back to reality. Far down the beach he saw Jap soldiers running his way, firing as they ran.

Almost in one motion, he popped the top, cranked open the port side window, unstrapped his belts, felt for his machete, emergency kit, and Colt .45, and dragged his bad leg out onto the inboard wing. He slid off the leading edge and crashed full force into the jungle. Frantically he tore through clusters of thick brush and charged ahead gaining speed through the occasional breaks in the growth. He tried to hold to a course that ran 90 degrees from the jungle's edge, and he hoped that what Greenie had once told him could be true.

It *was* true. About twenty-five yards into the jungle he came to a narrow path that ran parallel to the beach and the jungle line. It had been hacked through the growth, then packed down by foot traffic. Greenie had told the Gophers that the Japs often created these patrol paths so they could move quickly around an island's perimeter to where they were needed, all the while remaining under cover.

Instinctively, Lee turned left to run away from his pursuers. Then suddenly, he stopped. He was one man, running on one leg. They were many, each with two legs. He'd never outrun them. He turned and began running back toward them. If he didn't encounter more soldiers on the patrol path he had a chance. If he did, it was all over. He hoped the Japs followed his trek single-file in from the ship and didn't charge randomly through from the beach to the path.

Then, through the band of jungle between the path and the beach came the sounds of voices shouting to one another. As the voices became louder, Lee slowed. He considered stopping while they passed. But he needed to put as much distance between himself and the enemy as he could before they got through the brush and into the path. He bent low and tried to run as quietly as he could. He wished desperately for two good legs, and he wished even more that the Japs would follow their instincts and turn left instead of right when they reached the perimeter path. But what if they split up and chose both?

What would they expect *him* to do? Of course! They'd expect him to run deeper and deeper into the jungle. But while that might increase his chances for escape it would greatly reduce his chances for rescue. He decided to give his run one more burst and then cut off into the thicket back toward the beach, hoping that the unexpected might throw them off.

After a few hundred yards, Lee had to concede that his left leg could contribute no more. His movements had been reduced to *step-drag, step-drag*. He slowed and looked for a place to break to his right into the thicket. Something caught his eye, something that seemed foreign to the environment. He stopped, backed up a couple of steps and bent down. It was a watch, a GI wristwatch! The leather band was still buckled, but one end of the band had torn loose from the watch itself. It had to be Mo Brennan's watch!

He pocketed the find and turned into a small break in the brambles. He hunched over and moved carefully, With each step he tried to replace the vegetation behind him to its original state. Occasionally he cut a bushy branch and stuck it into the ground to help cover his chosen path. He moved as quietly as he could, as slowly as he had to, stopping often to listen. He was glad to hear the building crescendo of the surf. It would help cover any noises he made, and it meant he was close to where he wanted to be. He stopped, looked back, and listened once more. He thought he heard Jap soldiers' voices coming up the path.

Turning to take another step closer to the beach, Lee looked down and found himself staring into the muzzle of a Colt .45. A second look told him the weapon was cocked. And the third look told him he had found Mo Brennan.

"Christ, Marks, when I said, 'Come with me,' I didn't mean *forever*. What the hell *you* doing here?" Mo said in a loud whisper.

Lee reached into his sweaty shirt pocket.

"I came to bring you your watch," he said, flipping the timepiece at Mo.

"Huh? Oh, good eye, Killer. That means *they* won't find it. What's *that*?" Mo asked, pointing to Lee's wounded leg.

For the first time, Lee bent and looked at his left leg. The slug had entered his thigh from the side midway between the hip and knee. From the rather neat, round hole in his trousers blood had oozed out and run downward, soaking the trouser leg almost to the ground. But the bleeding was relatively slow, and the pain was tolerable.

"That's my corporate perk for covering my leader," he said. "That's what one gets after the field glasses, the daggers, the swords—and the dedication."

"After all your screw-ups, now you're bucking for a Section Eight? Killer, I'm *still* your commanding officer, whether you like it or not."

"And I suppose now I get the speech about sticking together?"

"Wrong again. I've got the ball on the two-yard-line and I've got 98 yards to go. My blocker's got a broken leg, so I go it alone. Can't have *him* slowing me down—Shssshh!"

Mo reached up, grabbed Lee's shirt, and pulled him to the ground. Then he motioned to his own Colt before slithering quietly to a spot a few feet away. Lee carefully drew his .45 from its holster. He didn't want to risk the noise made by cocking it.

He could hear Japanese soldiers working their way up the path. They were no longer shouting or even talking, and their movements were slow and hushed as though stalking nearby prey. The thought gave Lee a chill. *He* was the prey. It sounded like they periodically probed the thicket bordering the path with their bayonets. Lee hoped he had left no trail of blood when he turned off the pathway. He hadn't even thought of it.

He could barely make out the soldiers. Most visible were their old-fashioned leggings. He counted them as they passed by in single file, two legs...four legs...on up to ten legs. Just as he began to relax, a group of four more soldiers passed. One stopped for a second and probed near the entrance to their hide-away. Then he dropped the butt of his rifle to the ground, wrapped one arm around its muzzle and bayonet, unbuttoned his trousers, and pissed into the brush. When done, he buttoned up, grunted, and hustled on down the path to catch up with his comrades.

After several minutes of silence, Mo slid back over toward Lee. For moments, he said nothing, just looked at Lee. It seemed that his glare had softened. Lee thought for a moment that he was looking at the other Mo, the sincere, personable one. Then Mo tugged at his trouser pocket, finally extracting his flask. Never taking his eyes off Lee, he unscrewed the cap, took a long slug, then replaced the cap and shoved the flask back into his pocket.

"I thank you, Killer, for covering me out there," he said, pointing a thumb toward the beach. "You went beyond the call of duty. I thank you, my parents thank you, and all the citizens of the great state of Minnesota thank you. They *will* get to erect that statue. You're really a good—" Mo stopped, turned away, jammed his Colt back into its holster, and clamored to his feet. "You can't keep up with me, but I'll get out of here, and when I do I'll send help for you."

With that, Mo crawled out to the path, turned left, in the direction from which Lee had come, and took off trotting. He never looked back.

Lee found himself tumbling about in a mixing pot of feelings that was about to boil over. For a moment, Mo had come across like the loyal, trustworthy Mo he had come to like and respect. He missed that Mo. But when he thought of the Mo who had manipulated him and assailed him repeatedly, the Mo who just now ran off and left him here wounded, he could hardly contain his rage. If, by chance, they both made it back, he vowed he would beat the great Mo Brennan to a pulp, no matter what he had to use to do it and no matter what the consequences might be.

He rolled over onto his belly. Tears slid slowly down his cheeks. For the moment, the power that was Lee Marks had evaporated like steam from the boiling pot. And as the emotions finally settled, fatigue rolled in to the rhythm of the rolling surf.

Hours later, Lee awoke in shear panic. The jungle was black and silent, so quiet, like a huge, soundproofed cage. But as he stared upward to the ceiling of tree branches and palm fronds, he caught glimpses of light showing through— moonlight. A glance at his watch told him nothing. Too dark, but not too dark for the swarming mosquitoes.

His left leg throbbed, but he could think of little he could do for relief. He dropped his trousers, stripped off his shirt and undershirt. Tearing up the GI undershirt, he fashioned a thick wad over the wound and then bound it tightly with the remainder of the undershirt. He slipped back into his uniform shirt and pulled up his trousers. He stripped his fabric pilot's helmet off his head and toyed for a moment with the goggles. Could they be of any use to him? He couldn't imagine what good they could be, but just in case, he'd put the helmet back on for the time being.

Several moments of careful listening convinced him it was safe to move. He crawled gingerly toward the beach. A careful inspection gave him the courage to stick his head out for a look around.

He found a beautiful tropical beach night, complete with a half-moon shining down through clear skies onto a light, sandy beach that separated him from the rolling surf. A light southeast breeze brought the salty air of the sea to him, a fresh change from the dank smells of the jungle. He took a moment to refresh his sense of direction. The open sea he faced was to the south. Perhaps 800 yards to his right, to the west, rested his Lockheed Lightning, its nose buried in the jungle.

Was there anything in the ship that he needed? He saw no Japanese soldiers guarding it. Yes, he thought with a chuckle. He'd like to have the four fifty-caliber machine guns. He laughed to himself. In his present condition he couldn't carry even *one* of the heavy weapons, and if he could he had no means to fire it.

The radio? It probably still worked, unless the Jap soldiers had disabled it with their firing. Or maybe they had removed it from the plane. If it were still there, he could send out a call for help. He sat back and deliberated with himself on the subject. In the final analysis, it wasn't worth the risk. He might get a message off. But if he gave his position to the Allies, he would also be giving it to the Japs and helping their scanners pinpoint his location. He would be handing himself over on the proverbial silver platter.

Did he really *need* to communicate his predicament? His squadron mates knew he'd followed Mo down near Japen Island. And right out there on the beach rested a nine-ton marker with a large number 161 on its sides, impossible to miss from the air. No, he reasoned, the ship told them where he went down. He needed to tell them he was still alive and where he was. The more precisely he could give his location, the better chance the men in the rubber raft from a submarine or a dumbo had of getting him out without casualties. He had to find a way to send the message and not share it with the Japs.

Some time later, Lee stepped carefully out of the jungle to the edge of the sand. He carried his machete in one hand, and in the other he held a palm frond. Slowly, cautiously he began working his way toward the Lightning. As he moved he quietly swished away most of his footprints in the sand with the palm frond. He stopped every forty or fifty feet and listened intently before continuing.

When Lee was perhaps 500 yards from the ship, he turned and stealthily moved out onto the beach where he began a planned ritual. He took a step sideways with the bad leg, then dragged his right foot through the sand. At specific points he made sharp turns and moved off in another direction. Minutes later, he paused to check his work. There in the sand he had inscribed L M in twenty-foot letters. He retreated quickly to the jungle line and then turned for another inspection. He had hoped to make his etchings clearly visible from the air and yet keep the edges of the small trenches soft enough that they would not be spotted from the edge of the jungle. One of the obvious risks was, of course, that a Jap plane might fly over. He would then find out just how fast he could run on one leg.

As he studied his project he decided that a couple of edges needed a slight touch-up to make them less visible at ground level. He had just started back out onto the beach when a maelstrom of gunfire erupted in the jungle on the far side of the Lightning. Lee dropped onto the sand and lay there listening to a mixture of the loud *Bam! Bam! Bam!*, the unmistakable sound of the Colt .45 and the light *Pop! Pop! Pop! Pop! Pop!* of the enemy rifles. The louder reports had to be Mo. But from the sounds of the battle, the Japs were getting off about a dozen shots for each of his. Finally, after an intense flurry of rifle fire, it all stopped. Lee knew the rest of the story. The invincible Mo Brennan had gone down short of the goal line.

Lee resisted the temptation to lie there and deal with his emotions. He hurried out to his letters and touched up several edges. He had just made it back to the overgrowth when a staccato, sing-song dialogue mixed with laughter came from the other side of his Lightning. Lee quickly erased the last of his tracks and backed into the cover of the vegetation where he could safely observe whatever transpired on the beach. But if the soldiers should spot the letters highlighted by the moon, they'd be on him immediately.

The voices had reached the P-38, though their owners were all on the far side of the ship. Lee would like to have understood the conversation. One voice stood out, barking orders with the authority of command. A series of subdued bumping noises filtered into the discussions. Two soldiers appeared next to the cockpit on the far wing, the port side, then a third. With an apparent struggle they hoisted what appeared to be a heavy object over the side and into the cockpit. After some tugging and jostling to rearrange the posture of the object, they stood back and looked at their handiwork.

With a clearer look, Lee knew. They had dumped Mo's body into the cockpit. Were they going to set the plane on fire? One of the soldiers made another comment, then jumped down off the wing. In seconds he reappeared and again jerked Mo's body this way and that. When the task was done they stood back once more, making comments and laughing. They had tied one of Mo's arms up to the top framework of the cockpit. Why, he wondered, would they go to that trouble? Suddenly, Lee knew their plan! They had tied Mo's arm to the top to make it look like he was waving to something overhead. It was a trap, and Mo was the bait!

Lee pulled back into the brush. Their ruse could cause the deaths of three or four sailors or airmen in a rubber raft; it could cost a PBY Dumbo; it could even cost a navy submarine. At the very least it would bring about many hits on the scout plane or planes that came in close to investigate. And he had just flavored the bait by putting his initials nearby.

He listened. The voices faded into the jungle. He waited to see if they came up the pathway in his direction. They didn't. Apparently their base of operations lay to the west, away from him, not to the east. There seemed to be no sign of them setting up weapons. He reasoned that they would wait until morning to do that. And he imagined that their trap would include many powerful weapons, perhaps even mortars and small artillery. A wave of panic swept through Lee. He had to do something—and fast. He'd have to change his message. If the enemy set up all their gun emplacements on the other side of the Lightning, they might not spot his letters. He didn't like the size of that *if* but he couldn't come up with anything better.

Lee hurried out to his letters. Using his feet and the palm frond, he busily erased portions and revised the letters. When finished, he had converted the L M to N O and had added two crossed lines under the O, hoping that some pilot might recognize the skull and crossbones warning. He retreated quickly, brushing his tracks thoroughly.

Next he would move as far to the east as he could under the cover of darkness, then set up a new L M far from the trap. How far? That would be determined by how much ground he could cover on a gimpy leg that was already complaining of overuse. Lee struck out to the east. To move faster and avoid running smack into a Jap patrol on the interior path, he stayed on the edge of the jungle. He covered as much ground as he could in sixty seconds, then stopped to listen. Five of these cycles took him around a bend and out of sight of the Lightning. He felt a little more secure, but he was well aware that he might be running right into more Japs. It always came back to choices.

Fatigue set in rapidly. He had begun the trek with a walking pattern of *step-short step, step, short-step* and it had taken him a long way, perhaps a mile or two. When he realized his pace had dropped off to *short-step, drag, short-step, drag,* he knew it was time to set up his second message and find cover. He had just rounded another small point and could see no coastal enemy installations ahead. This had to be the place. He checked the surf. It seemed to be lighter here, Good. But could there be coral reefs out there to raise hell with rescue operations? Could be. Could he do anything about that? Not really.

Quickly, he tramped another L M in the sand, though the letters were smaller than those of the first edition. Then he crawled back into the jungle and searched out the best possible nesting place where he would have a good view of the beach and the sea. Before retiring, he checked his wound once more. He wished he hadn't. The activity had opened up the bleeding. His left trouser leg had become thoroughly saturated. He had to have left a trail along the edge of the jungle. He could use his outer shirt for another bandage, but would it do any good? Or would it simply expose him to more mosquitoes? Recalling that he had DDT in his emergency kit, he ripped up the shirt for a bandage and used his belt for a tourniquet. Then he powdered heavily with the DDT.

He cut some bushy branches to help conceal himself, smoothed out his indentation in the jungle floor to reduce the scratchy irritants against his bare skin and then retired for the night. Reviewing the trap he had seen being set, his two messages, and his long move to what he hoped was a better location, Lee felt he had done the best he could with what he had. Despite his best efforts, his rescue still depended on others and on circumstances that might well be beyond their control. He was surprised at how comfortable he felt in such a miserable bunk. It might…all work out…and it might…not…work…out…Lee's inner battery was dead. Two sleepless nights, a nightmare of a day, and a Jap rifle shell in his leg took him into a place of temporary comfort. The ease with which he was drifting off surprised him a little, but drift he did.

Hours later, out of the beautiful tropical morning came the distant rattle of fifty-caliber machine guns and many smaller ground-based weapons followed by a hair-raising *Zzzzooooommm!* The sound of twin Allisons zooming right over him would have brought Lee Marks back from the dead. He heard more gunfire, then *Zzzzooooommm!* There went another! He tossed back his cover of branches and struggled to his feet. Limping out onto the sandy beach, he turned to face the third Lightning. He pointed back in the direction of his ship, shook his head violently, and made a series of slashing motions across his throat. *Zzzzooooommm!* It was Sandy's ship. He waggled his wings and followed the others in a smooth turn out to sea. A second flight of four Lightnings circled high above the low level action as though awaiting their turn. Zzzzooooommm! The fourth P-38 roared past and banked toward the sea.

The four low-level ships made another strafing pass on the enemy troops hiding in the jungle near Lee's ship. One by one, Lee waved them on as they passed over and headed out to close ranks off shore. Lee had lost sight of the higher flight.

Then suddenly, a gigantic *Whooommmp!* Then another close behind it. *Whooommmp!* Lee had never experienced a napalm dropping from ground level, but he knew instantly what had happened. *Zzzzooooommm!* A huge, angry mass of flames and black clouds enveloped the jungle back to the west. A second Lightning followed up with napalm. *Whooommmp! Whooommmp!* Two planes of the second flight circled at about 3,000 feet, probably waiting to see if their jellied gas would be needed. The other six set up a long rectangular pattern, not unlike the one Lee had used in covering Mo. If the enemy resumed firing, there would soon be a P-38 firing down his throat.

In from seaward flew a PBY Dumbo. He circled offshore as the P-38s finished their job. Then he turned into the wind and settled into the sea. He taxied in half way and launched a rubber raft. In fifteen minutes Lee was hoisted up into the open bubble turret aft on the PBY. His rescuers clambered aboard as the pilot turned into the wind and opened his throttles. The ungainly bird rattled and vibrated its protests. Finally, with a series of loud slaps of the surf against the hull, the ungainly craft struggled into the air and headed for Hollandia.

A smiling sergeant brought Lee a blanket, a hot cup of coffee, and a candy bar, then set about checking his leg. Lee had forgotten about hunger. He had been so occupied with surviving, he'd not once thought of food. But he knew that, had he not been rescued, the subject would have come up—big time.

"That was a real piece of work," said the co-pilot who came back to check on Lee.

"Huh?"

"Those letters in the sand—pretty nifty. We all thank you. A lot of us could have gotten hurt. By the way, who was that in the P-38? At first they thought it was you."

"I, uhhh, guess a part of me *was* there," Lee mumbled. Then he continued, "That was Lieutenant Colonel Mo Brennan. Those bastards used him for bait. Ends up, they fried right with him."

Lee's statement brought back Burner Hedman's words, that he didn't care if the headhunters put him in the boiling pot—as long as he was dead first.

Epilogue

▼

"Want watuh?" asked the plump, bare-breasted native woman, her ever-present smile lacking two front teeth.

"Uhh, no thanks," replied Lee, struggling to keep from staring at the smooth, dark brown breasts. "But I could use some more paper."

"Papuh?"

"Paper," he repeated, waving the letter he held before her.

"Ah, ha, ha! Papuh! Papuh!"

In a minute she returned with paper. Pride glowed in her smile as she handed Lee a single sheet and turned away to check on another patient.

Lee had written the letter to Mr. and Mrs. Brennan a dozen times in his mind. He had written it twice on paper, two versions that differed by a hundred and eighty degrees. But each time he reread one of the two efforts, he flipped back to the contrasting version. He stared at the blank sheet for some time. Then he set it aside, swung his legs back up onto his hospital bunk, and stretched out on his back. He needed to think some more.

In five days at the Nadzab base hospital, his leg had healed rapidly. The Japanese rifle bullet had lodged against the femur but hadn't broken the bone. With the removal of the slug, the doctor had immediately pronounced Lee "on the mend." He had been wounded seriously enough to "qualify for a week off and a Purple Heart but nothing close to going home or doing a war bond tour." The doctor's last words had returned to prickle Lee's consciousness numerous times. Had the doctor somehow been privy to Mo Brennan's master plan?

As before, whatever he thought about eventually connected to Mo and brought Lee face to face with his dilemma. He shouldn't *have* to write to Mo's parents. It was *not* part of his job. Several times he had asked himself, "If I simply didn't bother to write the letter, who would know?" Only one living person knew about the promise, only one. But Lee would have to live with *that* person the rest of his life.

He had also promised to give Mo the best possible write-up. How easy it had been to agree to Mo's request. Lee was riding high at the time. He had temporarily lost track of the hurtful manipulations and angry punishments inflicted upon him. And he couldn't possibly have anticipated Mo's despicable decision-making on Japen Island. He still found it hard to believe that Mo Brennan had actually run off and left a wounded Lee Marks behind.

"My blocker's got a broken leg, so I go it alone," Mo had said. "Can't have *him* slowing me down."

The first few times Lee had replayed those words, the hurt they conveyed had depressed him. The next dozen times, Lee found himself so angry he thought he would burst. But the last few times he had begun to change his focus. He had begun to think more of himself and his own future.

Col. Sledge Hammer had flown down from Hollandia to see him. Sledge had been surprisingly soft and understanding. But he was all business when he informed Lee that his promotion to captain was being rushed through and that he would become the next CO of Gopher Squadron. In addition, Sledge had put Lee in for the Silver Star medal for gallantry in action while providing cover for Lt. Col. Brennan.

"But what about Greenie?" Lee had asked. "He has more experience and seniority."

Sledge had looked Lee in the eye and said, "I don't usually ask for input from my subordinates when making such decisions. But this time I asked Greenie how he felt about it. He said something about a promise you had made to him. Then he said, 'Even if I also make captain, I'd be more than pleased to serve under Captain Marks. The guy's a straight shooter.'"

"So it's final, were Sledge's words. "You've got two more days. I'll send Marv down with the Golden Goose to pick you up day after tomorrow. Then it's back to work."

As Sledge turned to leave, Lee spoke up.

"Uh, Col. Hammer—thanks for coming down."

Sledge grinned. "Oh, I didn't come down to see *you*. I needed some hours for my flight pay."

Sledge's visit had brought Lee around to focusing on the future. Yes, Lee thought, his own future counted here. And he would not take over a command while still dealing with demons. For five days he had played and replayed the events of the last weeks as well as those on Japen Island hoping to find the truth. He began to consider explanations that began as ludicrous and gradually drifted into the realm of the possible.

After all, if he *had* been able to keep up with Mo, he would in all likelihood be dead now. The more Lee processed that statement, the better he felt. Then, he even found himself wondering if perhaps Mo had abandoned him so as to draw the Japanese soldiers away, to save him from capture. He recalled the distant gunfire he had heard on Japen Island, the contrast between the *Pop!* of the light .30-caliber Japanese rifles and the powerful *Bam!* of the .45-caliber Colt that Mo carried. Lee knew he would never be sure, but it seemed that he heard Mo's weapon fire first.

In the final analysis, however, one thought outweighed all else. This was war—not a fraternity activity—but real God-awful war.

Lee sat up and swung his legs back over the edge of the bunk. He snatched up one of the letter drafts, crumpled it into a ball and tossed it into a nearby waste bucket. He picked up the other and began to read it once more for what he knew would be the last time.

As he reached the final paragraph, it was clear to him that he was doing the right thing. The tension of indecision drained away.

> *"...in addition to the outstanding leadership and the incredible achievements I've told you about here, I want you to know that on many occasions your son took risks to help his individual pilots out of tough, life-threatening situations, risks that went beyond the call of duty. Because of his last one I am alive...and he is gone. With all respect, I share your loss, Mr. and Mrs. Brennan. I have lost my commander, my mentor, my teacher, and my wing man. I can only hope that my actions through the remainder of this terrible war will justify in some small part the faith he had in me and the sacrifice he made."*
>
> *Yours truly,*
> *Lt. Lee Marks*

There it is, Mo, all I can do," Lee said aloud. "You're right, it's only *a paper statue*. But you have to admit, it won't attract many pigeons. And you know something else, Mo? You always planned for the future. You taught me that and I thank you.

"Who's to say I can't still execute the plan and go home a hero? After all, I have a pretty good start, with the kills and the medals. But understand this, Mo, I won't be shooting for medals—I didn't *plan* on winning a single one of them. And I don't know the first thing about selling war bonds, but if they ever want to send me home, I'll figure it out."

978-0-595-40768-2
0-595-40768-4

Printed in the United States
61293LVS00004B/256-285